The Taking

A Riverview Mystery

Other books by Michele Pariza Wacek

The Secret Diary of Helen Blackstone
(free novella available at MPWNovels.com)

It Began With a Lie (Book 1 in the "Secrets of Redemption" series)
This Happened to Jessica (Book 2 in the series)
The Evil That Was Done (Book 3 in the series)
The Summoning (Book 4 in the series)
The Reckoning (Book 5 in the series)

The Murder Before Christmas
        (Book 1 in the "Charlie Kingsley Mystery" series)
        Ice Cold Murder (Book 2)
        Murder Next Door (Book 3)

The Third Nanny

The Stolen Twin

Mirror Image

The Taking

A Riverview Mystery

by Michele Pariza Wacek

For my family, for always believing in me.

Chapter 1

It started like any other day.

My alarm woke me, dragging me out of an exhausted, unsatisfying sleep. Between my night terrors and inability to quiet my mind, it was a constant battle to get enough rest. I stumbled to the kitchen to get the first pot of coffee started—I usually went through at least two ... three, if it was a particularly trying day.

It was already feeling like a three-pot day.

I swept the empty wine bottles into the recycling bin and forced myself to drink a glass of water, all the while telling myself how I really needed to cut back on the nightly wine. Maybe that would make it easier to get up in the morning.

I pulled on my workout gear, laced up my shoes, and forced myself out the door for a run while the coffee brewed. I had to do it before my first cup, or I would never get it done. The moment I poured my coffee, I'd open my laptop. It was also why I had to hide my phone at night ... to stop myself from constantly checking my near constant notifications. Once I started, I wouldn't stop. And if I didn't go for my regular run, by the end of the day, I would be a hot mess—a seething mass of anxiety, overwhelm, and stress.

Then, I would really have too much wine. And ice cream.

Returning home sweaty, but much calmer (running always helped me refocus my mind away from my mountain of to-dos), I poured myself a cup of coffee with cream, stuck a frosted brown sugar and cinnamon Pop-Tart in the toaster, jumped in the shower, and was finally ready to face my day.

With my coffee at my elbow, I munched on my Pop-Tart and began my morning as I always did—with a knot in my stomach as I perused the different social media sites before opening my email, Slack, and text. Being the digital marketing director for an organic skin care and make-up line was a little ironic, as personally, I was barely ever online. I had Facebook, Twitter, LinkedIn, and Instagram accounts with a handful of posts on each, but absolutely no pictures of me. Not even my LinkedIn had a professional photo, which I knew was a no-no, but I didn't care. I had one very firm rule: No pictures of me online. Anywhere.

My no-picture rule wasn't because I hated social media, marketing, or even getting my picture taken. It was for self-protection. In fact, if you took personal photos out of the equation, I might have even turned into some sort of influencer with active social media accounts. I liked the strategy of online marketing.

What I hated was the stress of it all. The constant notifications and pinging and dropping everything to put out fires. By the end of the day, I was completely exhausted, and all I wanted to do was collapse on the couch with my customary glass of wine.

But I was good at it, and it paid well. So, despite the nagging feeling deep inside that I wasn't living the life I wanted, I sucked it up and did it anyway.

I had barely logged onto Twitter when my phone started blowing up. Already? Mondays were the worst. Even though I pretty much never took a day off and always at least checked in over the weekend, not everyone else did, so a lot of times, Monday morning became "deal with the weekend issues" morning. I sighed, rubbing my temples as I already felt the beginnings of a stress headache forming at the back of my eyes. Definitely a three-pot day.

I reached for my phone, dreading whatever calamity I was going to have to drop everything to take care of, despite being barely halfway through the report that was due no later than 3:00 p.m. *I probably should have done more on it over the weekend,* I thought. *Ugh. What had I been thinking?*

In retrospect, I wished it *had* been a dreaded work-related fire.

Tess, my assistant and friend, had texted. *Tori, have you seen the news yet? What is going on here in Riverview? I thought all the weird stuff only happened in Redemption. That poor baby.*

I froze, staring at the screen. *That poor baby.*

No, I just sat down, I texted back, my fingers numb and clumsy, misspelling two words. *What's going on?*

It's probably some weird accident, I told myself. *Or maybe a baby has been kidnapped.*

Which would be tragic, of course. Tragic and newsworthy.

But still completely different from what had happened to me.

As I waited for Tess to respond, I opened the website for *The Riverview Times.*

The front screen loaded as Tess's response came through.

Some woman is claiming someone kidnapped her real baby and replaced it with a changeling. So, she 'had' to kill it.

All the blood seemed to drain from my body. My vision darkened, narrowing to a pinprick until the only thing I could see was that one sentence. Two words kept repeating themselves over and over in my head until they were all I was conscious of:

Not again.

Chapter 2

The report I needed to be writing nagged at the back of my head as I parked the car and made my way to the hospital's entrance.

Once I got through the initial shock, I clicked my way to the full story. It was still fairly jumbled, as it was early in the case, but it appeared the woman in question (they hadn't released her name yet) had given birth at home at some point—the exact time wasn't clear, but it might have been as long as a day ago. The neighbors had called the cops because she was screaming nonstop. When the cops arrived, they found her in what seemed to be a psychotic state. She was covered in blood, screaming that the faeries had stolen her baby.

The deceased baby in question was also covered in blood, and he was taken away for further examination. It was determined the blood had come from the woman, not the baby. As the cops hadn't charged the mother with murder (at least as of yet) and the blood had come from the mother, I wondered where Tess had gotten the idea that the mother had killed the baby. I also wondered how many other people were assuming as Tess was. I instantly empathized with the mother. If she had nothing to do with it, she had no idea the battles in front of her to clear her name.

I knew all too well how it felt to be on the other side of false accusations.

Adding to the strangeness of the story was one peculiar detail; one of the neighbors had claimed to have seen someone leave her apartment. The figure was tall, with proportions that didn't "seem quite human." It was stooped, dressed in black, and carrying a bundle in its arm.

Like a baby.

The woman was admitted to a psychiatric hospital, and the cops were looking for the figure. If anyone had any information, they should call a tip line.

I wrote down the number, even though I wasn't sure why, since I didn't have any information.

It couldn't possibly have any bearing on what happened to me over twenty years before.

I closed the site and turned to my Slack and email, determined to put the story out of my mind. I already had too many to-dos to get through in a day. I didn't have time to worry about some random news story. I didn't even know the woman, after all. It had nothing to do with me.

But no matter what I did or how much I tried to distract myself with work, I found myself being pulled back in. I would regularly log onto the news site and Twitter feed, looking for updates. I even checked the local police newsfeed to see if they were updating.

Nothing was posted, but that didn't stop me from obsessing about it.

Eventually, I decided maybe a change of scenery would help my focus. I could go to The Coffee Clutch, a little coffee shop not far from me, to have a cup and maybe a sandwich. I packed up my laptop and phone and headed out.

Except instead of heading to the coffee shop, I found myself driving to the hospital where the unnamed woman was being treated.

"No one is going to tell you anything," I muttered to myself as I pushed open the front doors. "This is an absolute waste of time."

It didn't matter. I continued making my way to the psychiatric floor.

Maybe I just needed to be turned away to realize how ridiculous I was being. Then, I could put it behind me and focus on what really mattered ... like that report due in just a few hours.

Is that report what really matters? A little voice whispered inside me. *Or is it time to finally get to the bottom of what happened to Scott all those years ago?*

I pushed the voice away. Whatever was going on with this woman had nothing to do with what happened to Scott. And besides, I had made my peace with it. There was no reason to pick away at that particular scab.

If you made your peace with it, then why are you standing in the hospital right now rather than working on your report?

Curiosity, I decided. *That's all. Simple curiosity.*

Like the curiosity that killed the cat? Or that compels onlookers to pause to watch a train wreck?

I quit arguing with the little voice.

I turned the corner that led to the psychiatric ward, and my heart sank in my chest. Of course it would be locked. Why had I thought otherwise?

A woman was sitting behind a glass partition, long fingernails painted lime- green clicking away on a keyboard. Her pink hair was cut in a short, asymmetric style and shaved on one side, revealing the tip of a tattoo snaking up the side of her neck. As I studied her, wondering what I could possibly say that wouldn't make me sound like a nut and might actually compel her to let me in, a nurse in blue scrubs exited the door of the ward, allowing me a glimpse down a long hallway. A cop was standing next to a door near the end of the hall, a bored expression on his face. Another man, younger and exhausted-looking, faced him, leaning against the wall as if it was the only thing holding him up. There was something about him that seemed familiar, but I couldn't place him. As the doors began to close, he turned his head and saw me looking at him. Our eyes met, and I felt a distinct jolt.

He felt it, too. I saw his eyes widen as he straightened up, almost like he was going to come toward me, but then the doors clanked shut.

This was all a really bad idea. I knew I should just get out of there. Go back home or to the coffee shop and focus on that report ...

"Can I help you?" a nasally voice asked from behind me.

I turned. The pink-haired woman was staring at me. She was older than I had assumed when I first noticed her colorful hair and nails, tiny wrinkles already appearing around her eyes and lips. She loudly cracked her gum.

"No, I was just leaving," I said.

She gave me a suspicious frown. "You're here because of the woman, aren't you?"

"Really, I was just going."

"Are you a reporter?"

"No, no, nothing like that."

Her eyes narrowed. "Then what? You shouldn't be here gawking at her. It's not right."

Images rushed through my mind. Our front yard choked with reporters, flashes of light, microphones thrust into my father's face. *Who killed your son? Was it your daughter?*

Anger shot through me. "I know," I snapped. "I'm not here to gawk. I thought I could help."

Her eyes widened slightly as she reached for the phone. "Help? Do you know something?" Her demeanor had softened slightly. I wondered if maybe her prickliness had more to do with people showing up like ghouls to drool and gossip about the "sick" mother. Now that I thought about it, I could see how I likely appeared to fit that description. "Let me call the officer and have him come ..."

"It's okay," I said, moving swiftly toward the exit. "I have to go anyway."

This was a huge mistake. Had I really thought they would just let me stroll in and question that woman? Especially considering she was probably medicated up to her eyeballs and likely incoherent. I couldn't even imagine what I would say to the officer that wouldn't sound like a waste of his time.

Not to mention how I didn't want to talk to whoever that guy was standing with the cop.

She was still trying to call me back, but I kept walking, hurrying to put as much distance as possible between myself and the locked ward as quickly as possible.

What an absolute waste of time and energy. Plus, I had so much to do and was now even further behind. What was I thinking? I contemplated going back to therapy again. Obviously, I wasn't as healed as I thought.

As I stepped out of the frigid, over-air-conditioned crispness of the hospital and into the humid heat of the parking lot, my cell phone rang. Oh crap. That was probably work, wondering what happened to me. I fumbled through my purse before locating the phone.

It wasn't work. It was Nanna.

My stomach, already twisted in knots, seemed to flip inside out. I stared at the screen, wondering if there was a way to avoid talking to her, at least for a few days until I was able to get my head on straight.

But even as I considered it, I knew it was a lost cause. Nanna would keep calling and texting until I responded.

Sighing, I answered the phone.

"Tori! I'm so glad I caught you. Did you see the news?"

I tucked the phone between my shoulder and ear as I fished for my keys. "If you mean, did I see the story about the woman who claims someone stole her baby and left a changeling, then yes."

Nanna let out a deep breath. "Are you okay?"

"As fine as I ever am," I said.

"Tori, you know you can't fool me." There it was. The matronly disciplinarian I could never hide anything from when I was a teenager.

Nanna was my grandmother on my mother's side. She had taken me in once it became clear my mother's "temporary" stay in the beautiful, private psychiatric hospital was permanent, and my father was not equipped to raise a daughter on his own. I still saw both parents—my father one weekend a month and over the holidays, and my mother a couple of times a year. In a way, it was like I was the child of divorce, with both parents having visitation rights.

"I'll be fine," I said, softening my voice. "It was a shock; I'm not going to lie. But I don't see how it has anything to do with what happened to me."

"How are you sleeping?"

What she was really asking was how my night terrors were. "The Valium helps," I said.

"Maybe you need to get back into therapy," she suggested.

"Funny you should say that," I said. "I was just thinking I should make an appointment."

"I worry about you, you know," she said. "A girl your age. You should be dating, having fun with your friends. It's not normal to work all the time."

"Actually, in this day and age, it's very normal to work all the time," I said. "I'm trying to get ahead."

She snorted. "Oh, please. We both know you're not in love with your job. It would be one thing if you were doing what you love, but you're not. There's more to life than work, Tori. It's time to start living."

"I have to go," I said, opening my car door and trying to ignore the hollow feeling her words created inside me.

"Are you out somewhere?" she asked. "I keep hearing other noises."

"Yeah, I'm at a coffee shop," I lied. There was no way I was telling her where I really was. "I needed a break."

"Are you meeting someone?"

"No. I've got a report to finish. I'll call you later."

She sighed again, but didn't protest as I ended the call.

Nanna needed a hobby, I decided. She was always bugging me about my lack of friends and interests, but if she had more going on herself, she wouldn't be so focused on me.

Doesn't mean she wasn't right, the little voice said inside me. *After all, look where you are right now.*

I pushed the voice down. I had work to do. A lot of work. I didn't have any time to add more things into my life.

I started the car, intending on driving to The Coffee Clutch, but realized I was feeling way too much pressure to finish that report and should probably just go home. Especially since my stomach was too queasy for food. Instead, I stopped at a local kiosk for a large latte to-go and headed back to my apartment.

Once I arrived, I texted Tess to hold down the fort while I finished the report, turned off all notifications, and threw myself into getting it done. I was only 15 minutes late turning it in, which I considered a huge victory, even though I had to lie in the email to my boss, saying the reason I was late was because I thought I might be coming down with something.

In retrospect, however, I wasn't totally lying. I hadn't been acting like myself since that morning. There was such a thing as "temporary insanity" … maybe that was what had come over me.

I turned my notifications back on and, after a moment's hesitation, went into the kitchen to open a bottle of wine. Sure, I wasn't "officially" done with work, but there had been many times I had worked while enjoying a glass of wine. Or two. And it was getting close to the end of the day, being almost 4:00. Well, 3:30, but close enough. Especially with the day I'd had, I figured a glass of wine could only help. Plus, I would probably have to work late to catch up, so what would it hurt to get started then?

I was about to take a sip when there was a knock at my door.

I froze, the glass halfway to my lips. Who could it possibly be? My apartment building was locked—I had to buzz people in. And I had made a point of not knowing my neighbors. I liked it better that way.

An image flashed in my mind … the man at the hospital, the jolt as our eyes met. No, it couldn't be him. How would he even know who I was? It wasn't like I had given the pink-haired orderly my name.

It's probably a mistake, I told myself as I put the wine glass down on the counter and edged my way toward the door. Some-one went to the wrong apartment. It happened. No big deal.

I peered through the peephole and almost fainted.

There standing on the other side of the door was the man from the hospital.

Chapter 3

I had to be dreaming.

I squeezed my eyes shut, shaking my head slightly. There was no way it could be him. I figured my mind was playing tricks on me, conjuring him up when he was nowhere near my door. In fact, this was probably a sign that I absolutely needed to book that appointment with my therapist.

I took a second look.

It was definitely him.

No! I dug my fingers into my temple. Maybe it was just someone who resembled him. I closed my eyes again and tried to picture what the man in the hospital had been wearing, but it was all vague and nondescript. Maybe a blue shirt and jeans? I couldn't remember.

This is all stupid, anyway, I thought. It couldn't be him. It was clearly a mistake. This person had come to the wrong apartment. All I had to do was keep quiet and he would go …

The knock came again, making me jump and hit the door, slapping it with my palm.

Well, great, Tori. Now he knows you're here.

The day was just getting better and better. At that point, I figured I might as well open the door. How much worse could it get?

So, I did.

For a moment, we just stood there staring at each other. He was a little taller than me, well-built, with sandy-brown hair that went every which way, as though he had spent too many hours combing his hand through it. His bloodshot hazel eyes were ringed with puffy black circles, and his cheekbones were sculpted. As exhausted as he was, he was still really good-looking.

"Vicky," he breathed, almost like he couldn't believe it. "It is you."

I automatically stiffened. "I haven't gone by 'Vicky' in years," I said. "And who are you?"

"It's Cole. Cole Bennett. Remember me?"

I blinked. An image of a scruffy eight-year-old yanking on my ponytail filled my mind. "Cole? From Redemption?"

He smiled tiredly at me. "The same."

"But ..." I blinked again, trying to put the pieces together. "What are you doing here? How did you find me? And what were you doing at the ..." My words trailed off as more images clicked into place.

Cole had a sister. A twin sister.

His smile turned grim. "What was I doing at the hospital? I could ask you the same."

"Was it Missy?" My voice was barely above a whisper. I grabbed the side of the door, feeling like I needed support to stabilize myself.

Was it possible that Missy and I had seen the same vision? Even years apart and under completely different circumstances?

Was this the proof I had been looking for all my life?

Or was this some sort of cosmic joke being played on me?

Cole's lips pressed together. "Can I come in?" he asked.

I didn't move. On one hand, I wanted to know everything that had happened. Every single detail, no matter how small. And maybe, I could even convince him to let me talk to his sister.

But on the other, I wanted nothing to do with any of it. I could just close the door and go back to my wine and work.

Oh, man. My work. I was so behind.

"It's not a great time," I said. "I'm still working."

"You work at home?"

I nodded. "Yeah, and it's not quite 5:00, so you know ..." I forced a smile, willing him to leave and let me get back to my unsatisfying, overwhelmed, and stressful life.

But at least it was "normal." Mostly.

"This won't take long," he said. "Can we just exchange numbers and figure out a time and place to talk later?"

I hesitated. I wasn't keen on letting him inside, because it would be that much more difficult to get him to leave. But I also didn't have my phone with me, so I was either going to have to leave him in the hallway while I went to fetch it, or bite the bullet and let him in.

Tori, just let him in, a voice said inside me. *Do you want to talk to Missy or not? Stop being so difficult.*

I pushed the door open and stepped back, allowing him to enter my cluttered apartment and hoping he didn't notice the dirty dishes still piled up by the sink or the overflowing trash that really needed to be taken to the dumpster.

The first thing his eyes landed on was my full glass of wine on the counter. His eyebrows lifted in question.

I sighed. Now, he probably thought I was lying about working. "Do you want a glass?" I asked. "I normally don't drink this early, but it's been a day."

"Sure," he said, and gave me a crooked smile. "It *has* been a day."

I went into the kitchen to hunt for a clean glass. I tried not to look at the dishes in the sink. I promised myself I would wash them up after Cole left.

"So, what should I call you, since you don't go by 'Vicky' anymore?"

I didn't immediately answer, focusing instead on pouring the wine in a tumbler. "Sorry, I've been swamped at work and haven't had time to wash dishes," I said, hoping he didn't notice the unused dishwasher.

"No problem," he said. "So, what name are you going by now?"

He wasn't going to let it drop. "Tori," I said with a sigh. My hands trembled slightly, and it occurred to me that as much as I wanted to talk to Missy and see if there was a link between our stories, I also wanted to keep my private life private.

I had spent years burying my past, making sure no one could connect me to that terrified five-year-old girl. I changed my name and kept my online profile as low-key as possible. And now, because of a crazy impulse, it was all about to disintegrate.

I handed him the glass. "How did you find me?"

Our fingers briefly touched as he took it. He didn't drink, just held it in front of his face. We were close enough that I could smell his scent, a faint whiff of soap and shampoo mixed with his maleness. "It's what I do. I'm a writer."

My entire body went hot, then cold. "You're a journalist?" It was all I could do to not shove him out the door.

"Writer," he corrected. "Or blogger, to be more exact."

I was still suspicious. "What kind of blog?"

He looked a little self-conscious. "Cooking."

"Cooking?"

"Yeah. I've always had a passion for it, and I started it years ago when I was still working at my job. I used to work for a public relations agency writing articles and press releases, but now, the blog is my main focus."

The whole conversation was starting to feel surreal to me. Someone from my childhood who was now a cooking blogger had just arrived at my doorstep. I had questions, a lot of them, but I didn't want to get derailed from what was really important. "But that doesn't explain how you found me."

He took a quick sip of his wine. "Trust me, you didn't make it easy."

"Did you recognize me at the hospital?"

He nodded.

"So, then what? I changed my name."

"Yeah, I know," he said. "When I couldn't find you under 'Hutchinson,' I decided to check under your mother's maiden name. Luckily for me, there's only two 'Agnellos' in Riverview."

"But how did you find my mother's maiden name?"

"Her marriage certificate."

Silently, I kicked myself. Was it really that easy? I should have picked a completely random name. How could I have been so careless? I should have known it would be far more difficult to escape your past.

"I'm not going to say anything," he said.

"I appreciate that," I said, picking up my glass. "So, why are you here?"

"Why did you come to the hospital?"

I took a drink, my gaze sliding to the back of my laptop. I could picture all the messages piling up. "I'm not really sure," I said finally. "I didn't know it was Missy. I didn't know anything but what was reported. It made no sense to show up … I knew that even as I drove over there. But … I don't know."

He kept his eyes on my face as he took a sip. "Do you believe her?"

"I haven't talked to her, so I have no idea what I believe."

"Let me rephrase. How close is Missy's story to yours?"

I played with the stem of my wine glass. *Did you kill your brother?*

"I only know what I read in the paper," I repeated. "According to it, yeah, there are some similarities. But it would help if I could talk to her."

"I could try and arrange that," he said. "Right now, I can't even talk to her."

"You can't?"

He shook his head. "The doctors are still trying to stabilize her. And the cops have made it clear that the moment she's lucid, they want to interview her first."

"Can they do that?"

He shrugged. "I'm getting her a lawyer. At least she won't be questioned alone."

I looked away. As similar as our situations were, the differences were just as striking. I was a child, so I had been sheltered from the legal issues. But as an adult, Missy would be in a completely different position.

Cole straightened, tossing the rest of his wine down his throat. "I better get back to the hospital, and I know you have to get back to work. If you want to exchange numbers, I can text you tomorrow and give you an update on Missy."

I nodded, reaching for my phone. After we updated each other's contact information, Cole made his way to the door. "Thanks for the wine. I'll be in touch."

"Appreciate that," I said.

He was practically out the door when I called him back. He half-turned, still standing in the doorway. As exhausted as he looked with his red-rimmed eyes and puffy face, I could still see the vestiges of the young boy he once was, and I felt a jolt in my chest just looking at him.

"I hope Missy is okay," I said softly.

It wasn't exactly what I wanted to say. What I wanted to say was, "I hope she didn't do what some people are accusing her of … that it's all a big mistake … that there is a simple explanation for your sister giving birth to a baby and the cops finding it dead in her apartment." But I couldn't speak those words.

Especially given my history.

He gave me a knowing look, as if he understood exactly what I was trying to say. "Thank you," he said before quietly closing the door behind him.

I took a deep breath. I could still smell him in my apartment, that mixture of soap and shampoo and essence.

Okay, enough. Clearly, I was feeling vulnerable after everything that had happened, and what I really needed to do was get my head on straight. I had work to do, which was what I needed to focus on.

I picked up my wine and determinedly headed for my computer. At that moment, the only thing I needed to think about was getting caught up. I could deal with everything else then.

Chapter 4

I jerked awake, a scream frozen in my throat.

I scrambled into a sitting position, my back jammed against the headboard, my eyes straining into the shadows.

I knew I had seen it. The dark figure draped in shadows, the bundle snug against its chest, the long white finger pressed against its lips. *Shhh.*

But the longer I stared, the more the darkness broke apart, disintegrating into nothing.

There's no one there. I'm alone. It's just a dream. I'm not seeing things. I'm not crazy.

I tried not to finish that thought, but the words came anyway. *Of course he isn't here. There's no baby to steal.*

I ran my sweaty hands through my hair. My mouth was dry and thick, the result of too much wine. Again. I was getting a headache, as well, my temples starting to pound.

I reached for the water glass next to my bed, but it was empty. Had I filled it last night before going to bed? I couldn't remember.

I got up and padded into the kitchen, already knowing I wasn't going to fall asleep without help. I thought longingly of my Valium prescription, the pills nestled in my bathroom medicine cabinet, but it was too late to take one. I had lost a lot of time the day before already. I couldn't afford that happening again.

While I had managed to get the most pressing items taken care of the previous night before giving up, popping a microwave meal into the microwave and pouring more wine, I still had a lot to do. I needed to get the coffee started and get to work.

I went to the sink and drank two full glasses of water. My heart rate was finally slowing down, and I was feeling more like myself. The leftover chicken and rice meal was still sitting out, congealing in its cardboard container on the counter. My stomach turned, and I tried to shove the box into the overflowing garbage. I yanked the bag out to take it to the dumpster, and the next thing I knew, I was in full cleaning mode. I got rid of the garbage, scrubbed the kitchen and bathroom, and dusted. The only thing I didn't do was vacuum, as I didn't want to disturb my neighbors.

The whole time, I refused to let myself think. I would not entertain the thoughts bubbling up under the surface.

Not that I remembered much from that time. I was only five, after all. So many of my memories were mixed with what other people had told me.

After I finished cleaning, I took a long, hot shower, scrubbing myself with as much vigor as I had scrubbed the apartment … as if I could scour that part of my life away.

I dressed in black leggings and an oversized soft, pink tee shirt. I pulled my wet hair back into a ponytail and surveyed myself in the mirror. There had been a time in my life when people told me I had a "mysterious" beauty. Black hair, grey eyes, translucent, porcelain skin with high cheekbones, a petite nose, and a heart-shaped face. But now, I just looked drained of any sort of life-force. My skin was pale and unhealthy-looking, my eyes were bloodshot, and the bones of my face seemed to jut out, as if I had lost too much weight.

I sighed. I really needed to cut back on the wine. Maybe eat more salad, and actual lunch instead of pouring another cup of coffee. A healthier breakfast than Pop-Tarts wouldn't hurt, either. Maybe I could start making a protein shake or even boil an egg.

Of course, I would first have to find the time to shop for and prep actual food, rather than what I normally did, which was grab convenience foods whenever I went to the store for more wine, coffee, or cream.

I pressed my forehead against the mirror. I just needed more hours in the day. How did other people with families and relationships do it? Most days, I fought just to keep my head above water. I worked long hours, and then spent my weekends catching up on whatever didn't get done during the week, along with trying to get as many "normal" life tasks, like laundry and errands, done as I could before collapsing in front of the television. I barely found the time or energy to occasionally hang out with Tess and a few other local friends and attend my bi-weekly dinners with Nanna.

Although a lot of that was by design. I preferred keeping all my relationships at arm's length. That kept all the uncomfortable questions down. And dating? Forget it. The last thing I needed was that sort of headache in my life.

I finished up in the bathroom and headed to the kitchen to brew a pot of coffee and get an early start. I reasoned I could skip my usual run, as I had cleaned the apartment, instead.

I toasted my Pop-Tart, poured a cup of coffee, and settled in front of my laptop.

I was completely immersed in my work, unaware of the minutes flying by, when the beeping of my phone jolted me out of it. I glanced at the clock. Not even 8:00.

I frowned, rubbing my forehead before taking a sip of my now-cold coffee. The notifications and pingings were starting to flow in. Ugh.

For a moment, I thought about ignoring them. Most days, I didn't dig into notifications until later, when I had a chance to get some caffeine and sugar into my system. On the other hand, I had been working for a while already, returning emails and answering Slacks. It was possible someone who knew I was already working had decided to text me.

Well, the least I could do was get a fresh cup of coffee before diving into my texts, I reasoned. I got up, dumped out the cold coffee and refilled it, and then walked back over to my phone.

But it wasn't a work-related text.

It was from Cole.

Missy wants to see you. Can you come by later this morning?

My hands began to tremble. The shadowy figure in the night shushed me, a long, white finger the only clear image in the dark.

I should say "no," I thought. This wasn't a good day. I had a team meeting in just a little while and more meetings in the afternoon. I needed to focus on work, not on dredging up my past. That was better left for my therapist, who I *really* needed to call.

There was absolutely nothing I could do to help Missy. I knew nothing at all about her situation. Heck, I didn't even know she was in Riverview. Agreeing to see her would only raise her hopes that I could help, which would be cruel. It would be better for her if I didn't go. Better for both of us, really, as the most likely outcome would only be another night terror for me. I had enough trouble sleeping as it was … I certainly didn't need anything new in my life that might make it worse.

Nothing good could come of meeting with Missy. But an awful lot of bad was feasible.

I picked up the phone, fully intending to tell Cole that unfortunately, it was a bad day for me … in fact, the entire week wouldn't work. But maybe we could plan something for over the weekend or next week.

Instead, I found myself typing: *Would 11:30 work?*

Chapter 5

Cole was waiting for me when I arrived at the front of the psychiatric ward. He had on what appeared to be the same blue shirt and jeans he was wearing the day before, except the shirt was more wrinkled and sported a brown stain on the side, like he had spilled coffee on himself. I still wore the same oversized pink tee shirt and black leggings I had put on after my shower, but I had taken a few minutes to add a pair of gold hoop earrings, a chunky gold necklace, mascara, and lip gloss. I refused to let myself think about why I had taken the time to do that.

"She's with me," he said to the same pink-haired orderly sitting behind the desk.

"She still has to sign in," the orderly said, pushing a clipboard at me, her green nails pointing to the next available line, as if it wasn't obvious what I was supposed to do. Everything about her—her manner, her expression—screamed her disapproval. It almost felt personal. I wondered if she thought she was the reason I had left so abruptly after my prior visit.

Gingerly, I took the offered pen and filled out the form. I didn't particularly relish leaving a paper trail, but with Cole standing impatiently at my elbow, it seemed a moot point.

My hope was that after today, I would be able to get my life back. Yet again, I had spent the morning unable to focus, instead going back and forth between wanting to cancel and wishing the clock would move faster. The team meeting was painful and embarrassing. Twice, I had to ask people to repeat their questions, and once, while I was giving an update, I completely lost my train of thought and had to backpedal.

I was missing emails and notifications, even though I was trying to get back on top of everything. I knew other people were starting to notice. Tess sent me a text asking if I was okay and if there was anything she could do to help. I told her everything was fine, but I had a lunch appointment and asked her to cover for me. She immediately agreed, but I knew her antenna was up. I almost never had lunch appointments.

I still wasn't convinced I was doing the right thing, but it was too late now. I just had to hope that, after my conversation with Missy, I would be able to put the whole thing behind me.

Pink-Hair handed me a badge with the word "visitor" on it. I put it around my neck while noticing Cole didn't have one.

"Thanks, doll," Cole said, flashing a smile at her. She turned a slight pink as she pressed the button to open the door for us.

Ah. The mystery of the missing badge was solved.

"Thanks for coming," he said as he led me down the hallway that smelled of bleach and antiseptic. Our footsteps were loud against the tile floor.

I glanced at him in surprise. "Why would you thank me?" I asked. "I can't imagine I'll be of any help to Missy."

"Well, she may disagree," he said. "When I told her you wanted to see her, she really perked up. The most excited I've seen her."

I felt a cold pit settle into my stomach. I truly hoped my selfish need to revisit my past didn't end up harming Missy.

"How is she?" I asked.

"Well, you'll see in a moment. The meds have side effects, but we can at least talk to her. She's mostly coherent."

"Mostly." That didn't seem to bode well.

There was a different cop stationed in front of Missy's room. This one was older with a thick black beard and bushy eyebrows. He nodded at Cole and fixed his eyes on me.

"This is Tori. Missy asked to see her," Cole said.

The cop's gaze didn't waver. "Last name?"

"Agnello," I said.

"Mind showing me some ID?"

I did mind, but refusing would seem more suspicious. Wordlessly, I dug out my license to show him, telling myself that just because Cole found me didn't mean that this particular cop would have any reason to be suspicious.

He jotted down a few notes in a notebook before handing it back. He seemed bored. Just dotting i's and crossing t's. Nothing more.

Still, it made me uneasy.

Cole pushed open the door, and we entered the darkened room.

The first thing that hit me was the stench. The smell of sweat and body odor was very strong, made worse by how warm the room was. I tried to breathe through my mouth.

A bundle of blankets lay on the bed, which I finally realized was a person lying on her side, her back to the door. One hand was handcuffed to a metal bed rod.

A nurse monitored a row of machines that occasionally beeped. I wondered how she could stand to be in there. She glanced over at us. "Missy is pretty tired," she said. "I don't think it's a good time for visitors."

"I think Missy will want to see this one," Cole said.

The nurse didn't look convinced. She had bright-red hair that was pulled back in a French braid and a face covered with freckles. "I think it would be better if you let her rest. She's had quite the ordeal. Her body and mind have been through a lot these past few days."

"I know she's had quite the ordeal," Cole said. His body vibrated with anger, but he kept his tone civil. "But time is of the essence right now, so if she's up for it, I think we should talk to her."

The bundle on the bed finally stirred. "Cole?" The voice was faint, only slightly slurred. "Is that you?"

Just like that, Cole was at her bedside, reaching for her hand in the cuffs. "I'm here. I brought Vicky. Just like you asked."

I opened my mouth automatically to correct him, but realized it wasn't the time or the place. Of course Missy would know me as "Vicky."

"Vicky?" She struggled to sit up. "She's here?"

"I'm here," I said, but I stayed where I was. What I really wanted to do was run out of that hot, smelly, suffocating room, but I forced myself to stay put.

The nurse pursed her lips. "I'll give you ten minutes," she said. "But if she starts to get stressed, you have to promise you'll leave."

"We promise," Cole said, not looking at the nurse as he helped his sister to a sitting position.

I realized a few things as soon as Cole propped her up. First, it was no wonder the room stunk. Missy was covered with sweat. Her gown was sticking to her body, and her forehead glistened in the dim light. Second, there was no way I ever would have recognized her, although the side effects Cole had warned me about were likely responsible for some of that. Her face was puffy and creased, and her mouth drooped on one side. Her hair was plastered against her head with sweat, which made it impossible to tell what color it was, and her eyes were glassy.

She peered at me. "Wow, you didn't change much."

Seriously? That was the last thing I wanted to hear. Did that mean anyone who knew me back when I lived in Redemption would recognize me? Ugh. "How are you feeling?" I asked awkwardly in response. Under the circumstances, it was a stupid question, but I couldn't think of a thing to say about her appearance that wasn't an outright lie or just plain rude.

She barked a laugh. "Like crap. How do you think?"

I had nothing to say to that, so I busied myself looking for a chair to pull a little closer.

She watched me, her eyes narrow and hard in the fleshy folds of her face. Once I was settled in my chair, she leaned forward slightly. "I want to know why you did it."

I nervously glanced at Cole, who looked as surprised as I was. "Why I did what?" I asked.

"Sent him."

I shifted uncomfortably. "Sent who?"

She tried to move even closer, the handcuffs clanging on the metal bed frame. "The faery who stole my baby."

My mouth dropped open as Cole's eyes widened. "Missy, I don't think ..."

"Shut up, Cole," Missy said. Her eyes glittered. "She knows what I'm talking about. Why did you send the faery? Did you think he would return your brother if he had my baby? Why would you do this to me? What have I ever done to you?!"

Missy's voice was getting louder and louder as she fought to move closer to me. "This was a mistake," Cole said, trying to pull her back.

"Missy, I had nothing to do with what happened to your baby," I said.

"You lie," she hissed, baring her teeth. "You had the faery take my baby to save yourself, didn't you?"

You killed your brother, didn't you?

"No, I would never do that," I said, pressing myself against the chair. Something about the crazed look in Missy's eyes and the way she lunged at me dislodged some piece of memory I thought was long buried. My mother, screaming profanities at me, as they came and took her away. I blinked my eyes and gave my head a quick shake, willing those memories to go back where they were. "I would never hurt anyone," I said, and in that moment, I was sure my voice was higher, younger, like a child.

"This is all your fault," Missy screamed. "If the faeries hadn't come for your brother, this never would have happened to me."

The door to the room flung open then, and the nurse who had tried to kick us out came rushing in followed by two beefy orderlies and a man in a white coat with a stethoscope flying from around his neck. The orderlies pushed Cole out of the way and held a screaming, frothing Missy down while the doctor jammed a needle into her shoulder.

Missy panted, trying to buck them off, but whatever was in the needle worked fast, and her body went limp, her eyes fluttering closed.

The orderlies let go of Missy while the nurse started fiddling with the machines. "I told you to let her rest," she snapped. "She needs time to recover."

Cole looked shaken. "But she was fine earlier. We talked, and she didn't mention faeries. She just seemed confused as to what happened."

The doctor sighed, adjusting his stethoscope. He looked way too young to be a doctor, with his thick head of blonde hair and skinny body. "That happens. We're still trying to adjust her meds, but it's not uncommon for her to seem fine and then relapse."

Cole looked down at her. "Will she be okay?"

"We're trying," the doctor said. "She'll be out for a while now. If you want to try coming back later this afternoon, you can see if she's better."

During the exchange, I quietly stood up and started moving toward the open door. I was shaken. Whether it was from what Missy said or the memories that had come loose, I wasn't clear, but what I did know was that I couldn't get out of that room and away from the noise, stench of sweat, and drugs fast enough. The bearded cop was hovering in the doorway, watching the excitement. I stepped toward him, hoping he would get the hint and move.

He gave me a look, but stepped aside to let me through.

"Vicky, wait up," Cole called out from behind me.

I cringed. The bearded cop's eyebrows went up.

Great. The last thing I needed was a curious cop.

I waited for Cole in the hallway, figuring that running away would make him even more interested in me.

"I'm so sorry about that," he said. "I had no idea she would do that, or I never would have invited you."

"It's okay," I said as I started walking down the hallway toward the exit. "Not your fault."

"Can I buy you lunch? Seems like the least I can do."

"Not necessary," I said, speeding up my walk, although Cole kept pace with me. "I need to get back to work anyway."

"You have to eat," he persisted. "It's lunch time."

"Honestly, I don't think I have enough time," I said. We were at the end of the hallway, and I started pushing on the door, but it wouldn't open.

"You have to get buzzed out," Cole said, waving through the window at Pink-Hair who was still at her desk. "Look, it doesn't have to take long. We can just go down to the cafeteria here. The food isn't bad, actually."

The door buzzed, and I immediately shoved it open. "I really shouldn't," I said, even while recounting the promise I'd made myself that very morning to stop skipping lunch. This wasn't what I'd had in mind.

"Actually, you'd be doing me a favor," Cole said.

I shot him a questioning look as we both walked through the waiting area. I caught a glimpse of the expression on Pink-Hair's face, who looked a little distressed that Cole wasn't paying attention to her. "How would I be doing you a favor?"

"Because I really need to talk to someone," he said. He ran his hands through his hair, and I caught a glimpse of something—pain? Anguish?—in his eyes. "Everyone is assuming she's crazy, guilty, or both. I need someone who is maybe a little more understanding and compassionate to listen."

You killed your brother, didn't you?

"You mean someone who might also be a little crazy," I said bitterly. I couldn't get out of the hospital fast enough.

"No! Not that at all," Cole said, grabbing my arm. "Could you just stop for a moment? Give me a minute."

His hand was warm on my skin, warmer than I had expected, and it even tingled a little where he'd touched it. Despite myself, I paused and turned to meet his gaze.

"I feel like you're the only one who might understand," he said. "Not because I think you're crazy or anything else, but because you've lived through it. Something happened the night my sister gave birth just like something happened to you all those years ago. I have no idea if they're related or not ... logically, it doesn't make sense for them to be, but even if they aren't, your taking the time to talk it through with me would really help."

There was a touch of desperation in his eyes, and it hit me that no matter how this was impacting me, what he was going through was far worse. It was his sister who was in the middle of everything, and he had no idea how to help her.

"Okay," I relented. "You're right, anyway. I do need to eat."

He smiled in relief. It lit up his face, nearly taking my breath away.

"You won't regret it. Really, the food is better than you might think."

"I'll be the judge of that," I said.

Chapter 6

Cole wasn't wrong. The food *was* better than I expected. I had a grilled chicken salad, which was huge, with a nice raspberry vinaigrette dressing.

I was feeling quite pleased with myself. A salad AND lunch. So far, so good.

"This is all such a nightmare," Cole said, picking at his Reuben. "I still can't believe it's happening."

"Neither can I," I said. "The whole thing is bizarre."

"I'm just … I don't even know where to begin," he said, with a self-conscious laugh. "There's so much I want to say and ask you, but where to start?"

"Let's start at the beginning," I suggested. "When she first got pregnant. Was everything normal?"

"That's the thing … I'm not really sure."

I paused, my fork halfway to my mouth. "You're not sure?"

He exhaled a long, deep sigh. "So, I guess I'll just say it. Missy does have a history of bipolar issues."

I put my fork down. "Oh, Cole. I'm so sorry."

He nodded. "Thanks. It's not really something I like to talk about. She was first diagnosed in her senior year in high school. Luckily, we got her started on meds early on, and they worked. She was fine. She was living her life, holding down a job, paying her bills. At least on the surface, we thought she was doing well. But then she got pregnant, and everything went to hell." I couldn't see his face, as he was staring at his food, but everything about him—the slump of his shoulders, the way he poked at his meal—screamed how sad and discouraged he was.

"I take it the pregnancy wasn't planned."

He sighed. "I doubt it, but I don't really know."

I raised an eyebrow. "You don't know?"

He sighed again. "Quite honestly, I wasn't even aware she was dating anyone."

"It was a secret?"

He shrugged. "I guess. She doesn't talk about who the father is. Whenever anyone asks, she just offers this little self-satisfying smile, like the cat who ate the canary."

I was floored. "But you two are twins! She didn't even tell you?"

Cole was silent, his expression unreadable. It felt like he was trying to make up his mind about what to say or not say. "At first, all she would say was that she couldn't tell me who the father is. Which was odd, of course. I could tell how excited she was about being pregnant. She's always wanted to be a mom. She even started doing prenatal yoga, even though she always hated yoga before. She changed her eating habits and gave up coffee. But she just refused to talk about the father.

"I couldn't figure out why. Was it a one-night stand, and she was embarrassed? Had she gone to a sperm bank? Finally, one night after I had really been badgering her, she shared a few more details. Said she was in a relationship with the father of her child, and they were in love. She said they were going to get married and raise the baby together, but for now, she had to keep it a secret. When I asked why, all she would tell me was that he was famous, and they had to keep everything hush hush while he worked things out with his family.

"Of course, that made no sense. If he was famous, why would he care about what his family thought? Why would his family have anything to do with anything, anyway? Was the problem that HE was married and had a family? But she refused to explain. I thought she was making it all up because, for whatever reason, she wasn't ready to share the truth … at least not with me. I'll admit, it hurt that she didn't trust me, and I'm not proud of how I responded. We didn't fight or anything like that. I just ... I decided if she wasn't going to trust me, then I didn't need to be that involved in her life. So, I focused on my work and ignored her. In my defense, I had a lot on my plate, but still. So, it was a few months later when I realized she was off her medication."

My eyes widened. "You think she was delusional?"

"What else?" His voice was bitter, and he scrubbed his forehead with his hand. "I'm just so angry with myself for not seeing it at the time. She wasn't lying to me. She wasn't making up a story. She really thought some famous guy was the father. Probably some actor or singer. I should have known she wouldn't have done that to me. We have always been honest with each other. I should have realized then that there was a problem. Maybe I could have done something to have prevented this whole tragedy."

He looked so lost, so sad, I could feel my heart contract. "What about her doctor? Did her doctor know she stopped taking her meds?"

He nodded glumly. "Yes. She had done it all by the book and was apparently being monitored. They were trying other treatments, but clearly, they didn't work."

"Then I don't see how you can blame yourself. It sounds like it's the doctor's fault, not yours."

He ran his hands through his hair again. "You don't understand. Even then, I knew something wasn't right. I asked her, of course, if she was still being treated, and she said "yes" ... that her doctor knew, and she was being carefully monitored throughout the pregnancy. And she didn't sound like she normally did when she was trapped in a delusion. She sounded just like herself, except she was sharing this silly story. But she wasn't being manic. She was just ... normal. Still, I had a feeling something was off. I couldn't put my finger on what, and she was sticking to her story, refusing to budge. I got so angry at her when really, I should have listened to my gut."

I leaned forward. "You're not a doctor. You're her brother. It's not your job to monitor her medical condition. Especially since those drugs can cause birth defects. I'm not surprised she didn't want to take the chance."

He gave me a small, twisted smile. "I appreciate what you're trying to do, but truly, I have a lot to answer for. Yes, she was under medical care, but she was still living alone, and I knew it. I knew she had some friends stopping by to check on her and a neighbor who was keeping an eye on her, but that's not the same as family."

"Your parents couldn't help?"

He shook his head, his eyes on his plate. "My father is ... not well. He hasn't been for a while now. He had a stroke a couple of years ago, and he can't use the right side of his body, which means he can't really walk, dress, or eat. My mother takes care of him full-time. I know she was calling Missy every day, but that's not the same as going over to see her.

"And that's the thing. With so many people checking on her—her therapist, her neighbor, her friends—I told myself she was fine. I had my own life to focus on. I was working full-time plus launching my blog on Substack, so I was basically working all the time. When I found out she was off her meds, I did start checking on her more, but clearly, it still wasn't enough. And she did seem fine, even if sometimes a little scattered or extra emotional, but I just thought that was part of the pregnancy. Hormones, or whatever. But she must have been having episodes. How else do you explain what happened?"

"What about Missy's doctors? Do they have any insight?"

Cole pressed his lips together. "That's the other weird thing about all of this. Missy had an OB/GYN who I thought she liked. He had hospital privileges here, which is where she wanted to deliver her baby. She loved the new Duckworth Birthing Center and was excited about giving birth there. It's all she talked about at first … how she was going to give her baby the best birthing experience she could. She was determined to avoid what our mother went through with us, which, according to my mother, was pretty traumatic. Three days in labor, and she still ended up having a C-section. I don't know how a new birthing center could prevent that, but regardless, there was a time when Missy just wouldn't stop talking about it."

"Well, it does appear to be a beautiful center," I said. The Duckworths were one of Riverview's most wealthy and generous families. They donated money for new parks, a library remodel, and more. The birthing center was their newest donation. Viola Duckworth had a soft spot for new and expectant mothers, and over the years, she worked hard to attract some of the top OB/GYN doctors and surgeons to Riverview.

Cole rolled his eyes. "I get it. But she gave birth at home."

"That *is* weird. She must have changed her mind. But why?"

"Exactly," Cole said. "She went so far as to switch to her current OB/GYN because of the hospital privileges. Why would she suddenly change her mind at the last second and give birth at home?"

"Good question. Has Missy said anything about it yet?"

Cole sighed. "Not really. At least nothing that has made any sense." He scrubbed his face with his hands. The stubble on his face was getting longer, and I wondered when he'd last shaved.

"What do you mean?"

"Missy started talking about some sort of home check-ins she was getting, but it makes no sense. Who does house calls anymore? She insisted she was in some sort of program because she's bipolar, so a nurse came to the house for her appointments. At least, I think it was a nurse—Missy didn't specify exactly who was coming. I have a call into the OB/GYN to ask him about it, though I suspect all he's going to do is confirm there was no nurse … that this was all just another figment of my sister's disease. Just like the mythical famous boyfriend." He poked at his sandwich again, his body collapsed in discouragement.

I was the exact opposite. I found myself sitting straight up, every cell in my body vibrating in alarm. "What if she's telling the truth?"

Cole looked up from his barely touched sandwich. "What? Are you saying you believe a faery stole her baby and left a changeling in his place?"

"No, I'm saying what if Missy is right, and someone WAS trying to steal her baby ... but it was a human, not a faery?"

Cole looked puzzled. "I'm not following."

I leaned forward. "A strange woman who calls herself a nurse suddenly shows up at the home of a mentally ill pregnant woman who has little other support. She gains the pregnant woman's trust and is able to convince her to have the baby at home. Except something goes wrong, and the baby is either stillborn or ... well, clearly not going to make it. So, the nurse simply leaves, and the mentally ill mother is found having a breakdown with her dead baby, thus ensuring no one will believe her about the 'mythical' nurse."

Understanding slowly dawned across his face. "So, you think Missy is telling the truth?"

"To me, it seems to make the most sense. We need to talk to the doctor and find out if there was some sort of visiting-nurse program, but if there wasn't, wouldn't that be a perfect way to steal a baby?"

"But what if the baby was born healthy, and the nurse took it, leaving the mentally ill mother with no baby? Wouldn't the police realize there was a kidnapping going on and be looking for the baby?"

I cocked my head. "Are you sure that's what they would think?"

He looked even more confused.

"So, imagine this. The same scenario. A mentally ill pregnant woman gives birth at home. But there's no baby, and the mother keeps talking about a nurse who had come to the house. Are the cops going to immediately look for that nurse, or are they going to assume the mother did something to the baby?"

Understanding lit up Cole's eyes. "And by the time they realize someone may have actually taken the baby, the nurse is long gone."

I sat back triumphantly. "Exactly."

Cole didn't say anything for a moment. He simply sat there, as if processing what I had said and how all the pieces might fit together. "I don't know," he said at last. "What you say is possible. But I can't get beyond her delusion, which started months earlier."

"Don't you think that would make her more of a target, not less?" I countered.

He cocked his head, studying me. "Is that what you think happened to you?" he asked, his voice soft. "Your mom was targeted because of her disease?"

I stopped breathing. My ribs felt like they had suddenly turned to ice, and the shards splintered throughout my chest, tearing me from the inside.

Did you kill your brother?

Cole looked away, his expression contrite. "I'm sorry," he said. "I wasn't trying to bring up bad memories. It's just that your experience seems so similar to what Missy is going through. You must feel it, too. After all, you showed up. I was hoping maybe you would be open to talking about it."

I was silent. *Was* I open to talking about it? My initial gut reaction was no, absolutely not. I hadn't spent years of my life burying the past simply to dig it all up now.

But then, I thought about my life. My empty, unfulfilling life. Very few relationships. No other interests. All I did was work.

And when I wasn't working, I usually had the television on and a glass of wine in front of me. Could I even call that a "life"?

If I was really as okay as I told myself over and over, would I even be sitting at the table with Cole? Would I have even considered showing up at the hospital in the first place? Or would I have simply said how wild it was that someone else had a story so similar to mine, and gone back to my regular world?

Maybe it was time to start talking about what happened to me all those years ago instead of ignoring it, pushing it down, and numbing it with work and alcohol. Maybe getting myself involved with Cole and Missy's story was a subconscious cry for help.

Maybe it was time to finally come to terms with my past, once and for all.

Chapter 7

"I was really excited about becoming a big sister," I began, my voice low. "There's a lot that's jumbled. I'm not sure if some of the memories are even mine or what someone told me later, but that, I remember. I also remember my mother wasn't quite right for much of her pregnancy, but especially so near the end."

"Why do you say that?"

I shrugged. "It's hard to describe. The closest I can come is that she didn't feel like my mother anymore. I even remember telling my dad that I thought someone else was living inside my mother's body." I let out a bark of laughter that wasn't the least bit humorous. "Kind of ironic, after all that happened."

"Was she abusive to you?"

I shook my head furiously. "No, no, nothing like that. It was more that she was just … erratic. There were days she would barely get out of bed, and if she did, she would just sit at the kitchen table and cry. But there were also days when she would have all this energy, and she would play with me. She'd take me to the park, cook up a storm, paint the nursery. And then there were days you couldn't say anything to her, because the smallest thing would set her off. I remember once, she got so mad, she broke every plate in the cupboard. My dad was beside himself when he came home and discovered the kitchen floor covered in broken china, her sitting in the middle of it and me huddled in my bedroom. To this day, I don't know what she was so upset about. I'm not even sure she knew.

"Then, of course, there was the Day of the Faery Tales."

I rolled my eyes as I said it, mostly to hide the dart of pain that shot through me, tearing through the soft tissues of my chest and heart, reminding me why I never spoke of it.

I wasn't sure who had first dubbed it, but it showed up in a few articles after the fact and ended up catching on in the sick way true-crime stuff sometimes does.

It all started with two questions. I wasn't sure who first voiced them—the detective investigating the case, a journalist, or even my father—but once asked, they ended up changing the entire trajectory of the case.

How did a five-year-old know what a changeling was?

Who had told me?

The answer, of course, was my mother.

I clearly remembered the day. It was one of two memories burned into my brain.

I was playing in my room when my mother's voice called out, floating as if on a cloud. "Vicky, want me to read you a story?"

I had been so excited. I loved when she read to me. I was even more excited on that occasion, because I thought that meant she was "there," that day. Present. I dropped the dolls I was playing with and ran into the living room.

The moment I saw her, I knew something was wrong. She was sitting on the couch, but she wasn't still. She was fidgeting, her fingers plucking at the book on her lap, twisting her hair, her clothing. Her eyes kept darting around the room, unable to focus on anything. Next to her was a glass of clear liquid that smelled funny. Later, the doctors said she must have been drinking, based on what I had told them, but had she? I was only five. I could have gotten it wrong.

"Come sit next to me," she said, quickly patting the seat next to her. "Hurry up."

I didn't want to. I remember how my excitement shifted as I realized it was one of the times mommy was gone. That was how my five-year-old brain characterized her episodes. Mommy was there, or mommy was gone.

That day, mommy was most definitely gone.

Alas, mommy also got mad easily when she was gone, so I still obeyed her, even though I didn't want to.

I scrambled up onto the couch next to her, and she smiled, pressing herself against me. She didn't smell right. When mommy was there, she smelled like vanilla and raspberries, the scent of her bath soap and shampoo. When she was gone, though, she smelled like something else ... something foul. Next to me on the couch, she smelled like sweat and old socks.

She had a book on her lap that was filled with pictures, but it wasn't a child's book. The pictures were more like illustrations, and they were disturbing; human shapes twisted in oddly deformed poses, some with pointed ears and wings. Later, I found out it was a book of faeries, but more for adults than children.

She leaned close to me, her sour breath warm on my cheek. "Listen to me, Vicky. There's danger everywhere. You have to be careful."

Mommy often didn't make much sense when she was gone, but I had learned not to ask too many questions. "Danger?"

She nodded. "We're being watched," she said, dropping her voice. "Can't you see them?"

I jerked my head around, but the living room looked like it always did, albeit messier than it was before the pregnancy. It was strewn with dirty plates, stacked mail, newspapers, and my toys. "See who?"

She cupped her hand over her mouth. "The faeries. They're watching."

She proceeded to tell me a variety of stories about the faeries, or "fae." How they weren't to be trusted. How they loved to trick and hurt humans, sometimes even killing them. How they would lure humans into their land, where the humans would think they were spending an afternoon at a party, when in reality, hundreds of years sped by. When they were finally returned, nothing was the same. All their friends and family members were dead.

"You can't trust them, Vicky," she said, her eyes shifting constantly around the room. There was an odd sheen to them that made me shrink away and into the couch. "They only want to hurt us."

But she saved the worst for last.

The story of the changeling. She explained how a faery would sneak into a house and steal a baby, but leave one of its own to be raised in the human baby's place.

"You're going to be an older sister," my mother said, rubbing her swollen belly. She was quite far along at that point. "You have to watch out for your little brother. Promise me."

"I promise," I said, my eyes wide.

"You can't let the faeries get him."

"I won't," I breathed.

My mother took my hand and pressed it against her belly. I felt a kick against my palm. She laughed, a strange note straddling the line between delight and out of control. "See? Your brother heard you. He knows you're going to take care of him. You're going to keep him safe."

All these years later, and it still felt like a knife in my gut. *I was his big sister. I was supposed to keep him safe. I made a promise while he was in the womb.*

Instead, I was accused of killing him.

"Was she manic?"

I jerked my head up. I was so lost in the memory, I had nearly forgotten Cole was there. "I don't think so. Before the pregnancy, she was on medication for depression and anxiety, but like your sister, when my mother got pregnant, they didn't want her on the meds. My understanding is that when she was pregnant with me, she was more or less fine. It wasn't easy, but it wasn't that bad. When she was pregnant with Scott, though, that wasn't the case. Her schizophrenia symptoms started, possibly triggered by the pregnancy. It's also possible the pregnancy had no bearing on it … that she would have become schizophrenic no matter what.

"Later, the doctors said she was self-medicating throughout the pregnancy. Drinking or doing drugs. Of course, my descriptions of clear liquids that smelled funny didn't help matters.

"Anyway, as bad as things were when she was pregnant, they got even worse after she gave birth."

I paused, reached for my iced tea. My mouth was parched, like I hadn't drunk anything in days.

"Eventually, everyone realized she had a really bad case of postpartum depression. She wanted nothing to do with Scott. Wouldn't touch him. She barely even looked at him. Dad was the one trying to take care of him. Well, dad and me."

"That must have been a lot," Cole said.

I nodded, staring at the remains of my salad. "It was. He kept telling me my mom would be fine. That we were a team and could do it ourselves. Especially since I was such a 'good little helper.' Mom just needed a few days to rest, and all would be well. Of course, that wasn't what happened at all."

I turned my head, unable to look at Cole, instead focusing on a bearded doctor sitting at a table across the room, leafing through a medical journal and drinking a large cup of coffee. I could feel the decades-old shame flowing through my body like a drug. I hunched my shoulders, fighting the urge to curl in on myself. Even though I knew it was unwarranted (I was only five, after all … I couldn't possibly be blamed for any of it), I still to that day felt like somehow, some way, I could have stopped it.

You have to watch out for your little brother. Promise me.

"Again, I don't remember much other than she wanted nothing to do with Scott. But it wasn't just Scott; she didn't want anything to do with me, either. She mostly just stayed in bed, the door shut, the curtains closed, barely getting up except to go to the bathroom, hardly eating or drinking anything. I remember my father going in and begging her to at least have a cup of tea. But even that seemed beyond her.

"So, it ended up being me and my dad taking care of Scott. I loved my little brother. Dad would let me hold him and feed him his bottle. He was such a good eater." I could still remember holding him in my lap. Dad would prop me up on the couch, surrounded by pillows, as I held the bottle. Scott would gaze at me, his big eyes watching me as one of his tiny hands clutched my finger. He smelled like baby powder and formula—a warm, comforting smell. I blinked my eyes, trying to hide my face from Cole.

I was his big sister. I was supposed to keep him safe. How could I have let him down?

"Anyway," I said, dashing a hand across my eyes. "I guess it was about a week after we brought him home when all hell broke loose."

"How much do you remember?" Cole asked, his voice low. I was so thankful he ignored my emotions and just focused on the story, I could have reached across the table and kissed him.

"Everything and not much," I said with a bitter laugh. "While there's a lot burned into my brain, there's also a lot of holes.

"One thing I don't remember is how I got into my brother's room. My father said I was sleepwalking. Apparently, I had a history of sleepwalking, nightmares, and night terrors." I couldn't repress the shiver, thinking about those terrible nightmares as a child. But what I saw in Scott's room didn't feel like any nightmare I ever had. It felt different … grounded in reality. Even though parts of it made no sense.

"I remember standing in the doorway of Scott's room and seeing a figure bending over the crib. It was dressed in black. At first, I thought it was my father checking on him, but there was something … not right about it." My stomach clenched remembering. "There was this sound coming from the figure. It was like a high-pitched keening. Nothing like my father would have made.

"I remember asking, 'Who are you?' and the figure turned to me with a jerk. The face was white ... like, really white. Unnaturally white. And really thin and gaunt. It wasn't a normal face. It was something ... not human. I couldn't even tell if it was a man or a woman. And there was this smell." I wrinkled my nose. "It was this damp, rotting smell, like something was decaying. It was just a whiff, but there all the same.

"And when the figure saw me standing there, it put a finger to its lips like this." I demonstrated. "'*Shhh.*' Then, it gathered my brother up into its arms.

"I said, 'No, you can't take my brother! Stop!' But it didn't stop. It just smiled at me, this terrible smile, and said in this horrible, raspy whisper, 'Don't worry. Your brother has a little cold. I'm going to take him to get some medicine and bring him right back.'"

"I said, 'He's sick? Let me get my dad.' And the figure said, 'It's all taken care of. Don't worry. There's another baby here you need to take care of while I'm looking after Scott.'

"'Another baby?' I asked, and that's when I saw the bundle in the crib. I took a few steps toward it, trying to see the new baby. I was fascinated with the idea of another baby.

"But there was something wrong with it. It wasn't moving at all. I reached through the crib to poke it, and it was completely still.

"And that's when I began to scream."

The rest of the night was a blur, but I filled Cole in on what I did remember. My father came rushing into the room, his hair all stuck up on one side of his head, his eyes wild. When he saw the dead baby in the crib, it was like his entire body seemed to collapse in on itself, and his face aged about twenty years. "Vicky," he whispered. "What have you done?"

"The faeries!' I had screamed. 'The faeries took Scott! Just like in the story. There's a chang-ing in there!'

"My father had no idea what I was talking about. His face was full of grief and horror. It was only when the cops showed up that someone finally figured out that I wasn't saying 'chang-ing,' but 'changeling.'

"It was all very confusing and jumbled," I said. "The cops came and asked me some questions. I kept telling them the baby in the crib wasn't Scott—that the faeries took Scott and left a different baby in its place. But my father kept insisting it was Scott in the crib. There was no other baby. Later, a medical examiner said Scott died of crib death. It was no one's fault. I had been sleepwalking, you see. Night terrors. Maybe I had even been in the room when Scott had died, and my subconscious conjured up this terrible nightmare of him being taken and another baby being left in his place.

"As bad as all of that was, the worst was yet to come."

At some point during the commotion, our house full of strange adults, a dead baby, and a terrorized five-year-old who wouldn't stop screaming about the faeries, my mother appeared.

She looked terrible. Like she hadn't showered in days, which was likely accurate. Her hair was greasy and matted, and her nightgown filthy. Her skin looked grey and worn.

"What's going on?" Her expression was bewildered as she tried to take everything in. "Simon? What happened?"

"Ma'am," one of the cops started to say as my father tried to step between them. "Cora, it's okay, I'm handling it. Go back to bed."

"Sir," the cop said, trying to move my father aside, but my father was determined to keep the cops from talking to my mother by telling the officer my mother wasn't well.

I don't know who would have prevailed if I hadn't decided to step in. Of my many regrets, this was one of the biggest.

I launched myself at my mother. "Mommy," I screamed. "The faeries took Scott! Just like you said! They took him!" I threw my arms around my mother and buried my head in her waist.

Above my head, I could hear the adults talking. "Cora, what is Vicky talking about?" my father asked, his voice floating like a disembodied head.

At the same time came my mother's voice. "Is that true? Is Scott gone?"

More jumbled voices. I buried my face deeper into my mother's soft tummy. She smelled of dirty clothes and old sweat, but I didn't care.

Two hands grasped my upper arms and pried me off, not too lightly.

It was my mother. She held me at arm's length as she stared at me, a flat sheen to her eyes.

"Is this true?" she demanded.

I sniffed. "The faeries took Scott," I repeated. "Just like you said."

Her mouth went slack with horror. "You were supposed to protect him," she hissed.

"But the faeries ..." I started to protest, but she cut me off. "What did you do to your brother?" Her voice grew louder, rising to a shriek. She started shaking me, hard. "What did you do? Did you kill your brother? Did you?"

My head snapped back and forth, and I was lost in confusion. I do remember my father bellowing, "Cora," as rough hands pulled me away from her. There was a sharp pain in my mouth, and I tasted blood. I had bitten my tongue, at some point.

The next thing I remembered was my mother on the floor, still screaming at me, insisting I had killed my brother, the cops on top of her, forcing handcuffs on her. One of the cops was talking to my father, who looked completely shell-shocked. My mother's eyes were rolling around her head like a wild animal.

Finally, they hauled my mother to her feet. Saliva dripped from her mouth, and a long thin line hung from her chin. She was struggling, fighting with the officers even with her hands handcuffed behind her back.

Eventually, the adults must have remembered I was in the room, and I was ushered out and back to my bedroom, but the damage was done. The image of my mother getting dragged off by the cops as she screamed at me was branded into my brain.

Cole was staring at me, his mouth open in horror. "I didn't realize," he said. "I had heard bits and pieces, but not the full story. That must have required a lot of therapy to get over."

I smiled despite myself. "The therapy helped, but unfortunately, it didn't cure me."

His smile was equally grim. "I don't think therapy is designed to 'cure' anyone. But I digress. Was your mother committed, then? Or did she go to jail? I think I remember the cops suspecting she might have killed your brother."

"She was never charged with anything," I said. "The medical examiner eventually ruled that Scott died of crib death, so no one was at fault. I think there might have been some discussion as to whether my mother could have smothered Scott and not have left any trace, but there was no evidence of any foul play, so it was all dropped. But my mother still never came home.

"I remember my dad telling me my mom was going to be gone for a little while, so she could 'get better. 'Remember, Vicky, how she was taking her medicine here at home? Well, the hospital will give her her medicine now for a little while, and after she starts to feel better, she'll come home.' I don't know if my father knew then that my mother was never going to leave the hospital and was trying to soften the truth, or if he truly did think once she was stabilized, she would be fine. It probably doesn't matter."

"Where is she now?"

"Sunny Meadows."

Cole whistled. "That place is nicer than my apartment."

I raised my eyebrows. "You know it?"

He looked a little uncomfortable. "I took a tour of it a few years back. When Missy started getting bad. We had looked into a short-term stay just to help her get stabilized on her meds. Unfortunately, even a week's stay was out of our budget."

I turned away, feeling equally uncomfortable. My father owned a very successful construction company, which meant I never lacked for any material items. Even when I went to live with Nanna, I knew my dad was sending money to her. I was well aware of how lucky I was.

Money didn't buy happiness, but it sure made the struggle more comfortable.

"Do you see your mother at all?"

I shrugged. "Every few months." It was more like every six months, but Cole didn't need to know that. When I lived with Nanna, she would take me several times a year, but it was never a good experience. My mother was either too drugged out or too confused to have much of a conversation with. But at least she never screamed at me, so that was progress. Once I started living on my own, I dropped my visits down to twice a year. "It's been a long time."

Cole gave me a sideways smile. "Mental illness sucks, doesn't it?"

My answering smile was equally bleak. "No question."

We stared at each other for a moment, eyes locked, a strangely intimate moment born of two family tragedies.

Cole broke the gaze first. "So, you left Redemption, but your dad stayed. Where did you go? Here?"

I nodded. "My grandmother on my mother's side lives here. I moved in with her. Although you already figured all that out, didn't you?"

He grinned. "What about your dad's family?"

"I never knew them. My father was an only child of a single mother. She died years ago. He never spoke about his father, so I don't know if he even knew who he was."

"That's kind of sad."

"Yeah. It is."

Cole played with his sandwich, but he didn't ask the obvious follow-up question.

Why?

Why, after all the terrible things that had happened to my family, did I not live with my father? Especially since he appeared to be all alone in the world. No parents, siblings, or even cousins. His wife was locked in a psychiatric ward, and he sent his only child to live with her grandma. Why would he do such a thing?

The answer was, of course, because of all the terrible things that had happened.

My father, to his credit, tried. He hired a succession of babysitters to watch me when I got home from school and handle the grocery shopping and cooking. A housekeeper came in once a week.

But the older I got, the reality that it wasn't working became clear. My father worked all the time, so I barely saw him. Nanna started spending more and more time at the house, so I wouldn't be raised by babysitters, and eventually, she told my father it might make more sense for everyone if she took me to Riverview. My father didn't protest. In fact, I think he was relieved when I was finally gone.

Nanna made a point of making sure I saw my father as regularly as his schedule would allow—one weekend a month, holidays, sometimes a week or two in the summer. But there was always an awkwardness between us that never quite went away. I suspect we were both happier once I became an adult, and my visits were regulated to holidays and an occasional lunch or dinner if either of us happened to be in town.

"That must have been nice," Cole said. "To have a grandmother so close."

"Yes, I was lucky," I said. "Moving out of Redemption was the best thing that happened to me. Oh, wait ..." I put my hand up near my mouth. "I didn't mean to say that."

Cole let out a chuckle, but there wasn't much humor in it. "Why? Because I still lived there? Don't worry, I'm not offended. Moving out of Redemption was the best thing that happened to us, as well."

"So, what's your story?" I was relieved to not be the focus of the conversation, but I was also curious.

"With me, it was college. I was accepted here at University of Riverview, and once I moved out, I never went back. Missy, though ..." He swallowed and looked away. "Do you believe all the stories?"

"You mean about Redemption being haunted?"

"Yeah."

I laughed, but it was full of bitterness. "I saw my baby brother be taken by a faery and another baby left in his place. What do you think?"

"You were five years old. Children see things and have nightmares all the time. You don't have to live in a haunted town for that to happen."

He had a point. It wasn't uncommon for children to let their imaginations run away with them and see things that aren't there. It was even more common if that child already suffered from night terrors and had a family history of mental illness and schizophrenia.

The problem was, I didn't believe it.

The logical part of my brain knew I was being ridiculous. No one had snuck into Scott's room and stolen him. My father had told me over and over that it was Scott in the crib. The most likely, and most tragic, explanation was exactly what the doctors kept telling me: I had been sleepwalking. I walked into Scott's room while he was struggling to breathe. I was there when he died and imagined the rest.

It made perfect sense.

But I still didn't buy it.

Cole continued to study me, his hazel eyes more green than brown in the fluorescent light, waiting for me to answer. Suddenly, his eyes widened as understanding lit up his face. "You really think it was a faery."

"I didn't say that."

"You didn't have to."

I frowned, picking up my fork to dig at the remains of my salad. "I get that it doesn't make any sense. It makes far more sense that I imagined it."

"So, why don't you think you did?"

I didn't immediately answer. How could I possibly explain without sounding like a nut?

On the other hand, why did it matter if Cole thought I was as crazy as my mother? It wasn't like I was ever going to see him again after we finished lunch.

The thought made me sad, which also made no sense. I barely knew him. Even when we were children, we hadn't been friends. And while it was true finding a few more friends would be good for me, making friends with someone who was in the middle of the same nightmare I had experienced as a child was probably not wise.

So why was I fretting?

"It doesn't matter," I said. "It sounds crazy even to me. And it's not like anyone can do anything about it anymore."

"Try me."

There was something so warm and comforting about him ... even his gaze seemed non-judgmental. I reminded myself again that none of it mattered. The chances of seeing him again were pretty low, so why not tell him? It might even do me some good.

"There was just something so real about it," I said. "I've had night terrors before, and as real as they seem at the time, when I remember them later, there's almost a hollowness to them. Like they're just puffs of air—nothing substantial. Which of course, there wouldn't be. But this ... the air shifted as she, or he, or *it* glided past me. I even felt the touch of the black cloak against my arm. In all my nightmares and night terrors, I've never felt anything so ... *real*, like that. There was even a smell." I shivered, despite feeling unseasonably warm, even sweaty.

"What was the smell?"

I shuddered. "Death."

His eyebrows shot up, but he didn't say anything. After a pause, during which I tried to forget the stink that sometimes seemed to have coated the inside of my nose, I went on. "And there was the baby."

"Baby? You mean Scott?"

I shook my head. "No, I mean the baby that was left. It wasn't Scott."

Cole's eyes went very wide. "But the papers ..."

"I know what the papers said," I said curtly, cutting him off. "That it was him. But it wasn't. I know. I had spent hours holding him and feeding him. I knew what Scott looked like. That baby, whoever or whatever he was, didn't look like Scott."

"What was different?"

I frowned. "It's hard to describe. His face was thinner, flatter than Scott's. I didn't get a very good look."

"They let you see the baby after it died?"

"No, when that … that *thing* told me about the baby, I went rushing to the crib to look. That's when I saw the baby was all wrong. The face was all wrong. And I started screaming about the faery taking Scott. Later, when the cops and everyone were in the house, I tried to tell them the baby wasn't Scott. I tried to get them to show me the baby again, but they wouldn't."

"What did your father say?"

I snorted. "That it was Scott, of course. What do you think?"

"How did he explain the babies looking different?"

"That's just it—he said they didn't. He thinks the trauma of it all caused my mind to play tricks on me, so I could believe that Scott was still alive."

Cole was quiet for a moment, digesting everything I'd said. I put down the fork I had been using to poke at my salad and picked up my napkin to wipe my hands.

"I knew you wouldn't believe me," I said. "I don't blame you. It's pretty unbelievable."

"I didn't say I didn't believe you."

"Your expression does. I have to go."

"Vick … Tori, wait a minute." He leaned forward, putting a hand on my arm. I felt a jolt, like an electric shock shot up my arm.

He must have felt something similar, because he removed his hand almost immediately. "Just give me a moment. It's a lot to take in. And it's not that I don't believe you. It's just that I'm struggling to also not believe your father. Why would he lie, if it wasn't his child?"

I collapsed in my seat. "I know," I said softly. "It makes no sense." I could still remember the pain and grief on my father's face as he repeated to me over and over, "Honey, I know how terrible this is, but truly. Scott was the one in that crib. It was a terrible thing to happen, but he's up in heaven now, with grandma and grandpa."

"Yeah, that's what's so weird about it," Cole said. "Not just why your father would lie about such a thing, but also, if Scott had actually been kidnapped, why would the kidnapper leave a different baby? And where would the kidnapper even get one?"

I rubbed my temples, feeling a slight headache starting to form. I wished I was home and could open a bottle of wine. I definitely needed a drink after this conversation. "I know. Nothing about it makes sense. Unless ..."

"Unless?"

I gave him a crooked smile. "It really was a changeling, after all."

Chapter 8

Cole opened his mouth to answer when his cell rang. He glanced at it and held up a finger. "Give me a moment—I need to take this."

He turned away and answered his phone, keeping his voice low. I pulled my own phone out of my purse and winced when I saw the time. I needed to get back to work. I glanced over, considering leaving while he was on the phone, but that felt rude. So instead, I checked my email and Slack to see what was waiting for me.

"Sorry about that," Cole said as he hung up the phone.

"No worries, but I need to get going anyway."

"Think you could stay away for thirty more minutes?"

I glanced up at him. His expression was neutral, but excitement danced in his eyes. "Why?"

"That was Missy's doctor. He's in the hospital and can see us now."

"'Us'?"

He shrugged. "Why not? You're here, and you know the story. Aren't you the least bit curious about what happened?"

I was. I was a lot curious. It was one thing for this crazy story to have happened to me.

But to have it happen to someone else over twenty years later?

Yeah, I definitely had questions.

On the other hand, it really had nothing to do with me. I had a job to get back to, and honestly, I had no business teaming up with Cole for some amateur sleuthing.

I had better things to do with my time.

Like what? A voice inside me inquired, but I shoved it down. No, this had all been a nice little vacation from my regular life. But playtime was over. It was time to get back to work.

I opened my mouth, all set to tell him I couldn't, but instead found myself saying, "Okay, why not?"

He grinned. "Great. It shouldn't take long." He swept up the tray with his half-eaten meal and headed to the conveyor belt that rolled the dirty dishes into the kitchen. I did the same and followed after him.

"So, this is why you believe Redemption is haunted," he said, giving me a sideways look. "Because you think a faery took your brother."

I gave him my crooked smile again. "Crazier things have happened in Redemption. If such a thing could happen in this world, it would likely be in Redemption."

Redemption, Wisconsin, was an enigma. The town had a strange, haunted past that started in 1888 when all the adults suddenly disappeared. No one knew why … not even the children who were left behind. Since then, Redemption had been a hotbed of hauntings, bizarre disappearances, and more. A lot more.

People who lived there swore the town itself decided who stayed and who left. It was all very mysterious and strange.

Personally, I was glad to no longer be living there. Even the short time I spent visiting my father always gave me willies. I could feel the hair on the back of my neck start to stand up the moment I entered the city limits, and I wouldn't relax until I left again.

Cole slid his tray onto the conveyor belt. "Scarily, that makes a lot of sense," he said. "I personally was never all that comfortable living there. I'm much happier here."

"Same," I said. I fell into step beside him as we left the cafeteria and started snaking our way through the hospital corridors. "What about your sister?"

"Oh, Missy hated Redemption. She had terrible nightmares when we were kids. She was sure the house we lived in was haunted." He shook his head, a bemused expression on his face. "I never saw any evidence of ghosts, but it also never felt like home to me. I always felt unwelcome in that house." He gave me a self-conscious smile. "I've never said that to anyone before, but if anyone would understand, I suspect it would be the girl who thinks a faery stole her brother."

"It makes total sense to me," I assured him.

"Well, over the years, my parents would try and move, but something always fell through, and we'd have to stay. The house wouldn't sell, or the buyer would cancel, or a job offer would fall through. So, we had to wait until we graduated before we were able to leave. My parents are still there, though."

"Yeah, my dad is, too." We were quiet for a moment as we reached the elevator. Cole pressed the button to go up.

"It's weird, though," he said. "Missy was here in Riverview when she gave birth. She wasn't in Redemption."

"Then it was probably not the same faery," I said drily as the doors opened.

Cole laughed … the first true laugh he'd probably had in days. "Probably not. Although," his expression changed, becoming thoughtful again. "It IS wild, don't you think? You both having such similar stories? The only thing that's truly different is the location."

The elevator doors opened, revealing a tired med student and a couple of nurses, and saving me from answering.

It WAS wild, but it certainly couldn't be related. There was just no way.

My involvement and interest were simply as a curious on-looker. Nothing more and nothing less.

Because what happened to Missy couldn't possibly have anything to do with what happened to me.

Could it?

* * *

We found Missy's doctor standing by the nurses' station on the birthing center floor. Unlike the ward Missy was on, which had walls painted beige and looked cold and clinical, these were a warm, welcoming yellow edged with ducks and teddy bear wallpaper.

He was a middle-aged, tall, lanky man with dark-red hair and gold-rimmed glasses. His name tag read "Dr. Greene." As we approached, he glanced up from the paperwork he was doing and pushed them up on nose. "Cole Bennett? Missy's brother?"

"That's me."

Dr. Greene shook his hand before glancing at me. "A friend of the family," Cole said, introducing me.

Dr. Greene nodded. "I'm so sorry to hear about Missy," he said. "I don't know how much help I'll be, as there are some things I can't talk about. Not to mention I'm not her doctor anymore."

Cole blinked. "Wait. What?"

Dr. Greene looked flustered. "Oh. Didn't Missy tell you? Here." He scooped up his files and gestured for us to follow him, leading us to a semi-private waiting area off the main hall-way. "Have a seat." He waved to a small couch, almost like it was his office, as he sat down in an overstuffed chair across from us.

I gingerly sat. The couch was so small, I was nearly touching Cole. I told myself it wasn't a big deal.

"I don't understand. Are you her doctor, or do I have the wrong Dr. Greene? I'm sure that's the name she gave me."

"No, it was me," he said.

"Then what happened?"

"It was about a month ago. She canceled her appointments. When my secretary called to reschedule them, she said she had decided to find another doctor."

"Did she tell you who? Or why?"

He shook his head. "No, we asked her if she wanted us to send her medical records to another OB, and she said, 'no.'"

"Why would she do that?" Cole muttered.

Dr. Greene adjusted his glasses. "You'll have to ask her."

"Do you think it had to do with the nurse who was seeing her at her apartment?"

Dr. Greene gave Cole a strange look. "Nurse?"

Cole sighed. "Missy had said there was some program at the hospital that qualified her for in-home care. A nurse was visiting her each week."

"I don't know anything about that."

"She said it was affiliated with this hospital."

"She must have been mistaken. We don't have any program like that."

"Does any other hospital around here have one?"

"Not to my knowledge."

Cole rubbed his forehead. "What about her health? And the baby's health? Is there anything you can tell me about that?"

"Unfortunately, no."

Cole gritted his teeth in frustration. "You know she was bi-polar, right?"

"Correct."

"Didn't it bother you that a bipolar patient stopped seeing you?"

"Of course it did," Dr. Greene said. "Which is why we reached out. We followed all the protocols. But she's an adult. We certainly couldn't force her to be our patient. If she wanted to go to someone else, that was her decision."

"But if you were worried about the baby, couldn't you have hospitalized her?"

"Her therapist is the person who could have committed her, if she thought Missy was a danger to herself or her baby."

Cole didn't immediately answer. Instead, he started grinding his teeth, and I could see a muscle jump in his jaw.

"What about drugs and alcohol?" I asked. Both Dr. Greene and Cole stared at me. I hadn't intended on saying anything, but the question seemed to fly out of my mouth.

"What about them?"

"Do you think Missy was self-medicating? And maybe that's what happened to the baby?"

"I really can't share anything about Missy's state of mind," Dr. Greene said.

I leaned forward. "But is it possible?"

He shrugged. "Anything is possible. If you're asking how Missy was doing, again, that's not something I can comment on."

"What if we told you that the baby showed signs of having been exposed to either drugs or alcohol while it was in the womb?" I persisted. Cole glanced over at me, an eyebrow raised in surprise, but I ignored him. "Would that surprise you?"

Dr. Greene straightened his glasses. "Surprise me? No, as I said, anything is possible. If that's what the M.E. found, I wouldn't question it."

"I guess what I'm asking is … well, there are some patients you might have more difficulty imagining drinking or doing drugs while they were pregnant, so you might be inclined to question the M.E.'s ruling. Maybe offer an alternative theory. I was wondering if Missy fell into that camp, or if, in her case, it would be consistent with what you knew about her?"

Dr. Greene folded his arms across his chest. "The vast majority of my patients do not cancel their appointments in their last trimester, nor do they switch to a different doctor. Unless there is something wrong with the fetus, and they require a specialist, but even then, that's usually determined earlier in the pregnancy. I would consider a patient with a healthy pregnancy doing so as acting erratically, and a patient acting erratically in one area would have a high probability of acting like that in another area. Does that answer your question?"

I sat back. "Yes, thank you."

Dr. Greene pulled his cell phone out of his pocket and glanced at it. "If you have no more questions for me, I must excuse myself."

"I appreciate your help," Cole said.

Dr. Greene gave us both a curt nod before standing up and striding out of the room.

"What was all that about the drugs and alcohol?" Cole asked.

"A hunch," I said. "Something is just starting to feel fishy to me. Like this is too pat. If it turns out Missy was abusing drugs or alcohol while she was pregnant, then this is all a moot point. But if she claims she wasn't …"

"Then she's been set up," Cole finished. "If whoever this so-called nurse is convinced her to stop going to Dr. Greene, and if no one believes the nurse exists, then it looks bad for Missy."

"Exactly. I wonder about Missy's therapist," I said. "I wish we could ask her some questions. It would be interesting to know if she knew that Missy stopped seeing Dr. Greene."

"I don't know if she would tell us that or not," Cole said. "She left me a voicemail message saying she was too busy to meet with me. And even if she wasn't, it was a waste of time, as she couldn't discuss Missy, anyway."

"That seems a little rude," I said. "Dr. Greene couldn't share much either, yet he still made the effort. You'd think she'd at least give you the courtesy of talking to you. You're Missy's brother, after all."

"You'd think," he said. His cell phone buzzed, and he fumbled around to grab it.

"Oh, I have to go," I said, standing up as I dug into my purse for my own phone. I suddenly realized how long I had been at the hospital—first Missy, then lunch, and then Dr. Greene. I snatched it up, my heart sinking at the full screen of notifications. "I really need to go."

"Of course," Cole stood up as well. "I have to take this myself."

We stared at each other awkwardly. I tried to figure out what to say. See you around? I suspected we both knew that wouldn't happen. A friendship built on a semi-shared tragedy wasn't a solid foundation for anything lasting. I should know. Exhibit A—my relationship with my father.

Keep me posted on your sister? That sounded a little ghoulish, considering there was a dead baby involved. On the other hand, maybe he wanted me to show interest. He invited me to meet with the doctor, after all. Maybe he really was looking for someone to help him investigate.

And there was no question I wanted to know what happened.

"I'll call you with any updates," he said.

"Please do," I answered.

He nodded once. I slipped past him and was heading to the door when he called me back. I turned.

"Thank you," he said.

"For what?"

"For listening. For coming with me. For not assuming Missy is guilty."

I flashed him a crooked smile. "I'm the last person who should assume anyone's guilt or innocence."

"You know what I mean."

I looked directly into his eyes. "I do."

We stared at each other for a moment. I could see the boy he once was, lost and confused, any my heart broke a little for him.

I ducked my head and turned to leave. This time, he didn't stop me.

I most definitely didn't need to start any sort of friendship or relationship or anything else with someone whose twin sister was currently committed to a mental hospital amidst questions around what happened to her baby.

No matter how much he looked like he needed a friend.

The best thing I could do, for both of us, was keep my distance.

Chapter 9

I arrived at home to a virtual stack of messages and notifications I needed to address. Tess, my assistant, was the most vocal, having left multiple texts, Slacks, and even a voicemail. She was sure I had been kidnapped or involved in some kind of accident, as I usually wasn't that hard to reach.

When I told her I was having lunch with an old friend and time got away from me, she instantly perked up. "How old?" she asked. "And could this be a male friend?"

I could feel my cheeks burning as I assured her it was strictly platonic.

"Oh, no you don't," she said. "I want the deets. Drinks on Thursday. I'm not taking 'no' for an answer."

I reluctantly agreed, mostly because she was a great person to cover for me the handful of times I did want to take a little time for myself during a workday, this week excluded. Regardless, I was sure I was done needing time off. The moment Missy was stable, she would be able to answer questions, and the mystery would likely be solved. My services would no longer be needed. However, in the highly unlikely case that I did end up taking a longer lunch hour or breaks during the day in the future, I wanted to be able to count on her.

For the first time since the whole Missy business began, I found I was able to focus on work. So, I spent the afternoon getting caught up and was barely aware of the time passing.

In fact, I had put Missy and Cole aside so completely that near the end of the day, when my phone buzzed with a text, I picked it up, assuming it was something to do with work, even though my work colleagues rarely texted me.

It was Cole.

What are you doing tonight?

I stared at the phone unable to comprehend the message. Was he asking me out *on a date?* Did I even want to go on a date with him? I could feel my heartbeat speed up, and my palms were suddenly sweaty. *This is silly*, I lectured myself silently. *I'm not in high school anymore.*

But why would he ask me on a date? What would we even talk about? We already spilled our guts that afternoon. What was left to discuss?

Catching up on work. I finally typed back. *You know, to make up for my extra-long lunch.*

Can you take an hour to come talk to the neighbor with me?

Neighbor? What was he talking about? I was starting to wonder if he even meant to be texting me.

I was trying to formulate a way to ask him if he meant those texts for me without sounding too rude when another message appeared.

The neighbor recanted.

I was completely lost. I typed a question mark in response.

The three bubbles appeared, then disappeared, and then my phone rang, startling me so, I almost dropped it.

Of course it was Cole.

"I thought it was easier to call than type," he said breathlessly when I answered. He sounded like he had been running. "Missy's neighbor. Do you remember? He said he saw someone leave Missy's house the night of the … the incident."

I had completely forgotten about the witness. "That's right …. there was a witness. So, Missy isn't crazy at all."

"Yes, but he recanted," Cole said.

"What do you mean, 'he recanted'?"

"He called the cops this afternoon and told them he had been mistaken. He hadn't seen anyone at all. He must have been dreaming."

"What?"

"I know! That's why I want to go talk to him. Do you want to come with?"

I paused. Did I? I hadn't been lying when I told him I needed to catch up on work that evening. And doing so would be a better use of my time than tracking down this neighbor on a case that had nothing to do with me.

Yes, it made far more sense to say "no."

The problem was, I wanted to go.

I wanted to know what happened.

"Honestly, it will only be an hour, hour and a half tops," he said into my hesitation. "You'll have plenty of time for work."

"Okay," I said. "If you think it's really not going to take that long."

"I do," he said. "I have to get some work done myself later. Needless to say, I haven't done much of anything since this whole thing happened."

"Where should I meet you?"

"I'll text you the address."

I hung up, then headed into the bathroom to check my appearance. *Really, it shouldn't matter*, I told myself as I undid my hair from its ponytail, let it fall around my shoulders, and added lip gloss. *He just saw you a few hours ago*, I reminded myself as I picked up my mascara and then put it back in the drawer. *This isn't a date. We are investigating what happened to his sister.*

I took one last look in the mirror and headed for the door.

* * *

Cole was already there when I arrived.

He had parked in the street, a few doors down from Missy's apartment complex, and was standing outside his car. He leaned against the driver's door, playing with his phone. He wore the same outfit as earlier, except he had added a jean jacket, which made me wonder if I should have grabbed a light jacket, too. Even though it was nearly June, it could still get cold when the sun went down. He looked up as I parked right behind him.

"Any trouble finding the place?" he asked as I got out.

"Nope, it was easy."

Missy lived at the end of a quiet, residential street. There were dozens and dozens of smaller buildings within the giant apartment complex, all sprawled across the well-manicured lawn. Each smaller building appeared to house four apartments, two above and two below, complete with balconies overlooking the front and garages and driveways in the back. A cobbled pathway meandered through the mature oak, maple, and pine trees, and pots of marigolds and geraniums dotted the balconies. Further down, I could see what appeared to be some sort of community center complete with a huge pool. The sun was starting to set, and it cast a warm, orange glow over the dark-brown siding, making it look almost like a collection of cottages.

"This is nice," I said as I fell into step next to Cole.

"Yeah, it sure is," he said, his mouth a sideways slant. "They're actually condos, not apartments, in case you were wondering. Definitely nicer than my place."

"Nicer than mine, too," I said. "She must be doing well."

"Yeah, looks like it," he said.

I glanced at him. "You don't know?"

He shrugged. "She has some sort of administrative job with the university. With the pregnancy, she had dropped down to half-time, but she was still able to keep her health insurance, which is important. But I don't know." I followed his gaze as we started walking down the quiet sidewalk. Up ahead, a mother herded her two kids through the front door, one of them whining about wanting to go to the park. "I'm pretty sure she hasn't been working at all for at least the past three or four months. I don't know if she was able to start her pregnancy leave, or if she was able to take a longer leave for her illness, or what. But regardless of her current employment status, I'm not sure why she made the decision to move here. It was right after she got pregnant that she moved in."

"I guess she wanted to make sure she was living somewhere nice when the baby came."

"I'm sure that was the reason. But it's still … weird. The timing. She knew she was going to have to drop down to at least half-time since she had to be off her meds, which meant her salary was cut, and she also must have known that it was quite possible she wouldn't be able to work at all at some point. I also don't think she was planning on going back to full-time any time soon after the baby arrived. So, she had less money coming in, but moved into a more expensive place. It doesn't really add up."

"Maybe the father is helping."

"That's probably the answer, but I would feel a lot better if I knew who the father is and could verify that."

"Missy never told you? I mean, about how she is able to afford this place?"

He shook his head. "I'm not even clear if she actually purchased the condo or if she's just renting it. She was very tight-lipped about it … just said she had plenty of savings, and it was a good place to raise a baby—much better than the run-down duplex she was in before. Which I agree, the duplex WAS a dump. But she chose it partially because of how cheap the rent was. She wanted to make sure she could still pay her bills if she had a relapse and needed to take time off of work. But that's Missy. Always planning, always responsible. At least, until she got pregnant. Then, when you'd think she'd become even more cautious with her finances, she does this, instead." He shook his head.

"Personality changes aren't uncommon with people who have bipolar disorder," I said cautiously.

"You don't think I don't know that?" he said curtly. "Believe me, I questioned her about it. But she sounded reasonable. She said she had savings and a plan, and she wasn't going to raise her child in that duplex. And I thought, 'Well, maybe she does have a plan. She usually does.' But whatever her plan was, it definitely veered way off-track. There, that's her condo." He paused and pointed to the only one covered with yellow crime-scene tape, the ends fluttering in the breeze. On the small porch next to the door was a glass table, two chairs, a small clay stand-alone fire pit, and a basket of dead flowers.

"And there," he pointed to the condo in the building next to Missy's, "is the neighbor's … the one who witnessed the person leave and has now recanted."

"I'm surprised he was the only one," I said, slowly scanning the area. "That's a long walk to the street."

"I think whoever he saw went out the back, by the garage," Cole said, leaving the cobbled path and walking across the lawn between the two buildings. "See?"

The street behind the condos was more like an alley, and on the other side of it were dense woods, already full of shadows.

I could feel my throat start to close. If it was a faery, how easily it could have simply melted into the trees and disappeared into the darkness. No one would ever know.

"Well, are you ready to have a chat?"

I glanced at him, glad to have a reason to stop staring into those woods. I could almost feel eyes staring back, watching me, hidden in the gloom. Eyes that knew too much.

I gave myself a quick shake. I was letting my imagination get away from me.

Cole noticed the movement. "Cold?"

"A little," I said, rubbing the goosebumps on my bare arms. "It's cooled off since the sun went down."

He stripped off his jean jacket and wrapped it around my shoulders, despite my protests.

"I'm fine," he said.

The jacket smelled like him, the faint scent of woodsy soap and his essence. I shivered a second time, and tried to cover it up by pushing my arms through the sleeves.

"Why did you ask me to come with you?" The question was out of my mouth before I even realized I was going to ask it. He looked surprised by it, as well. "I mean, it's not like you need me or anything," I said, trying to soften the bluntness. "I'm not sure how I can really help."

"You're a bigger help than you know," he said. "Everyone else thinks I'm delusional. Even my mom."

"'Delusional'? I don't understand."

He sighed, running a hand through his hair. "They think Missy is, well, maybe 'guilty' is too strong a term. I don't know if anyone thinks she did anything on purpose, but according to the initial M.E. report, it's looking like the baby died from natural causes. And maybe Missy is partly to blame ... maybe she was drinking, or using drugs, or otherwise not taking care of herself during her pregnancy. Maybe it's her therapist's fault for not monitoring her well enough. Or maybe it's just bad luck. But that's all this is. It's a tragedy, sure, but nothing criminal. There's no stranger who stole her baby, no baby swap, nothing like that. They think I'm wasting my time and should focus on helping Missy get better. They want to let the cops worry about investigating."

He looked so lost and alone, standing there in his stained and wrinkled blue shirt, his eyes haunted. "So, why are you?"

He blinked, as if coming out of a trance. "I'm sorry?"

"Why are you investigating? Why don't you think your mom and friends and family are right?"

"Because it doesn't feel right," he said. "I know how that sounds, and I get that it certainly looks like they're right, and I'm wrong. But I just can't shake the feeling that there's something off with this whole thing. I can feel it in my gut. It's not adding up, and I don't know why."

"I can see why you'd feel like that," I said. "There is some weirdness to this whole thing, for sure. I can't put my finger on it either, but it doesn't feel cut-and-dried to me, either."

"See!" He flashed me a smile that was part relieved and part excited. "You do understand. And it's so helpful to me to have someone to talk things through with. So, thank you."

I smiled back, trying to quash the flair of disappointment that shot through me. I was a sounding board, nothing more, chosen for my probable gullibility. This likely was a wild goose chase that would end with Cole's broken heart as he came to terms with there being nothing anyone could have done to prevent this horrible tragedy. I was probably doing him a disservice.

Yet … I hadn't been lying. Something did seem fishy about the whole thing. It all felt way too pat. Missy had some sort of mental breakdown. Period. End of story. Never mind any inconsistencies or witnesses from assumingly sane neighbors.

Of course, as I appeared to be the only person on the planet who believed Scott may still be alive, I was probably not a good judge of what seemed "fishy."

Cole took a step to the side as he swung his arm in a flourish. "Shall we go talk to Mr. Naden?"

"Sure," I said as we both started back through the grass and toward the door. "Although do you really think he's going to admit to anything? There's probably a reason he recanted. I'm not sure your asking is going to change that."

Cole's mouth was a flat line. "I can only try. He always liked Missy. I'm hoping once he sees me, he'll decide to open up.

But if nothing else, I should get a sense of whether he's lying or not."

We stepped onto the small, cement landing, which was bare other than a welcome mat. Cole pushed the doorbell, and we listened to the chimes echoing inside.

Almost immediately, we heard footsteps, and then, the door cracked open. "What do you want?" came the wavering voice on the other side of the door.

"Mr. Naden? I'm Cole Bennett, Missy's brother," Cole said. "We met a couple of times when I was here visiting Missy?"

"Oh, yes." The door opened wider, revealing an older, gray-haired man, his face wreathed in wrinkles. He wore a dark-green wrinkled tracksuit. "I think I do remember you. I'm so sorry about what happened to Missy."

"Thank you. I was wondering, do you have a few minutes? I was hoping we could ask you a few questions."

Naden's face closed down. "I don't know," he said hesitant-ly. "I'm sure there's nothing I can help you with."

"Let me be the judge of that," Cole said, with a disarming grin. "I promise I won't take too long, and it would really help put my mind at ease."

I could see the struggle waging on the old man's face. On the one hand, it was clear he wanted to help, but there was something stopping him. It almost looked like fear.

I wondered why.

"Okay," he said finally, holding the door open. "I only have a few minutes, though. My dinner is almost ready."

"It should only take a few minutes," Cole assured him, step-ping through the door. "By the way, this is Tori. She's an old childhood friend. We grew up together."

"Not too old, I hope," I said drily, following after him and trying not to wrinkle my nose as the stench of used litterbox and chili hit me.

Naden let out a wheezy laugh. "Both of you are babies, especially compared to an old guy like me."

He led us to a dark living room filled with stacks of newspapers, magazines, and other various pieces of paper. Stained coffee mugs and plates with crumbs dotted the room. A huge grey cat was curled up on the green plaid couch covered with a hefty amount of animal hair. One of the cat's eyes opened as we approached, but it didn't move.

"Don't mind Sebastian," Naden said, waving an arm toward the cat. "In fact, if he's in your way, you can push him off."

"It's okay. I like cats," I said, gingerly sitting down. The cat blinked one green eye at me, but still didn't move.

Naden sat in an armchair across from me, and Cole took the other chair. "It's just such a shame what happened to Missy," he said, his voice sad. "I know how much she was looking forward to her little one's arrival."

"Yeah, it's very sad," Cole said.

"How is she doing? There hasn't been an update yet on the news."

"She's okay … physically, at least. She's still in the hospital, because they're still trying to get her meds stabilized."

"Such a shame," Naden said, shaking his head.

"How was she during her pregnancy?" Cole asked. "Did you notice anything strange?"

Naden raised an eyebrow and let out a guffaw. "Strange? All women are strange when they're pregnant."

"Well, that's true," Cole conceded. "But more strange than normal, I guess. Like, did you hear any weird noises, or see her do anything that seemed off?"

The old man shook his head. "I will say she kept more and more to herself the further along she got. When she first moved in, she would sit outside a lot, even when it started getting chilly. She'd be out there all bundled up, with a fire going in the fire pit and drinking a mug of cocoa." He swallowed, almost like he was a little misty at the memory. "She would always wave to me if I was outside and invite me over for a cup.

"So, when it started warming up, I thought I'd see her outside again, enjoying the warm spring air, but I didn't. It's a shame, really. Being outside is good for the baby, too."

"What about visitors?"

He shrugged again. "Just the same as always. A couple of friends, especially that dark-haired one, and Maryanne from upstairs."

"No one else? Like a doctor or a nurse?"

"Not that I noticed. Of course, someone could have come and gone while I was doing something else. I don't always notice who is coming or going."

I very much doubted much of anything got by Naden. Those watery blue eyes probably saw quite a bit that went on in the neighborhood.

"What about that Saturday night?" Cole asked.

Naden shifted uncomfortably in his seat. "What about it? I already told the cops I didn't see anything."

"But first, you told them you did," Cole persisted.

"I was mistaken," he said. "I got confused. That happens sometimes, late at night."

Cole leaned forward. "Look, I'm not here to get you in trouble or even to have you talk to the cops again. But she's my sister." His voice cracked. "I have to know. Did you see something? Anything?"

"I think you should leave now," Naden said, awkwardly getting to his feet. "My dinner is ready, and I have to feed the cat."

Cole looked like he wanted to protest, but I caught his eye and gave a quick shake to my head. "Thank you for your time," I said, standing up. "We appreciate it. And if you do remember anything, maybe you can reach out to us?"

Naden was nodding. "Of course, of course. Be happy to. And please give Missy my best. I really hope she's going to be okay."

"Of course," Cole agreed as Naden hustled us out of his home.

"Well," Cole said as we stood on the front walk, listening to the sound of the door shutting behind us and the locks turning. "I guess you were right. He wasn't going to share anything."

I squinted as I looked around the collection of condos in the fading light. It had grown quite dark, even though we had only been in Naden's condo for a short time, and the shadows were long, stretching out across the yards.

"You were right as well, though," I said.

He gave me a quizzical look. "How so?"

"It wasn't a waste of time."

"What do you mean?"

"Well," I glanced back at the closed door. "We still learned something pretty important."

"What?"

"He's afraid of something. I think he's lying."

Chapter 10

"What did the other neighbor say?" I asked, still standing on Naden's stoop. "Maryanne, right? Did you have a chance to talk to her?"

He frowned, digging out his phone and scrolling through it. "I reached out, but she didn't get back to me. I've been so busy, I haven't even had a moment to follow up."

"What about the friends who were stopping by?"

He shook his head, still scrolling through his phone.

I squinted around the quiet neighborhood, peering through the darkness. "How well do you know Maryanne?"

"What do you mean?"

"Do you think we could just stop by now and see what she says?"

He blinked. "Don't you have to get back to work?"

He was right. I did have things to do. On the other hand, there was an excellent chance my sleep issues would get me up at the crack of dawn the next day, and I could just get an early start.

I shrugged. "We're here, right? Maybe we should just see if she's home?"

He grinned. "I like the way you think."

I smiled back, feeling a warmth spread through my chest and trying not to think about what it meant. "Well, let's give it a whirl."

Maryanne, as it turned out, lived right above Missy. We climbed the short flight of stairs to the door, which, like Naden's, had a welcome mat, but unlike Naden's, was heavily decorated with pots of blooming petunias and daffodils, wind chimes, and a couple of clay garden gnomes.

Cole rang the doorbell, and we listened to the footsteps inside.

There was a pause for a long moment, almost as if whoever was on the other side was trying to decide whether to open the door or not, but as Cole reached forward to ring the bell again, the door opened, revealing a middle-aged woman who was, to put it simply, trying too hard. She had on yoga pants and a top, both revealing a toned body that appeared to be no stranger to yoga class. The line of sweat down the front indicated she'd just gotten back from class. Her blonde hair was a little brassy, like it had come from a bottle, and was pulled up in a knot on top of her head. Her thickly applied makeup was smeared.

"Cole." Her smile was forced. "I'm so glad to see you. How's Missy?"

"She's doing better. I know we're showing up unannounced, but I was wondering if you have a moment? We'd love to ask you a few questions."

Maryanne hesitated. "I just got home from yoga," she said. "I haven't had a chance to shower or anything."

Cole flashed her his charming grin. "Only ten minutes. Maybe less. I promise. It would really mean a lot if you could give us the time."

She wavered, obviously taken in by Cole's charm. Finally, she pushed the door open. "It's fine. I was going to open a bottle of wine, anyway. Do you want a glass?"

"Sure," Cole said. "Oh, and this is Tori, a childhood friend of ours."

"Hi Tori," Maryanne said. "Would you like some wine?"

"Sure."

The front stoop wasn't the only thing that made Maryanne's condo different from Naden's. Hers was clean and tastefully decorated in soft pastels with lots of throw pillows and knick-knacks. She led us into the kitchen, equally spotless and newly remodeled with a granite countertop, maple cabinets, and stainless-steel appliances. It smelled strongly of a lemon-scented cleaner.

"Have a seat," she said, waving us toward the glass-topped kitchen table. "Is Chardonnay alright?"

Cole and I agreed it was, and Maryanne went to work uncorking the bottle.

"I'm sorry I didn't call you back," she said. "It's just been crazy around here. I have barely had a moment to myself. This was the first time I was able to go to yoga since it all happened."

"I get it," Cole said easily. "It's been pretty crazy for me, as well. Otherwise, I would have followed up with you."

Maryanne took out three stemless, gold-rimmed wine glasses from the cupboard. "It's been so terrible," she said. "I can't believe what happened. Everyone is just completely shocked that something like this could happen in our little community. The board even had an emergency meeting about it. Like I had the time for that, especially since I had to squeeze in an interview with the cops. My phone has been blowing up, too. It's just been one thing after another." She brought the glasses of wine over, placing one in front of each of us. I noticed how still Cole had gotten, even though he tried to keep a smile plastered across his face.

Maryanne didn't notice as she returned to fetch her own glass. "So, how can I help?"

Maybe not make it all about you, I thought, but refrained from saying it. Cole took a rather large gulp of wine.

"When was the last time you saw Missy?"

Maryanne settled in a chair next to Cole as she took a sip of wine. "I saw her the Tuesday before," she said.

Cole furrowed his brow. "Tuesday? I thought you were seeing her at least three times a week?"

Maryanne nodded as she took another sip. "I was, but in the last month or so, I tapered my visits off, since her other friend started coming by more."

Cole was lifting the wine glass to his lips, but he paused. "'Other friend'?"

Maryanne nodded. "Yeah, the one with the glasses. Sarah, I think her name is?"

Cole carefully put the glass down onto the table, making a light "chink" sound. "I don't think Missy has a friend named 'Sarah.' Are you sure that's her name?"

Maryanne frowned. "Pretty sure. Or maybe it was Sierra? Or something that sounded like 'Sarah'?"

"Do you remember her last name?"

She shook her head. "I don't think she ever told me her last name. It was a quick meeting. Sarah and Missy were on the front porch as I was coming back from yoga. Sarah was leaving, and Missy introduced us. The next time I stopped by, Missy told me I didn't have to come as often anymore. Sarah was going to fill in the gaps." Maryanne paused to take a drink. "Didn't Missy tell you any of this?"

"Missy isn't herself quite yet," Cole said briefly. "They're still stabilizing her meds. So, can you tell me anything at all about Sarah? What did she look like?"

Maryanne screwed up her face. "Well, she has brown hair and tortoise-shell glasses. They're really big and take up a lot of her face. And she's pretty tiny. Missy looked huge next to her. Of course, Missy was also seven months pregnant. Does that help at all?"

"Yes, it does. Thank you."

Maryanne nodded and picked up her glass. There was a smudge of pink lipstick on the side. "Why are you asking all these questions, anyway? Or ..." a look of horror crossed her face. "Do you think Sarah may have had something to do with what happened to Missy?"

"I have no idea," Cole said quickly. "This is the first I've heard of a 'Sarah.' I'm just trying to get to the bottom of what happened. Maybe this Sarah person has a clue."

Maryanne's face seemed to shut down. "It seems pretty obvious, doesn't it? Missy had a breakdown, probably because she wasn't on her medicine anymore. Not that I blame her. I get that she was trying to do the best she could for her baby, but unfortunately, that's probably what caused this tragedy." She reached over and started adjusting the yellow ceramic salt-and-pepper shakers and matching napkin holder, which were sitting in a perfect circle in the center of the table.

"So you didn't see or hear anything that night?"

Maryanne shook her head as she moved the napkin holder a quarter of an inch to the right. "No," she said quickly. "I didn't hear anything."

Cole looked skeptical. "You didn't hear the screaming?"

Maryanne looked faintly embarrassed. "Ear plugs," she said. "Plus, I sleep pretty deeply."

"Who called the cops that night?"

"I don't know. I thought it was Naden. Wasn't it?"

"I'm sure the cops told me it was you."

"Me? Oh no." Maryanne was clearly flustered. "I mean, I talked to the cops, sure. Especially since I had been seeing Missy. And I saw the lights and sirens when the cops arrived. My bedroom overlooks the street, so that woke me up. But no, I wasn't the one who called them. There was probably a mix-up somewhere."

"Oh, that's probably what it was," Cole said, but I could tell by his expression he thought it was Maryanne. "So, did you notice anything at all that was strange?" he asked, deliberately changing the subject. "Especially that last week or two?"

Maryanne pursed her lips as she considered. "Well, other than the fight with Beth, I really didn't notice anything."

Cole's eyes grew wide. "Fight with Beth?"

Maryanne nodded as she sipped her wine. "Yeah, I thought you knew."

"No, Missy didn't tell me. When was this? What happened?"

"Well, it was at least two weeks ago." Maryanne tapped a long, manicured nail against the side of her wine glass. "Maybe three. I can't quite remember. But I do remember them screaming at each other."

"About what?"

"I couldn't make out specific words, just that they were both clearly upset."

"How do you know who it was?" I asked, breaking into the conversation.

Maryanne stared at me, blinking her eyes. "I'm sorry?"

"I was just wondering how you knew who Missy was arguing with."

"Oh, well, I heard a commotion outside and went out to my balcony, which is where I could see them. Normally, I wouldn't be so quick to find out what was happening, but I wanted to keep an eye on Missy."

"So, you were inside when you first heard them?"

"Yes, that's what I just said," Maryanne said, clearly exasperated with me, but then, she seemed to realize why I was asking. "I was in the living room," she explained quickly. "It's closer to the outside. All I heard were muffled voices when I was in the living room, which is why I went on the balcony. I wanted to make sure Missy was okay."

"Plus, you weren't wearing ear plugs, like you do while you're sleeping," I said.

She looked relieved. "Right. Yes. They block out a lot." She gulped down the rest of her wine. "Do you have any more questions? I'm afraid I've run out of time. I just remembered I'm meeting a friend tonight for drinks and dinner, and I still have to get ready."

"That's fine," Cole said, tossing the rest of his wine back as he stood up. I quickly finished mine, as well. "I appreciate your help."

"Of course." Just like Naden, Maryanne ushered us out the door in record time. "If there's anything else I can help you with, you know my number."

"I do," Cole said as she shut the door behind us.

Cole and I glanced at each other. He looked as baffled as I was. Without a word, we headed down the stairs and back to our cars.

We didn't speak until we were well on our way down the path, the cool evening air fresh and clean, a welcome scent after the cloying lemony chemicals in Maryanne's condo. "Think whoever got to Naden got to her, too?" Cole asked.

"Sure seems like it." I glanced behind me, noticing how quiet the community was. It was a nice spring night, even if it was a little on the chilly side. Why wasn't anyone outside enjoying it? What felt like a charming, quiet, upscale complex suddenly felt creepy and oppressive. Were there more people hiding behind closed doors and shut blinds, watching us? I was sure I could feel their eyes lingering on the back of my neck.

"It doesn't even make any sense," Cole mused. "By all accounts, Missy was screaming that night. Everyone in the whole neighborhood was likely woken up by it. Why would Maryanne lie about something like that?"

"She's clearly nervous about something," I said. "And that question caught her off guard. Maybe she just reacted and didn't think it through."

"Maybe," Cole said. "I will say, though, that if I had a feeling before that something was off, it's turned into a bullhorn. Whoever thought it would be a good idea to scare the neighbors into pretending nothing happened might want to rethink their strategy."

"Yeah, but if no one talks to us, it's going to be difficult to figure out what did actually happen." I pursed my lips thinking. "Who is Beth?"

Cole stumbled, but caught himself quickly. "Beth? She's one of Missy's friends who was keeping an eye on her."

"Did you reach out to her? Maybe she knows something. And more importantly, if she doesn't live here, maybe she hasn't had the same experience as Naden and Maryanne and would be willing to talk to us."

"That's true. I'll reach out to her."

I eyed him. His head was down, staring at his feet. "You mean you haven't yet?"

Even though it was dark, there was enough light from the overhead lamps for me to see a faint blush creep up his neck and cheeks. "I ... uh ... well ..."

I stopped walking and stared at him. "Did you date her or something?"

His face was really red. "It wasn't for very long. A few months or so. But ... yeah. We dated. It was never serious."

My eyes narrowed. "Then why are you so nervous about contacting her?"

He sighed. "Because the whole thing was a mistake. A big one. On my part. Beth and Missy had been friends since high school. She was one of Missy's closest friends. She was there through Missy's initial mental breakdown. In fact, she was a huge help to us, as we worked together to get Missy stabilized. I really liked her. As a friend. I knew she had a crush on me, but nothing ever happened. Until at a New Year's Eve party a year and a half ago. I had too much to drink. Way too much to drink.

And we ended up hooking up that night. When I woke up in her bed the next morning with a horrible hangover, she was so sweet about the whole thing. I thought, 'Well, maybe this is a sign. Maybe it's like in the movies, when you're friends with the girl next door forever, and then one day, you wake up and realize she's the love of your life.'"

"I take it that isn't what happened," I said drily, noticing his pensive expression.

He gave me a wry smile. "Not by a long shot. After a few months, I realized it wasn't working for me, so I broke it off. She didn't take it well. The whole thing was a cluster. Beth was a wreck. Missy was furious with me for even going down that road. She was sure she was going to lose Beth as a friend. Anyway, long story short, Missy and Beth eventually mended their relationship with the unspoken agreement that I would keep my distance."

I chewed on my bottom lip. "That's a toughie. On the other hand, this is a pretty extraordinary situation. I mean, maybe you could send a text and just explain the situation and see if she would be willing to talk to you for Missy's sake."

"Yeah, maybe that's what I need to do," Cole said, running a hand through his hair. "I don't know her other friend, Renee, I think her name is, but especially now that we know Beth and Missy got into a fight, I think we need to talk to her."

"If you really don't want to do it, you could always ask Missy," I said.

Cole pressed his lips into a straight line. "I don't think that's going to be possible for a while," he said.

"Oh no, she's not responding to the drugs?"

Cole shook his head, jamming his hands into his pockets. "No, she is responding, which is part of the issue, believe it or not. She's gone into a depression about losing the baby and is refusing to talk to anyone, including me."

I reached forward to put my hand on his arm. "I'm so sorry."

Cole hunched his shoulders, but didn't shrug me off. "Thanks. It's just really difficult, because I don't know how long this will last. If it was just a phase, the doctors could give me an estimate as to when she might come out of it, but because she's grieving as well, it's impossible to know."

"I guess you're going to have to reach out to Beth."

"Yeah."

We gazed at each other. I was suddenly conscious of how I was still touching his arm, his skin warm under my palm. I dropped my hand and took a step back. As if it were a signal, we both started walking again.

"Thanks for coming today," he said. "Although it took a little longer than I thought. I hope that doesn't mean you'll be up too late."

"I'll probably just get an early start," I said. "I don't sleep much anyway."

He glanced at me, giving me a slanted smile. "I don't, either."

I could feel the tension between us, like a living, breathing creature. I eased further away, trying to put some space between us. The last thing I needed was to get involved with someone who was in the middle of such a traumatic and chaotic situation.

"You'll be okay, right?" I asked as cars came into view. "I do need to get home."

"Yeah, I'm fine. Thanks again," he said, pausing at his car. But he didn't get in. Instead, he stood by the driver's side door watching me walk away. He continued to watch me as I got in my vehicle, started it, and drove off.

My stomach growled, and I realized I was hungry. I had missed dinner. I tried to focus on what I wanted to eat instead of the feeling of the warmth of his arm under my hand. It seemed like I could still smell him, too—almost as if he was sitting next to me in the car.

Man, I had to pull it together.

It was only when I pulled into a drive-through that I realized I was still wearing his jean jacket.

Chapter 11

It was the middle of the afternoon when Cole texted me. *Beth is willing to talk after work tonight. Wanna come? You can bring my jacket back then.*

When I arrived home the night before, I had texted Cole, apologizing for keeping his jacket and asking if I should drop it off. He responded by telling me to return it the next time we saw each other. My insides felt warm and fuzzy at the thought of seeing him again, until I squelched it down.

I'm not some silly schoolgirl, I reminded myself. *I'm a grown woman who knows the score. Whatever this is between Cole and me, it isn't built for the long haul.*

Now, reading his response and realizing his "seeing me again" meant seeing him with his ex-girlfriend, I felt oddly deflated.

Are you sure you want me there? I texted back.

The response was immediate. *Positive. I told you, you've been a huge help.*

I took a moment to reply, as I felt torn. I definitely wanted to hear what Beth had to say. Did she know who this mysterious Sarah was? And why was she fighting with Missy?

And I would be lying if I said I wasn't simply curious about Beth.

However, theirs was a bad breakup. It would probably be super uncomfortable. Was that really how I wanted to spend the evening?

Screw it. I definitely wanted to get a look at Beth.

Okay, I'm game, I texted back.

Great. He responded. *It's easy for me to pick you up, since I'm going right by your place. Or would you rather drive?*

I paused again. What did I want? I liked the idea of driving myself. Him picking me up felt like a date, which I knew this absolutely was not.

But I kind of liked the idea of him picking me up, as well. Even if it was so we could spend the evening with his ex-girlfriend.

Pickup sounds good.

Great. Be there at 6.

I glanced uneasily at the clock. That only gave me three hours or so to get all my work done.

I was most definitely behind. Although I was starting to realize that I was pretty much perpetually behind. Make that always behind. Working nights and weekends still wasn't enough to get through my to-do list.

Despite putting in fewer hours lately, I still somehow seemed to be getting about the same amount of work done.

I felt like there was something important in that realization, but I didn't have time to think about it. I had work to do.

I stopped at about a quarter to six to give myself a few minutes to get ready. I was still wearing black leggings, but I changed into a red tunic that I knew looked good with my black hair and grey eyes. I brushed my hair, leaving it loose around my shoulders, and dotted some concealer around my eyes before adding mascara and lip gloss.

Cole texted me to let me know he was in the parking lot, and I grabbed my keys, purse, black leather jacket, and his denim one.

When he saw me come out of my apartment building, he flicked his lights, but I could have probably found him anyway. His was the only car idling in the middle of the parking lot. He drove a black, late-model sedan that looked like it could use a good wash.

"I brought your jacket," I said as I settled into the seat next to him.

"Just toss it in the back seat, please," he said.

I did, trying not to make my examining of his car too obvious. I noticed a strange, foul odor, almost like rotting food, but the car appeared to be mostly clean.

"Is there something in the trunk?" I asked, wrinkling my nose.

He gave me a funny look. "Trunk? Oh. The smell. I was hoping it would clear up by now." He gave me a sheepish smile. "I have been more or less living out this car since what happened with Missy, so I sort of accumulated a lot of old food packages. I threw them all away before I picked you up, but I guess I should have aired the car out a little better."

"Hey, I get it. It's not a big deal. You just reminded me a story from one of my coworkers. A few years back, the company her father worked for gave away free frozen turkeys to all their employees for Thanksgiving. Her father put it in his trunk and promptly forgot about it, driving around for weeks as the turkey thawed and rotted. The smell permeated everything."

"Ugh." Cole made a face, then laughed. "Oh, that must have been awful."

"She said it was."

"Well, I can reassure you there are no frozen or unfrozen turkeys in my trunk."

"That's a relief."

We were quiet the rest of the drive to Beth's apartment. I could tell Cole was nervous by the way he switched between drumming his fingers on the steering wheel and running a hand through his hair. I wondered if I should try and distract him with conversation, but I didn't know what to say.

Luckily, the drive was short, and it wasn't long before we were pulling into a parking lot.

"When is she expecting us?" I asked as he turned the car off.

"Any time after 5:30," he said, running a hand through his hair again. "I thought I'd give her a little time to get settled after work."

"And she's okay with us talking to her about Missy?"

"I think so. We texted, so I couldn't hear the tone of her voice, but I asked her if she would be willing to do a ceasefire tonight for Missy's sake, and she said 'yes.'"

He turned his head to gaze out of the side window, but he made no move to get out of the car. I shifted uncomfortably in my seat, wondering what, if anything, I should say.

"Would you feel more comfortable texting her to let her know we're here?" I asked.

He shook himself, like he had been lost in thought, and reached for the door handle. "No need. Let's just go in."

"But if you're uncomfortable ..."

"I'm not," he cut in. "I was just ... well, I guess being here brings back some old memories." He gave me a self-conscious smile and opened the car door.

I wondered what "brings back some old memories" meant exactly, when he was the one to break it off. Or did it mean he didn't tell me the complete truth about why they weren't seeing each other anymore? *Not that it matters*, I told myself firmly. *It's not like we're dating or anything.*

Still, a sad little pain embedded itself in my heart.

A lanky, scruffy guy with wild black hair and tattoos up and down both arms was exiting the building as we reached the entrance, and Cole was able to grab the door and keep it open, so we didn't have to buzz Beth to let her know we were heading in.

The lobby was spacious—rows of mailboxes on one side and some couches and chairs grouped around a couple of tables on the other. A pair of glass double doors next to the elevator led to what appeared to be a workout room. The floors were covered in pale, beige tile, and the walls were painted off-white. It was all very plain, respectable, and boring.

We went up the elevator to the fifth floor, and Cole led me to a nondescript brown door in the middle of the hallway. He knocked.

The door opened, and that sad little pain in my heart morphed into a much bigger one when I got my first look at Beth.

She was gorgeous. Thick, golden hair cascaded down her back and shoulders in an array of curls. Her huge, dark-blue eyes were rimmed with thick, black lashes, and her face was perfectly heart-shaped with rosebud lips. She was still dressed for work in an off-white, silk, sleeveless blouse with a cowl neck and tailored black trousers.

She and Cole stared at each other for a moment before her eyes slid to me, and those perfect lips turned into a frown. "Who are you?"

"This is Tori," Cole answered, as I was too busy gaping to form words. Hadn't Cole told her he was bringing me? "She's a childhood friend."

Beth's eyes shifted back to Cole. "Why did you bring her?"

"She's helping me get to the bottom of what happened to Missy," he said. "Is that okay?"

Her mouth tightened, and for a moment, I was sure she was going to refuse, but then she stepped back, leaving the door open.

Cole gave me a quick glance, mouthing "sorry" at me before following her in.

For a moment, I wondered how weird it would be if I were to just leave right then and there. Did I really want to get in the middle of whatever was going on between Cole and Beth? The tension was already through the roof.

But then what would I do? Sit in that plain, boring lobby until Cole appeared? Maybe I should have driven myself, after all, which made me wonder if this was the real reason Cole wanted to drive—so I wouldn't have an easy escape.

I followed Cole into the apartment.

The door opened into a living room that appeared to be a mishmash of styles. A huge flat-screen television stretched out against one wall with an old, sagging brown couch across from it. A scuffed coffee table was in front of the couch, one side covered in piles of mail and the other with an open bottle of wine and two stemless wine glasses, a sea turtle etched in the glass. Next to the couch were two relatively new-looking green armchairs, and near them was a shelf filled with knickknacks and old paperbacks.

"I'll get another glass," Beth said coolly, and she disappeared into a room on the right.

Wine? I raised my eyebrow at Cole. He shrugged.

She came back with a glass that didn't match the two on the table and started pouring. "It might be easier to sit in the kitchen," she said.

"Or we can just rearrange these chairs," Cole offered, gesturing to the two armchairs. "Like we used to."

Beth handed the odd-man-out glass to me. "If you want to move them, be my guest. Just as long as you move them back."

Cole dragged the two armchairs over, so they were closer to the couch. "There, that's better," he said, accepting the glass from Beth, who flashed him an indulgent smile.

I swallowed half my wine. Definitely should have brought my car.

"Sit," she said, gesturing. I was about to sit on the couch, as I was already feeling like a third wheel, but Cole gestured for me to take the armchair next to Beth. I perched awkwardly on the edge.

"Still have your roommates, I see," Cole said, looking around.

Beth nodded. "There are three of us," she said to me. "And the apartment came furnished. It just seemed easier to use what they gave us, as the whole point of us living together is to save money. Except the television, obviously. That's Jasper's. So, anyway, that's why it looks like a college apartment in here. Because it sort of is."

"You live with a guy?" I asked.

"Two guys, actually. Dave and Jasper. It's not what you think, though. They're both gay, but they aren't involved with each other. At least not anymore. It's a long story. But it's been working for us." She turned those huge blue eyes to Cole. "How's Missy?"

"Physically, she's fine. Mentally ... well, it's a struggle."

Beth gave him a sympathetic look. "Is she back on her meds?"

"Yes, but it's still bad. She's barely acknowledging visitors. Although," he cocked his head and studied her. "Maybe she'd respond to you. I could add you to the visitor list."

Beth laughed, a harsh, cold sound. "I doubt it," she said. "We had a pretty big fight near the end of her pregnancy. I'm assuming that's why you're here? One of the neighbors has a big mouth, I'm guessing. Probably Maryanne."

"You assume right," Cole said with a grin. "So, 'fess up. What was the argument about?"

Beth rolled her eyes as she sipped her wine. "What do you think? Sarah."

Cole leaned forward. "So you know Sarah?"

"I saw her a couple of times. That's it."

"Who is she?"

Beth looked surprised. "Don't you know?"

Cole shook his head. "The first I heard about her was when Maryanne brought her up."

"Wow." Beth sat back, balancing her wine glass on the armrest. "I thought everyone knew. That's all she talked about. 'Sarah said this,' and 'Sarah doesn't think I should do that.' You couldn't shut her up about Sarah."

"Well, she kept her mouth shut around me," Cole said. "So, again, who is she?"

"She's a midwife, I think. Or maybe a doula. Something like that."

Cole looked perplexed. "A midwife. Why would she start seeing a midwife? I thought she was happy with Dr. Greene."

"I thought she was, too. Until she wasn't."

"Is that why she stopped going to Dr. Greene? Because she decided to use a midwife?"

Beth shook her head. "I don't know anything about that. She didn't tell me she stopped seeing Dr. Greene. Although I guess it shouldn't surprise me. Clearly, she was only listening to Sarah in her final trimester."

"Then, what? How did she even meet Sarah? I don't understand."

Beth sighed. "I'm not completely sure how or when they met. I think there was some sort of incident during her second trimester."

Cole looked alarmed. "Incident?"

"Everything was fine," Beth said quickly. "I guess you didn't hear about this, either. Something happened to Missy while she was drinking a decaf latte. You know how much she loved her lattes. She was pretty good about giving up coffee, but once or twice a week, she would treat herself to a decaf. Anyway, something happened. I think she was cramping or something. I don't quite remember. But Sarah just 'happened' to be there." Beth grimaced while making the quote signs in the air with her fingers. "Lucky break, eh? Anyway, Sarah helped her through it, and they ended up becoming fast friends."

"Just like that?"

Beth took another sip. "Yep. Just like that. Next thing I know, Sarah is coming over four or five times a week to help out, and whatever Sarah says is law. There was just no talking to Missy about anything. Renee was edged out first. After a couple weeks, Missy told her she didn't need the help anymore, because Sarah was handling it. She then tried to tell me she was fine, but I wasn't having any of it. Why would someone she just met choose to be a voluntary caregiver? It made no sense to me."

"Are you sure it was voluntary?" I asked, speaking up for the first time. Both Beth and Cole glanced at me in surprise, like they had forgotten I was there. Which was why I had decided to speak up. Cole hadn't looked at me once since sitting down, and I found myself wondering again about that break-up story and whether there was more to it than what he had said. "You said she was a midwife or doula," I continued. "So, maybe this was some sort of paid arrangement."

Beth shook her head firmly. "No. I asked that. Multiple times, even. Because it was the only thing that made sense to me, as well, but Missy kept insisting Sarah was doing this out of the goodness of her heart. Missy claimed Sarah had experience with bipolar disorder ... that it ran in her family, too, so she was 'uniquely qualified,'"—there went the air quotes again—"to help Missy though this."

"You don't think that was the truth?" I asked. While I definitely had my doubts about the goodness of Sarah's heart, it wasn't out of the range of possibility that she had seen a family member struggle with the same mental disorder and wanted to make a difference for someone else.

Beth turned to me, squaring her shoulders. "Have you ever had to deal with a family member or friend having a breakdown? Do you have any idea how stressful that is?"

"Beth," Cole started to say, but I held a hand up.

"Yes, in fact, I do," I said. "My mother."

Beth at least had the grace to look a little chagrined. "Then you know," she said. "You know what a huge sacrifice it is to be there for someone when she's in that state. So, why would Sarah put herself through that, if she wasn't getting paid or isn't a long-time friend? It doesn't make sense."

"I think you're probably right, but to play devil's advocate, I have seen people put themselves through all sorts of crazy things when trying to make up for some family wounding," I said. "And what's the alternative? That she went through all that hassle to what, steal Missy's baby?" Of course, that was exactly what I thought had happened, but I was curious to see how Beth would react.

Beth pressed her lips tightly together. "Now you sound like the cops," she said darkly, reaching for her wine. I noticed she had the same lipstick smear on her glass that Maryanne had left on hers. It even looked like the same shade. I wondered what the odds of that were.

"The cops?" Cole asked. "You talked to the cops?"

Beth gave Cole a sour look. "Of course I did. Weren't you listening? Maryanne seems to be telling everyone about our fight, including the cops."

"Did they know who Sarah was?"

Beth shook her head. "I doubt it. They were asking me if I knew Sarah's last name or where she lived or worked. Which I don't." She glowered at Cole. "So, don't ask. I saw her a couple of times. That was it."

"What did she look like?"

"Pretty average-looking. Brown hair cut short. Oversized brown glasses. A little older than us, maybe early- to mid-thirties. Nothing really stood out."

"Great." Cole rubbed his forehead. "We're never going to find her."

"Well, Missy may know more," Beth said. "I get you can't ask her now, but eventually, you'll be able to."

Cole sighed and kept rubbing his head. "Maybe," he said, but he didn't sound very convinced. "The problem is, I don't know how long it will be before she's in any state to answer questions. A few days. Next week. Longer. And the more days that go by, the less likely we'll be able to figure out what happened."

Beth's gaze softened. "I wish I could help. Believe me, if I could go back in time, I would definitely make different choices."

"You're not the only one." Cole stopped rubbing his head and picked up his wine. "Okay, so I know the fight was about Sarah, but what exactly happened?"

Beth dropped her gaze to her drink. "It wasn't one of my finest hours," she confessed. "And I don't know how much help it will be. I could tell something was off the moment I arrived. First, Missy wouldn't let me in. She said she didn't need any help that day, as Sarah had already been by. I kept insisting, though. I mean, we were friends, right? Why couldn't we hang out together? Finally, reluctantly, she opened the door. But the whole thing was a disaster. She was super paranoid ... kept asking me why I was coming around. What was I after? Was I going to steal her baby? Was I in cahoots with the faeries to steal her baby?"

You can't let the faeries get him.

Her delusion had started weeks before she gave birth? Just like my mother's? How could this be? What were the odds?

My whole body stiffened, as if a faery had just snuck in and cast some sort of spell, freezing me into place. But Cole had the complete opposite reaction—his entire body jerked on the chair. Beth didn't notice either of them, as she was still studying her wine. "She was worried you'd steal her baby?" Cole asked, his voice strangled in his throat.

Beth nodded. "I know. The whole thing was freaky. What a delusion to be trapped in. And it made me wonder, what poison was Sarah feeding her? Anyway, I kept trying to reassure her, but she just got more and more agitated, insisting her baby was in danger, and Sarah was the only one who understood.

"Finally, I just snapped. Said maybe Sarah was the one who was trying to steal her baby, and how could she not trust me, after all we'd been through? She started screaming at me to get out and not come back. So, I did."

Beth raised her glass to her lips, and I noticed her fingers were trembling. So much so, the wine sloshed inside. I wondered if any of it would spill on that beautiful silk blouse. "I know how it sounds," she said, her voice quiet. "Arguing like that with someone who is bipolar and not properly medicated because of her pregnancy. I shouldn't have let her get to me like she did."

Cole cleared his throat. "You're human. I know once she's herself, she'll understand." He still seemed a bit shaken, probably for the same reason I was.

Don't let the faeries steal your brother.

"Do you see why I'm so suspicious of Sarah? Even if Maryanne hadn't told the police, I was planning on going in to talk to them. It's possible, of course, that Missy landed in that delusion all on her own without anyone's help, but it does make you wonder."

I was desperate to catch Cole's eye. The last thing I wanted was for him to bring up what had happened to me.

Had Sarah been the one to put that idea into Missy's head? If it had been her, she would have been way too young to have known my mother when she was pregnant, so as strange as the whole thing was, it must just be a terrible coincidence.

Or had Missy's disease reached into her subconscious and plucked out a story from my past, dragging it out of her broken mind and into a full-fledged delusion?

Of all the possible scenarios, that seemed most likely—that Missy's delusion came straight out of my family's misfortune.

But, if it was all in Missy's head, why would Naden say he saw someone leave her condo and then recant?

What was he afraid of? What was Maryanne afraid of?

We definitely had more questions than answers. What we really needed to do was find the mysterious Sarah.

"One last question," Cole said. "Did Missy ever tell you who the father was?"

Beth's eyes went round. "You mean you don't know either?"

"Nope," Cole said. "Apparently, it's a big secret." He rolled his eyes.

"Yeah, I heard the same thing," she said.

"So, she never talked about who she was dating?"

"I didn't even know she WAS dating," Beth said.

Cole nearly spilled his wine on his shirt. "Seriously?"

Beth nodded. "We weren't seeing each other as much, but I didn't think too much about it. She said she was busy with work, some big project or something. That happened from time to time, so it didn't strike me as odd. But then, the next thing I knew, she was telling me she's pregnant, and no, she couldn't talk about the father, but someday, she'd tell me. I assumed she was embarrassed, like maybe she had spent a night or two with that guy she'd dated—Leo, I think his name is—again, or something equally as disastrous. But now, after everything that's happened, I don't know what to think."

"You and me both," Cole sighed. We sat in an awkward silence for a moment, all three of us likely wondering how we were supposed to politely end this strange little encounter. Finally, Cole broke it by making a big deal of tipping the last dregs of wine into his mouth. "We probably should get going. Thank you for agreeing to see us."

"Anything for Missy," Beth said. "You'll let me know when she's better, right?"

"Of course." Cole stood up as I swallowed the last of my wine. "I'm sure she'll want to see you."

"I hope you're right." Her smile was sad and her face pensive. "I don't know. It felt different this time."

"It's just been a while since she's had a breakdown. You've forgotten how bad it can be." Cole flashed her a comforting smile, but there was a strain to it, like he had been feeling the difference, as well. That there was something different about this time … something worse. "I'll be in touch."

"It was nice meeting you," I said awkwardly, even though it didn't feel all that nice. "Thanks for the wine."

Beth inclined her head in return, but there was a coldness in her eyes that hadn't been there when she looked at Cole.

I waited until we were in the hallway with the door firmly shut behind us before I hissed into Cole's ear, "Why didn't you tell her I was coming?"

Cole glanced quickly behind him and gave me a sheepish look. He waited until we were by the elevator before answering. "I'm sorry. I was a little afraid she would say 'no,' if I did. She has a horrid jealous streak."

I glared at him. "Do you have any idea how uncomfortable that was for me? Probably for her, too. She was trying to do something nice for you, and you lied to her."

"I didn't lie," Cole corrected as the elevator door opened and we got in. "I never said I wasn't bringing anyone else. I just … failed to mention you."

"A lie by omission is still a lie."

He held up his hands. "Okay. You're right. I owe you both an apology. Would you let me buy you dinner to make it up to you?"

I blinked, feeling blindsided. "Wait. Are you actually asking me to dinner after putting me in a super -awkward position and then forcing me to sit there and watch you two flirt?"

"We weren't flirting," he said.

"It sure looked like you were to me."

"We're friends," he insisted. "Or at least we were. Good friends. The three of us spent a lot of time together. Hence, again, why Missy was so pissed off at me. But it's nothing more than that."

I wasn't sure I believed him, especially with that final glare from Beth still lingering in my head, but I also wasn't sure it was worth arguing about.

"So, about dinner," he said. "Is that a 'yes'?"

The elevator door opened, and I stalked out of it toward the front door. "I have work to do," I said.

"You have to eat, as well."

I didn't answer, just kept walking toward the car. My instincts were screaming at me to decline. I was already spending way too much time and energy on whatever this non-relationship was. Having dinner with him in a restaurant felt like crossing a line—one that really ought not to be crossed.

"There's a great Irish pub here," he said behind me as I reached the car. "They have a really tasty beer-battered fish and chips. Want to try it?"

I turned to face him. "Did you plan all of this? Offering to drive and then not telling Beth so you would have an excuse to ask me to dinner?"

I thought he would get angry and rescind his dinner invitation in the process, but instead, he had the opposite reaction. His lips quirked up into one of his charming grins, and he shoved his hands into his pockets. My heart flipped inside out. "Man, when you put it that way, I sort of wish I had been that calculating. But alas, no. I offered to drive because your place is on the way, and it made more sense than taking two cars. And I'm offering to take you to dinner because I appreciate all the time and energy you're putting into helping me get to the bottom of this, not to mention I really wanted to talk through what Beth just shared. So, what do you say? Irish pub, or would you prefer somewhere else?"

I still wanted to say "no." The fact I felt a little deflated that he only wanted to buy me dinner to thank me and talk through the investigation bothered me a lot more than I wanted to admit.

It would be smart to go home.

Unfortunately, I wasn't all that smart.

"I love a good fish and chips," I said quietly as I opened the passenger door.

Chapter 12

The Irish Wolfhound was busier than I expected for a Wednesday night, although most of the crowd was concentrated in the bar. People dressed in professional clothes were clustered around tables with mugs of beer and glasses of wine in front of them, likely moaning about their bosses and jobs. The restaurant part was only half-full, so we had no trouble getting seated.

"The bangers and mash are pretty good, as well," Cole said as we slid into the rust-colored vinyl booths. The tables were made of highly polished warm wood, and festive lights in green fixtures hung from the ceiling. "Oh, and they of course have a decent Irish stew."

"I'm getting the sense you come here a lot," I said drily. I wondered if the proximity to Beth's apartment was part of the reason.

"My fantasy football league meets here fairly regularly," he said. "So, yeah, I guess you could say that."

I picked up my menu, firmly telling myself even if Beth was an additional reason for his frequenting the place, it wasn't any of my business. Nor was Cole under any obligation to tell me.

Both of us waited to bring up the investigation until after we had ordered (I decided on the fish and chips after all) and our drinks arrived, a black and tan for him and a wine for me.

"So, what do you think?" Cole asked, picking up his beer.

"I think someone needs to talk to Sarah," I said. "Hopefully, the cops are looking for her."

"Hopefully, but unfortunately, there isn't much to go on," Cole said. "All we have is a first name and that she was either a midwife or a doula. And a sketchy description."

"We might not even have that," I pointed out. "Sarah could have lied about both her name and her profession."

Cole winced. "Don't even say that. This is already difficult enough. That would make it impossible."

I picked up my wine. "It's also possible Missy was confused. Not by Sarah's name, but her profession. I mean, she was talking about being seen by a nurse coming to her home. Was she talking about Sarah? And, if she was, why would Missy tell you she was a nurse, if Sarah told Beth she was a midwife or doula? Was Missy confused because of her condition? Was she lying to one of you? And why?"

Cole looked like he might be sick. "This is getting worse and worse."

"I'm not trying to depress you … just talking through all the options. It also might be as simple as Missy thinking you'd accept her seeing a nurse more readily than a midwife. Do you think it might be worth tracking down Missy's other friend who was helping her? What was her name … Renee? Maybe she has something more on Sarah."

Cole stared glumly into his beer. "I don't know. Maybe. It feels like a long shot, since neither Maryanne nor Beth knew anything. I'd have to track down Renee's contact information first." He cocked his head and studied me. "So, if you had to guess, what do you think Sarah's involvement is? Do you think she was after Missy's baby?"

I gave him a surprised look. "Don't you?"

Cole shrugged. "I don't know what I think anymore."

"To me, it seems obvious Sarah targeted Missy, which is why I think the possibility that Sarah didn't use her real name is high. I know what I'm about to say is going to sound awful, and I don't mean it to, but if you look at Missy's situation, she's unfortunately a good target. She lives alone; the father doesn't appear to be in the picture; she's not only bipolar, but also off her meds. If you're looking to steal a baby, it's pretty perfect."

Cole's expression was pained, as though it physically hurt him to hear those words, and he took a long drink from his beer. "I should have been there for Missy."

"Hey," I said, leaning forward. "It's not your fault. Unless you moved in with her, which it doesn't sound like she wanted, I don't know if you could have stopped what happened."

"You don't know that," he said.

"She had friends and a neighbor keeping an eye on her. Quite frequently, it sounds like."

"Friends aren't the same as family." He rubbed the stubble on his chin, his eyes haunted. "Maybe if I had seen what was going on, I could have gotten her into a hospital where she could have been watched by professionals and stayed far away from this Sarah person."

"You and I both know how difficult it is to get someone committed against her will," I said. "It doesn't sound like Missy was violent, and she wasn't threatening suicide. I don't know if there's anything much you could have done. The only person who maybe could have done something is the therapist. She's the one who should be answering for this fiasco."

Cole sighed, his face sagging into a defeated expression. "Maybe. You're probably right. It's just so … depressing. Maybe I should have moved in. It wouldn't have killed me to live with her for a few weeks."

"You're assuming she would have agreed to that," I said. "Which might not be the right assumption."

"Well, we'll never know now, will we?" Cole said bitterly. "I should have at least asked. At least tried."

"Hey, you're here now," I said. "You're trying to get to the bottom of what happened."

"Yeah, after the fact. Like that's going to help anything."

"You don't know that it won't."

He eyed me warily. "What do you mean?"

"The way I see it is, there are two possibilities," I said, pausing to take a sip from my wine. Across the way, a plump, older woman with hair way too red to be natural was sniping at a teenaged girl, who looked like a younger, prettier version of the irritated woman, with a gorgeous mane of strawberry-blonde hair. The girl was staring at her phone and kept rolling her eyes every time the woman, who I assumed was her mother, told her to pay attention. "The first is that Sarah targeted Missy with the intention of stealing her baby, but unfortunately for everyone, the baby was either stillborn or died shortly after birth, so Sarah left without a baby. Worse, she left Missy alone with her crazy delusions and whacked-up hormones, which likely made everything that much more traumatic."

The waitress chose that moment to deposit our food. The fish and chips looked and smelled wonderful—the fish was flakey, and there was a huge portion of fries. Cole's bangers and mash also looked tasty, but Cole didn't look all that interested in eating. He picked up his fork, but rather than cut the sausage, he stabbed at it. "I will never forgive myself for not being there for her," he said after the waitress left.

I wanted to reach over and put my hand on his, to try and get him to relax. "There couldn't have been much for you to do except maybe get Missy to the hospital a little quicker, so they could get her stabilized a little faster. Luckily for Missy, she was so loud, the neighbors heard her and called an ambulance. I'm so sorry they couldn't help the baby."

Cole eyed me, and his sausage-stabbing became more aggressive. "That doesn't really make me feel any better."

I gave him a sad smile. "If that's what happened, it was a terrible tragedy."

Cole stopped his stabbing and started shoving food around his plate instead. "That's the most likely scenario, especially since Missy was found with a dead baby. But what's the other possibility? The baby lived?"

"Yeah, that's exactly it."

Cole stared at me. "Seriously? You think Missy's baby lived? Then why was there a dead baby with her?"

"Missy was telling the truth," I said matter-of-factly. "Someone stole her baby and replaced it with a dead baby."

Cole kept staring at me, his expression becoming more and more horrified. "You know what you're suggesting, right? That Sarah actually brought a dead baby with her to my sister's house."

"I know it seems a little unrealistic ..."

"*A little*?"

"But think about it. It would actually explain everything," I said.

"Everything except for how someone could get her hands on a dead baby."

"Maybe Sarah really is a nurse," I said. "What if she works at a hospital? She could have stolen one from there."

Cole made a face. "Yeah, but isn't there a timing thing? It couldn't have been sitting around for too long, or the M.E. would know there was a problem."

"Maybe the baby died that day," I said.

"But just because Sarah wanted Missy to give birth doesn't mean Missy would go into labor."

"Sarah could have induced Missy," I said.

Cole's jaw dropped. "Seriously?"

"It's possible."

"Yeah, but ... why?" Cole asked. "There has to be easier ways to get a baby."

"Unless Sarah is part of a black market," I said. "Infants are worth a lot of money. The risk might be worth it."

"The risk of stealing my sister's baby, sure," Cole said. "I get that. But why go through all the trouble and headache to swap it with a dead baby? First of all, that can't be easy to do. And why would you? What purpose does it serve?"

"Yeah, that's where I get stuck, as well," I said. "It does seem really elaborate, when just snatching a baby and disappearing makes far more sense. Sarah could have even drugged Missy when it was all over, so by the time Missy woke up and was able to call someone for help, Sarah would be long gone. Why add that extra layer of complexity?"

"Yeah, that's why I think what really happened is your first theory," Cole said, his voice discouraged. "And as soon as Sarah realized what was happening, she cut her losses and ran, leaving Missy in a terrible state."

"You're probably right," I said. Everything Cole said made perfect sense. This was a baby-snatching gone horribly wrong.

So why did I have this nagging feeling that it wasn't the truth?

"Which means," Cole said darkly. "That Sarah needs to pay. What she did to my sister was heartless and cruel. Leaving her there confused and disoriented and trapped in a delusion. She deserves to be punished."

"She deserves something," I agreed. "And we need to stop her before she does this to another vulnerable mother-to-be. But we have to find her first, which probably means waiting for Missy to talk to us."

Cole shook his head. "We've already wasted too much time," he said. "The longer this goes on, the less likely the police or anyone else will find her. We need answers now."

I picked at my fish. "Other than Renee and Missy's therapist, I can't think of anyone else to ask. I guess we could start with Renee …"

Cole snapped his fingers. "The therapist. That's it. Yes, let's talk to her."

I gave him a confused look. "She's not going to talk to you. You've tried."

"I'm not going to ask her about Missy's condition, but about Sarah."

"But isn't that part of confidentiality?"

"Why would asking about Sarah be confidential?"

"Because Missy talked about her in therapy."

Cole shrugged. "Maybe, but I don't think that's how it works. I'm not asking about Missy's medical condition or what she said in therapy. Just details on who Sarah is. It's worth asking the question, at least."

"That's true. She just hasn't been very forthcoming," I said. "Or has she finally called you back?"

"No, she hasn't, which is why I think we need to just show up at her office. Unannounced."

"You think she'll see you?"

Cole smiled. "We'll see. Want to come? I'll text you the details tomorrow."

I looked at him suspiciously. "You don't know them now?"

"Let's just say I haven't worked everything out yet," he said mysteriously. "I need to make a few phone calls. But I should know more tomorrow. Is that a 'yes'?"

"Why not?" At that point, I was in so deep, I might as well see it through. So far, no one at work seemed to have noticed my diminished hours, which I probably needed to thank Tess for. Tess. I'd almost forgotten. "Oh wait, is tomorrow Thursday? I can't. I'm meeting some friends from work for a drink."

"What time?"

I frowned. "I don't know. Six, maybe? Maybe a little later."

"We should be able to do this before you meet them," he said. He grinned at me, and my heart stuttered. "I promise, we'll make it quick."

Of course, I was in.

Chapter 13

Cole's idea was to wait in the parking lot until Dr. Broomer left her office.

"What if she's working late?" I asked. We were sitting in Cole's car, which was parked in the street facing the parking lot and the small office complex Dr. Boomer worked in. We had already seen a stream of professionally dressed people exit the building and drive off, leaving only a handful of cars left, including a shiny baby-blue BMW that stuck out like a sore thumb.

Even though I joined Cole in his car, I had learned my lesson the day before and driven myself. The last thing I wanted was to get stuck and not be able to meet Tess, or worse yet, have Cole accompany me to the bar. I felt hot and cold just imagining Tess's raised eyebrow as she checked out Cole and the questions she would pepper me with.

No thanks.

But I could worry about Tess later. I still needed to get my head around Cole's so-called "plan."

"She's not," Cole answered my question.

"How can you be so sure?"

"Because I called."

I eyed him. "You called and asked what? 'What time will Dr. Broomer be leaving, so I can meet her in the parking lot'?"

He rolled his eyes. "Don't be silly. I called and pretended to be a patient and tried to make a late-afternoon appointment, but the latest available was 4:00, so I figure that means she'll be done sometime after five."

That made a certain amount of sense, although it still felt like a long shot. What if she stayed late to do paperwork? "Have you ever met Dr. Broomer?"

He shook his head.

"So, how will we know if it's her?"

"I looked her up online and found a pic."

"Hopefully, one that actually looks like her."

Cole huffed a loud, exasperated sigh. "You are such a Negative Nancy."

"I'm not negative. Simply skeptical."

"A little faith can go a long way."

"Faith has nothing to do with it," I said. "If your best plan is to accost the therapist who refuses to return your phone call in the parking lot, you may need a new one, and quickly."

Cole started to answer, but then the door to the office swung open, and a woman emerged carrying a black briefcase and matching purse. She had frizzy, greying hair and was dressed in a grey suit with a pale ivory shell and grey pumps. Despite being professional and put-together, the overall effect was colorless and drab.

"That's her," Cole said, immediately shoving open the door. I quickly followed.

"Dr. Broomer?" Cole called out as the woman strode across the parking lot, her heels clicking on the asphalt, toward the BMW.

She paused, keys in hand. "Yes?"

"I'm Cole, Missy's brother," he said, continuing to walk toward her. "I was hoping I could ask you a couple questions?"

She quickly resumed walking. "There's nothing to say. Doctor-patient privilege."

Cole reversed course to cut in front of her. "You haven't even heard my questions yet."

"I don't need to. There's nothing I can say. I'm sorry." She didn't sound sorry at all. She sounded impatient, and something else I couldn't quite put my finger on.

Cole positioned himself between her and her car, forcing her to stop. "It will only take a minute." He flashed his most charming grin.

"I don't have time for this," she said. "I have to be somewhere." She tried to move past Cole, but he smoothly countered, side-stepping to remain in front of her.

She huffed a loud, exasperated sigh. "Please step aside, so I can get to my car."

He grinned again. "Not until you answer my questions."

Now that I was closer, I could see the expensive fabric and cut of her suit and her designer shoes and bags. Her nails were done as well, a French manicure, and I caught a whiff of subtle-yet-elegant perfume.

She shifted impatiently. "Fine. What's your question?"

"Who is Sarah?"

Dr. Broomer blinked in surprise. She was clearly caught off guard, probably having expected a question about Missy's mental state or something she had said. "I'm sorry?"

"Sarah. She was Missy's midwife or nurse or something. Who was she?"

"I ... I ... I don't know any Sarah."

"Of course you do," he said. "You were one of Missy's primary caregivers during her pregnancy. You would have known about all her medical decisions."

"I can't discuss her medical decisions," Dr. Broomer said swiftly.

"I'm not asking you to," Cole said. "All I want to know is who Sarah is. Ideally, her contact information, but at the very least, I would be happy with a last name. Maybe a place of employment, as well."

"I ... I would have to check my records," Dr. Broomer said faintly. "I see a lot of patients. There's no way I can mentally keep track of those types of details."

"Okay," Cole said reasonably. "I can wait."

Her jaw worked. "I can't now," she said. "I have to be somewhere. I told you. In fact, I'm late, so I really must go."

"Tomorrow, then," Cole said. "Can you check her records tomorrow and get back to me?"

"I have a busy day tomorrow," she said. "I'm not sure if tomorrow will work. But hopefully, over the weekend."

"You have my number?"

"I'm sure I do somewhere," she said. "But you can call my office tomorrow and give it to my receptionist. And now, I must insist. I have to be on my way."

Cole took a step backward, gesturing his arm with a flourish. Dr. Broomer gave him the side-eye as she hurried to her car. We watched her get in, throw her bags on the passenger seat without a glance, and quickly pull her car out.

"She didn't even put her seatbelt on," Cole mused as we watched her drive out of the parking lot, her tires squealing on the pavement.

"Something spooked her," I said. "You could see it in her eyes."

Cole shot me a sideways glance. "How much do you want to bet I don't get a call by Monday?"

"Oh, I think you'll get a call," I said. "She'll either say she found no mention of a Sarah, or that Sarah was one of Missy's friends helping out, and she doesn't know anything about her being a midwife."

Cole's face fell. "Oh man. You're right."

"It will be the same thing she tells the cops if and when they turn up."

Cole blew out a lungful of air. "And we just gave her a heads-up, so she'll be prepared when the cops get to her. Maybe this wasn't such a great idea after all."

"I wouldn't say that," I said. "That was some outfit she was wearing. It looked new, along with that car."

"She did look like she went on a recent shopping spree."

"Think she's maybe gotten an influx of cash recently?"

Cole eyed me. "You think she's in on it?"

I shrugged. "I have no idea. I'm just saying she has expensive tastes. I know therapists can make decent money, so maybe there's nothing to it. But it would be interesting to know if her tastes have, shall we say, upgraded, in the past few months."

Cole paused to ponder what I was saying. "Interesting."

"It's especially interesting when you couple that with the fear in her eyes when you asked about Sarah."

Cole gave me an unreadable look. "It reminds me of what happened to you."

The sun ducked behind a cloud, plunging us into darkness. The breeze, delightfully warm just a moment ago, had a sudden chill to it. I shivered. "What do you mean?" I asked, even though a part of me didn't want to know. That part of me wanted to turn and race back to my car, leaving Cole standing there with his too-knowing, penetrating gaze, and pretend this entire week never happened.

"You know, what happened with your father," he said.

Something inside me slithered and uncoiled, something dark that I would much rather ignore. The urge to run intensified, but my feet seemed stuck to the earth, unable to move. "I don't know what you're talking about."

"The money," he said, and he let out a little, uncomfortable laugh. "I mean, I'm sure it was just coincidence, but the timing was weird, you know? His business was failing, headed to bankruptcy, actually, and suddenly, right around the time your brother dies, something shifts, and he's back to making money."

My tongue felt like it had swollen up and was too big for my mouth. "You must be mistaken," I said, amazed by how clear and steady my voice was, even with my too-big tongue. "We never had any money issues. My dad's business was always successful. Always. You're just confused or … or something. Besides, you were the same age is me when it happened. You couldn't possibly be remembering it correctly."

He cocked his head and studied me. "It was all over town," he said. "People talked about it. My parents mentioned it a few times over the years. You really don't know?"

Finally, I was able to pry one of my feet from off the ground. "I have to go," I said. "Tess is expecting me."

"Okay," Cole said, his expression concerned and a little confused. "Tori, I wasn't trying to upset you …"

"I'm not upset," I said. Now that I could move both feet again, I was already feeling better. "I'm just late. Talk later?"

"Okay," he said again. "I'll text you."

"Great," I said, quickly turning to head to my car. As I opened the door, I stole a quick peek over my shoulder. He was still standing in the same place I'd left him, the unreadable expression back on his face.

***

I sat straight up in bed, a scream trapped in my throat. Sweat glistened on my skin, and I was sure I could see *him* in the room, a bundle wrapped in his arms.

Don't worry. Your brother has a little cold. I'm going to take him to get some medicine and bring him right back.

I clapped my hands over my eyes. *No! There's no one there! It's just a figment of my imagination. I'm alone.*

I kept my eyes tightly squeezed, refusing to let myself look, but I couldn't stop myself from listening, from straining my ears over the raspy sound of my own harsh breathing. Was that a rustle I heard? The soft sound of a footstep?

Finally, I got myself under control enough to peel my fingers away from my eyes.

I was alone.

I got out of bed and padded to the kitchen for a glass of water. My mouth was dry and filled with a coppery taste, and I could still feel my heart thudding in my chest. I seriously doubted any more sleep was in my immediate future, but maybe once I had some water and walked around a little, I would calm down enough to at least try.

Although, in retrospect, I shouldn't have been at all surprised that I was up with another attack. The evening had been a mess. First, Cole and whatever horrible thing he was insinuating, and then the whole disaster at the bar. I hadn't wanted to meet Tess anyway, as I was too upset by what Cole said, but I couldn't think of a decent excuse to get out of it. Tess wouldn't buy the headache or not-feeling-well excuse, even though I truly wasn't. My stomach was churning unpleasantly, and I felt like I might throw up. But she would pepper me with questions until she was satisfied, which might take a while, so I bit the bullet and showed up at the bar.

She was waiting for me with another girl who worked in accounting. Her name was Geri, and she had always reminded me of a fox, with her sharp face and long, thick, reddish-brown hair.

"So, tell me all about it," Tess said as soon as I had a drink in front of me. She wagged her carefully waxed and shaped eyebrows up and down. Tess was always carefully made up, as if trying to conceal the extra pounds that rounded out her face and the fact she was fast becoming an aging cheerleader. "And don't leave out a single detail. I don't care how naughty it is."

"Truly, it's nothing like that," I protested.

Both Tess and Geri gave me a look. "Uh huh," Tess said, drawing the sound out. "You expect me to believe that? You, who never misses a moment of work."

Inwardly, I groaned. I knew this was going to be an issue. I should have taken my chances with the sick excuse. "He's an old childhood friend," I began.

Tess's eyes widened. "I knew it!" she crowed. "Of course he is. What does he look like? Spare no details."

"It's really not like that," I insisted again. "He looked me up because he's having a family issue."

Tess gave me a skeptical look. "Yeah, right. 'A family issue.' After all this time? Sounds like an excuse to me."

A sudden bolt of inspiration struck me. "It's his mom," I said. "He's having the same issues I had with mine, and he wanted help."

Tess's expression immediately transformed into sympathy. "Oh. That's rough. I'm sorry." Geri looked away, her face a strange mix of pity and uncomfortableness.

"It's fine. I'm fine," I said, trying not to show my relief. Tess didn't actually know the truth about my mom. No one did. They all thought she had Alzheimer's. And what I was saying about Cole wasn't wrong … exactly. I was helping him with a family member, and one of his parents was having some medical problems. It was close enough to the truth.

The conversation bounced around for a while, covering all the usual topics: work, Tess's complicated dating life, and Geri's jerk of a boyfriend. I had just begun to relax when Geri brought up the second topic I had been dreading.

Missy.

"Can you imagine?" she asked, shaking her head, her tone full of outrage and all kinds of judgement. "Leaving a pregnant bipolar woman all alone to fend for herself. What was the family thinking?"

"I know," Tess said. "It's a terrible thing, but what did anyone expect? The family is the one who should be investigated, not the mother."

I sat there, frozen in my seat, the words trapped in my throat. *It's not what you think. The family did the best they could. It's not their fault.*

But I couldn't do it. The image of the shocked look on Tess and Geri's faces as they turned to stare at me ... "How would you know?" they would ask. And I would have to answer.

So instead, I let the words burn inside me, hot like acid. I listened to them talk, dissecting who was culpable and who wasn't and who should have known better as I steadily grew more and more nauseous. Finally, I stumbled to my feet, sure I was going to throw up. "I have to go," I mumbled to their surprised faces. "Sorry, I didn't realize how late it is. I missed so much work this week because I was helping my friend. Really behind. See you tomorrow?"

"Sure, Tori," Tess said as I threw some bills onto the table and fled into the night.

As I took a glass from the cupboard and filled it from the tap, I realized I still felt slightly ill thinking about that exchange. And I wondered how Cole would handle it—Cole, who was already beating himself up and thought he was to blame—contending with people he had never met, who had never had to deal with a mentally ill family member, judging what he did and didn't do ...

No. I had to stop. There was nothing more I could do, and it was time to get back to my own life. Cole could handle it. He didn't need me.

I slowly drank the water, the coolness soothing the sticky dryness in my mouth and throat. I pressed the glass against my sweaty cheek, breathing deeply as I calmed myself. It was just a bad dream. That was all. A bad dream triggered by getting myself involved in something I had no business getting involved in. Worse, it was the second bad dream that week. If I was looking for a sign to step back and tell Cole I was done, it was staring me in the face. Was this the price I wanted to pay for running around playing amateur detective? I already struggled with getting a good night's sleep … did I want to add daily nightmares to the mix?

No, the smart decision would be to stop the madness.

The problem was, I didn't want to be smart.

I refilled my glass, but I didn't drink—simply cupped the cool glass between my hands. It wasn't just that I wanted to keep seeing Cole, although that was bad enough. There were a million reasons why getting involved with Cole was a bad idea, not the least of which being that I wasn't even sure whether he was interested. Or if he still wanted to be with the gorgeous Beth. No, if I was being really honest, while there was no question Cole was part of the reason I wanted to stay involved, there was something else driving me. A deeper reason. Something I had refused to let myself even consider, as the pain it brought me was too intense.

The real reason was how much I loved investigating. How it made me feel alive. How this was what I wanted to be doing, instead of spending my days trying to convince people to spend their money on expensive makeup and shampoo.

There was a time, long ago, before my life fell apart a second time, when I truly thought I was going to become a true-crime writer or journalist. How much I loved the hunt, the sifting through clues, the uncovering of secrets people thought they'd buried.

But then, it all came to a crashing halt. And I buried that dream, instead choosing a career that kept me constantly busy, juggling multiple projects and putting out fires.

I didn't have any time to think. Only react.

And now, standing in my kitchen, in the quiet, early morning hours without any emails, texts, or messages pinging at me, I realized just how empty it was.

But what were my choices? Continuing digging around Missy's life, even though it was clearly bringing up all sorts of things I would rather stay buried? Did I really want to do that to myself?

Even more than that, was it even something I *should* be doing? So far, my mental health had been pretty good, but it was certainly possible I carried the seeds of a mental breakdown, same as my mother. What if my poking around caused one of those seeds to sprout into my own breakdown?

No. I couldn't risk it. For so many reasons, I needed to step back. It was the right thing to do, even if it felt like tearing one of my own limbs off.

Exhaling a deep sigh, I turned around, intending to sit at one of the stools in front of my long counter for a few minutes before seeing if I was ready to try to sleep again. I glanced around my kitchen, noticing how the moonlight slanted across the room, draining the room of color and giving it a silvery, unreal quality.

Suddenly, a memory sliced through my mind. Another time, another kitchen, the same silvery-grey light filling the room. My father, sitting at the kitchen table in the dark, surrounded by piles of paper, a glass of whiskey next to his elbow.

Jumping when he saw me. "Vicky, what are you doing up? You should be in bed." He tried to smile at me, but there was something off with his face—like jigsaw puzzle pieces that didn't fit together properly.

"Daddy, what's wrong?"

"Nothing is wrong, sweetheart," he said, his eyes darting behind me. "Where's your mother? Is she still in bed? You can't disturb her, you know. She needs her rest. Now, hurry up and go back to bed."

Another memory. Still in the kitchen. My mother at the sink, peeling potatoes for dinner; my father taking ice out of the ice tray, a bottle of whiskey next to him, and me, coloring at the table.

"The bank called," my mother said. "The check to the grocery store bounced. I told them there must be some mistake."

My father's hands shook as he plopped ice cubes into his glass. "I'll call them tomorrow and get it taken care of."

"Well, good, because they wouldn't listen to me," she said. "They kept insisting we were overdrawn. I told them that was impossible."

My father splashed some whiskey over the ice and took a quick swallow. "I'm sure it's nothing," he said. "Probably some sort of administrative screw-up. I'll have Brenda take care of it."

"Good," my mother said, moving the peeled potatoes to the stove. My father added more whiskey to his glass. "I'm trying a new recipe tonight. I hope you'll like it."

"I'm sure it will be wonderful," he said, his voice toneless.

My feet were cold. I looked down and saw I was standing in a pool of water and broken glass. At some point, I had dropped my glass, and I didn't even hear it break.

It took me a few minutes to get my bearings. I was no longer five, but an adult, living in my own cramped apartment.

I carefully knelt on the floor with the intention of picking up the glass before I stepped on any of it, but instead, I found myself curled into a ball, the water soaking into my sleep shorts.

What had just happened?

Were those actual memories, or something my mind made up, inspired by what Cole said?

Suddenly, I was furious. What was Cole thinking? Why would he say such a thing to me? Did he honestly think my father would sell his own flesh and blood because he was having business troubles? Everyone had money troubles from time to time. That was just the nature of the beast. But nobody sold their children, or whatever Cole was implying, because of it.

It didn't make any sense, anyway. Scott hadn't been taken. He was found in his crib. That's what everyone said, anyway. And more than that, it was the only logical explanation.

I needed to stop the silly notion that Scott had been taken. All it was doing was hurting myself.

Don't worry. Your brother has a little cold. I'm going to take him to get some medicine and bring him right back.

I clapped my hands over my eyes. No! I wasn't going there. My father had nothing to do with what happened! He loved me, my mother, and Scott. The hours he would walk around the house jiggling Scott while he cried, how he tickled him until he laughed, and played airplane with him.

This was all absurd.

What was even more absurd was me sitting in the middle of the kitchen floor, surrounded by broken glass, my clothes dripping wet and wanting nothing more than to pick up the phone and start screaming at Cole.

But I knew it wasn't Cole's fault. It was mine.

I was the one who involved myself by going to the hospital in the first place. If Cole hadn't seen me there, he never would have tracked me down.

I had no business getting involved. It was bringing up too many terrible memories that I was clearly unequipped to handle on my own. It wasn't Cole's fault that he'd said something that triggered this latest episode. He couldn't have known.

No, what I needed to do was stop all this nonsense. No more investigating, no more digging around in my family history. None of that. Period. End of story.

I was completely disgusted with myself. I should know better. Every single time I had started down this path of investigating something, whether it was my family's tragedy or someone else's, it always ended the same way. Something shattered into pieces around me. This time, I was lucky it was only a glass, and not my life.

I began to carefully pick up the jagged pieces while I made a plan. First, I needed to text Cole and tell him sorry, but I can't help anymore. Next, I needed to call Dr. Adams and book an appointment.

Third, I needed to make a commitment to myself—no more investigating. No matter how much my soul longed to do it.

I stood up and carefully picked my way to the garbage, the moonlight glistening on the sharp edges of the glass in my hands, sparkling like jagged diamonds.

It was time to get my life back.

Chapter 14

"You're awfully quiet this evening," Nanna said as she passed me the dinner rolls.

I gave her a faint smile as I took a roll. Nanna had made one of my favorite meals, chicken piccata with wild rice, but my stomach was so twisted up in knots, I wasn't sure if I was going to be able to get any of it down. "Sorry. Had a bad day."

"Bad" was actually an understatement. It had been awful.

Despite how clear I felt in the middle of the night, the morning sun brought confusion. I had gone back to bed, sure I would have no issues falling asleep with my new plan intact. But instead, I ended up tossing and turning before falling into a fitful sleep full of nightmarish creatures and faceless shadows that pursued me endlessly. I awoke exhausted and irritated at myself for even attempting to go back to bed. Why didn't I just stay awake? I could have gotten so much done. Instead, my brain was thick, foggy, and full of doubts and questions. Maybe I hadn't made the right choice after all. Maybe, rather than constantly trying to bury anything that made me uncomfortable or upset, I should face it and deal with it.

But then, I would see my mother's face in my mind's eye, slack with drugs, a line of drool trailing down her chin, and I would tell myself *no, this is the only way*. Maybe for other people, facing their demons and traumas was what they needed to do to heal.

But for me, the cost was too high. If I was wrong, my mind could break like my mother's. I couldn't risk it.

Instead, I tried to get back into my old routine. I started the coffee, went for my run, enjoyed my normal Pop-Tart with a cup of coffee, and settled down in front of my computer.

But I couldn't focus. I just kept staring off into space, my mind spinning with the memories of my father, the tightness around his eyes, how his hands constantly shook, the smell of whiskey following him like a cloud.

Over and over again, I turned over those shards of memories, trying to determine if they were real or imagined.

If my father had been having financial troubles, surely, I would have remembered something before now.

Surely.

Then, something would snap my attention back to the present, and I would shove the memories away, determined to do better.

But before I knew it, I was drifting away again, my traitorous brain sorting through the unreliable scraps of my memory, seizing on anything it could find to prove once and for all that Cole was wrong … that there was nothing strange at all about my father's behavior.

Cole.

I needed to tell him I was done. I also needed to call my therapist and make an appointment. The sooner the better. Hopefully, she could give me some new tools to help me stuff all the unwanted thoughts and emotions back in the box. Maybe there were some drugs that could help. I had been leery about medications, not even wanting the Valium prescription I had for my night terrors, so as to never risk turning into the husk my mother had become. But maybe that was the only real solution.

I decided to start with my therapist. I reached for my phone, dialed the number, and hit the "call" button.

"Hello?"

It was a man's voice. A familiar one, which made even less sense considering I was fairly certain Dr. Adams's receptionist was a woman. "Hi, I want to make an appointment with Dr. Adams, please."

Long silence. "Tori? Is that you?"

My stomach seemed to turn inside out. "Cole?" Oh, no. I had no intention of talking to him. I was going to text him.

"Yeah, I wanted to call and make sure you're okay after last night. Is something wrong?"

"Wrong?" There were all kinds of wrongs going on, but nothing I particularly wanted to share.

"Yeah ... you're trying to make an appointment with Dr. Adams?"

"Oh. That. I'm fine. It's nothing ... just a ... routine check-up. So, what's up?" I was still feeling discombobulated and wanted a minute to get my thoughts sorted out, and the best way I could think of allowing for that was to let him talk.

"Well, I ..." Now it was his turn to sound uncomfortable. "I guess I wanted to apologize."

"Apologize? For what?"

"Well, for yesterday. I didn't mean to insinuate anything with your father. I thought ... well, I guess I thought if it was true your father was having financial issues, then you would have known about it. But you know, small-town gossip and all." He cleared his throat.

"Gossip isn't usually true," I said, even as the memory of my dad sitting in the dark, surrounded by paper and the smell of whiskey, danced in front of my eyes.

"I know that. And ... well, I'm sorry. I was out of line, not to mention it's none of my business."

"Yes, it's not your business," I said, my voice harsher than I intended. I snapped my mouth shut. *Tori, what is your issue? The man is trying to apologize, and you bite his head off.* "I'm sorry," I said. "That was uncalled for. Thank you for apologizing. I'm … I'm not myself this morning. I didn't get much sleep."

"Oh, that sucks. Was there a reason, or you just couldn't sleep?"

Tell him! It was a golden opportunity. I couldn't have scripted anything more perfect, yet still, I hesitated. I knew it was the right thing to do. I couldn't keep going down this road. It was too dangerous for my mental health.

Still, for some reason, I found myself unable to say the words.

"Tori? Everything okay?"

I sucked in a deep breath. Now was the time. "Not really," I said.

"Oh? What's going on?"

I glanced over to the sun streaming through my kitchen window. It looked like it was going to be a lovely sunny day—completely opposite from my grey, stormy thoughts. "I can't keep helping you," I said, my words coming out in a rush.

There was an uncertain pause. "What?"

"Investigate what happened to Missy. I … I can't help you anymore."

"I don't understand. Is this because of what I said yesterday?"

"No. Yes. It's just … I have my own life. I'm so behind, and this is taking so much of my time …"

"We don't have to do anything during work hours," he interrupted. "We can keep it to nights and weekends."

"That's not going to work, either. I work a lot of nights and weekends."

"You can't take off nights and weekends?" His voice was disbelieving. "Are you mad at me?"

"What? No, of course not."

"Then I don't understand." He sounded bewildered. "I thought you and I were on the same page. And you're good at investigating, so I assumed you were enjoying it, on some level."

"I was. But ... that's not the point."

"Then help me understand."

"I just ..." The last thing I wanted to do was tell him how badly it was affecting me, but he was giving me no choice. "I'm ... I'm not sleeping very well, and I just ... I can't."

There was a long pause. "This *is* because of what I said yesterday," he said, his voice flat. "About your father."

"What? No."

"He WAS having financial issues, wasn't he?"

"What?" My voice came out in a squeak. "No! I told you he wasn't."

"I know what you told me. But something isn't right. Are you being threatened?"

"*What?*"

"You can tell me if you are."

"What are you talking about? No one is threatening me."

"Something is going on," he repeated grimly. "All these people suddenly afraid to talk. What is it?"

"I assure you, no one has talked to me or threatened me," I said.

"Then why? And no, I don't buy the needing-more-time-to-work and not-sleeping excuses. You told me you weren't sleeping well before this started. So, something's changed. What?"

"I just ..." I was so exasperated. "Look, I can't tell you ..."

"Because you ARE being threatened."

"No, I'm not. It has nothing to do with that. It's just ..." I paused, struggling with my words. "I just ... I'm having flashbacks, okay?"

"Flashbacks?" His voice was puzzled, but calmer.

"Bad memories, I guess you would call them. They're ... they're ... resurfacing. And I just ... I worked so hard to put that time of my life behind me. To keep it in the past and move on. And now, being involved with you and this case ... it's all coming back. And I just can't. I can't do it anymore."

I stopped, breathing hard. I had said more than I'd wanted. But at least I had still been able to keep most of it a secret.

He was quiet for a bit. "Tori, have you considered it may be time to deal with those memories?" His voice was gentle.

I was already shaking my head violently, even though he couldn't see me. "No. Absolutely not."

"Why?"

"I said 'NO.'"

"Okay," he said. "I'm not going to push you, but I really think you ought to consider it. Sometimes, things get worse before they get better. Have you heard the saying, 'The breakdown is just before the breakthrough'?"

My entire body seemed to freeze. Oh no. No breakdowns here. I couldn't risk it. I might never come back together again. "Look, I have to go," I said. "I hope you find out what happened to your sister. I really do."

"Thanks," he said. "But think about what I said. You have a knack for investigating. I would hate to see you neglect that talent because you don't want to face what's buried in your past."

"Goodbye, Cole," I said and hung up the phone. I was too angry to do anything else, and I was afraid if I stayed on the line, I would say something I'd regret.

It took a while for me to calm down. I alternated pacing around the apartment and drinking more coffee before I finally felt calm enough to focus on work. But even then, it was tough. Cole's words kept haunting me.

Have you considered it may be time to deal with those memories?

Every time they pierced my brain, I squeezed my eyes shut and concentrated on forcing them out. Yet they persisted, continuously showing me the images of my father, the worry, the whiskey ...

After a day of getting nearly nothing done other than fighting with myself, I finally decided to admit defeat. As much as I didn't want to dig into my past—as afraid as I was that it might end up triggering a bigger breakdown—I knew I couldn't go on the way I was.

I figured I could start by asking Nanna a few questions. Especially since I was having dinner with her that evening. In a way, it felt meant to be ... like something was pushing me toward at least getting to the bottom of one piece of what had happened to my family all those years ago.

Sitting at the same kitchen table I'd shared with Nanna growing up, enjoying one of my favorite meals, I watched her purse her lips as she handed me the salad, her sharp, penetrating grey eyes not missing a thing. Her hair, once as black as mine, was now a beautiful, soft silver, which matched her eyes that were also a mirror image of mine. Looking at her as she sat, back ramrod straight, I felt the familiar pang in my chest. Everyone always said I was the splitting image of my mother, who took after her mother, but that was before her disease ravaged her beauty. Now, she was just a shell of herself, trapped in an expensive treatment facility.

And again, I found myself wondering about my father's financial situation.

I gave myself a quick, hard shake and focused on filling my bowl with salad.

"I wondered how you were faring this week," Nanna said. "That case and all."

"What case?"

Nanna gave me a look. "You know quite well what I'm talking about," she said. "That poor girl who lost her baby."

"I've been so busy, I haven't had a chance to watch the news," I said, which was true. I hadn't looked at it at all that week.

Nanna's eyes remained fixed on me. "You don't need to look at the news to struggle with the story. How have you been sleeping?"

I could never hide anything from Nanna. "Not good," I admitted.

"Night terrors?"

"Among other things."

She shook her head, her eyes softening. "Have you called your therapist yet?"

After hanging up with Cole, I had been too flustered to remember to return to my original task and still needed to book an appointment.

"Next week."

"Make sure you do."

"Yes, ma'am."

A hint of a smile touched her lips. "Don't think you're too old to be put across my knee."

It was a running joke. Nanna had never laid a hand on me.

"No, ma'am."

"Good, glad we got that sorted out."

I picked up my fork and poked at my chicken. It smelled delicious, but my stomach revolted. The image of my father's strained face, the smell of whiskey, haunted me.

Nanna put her knife and fork down with a clatter. "Out with it," she said. "You're letting my good food get cold."

"It's nothing," I said, reaching for my wine. Maybe that would help dampen my memories.

"It's not nothing, or you would be eating. So, what's going on?"

A part of me didn't want to ask. It felt like even giving voice to the question would somehow legitimize it. If I didn't ask, then it never happened. My traitorous brain had made the whole thing up because, well, Cole. He had planted the idea, after all.

On the other hand, I knew by now that Nanna wasn't going to leave it alone until I broke down and told her.

"Was dad having financial issues when mom was pregnant with Scott?" The moment it was out of my mouth, I wanted to stuff it back in. It sounded so terrible, once the words were out and floating there in the warm, comforting kitchen.

Nanna looked surprised. "Why would you ask such a question?"

"I ... um ..." My voice faltered, and I stared at my plate. "I had some weird memories pop up this week, and I was wondering if they were real or not."

Nanna sighed, a heavy, deep sigh, and adjusted her silver-framed cat glasses. "It was a difficult time," she said. "I don't know all the details. Your father did a pretty good job hiding everything from your mother, but yeah. There was trouble."

I reached for my wine, needing something to wet my suddenly dry mouth. "What happened?" I croaked out.

"Like I said, I don't have all the details, but my understanding is that he lost a couple of big projects, and that caused him to have some issues with the bank. Eventually, it got straightened out, but it nearly killed him. Cora was in no position, especially near the end of her pregnancy, to notice anything, but Simon did have a scare."

"A scare?"

Nanna grimaced. "With his heart. He went to the emergency room, sure he was having a heart attack. He wasn't, though. It was all stress. But it was pretty scary."

I stared at her. "I don't remember that at all. Why don't I remember anything?"

"Well, you were pretty young. You were, what, four or five? I'm not surprised you don't remember."

"So, then what happened? How did he get it straightened out?"

"He finally landed a couple of big projects, which allowed him some room to negotiate with the bank. It was right around the time Scott was born, so I know it was a huge relief for him."

"Really?" I thought about those early days, when he and I were the ones taking care of Scott while mom spent her days in the bedroom ... how patient he was, no matter how fussy Scott was being. "That must have been why he was so relaxed after Scott was born."

"I'm sure it took a huge load off his mind."

I picked up my fork and took a bite of my chicken. Suddenly, I was famished, like I hadn't eaten anything all week. It surprised me, because even though Nanna was confirming my earlier memories, somehow, I found the conversation comforting. Nanna didn't seem to think it was any big deal that my father had some financial issues. It was just like what I had been telling myself. Things like that happen, and I shouldn't have gotten myself worked up about it.

"It had been a tough year," Nanna continued as she buttered her roll. Her voice was quiet, almost like she was talking to herself. "For all of you. It was ..." she shook her head. "So difficult. When Scott was born, it felt like a fresh start. Like everything was going to go right for you and your parents. It felt like such a gift. And then ..." briefly, she closed her eyes, but not without my noticing the sheen of tears reflected there. "Well, it's no use talking about it now. What's done is done."

I stopped mid-chew, the familiar chest-tightening closing my throat. Nanna, my rock, even though I know she must have suffered terribly herself. Not only had she lost her grandson, but she basically lost her only daughter, as well. And then, if that wasn't enough, she brought her only granddaughter into her home to take care of her, at a time in her life when she should have been spoiling her grandbabies, not raising them.

"I'm sorry," I said.

She darted a glance at me. "You're sorry? What do you have to be sorry for?"

What did you do to your brother?

"I don't know. For everything, I guess," I said. "For not thanking you for what you did for me ... for not being able to stop what happened to Scott or mom ..."

"Hush." Nanna reached across the table to grasp my hand. "None of that. I loved having you live here with me. I was happy to be able to help out your father. He was a good man, he just ... well, he had a really difficult childhood. He was doing the best he could, but becoming a single parent was just too painful for him. As for Scott, there was absolutely nothing you or anyone could do for him or your mother. It was all a terrible tragedy. But something good did come out of it."

I could feel tears gathering at the back of my eyes. "What?"

Nanna looked at me with so much love. "You, sweetheart. I am so grateful for our closeness."

I picked up my napkin to dab at my eyes. "Now look what you've done. You made me smear my mascara."

"Oh, like you need any," she sniffed and picked up her fork. "Anyway, things are definitely looking up. Your mother has been in a wonderful mood lately."

I picked up my fork. "Really?" I tried to keep my voice polite and interested, but even under the best of times, when Nanna told me about my mother, I would feel depressed and guilty. And after the week I'd just gone through, the last thing I wanted was to talk about her.

Nanna nodded. "Yes, she's been in an almost, well, giddy mood. If I didn't know better, I would say she's fallen in love. She's been like this for a few months now. I don't know what changed … maybe they finally got her medication right or something, but she's been a joy to visit. You should really go see her."

"Maybe I will," I said, even though I knew I likely wouldn't. At least not for as long as I could possibly delay it. Despite the cheery spin Nanna put on it, I always found it depressing and discouraging—not only a living reminder of a wasted life, but a warning that one day, I could end up in such a place.

I think Nanna understood that on some level, which is likely why she never pushed it. However, she also never failed to bring it up … to try and persuade me otherwise.

The conversation turned to other more pleasant things. I was able to not only finish my meal, but also enjoy a big piece of homemade coconut cream pie, my favorite.

It wasn't until I was home, tucked in bed and starting to drift off, when the uncomfortable little darts that had been poking me most of the night found their mark.

I opened my eyes, finally realizing what the nagging, teasing question hovering at the side of subconscious had been about.

Why was the year before Scott was born so difficult? Was it only the financial pressures? Or was there something else?

Chapter 15

"Such an unexpected surprise," my father said, offering me a faint-but-pleased smile over the menus. We were in Mario's, a cute little Italian restaurant with red-and-white checkered table-cloths, fat red candles in wine bottles, and delicious aromas. It was my father's favorite restaurant, and where we normally met whenever I visited Redemption.

It didn't matter how much I told myself I was making a big thing out of nothing. Of course it would have been a terrible year. Not only was my father having serious financial issues, but my pregnant mother was off her medications and slowly going mad. Wouldn't that be explanation enough?

But there was something about the way Nanna's jaw had tightened … the way she wouldn't meet my gaze, instead focusing way too closely on cutting her chicken into tiny pieces.

Nanna was hiding something.

But what?

If I had caught it at the time, I could have questioned her then. I still might not have gotten the whole truth, but it was possible I could have caught her off guard enough to let something slip.

Now, though, it was too late. Nanna would surely clam up, and there wasn't anything I could do about it.

Which left me two choices:

Let it go, which was the smart decision, as there most likely wasn't anything there.

Or ask someone else.

Since my mother was out, that left only one other person.

And there he was, sitting across from me.

I smiled back, hoping it didn't look as anxious as it felt. "I'm glad it worked out, and we could meet for lunch."

"Yes, you caught me on a light day. Wine?"

I nodded as he picked up the wine list.

The waiter came to take our order. He was very tall, thin, and young. His brown hair was pulled back in a neat ponytail, and he had a severe case of acne across the bridge of his nose. I wondered if he was even old enough to bring us our wine. My father ordered a bottle along with a fried zucchini appetizer and lasagna, which is what he usually got. I ordered a Caesar salad with chicken and hoped I would be able to get it down. My stomach was already churning.

My father shot me a look after the waiter left. "Is that going to be enough, honey?"

I reached for my water glass as I forced another smile. "Positive. I went to Nanna's for dinner last night, and I'm still full."

"Oh, yes." His eyes had a faraway look. "I do miss Nanna's cooking. She had the most wonderful meatloaf and mashed potatoes and gravy. It's been a while."

I bit my tongue before the words tumbled out of my mouth. *Why don't you give her a call? I'm sure she'd be happy to have the two of us to dinner and make meatloaf.* But I didn't want to upset him, as I had come for information. Besides, we both knew why he would never call her. He wouldn't be able to bear sitting across from his wife's mother, knowing that even while he faithfully paid the bills, he hadn't visited her in years.

No, it was better to just long for the taste of the meatloaf.

The waiter brought our wine, and like an old pro, deftly opened it in front of us. *Maybe he just looks a lot younger than he is*, I thought as I watched him interact with my father, handing him the cork so he could sniff the wine.

Then, I found myself seeing my father in a whole new light. He was still a good-looking man, even after all these years. A little too thin, but handsome. His salt-and-pepper hair was still thick, and he had a strong jaw line and high cheekbones. For the first time, I found myself wondering why he never remarried or even had a girlfriend. I was sure it wasn't because of a lack of interest, even with the scandal all those years ago. Some widow would have happily overlooked that unfortunate incident for the security of being with a financially well-off and good-looking man.

Yet he stayed true to my mother, even still wearing his wedding ring. Despite never visiting her.

Why?

"So, do what do I owe this pleasure?" he asked after the waiter filled both our glasses and disappeared.

My mouth was dry, and I reached for my wine. "What, I can't come see my own dad?" I asked, trying to inject a note of teasing into my voice, but feeling it fall flat.

"Well, of course," he said. "You know I'm always happy to see you. I just didn't know if there was another reason."

Was he referring to Missy? He must have heard about it. Redemption wasn't that far away from Riverview, not to mention all the other similarities and connections.

But that would be quite unlike my father. He hated talking about that time, and in fact did everything possible to avoid answering any questions about it. "What's past is past," he would say. "It's not going to do anyone any good, least of all you or your mother, to talk about it." Yet another reason why I had tried so very hard to forget it. I knew the chances of getting a straight answer out of my father were slim to none, and it was likely going to end up being an overall unpleasant experience.

But I was also unable to let it go.

"Well, it has been a crazy week," I said cautiously. Could that turn into the opening I needed?

He sighed, pinching his nose. "So, they've been bothering you, as well."

I gave him a puzzled look. Maybe I had misread the situation after all. Wouldn't be the first time I had gotten my father completely wrong. "Who?"

"The media, of course."

The media? Why would the media be bothering me? Or my father? Unless …

"They're calling you about Missy," I said. I could feel the skin at the back of my neck start to crawl, sure there was someone behind me staring at me. My own eyes started darting around the room, looking for some journalist lurking by a table, pretending to eat but really trying to listen to our conversation. But from what I could see, all the tables were filled with groups or couples who were focused on their own conversations versus the rest of the room.

Although there WAS a lone male diner sitting in the corner. Glasses, hair in a man bun, a loose beige shirt. He was scribbling furiously in a notebook. What was he writing? I didn't think he could hear us from where he was, especially with how noisy it was, with everyone talking and laughing.

But still …

My father glanced at me. "Luckily, it's just the local media this time, but yes. Haven't they been calling you?"

I shook my head. "I changed my name, remember?" Although I didn't add that doing so hadn't stopped Cole from finding me.

He picked up his wine. "I didn't think that would stop them. Vultures. Every one of them." His voice was uncharacteristically bitter. His hand shook slightly as he took a sip, his face hard, but then his features smoothed out. "Enough unpleasantness. What's new?"

It was now or never. He had barely cracked open the door, but it was clear it wasn't going to get any wider. "Well, actually, I have a few questions I was hoping you could answer."

His expression became guarded again. "Like what?"

The waiter appeared with a basket of garlic knots. I reached over to take one, not because I was hungry, but because I wanted something to do with my hands. Across the room, the man at the table had paused his scribbling and was peering around the room as he took a drink. I tore my eyes away—the last thing I wanted to do was call attention to myself. "Can you tell me a little about the year before Scott was born?"

"Why would you want to talk about that? What's the point? It was over twenty years ago."

"I know, but I had things come to the surface this week, and I feel like I need closure."

He narrowed his eyes. "'Things'?"

"Memories," I said, reaching for my wine and taking a quick swallow. Courage in a bottle. "At least I think they're memories. Which is why I want to talk about them. I have questions."

He picked up his wine again, not meeting my eyes. "I still don't see the point. Nothing is going to change."

I started pulling the roll apart into smaller pieces. "I know we can't change what happened, but that doesn't mean it isn't still affecting me."

"What are you talking about?" He shot me a reproachful look. "You're doing fine. You have a good job, you're making good money, you have friends ..."

Suddenly, I was furious. "I'm a workaholic," I cut in, the words erupting out of me like hot, bitter lava. "I don't have any friends, because I work all the time. I don't have a relationship, either, for the same reason. I have no hobbies, and other than running five miles nearly every morning, I have terrible health habits. I can't sleep, and I have night terrors. And worst of all, I'm working all these hours at a job I don't even like."

He blanched. "I'm sure you're making it out to be worse than it is. And even so, how would rehashing the past change any of that?"

"I don't know," I said, my voice rising as the words kept flowing, burning my throat, my tongue, like acid. I had no idea where they were coming from—what dark, twisted well inside me kept spewing them out. "I have no idea if it will change anything or not. But I have to try. I have to do something. I can't keep living like this. It's not living. I don't know what it is, but it's not that. I have to figure out how to change, because I don't want to end up …" I snapped my mouth shut, terrified of the words that were about to escape my mouth.

I don't want to end up like you.

My father's face was white. It didn't matter that I didn't finish the sentence, as we both knew what I was about to say. He reached for his wine again, finishing the glass and picking up the bottle to refill it, only shaking slightly.

I stared miserably at my garlic knot, now in pieces on my bread plate. As quickly as the flood of words appeared, they had dissipated, leaving me feeling weak and slightly ill. The smell of garlic was strong in my nostrils, making me even queasier. Normally, I would love it, but in that moment, it just made my stomach turn. I felt like I should apologize, but I didn't know how.

"What do you want to know?" His voice was soft and a little hoarse. I glanced up in surprise. His face was still pale, but not quite as white as before, although his expression was somewhere between resigned and sad.

I reached for my wine, trying to formulate my thoughts. I hadn't expected him to be open to my questions. "Was your business in trouble that year? Financially, I mean."

He flinched. "Yes," he said, his voice still low. "I had lost a couple of contracts. It was a difficult time. I even considered bankruptcy at one point."

My eyes widened. Nanna hadn't made it seem that dire. "How did you pull yourself out of it?"

He moved his wine glass around the table. "Hard work. Late nights." He glanced at me and gave me a sad smile. "I hated not being around more for you, but at the time, I truly thought you were okay. I didn't realize how sick Cora had gotten. And …" he swallowed hard. I could see his Adam's apple bobbing. "I wonder what else I missed, because I was so consumed with the business."

The man in the corner stood up suddenly. He tucked his notebook in a backpack and headed out of the restaurant. I felt something loosen in my chest. Not a journalist after all. *See, Tori? It's all in your head.* "Someone needed to pay the bills," I said, wanting to pass some of the relief I was feeling to my father. "You need to know I don't blame you. For any of it."

He nodded, still not meeting my eyes.

I cleared my throat. "So, was there anything else that happened that year?"

He shot me a quick look. "What do you mean?"

"Just, well, anything else. Mom got pregnant and went off her medications, and the business went south, but eventually, you got it back on track. Was there anything else that happened that year?"

He blinked at me in confusion. "Isn't that enough?"

Listening to myself and the conversation, I felt like my father was right. That WAS more than enough, and I didn't know why I was pushing it. Clearly, I had seen something that didn't exist on Nanna's face. But now that I had gone so far, I had to finish it. "Nanna had mentioned something about a fresh start after Scott was born," I said.

"You talked to Nanna?"

"Not a lot," I said quickly. "She was the one who asked me if I was having any, well, flashbacks about that time. And she was the one who said when Scott was born, it was like a fresh start for our family."

My father relaxed slightly. "Oh, yes. It did feel like that, in a way. A couple of new projects finally came through. The papers were signed, and they weren't starting for a few weeks, so I got to spend a few days at home taking care of you and Scott while your mother recovered." He paused, a faraway look in his eyes, as if remembering that time—maybe the smell of baby powder and the way Scott would wrap his fingers around your hand as you were feeding him. "It seemed like a good omen."

A good omen. Again, I pictured Scott, his huge blue eyes, his long lashes, his chubby arms and legs.

And again, I compared that image to the dead baby in the crib, the skinny arm thrown over his head.

I reached for my wine again. "Looking back, it unfortunately seems more like the lull before the storm."

He half-smiled. "Yeah, sadly, I guess that's exactly what it was."

The picture of the too-skinny arm kept blinking in my brain. "Dad, are you absolutely sure it was Scott?"

He stilled. "Tori, don't do this." His voice was tired.

"No, listen ..."

"No, you listen to me." He leaned forward, a faint flush across his cheekbones. "Look, I know this week brought all sorts of things up that really should have stayed in the past. But Tori, you have to stop this. It was all just a terrible tragedy."

"But it didn't look like Scott," I burst out, feeling a little desperate. "Couldn't you see it? It wasn't him."

My father sat back and pinched the bridge of his nose. He looked exhausted. "He was dead, Tori," he said, his voice hard. "Babies look different when they're dead. And you were a child suffering from a night terror. You aren't remembering it correctly."

Our food arrived, interrupting our conversation. I stared at my salad, feeling both terrible and sick to my stomach. As uncomfortable and awkward as my relationship was with my father, I wanted it. Other than Nanna, he was my only real family. I didn't want to alienate him.

But I also wanted the truth.

"I'm not trying to bring up bad memories," I finally said. "It's just … it's never felt right to me."

"It shouldn't feel right to you," he said, refilling his wine glass. "It was a horrible thing."

I watched him finish filling his glass, put the bottle down, and take a drink. "Do you know I still have night terrors?"

If possible, he looked even more sad … his face aging, his skin turning grey in the warm restaurant light. "Oh, Tori."

"I still see him," I said. "The figure in the room."

He sighed. "I don't know what to say. It was a terrible, terrible thing. I would give anything to have been the one to have found Scott that night and saved you from that nightmare."

A nightmare. Was that really all it was?

"The thing is, with Missy …"

My father looked blankly at me. "Missy?"

"She's the girl who thought her baby was stolen by faeries. I went to school with her and her brother. Did you know that?

He looked a little shaken. "No. But now … I wonder if that's the connection the reporters made.

"I don't know about that," I said. "But look. She is bipolar. Mom was sick, too, even if we didn't know how much so. And it's just weird that two people who were connected to me, two mentally ill people, had the same delusion. How can that be possible?"

His eyes widened. "None of this is your fault, if that's where you're going with this."

I shook my head. "No, I know that. But it can't be coincidence that two people who are not connected to each other and are separated by, well, decades, came up with the same delusion."

"I don't agree," he said firmly. "Look, your mother, well, I have no idea where your mother got her ideas. But your friend, she probably just remembered our story. I don't think it's anything other than that."

What my father said made sense. Especially since my saying out loud what had been lurking in my heart all this time sounded even crazier than it had while I was stewing on it.

Nothing I believed, deep down inside, made any sense—not that Scott had been taken, or that there was some mysterious connection between my mother and Missy. Those were silly ideas. I sounded like some sort of nutty conspiracy theorist. Even what I had been originally seeking from my father—some life-shattering event I couldn't remember that had maybe happened the year before Scott was born—seemed silly at that point.

My father was right. There had been enough stressful things. I didn't need to add anything more.

It was all just crazy thinking. And I needed to let it go.

So, why couldn't I?

Chapter 16

I was exhausted by the time I got home. The strain of the past two days, dealing first with Nanna and then my father, had taken its toll. Actually, the strain of the past week had finally caught up with me.

At least it was almost Sunday. My plan was to do as little as possible the next day, despite knowing it would make me even more behind on Monday. I needed the rest. I couldn't afford to keep pushing myself and risk having a breakdown.

Besides, with Cole and his investigation out of the picture, I could work as much as I needed to the next week to get caught up.

I put the remainder of my salad in the fridge and went to pour a glass of wine. At least my father and I had ended on a good note. Once we had moved the conversation away from the past, everything was okay. A little stilted and awkward, but okay.

As okay as it ever was with my father.

I had just finished pouring when the buzzer sounded from downstairs. I picked up my wine and headed over to the intercom, assuming it was someone who had gotten the wrong apartment. I wasn't expecting anyone, and every now and then, there was a mistake, and it was usually a delivery person.

I clicked on the button. "Hello?"

"Tori?"

I froze. It was Cole.

I had no idea what to do. Tell him to go away? Let him in? Argh. I was too tired to deal with whatever he wanted.

"Hello? Tori, are you there?"

"I'm here," I answered. "Why are you here?"

"Because I want to talk to you," he said.

"Why?"

"I'll tell you when you let me up."

"I thought we both said everything we had to say yesterday."

There was a sigh. "Tori, please. Will you give me a chance? I promise I won't stay long if you have plans."

I yelped a laugh. The only plan I had was for an early night in my bed, so I could catch up on some sleep. But he didn't need to know that.

I chewed on my lip as I considered what to do. A part of me, the part that constantly nagged me not to forget to call for an appointment with Dr. Adams first thing Monday, wanted me to tell him to go away and not contact me anymore. I could be nice about it, but I needed to do it.

For the sake of my own mental health.

But another part of me thought I should let him in. We were friends, right? It's not like we had been together and broken up or anything, so why should I send him away without listening to him? What could it hurt?

No! The first part yelled. *Do NOT let him in. You know what will happen. You're going to get sucked back into this investigation, and that means the nightmares will continue. And who knows where that will lead?*

Give him a chance, the other part urged. *He had a difficult week, as well. It won't kill you to hear him out.*

I took a deep breath and hit the button that unlocked the door, over the loud objections reverberating in my head that it very well might kill me to hear him out.

The objections continued as I ran to the bathroom to check my appearance. *I don't need to look good to let him say what-*

ever he came to say, I argued with myself. *And furthermore, I'm being foolish.*

I ignored all of it as I flipped on the bathroom light and studied myself in the mirror.

Luckily, I still had on the white, lacy peasant top and skinny jeans I had worn to lunch with my father. I quickly fluffed up my hair and touched up my mascara and lip gloss.

There was a tentative knock at the door. I took a final look in the mirror, wishing I had a little more time, then went to the door.

Cole gave me a sideways smile. "Hey." He was freshly shaved and showered, and he was wearing a clean, button-down, teal, short-sleeve shirt and jeans.

"Hey," I said, feeling strangely awkward and uncomfortable. Now that I was face to face with him, I wasn't sure what to do. "Did you want to come in?" I felt like an idiot. Of course he wanted to come in. Otherwise, he would have just called or texted.

Luckily, Cole didn't say anything as he stepped inside. He seemed as unsure of himself as I was. We stared at each other in silence. I wanted to ask what he wanted, but I was still holding the glass of wine I had just poured, and it felt rude to at least not offer him some. "Do you want some?" I asked, indicating the glass I held. "I just opened the bottle."

"I'd love some."

I went to fetch a second wine glass, glad to have something to do with myself. He followed me into the kitchen, leaning on the counter. "Sorry to stop by unannounced like this."

"It's fine," I said as I handed him his wine. "I'm assuming you have a good reason for it?"

He nodded, shifting his weight from one leg to the next. "I wanted to apologize. In person."

I did a double take. I hadn't been expecting that. "Why?"

"Because I was completely out of line on Friday. You've been nothing but helpful to me, and I had no right to get upset with you when you told me you didn't want to be a part of the investigation anymore."

"You don't have to apologize for that," I said. "I can see why you got upset. Witnesses ARE recanting their statements and acting strangely, and it sure seems like they're doing it under duress, so it makes sense you would immediately think I had had been targeted, too."

He ran a hand through his hair. "Yeah, but I still was out of line. I know this is taking a tremendous amount of time and emotional energy, and it's not fair of me to ask that of you. It's one thing for me to be so invested … she's my twin. But I shouldn't expect that from anyone else."

"It's not that," I said, before realizing it sort of was. But Cole seemed so dejected, my initial impulse was to try and reassure him. "Well, not that exactly," I amended. "I loved helping with the investigation, truly. I just, you know, have a lot going on at work, and I need to focus there."

"No, I get it," he said. "You don't have to explain." He flashed one of his crooked grins that made my heart stutter. "And I think I owe you another apology, as well."

"For what?"

He looked embarrassed. "I shouldn't have brought up your father, or your family, or how you're dealing with your family. It's none of my business, and honestly, with the mess my own family is in right now, I really ought not to talk."

"It's fine. I shouldn't have gotten so upset. I don't even know why I did." I let out a little uncomfortable laugh. "Turns out my dad did have some financial issues the year before Scott was born, but it wasn't a big deal. He was able to turn it around."

He shot me a curious look. "Oh. So, it was true, then."

"Yes, but it didn't mean anything," I said quickly. "Businesses lose money sometimes. That's just what happens."

"I get it," he said.

"It was a stressful time," I continued. "My mother was deteriorating mentally. I was so young. Add to that business troubles, and it's no wonder my father was stressed."

"I get it," Cole said again, holding his hands up. "You don't have to convince me. Honest."

It was like he had thrown cold water over me. I blinked stupidly at him, suddenly realizing how I must have sounded to him. "Sorry," I said. "I didn't mean to go on and on."

"It's okay," he said. "You don't have to be sorry. I get it. It was a terrible time in your life, so of course it's going to leave its mark."

"No, I ..." I blew the air out of my lungs. "I actually did what you said."

"What do you mean?"

"I ..." I felt like an idiot, but I also felt like I needed to explain. Cole made an effort to come to my home and apologize to me in person, and it wasn't right to keep the fact that he had a point from him. "When you brought up my father and his financial issues on Thursday, I didn't actually know about it. No one in my family had ever mentioned it. That's why I reacted the way I did. But then ..." I paused to gulp down a mouthful of wine, debating whether I should tell him about my nightmare and the memories resurfacing. "Well, let's just say I thought about what you said, and I decided to talk to Nanna and my father about what happened. That's when I discovered you were right."

"Ah," he said.

"So, anyway. I'm sorry I got upset with you."

"I don't think it's necessary to apologize," he said. "You were pretty young when all of that happened. Why would you remember? And why would your family talk about it afterward? Your brother's death would have trumped any financial problems, especially since it seems like they had been resolved by then."

"That's true," I said, but I still felt the little niggle that something wasn't right.

"Anyway, I probably should get out of your hair," Cole said, swallowing the last of his wine. "I'm sure you have things to do. Plus, there have been a few breaks in the case that I need to follow up with."

My ears perked up. "Breaks?" Inside, I could hear a part of me scream in frustration.

He nodded. "Yeah. I finally heard back from a few people. But I know you said you don't want to be a part of the investigation anymore, and I want to honor that."

Let him go, a voice in my head howled. *You remember what happened the last time you wanted to be an amateur sleuth. Do you want that to happen again?*

I pushed that voice down. Just because I listened to the updates didn't mean I was going to help with the investigation again. Plus, it was a Saturday night. It wasn't like I had any other plans besides channel-surfing.

Besides, I was super curious as to who had called him back.

"I'd love to hear what happened," I said. "Only if you have a few minutes, of course."

His face brightened. "Yeah, I'd love to tell you."

I picked up the bottle of wine and offered it to him. He held out his glass, and I topped off both of ours before gesturing for him to join me in the living room.

"So, first off, I heard from Dr. Broomer," he said once we were settled, him on the ugly plaid couch and me perched on the gold chair. Both items were used. One of Nanna's friend's sons gave me the couch, as he had just gotten married and was buying a new living-room set, and the chair was from another of Nanna's friends who was replacing it with a La-Z-Boy recliner. I had been meaning to buy new furniture myself for a couple of years, but I never found the time. Still, every time I had a guest over, I found myself promising to finally get it done.

I raised my eyebrows. "Really? That was fast."

"Yeah, I thought so, too. Anyway, it was exactly as you predicted. She said she did find mention of a 'Sarah' in her records, but Missy had described her as a 'friend.' As far as Dr. Broomer could tell, there was nothing suspicious about it."

"According to Beth, the way they met was suspicious," I said. "And don't you think Missy would have told Dr. Broomer about that? It seems like something that would have come up … Missy getting dizzy at a coffee shop and a midwife just happening to be there to help."

"I think we both know the answer to that," Cole said grimly. "But Dr. Broomer left a message, so I couldn't ask. She also made it quite clear she was done answering any sort of questions from me. As she put it, any more questions about Missy's therapy would need to be directed to Missy."

I rolled my eyes. "Of course. So, what's the second piece of news?"

Cole picked up his glass, a faintly smug look on his face. "I finally tracked down Renee. It took a bit of sorting through Missy's social media friends lists, but I did it."

"Were you able to talk to her?"

"Yeah. She couldn't help with anything having to do with Sarah, unfortunately. I'm not sure how we're going to track down Sarah without Missy. And the cops, well, that's a separate update. But going back to Renee … what she did tell me was that she may have seen a text on Missy's phone from the father."

"Really?"

Cole sipped his wine. A lock of his brown hair fell across his forehead. "Yep. She was over one afternoon, and she and Missy were in the kitchen talking. Missy had her phone next to her on the table and had gotten up to refill their drinks when the text came."

"What did it say?"

"How are you doing, gorgeous?"

I frowned. "That's pretty nondescript. How can she be sure it was from the father?"

"Because of Missy's reaction. The text wasn't connected to a name, just a letter. W. While Missy was in the kitchen, Renee called out, 'So who is W, and why is he wondering how you're doing today?' Missy turned a deep shade of red and ran back to the table to grab the phone. She was really flustered, but said it was 'nothing.' Renee, of course, said she wasn't acting like it was nothing, and Missy said it was no big deal. Just a friend who was helping her out. That was all Missy would say about it, no matter how much Renee bugged her. So, she was pretty sure it was the father."

"W," I mused. "Did Renee know who that initial might belong to?"

Cole shook his head. "No, and neither did Beth."

I gave him a startled look, my hand jerking as the wine sloshed in the glass, dangerously close to spilling on my blouse. "You talked to Beth?"

"I texted her. Neither Renee nor Beth knew any guy with a first name beginning with a W, although Beth did know someone whose last name did. It was 'Witherspoon,' believe it or not."

My eyes widened. "Someone related to Reese Witherspoon?"

He flashed me a lopsided smile. "That was precisely my thought. Maybe this celebrity thing was real after all. But, alas, no. No relation to Reese. And Beth wasn't even sure if Missy had ever even met him."

"Did you check Missy's social media friends?"

"Not yet. I need my computer."

"Why?"

He sighed. "Reporters. They figured out my cell phone." He fished his phone out of his pocket and shoved it onto the table with a clatter. "I've had it turned off most of the time, as well. I thought maybe that was part of the reason why you decided you didn't want to help anymore ... because you were also getting harassed."

I shifted uncomfortably on the chair. "No, they haven't found me yet." But I was starting to wonder. Between my father and Cole, I was pondering how long I had before the media did figure out who I was. Just the thought of it left me with an icy-cold feeling of dread. Maybe it was best that I was stepping away from helping Cole. "Why are the reporters calling you?"

"Because of the cops." He spat out the words, gritting his teeth as he reached for his wine. "The medical examiner released the baby's autopsy results."

"And?"

"Along with a lot of other issues, including being malnourished and too small, there was heroin in his system."

My eyes widened. "Oh no. That's why the baby died?"

"The baby never had a chance," he said grimly. "It was stillborn."

"I'm sorry," I said lamely, knowing those words weren't going to help anything, but feeling like I needed to at least address it. It was his nephew who had died, after all.

He inclined his head briefly.

"So, what are the cops going to do with that information?"

"As far as I can tell, nothing," he said, his voice shaking with anger. He ran his hand roughly through his hair. "Which makes no sense! This is proof the baby isn't Missy's."

"I'm not sure I'm following you."

Cole got up and started pacing, too agitated to sit. "Missy didn't use heroin. Never. So clearly, the baby wasn't hers."

I watched him as he strode around the couch. "What did the cops say when you told them that?"

"That I couldn't be sure," he said disgustedly. "After all, I wasn't living with her. I hadn't seen her much, so how did I know what she was or wasn't doing? I said, 'Talk to her doctors.' She's still in the hospital; she's been in the hospital for a week now. Wouldn't her doctors know if she was going through heroin withdrawal? Wasn't she tested for drugs when she was admitted?" He pressed the heels of his hands against his eyes.

"Well, was she?"

"Yes, but the results were inconclusive," he said.

"What does that mean?"

He let out a big sigh and came back to the couch. "I'm not entirely sure. Part of the issue is that heroin has a short half-life in the body, so it doesn't show up in blood or saliva. And it only lasts two days in urine. It's possible, if she had been doing heroin, that her last dose was before that. I'm also not clear when they started her back on her bipolar medication. If they gave her something before they tested her blood and urine, that may have tainted the results, as well. Hence, the inconclusive results." He reached for his wine.

I thought about Missy lying in the hospital bed, drugged up and full of wires, her thin, white arms exposed by the hospital gown. "But she doesn't look like a heroin user," I said. "I mean, there were no track marks."

"I said that, too," he said grimly. "Of course, you don't have to inject it. You can snort or smoke it. Either way, it doesn't look like the cops are going to follow up at all."

"Well, just because they won't right now doesn't mean they never will," I said. "Once Missy finally decides to talk, who knows what she'll say? The cops might open her case sooner."

"They might," he said, but he didn't sound very optimistic.

"How is she doing?"

He sighed again. "Not well. She's severely depressed and still refusing to speak or eat."

My heart went out to him. "Oh, Cole."

"I know you get it," he said. "That's part of the reason they haven't released her yet. They want to make sure she isn't a danger to herself or anyone else. So, yeah. Who knows when she'll be ready to talk, and how cold all the leads will be then? At this point, I don't have a lot of hope we're ever going to get to the bottom of what happened that night."

For an answer, I gave him a sad smile. I was the last person to tell him to look at the bright side. I was living proof that you don't always get to the bottom of everything that happens in life.

He finished his wine, but didn't set the glass down. Instead, he spun it by its stem, his expression brooding. His face was thin, his cheeks hollowed, and his shirt hung loosely around his chest.

"When was the last time you ate?" I asked him impulsively. *Are you out of your mind?* The little voice of my Negative Nancy asked. *It's just dinner,* I answered.

He eyed me. "I don't know," he said. "Lunch, maybe? No, it was breakfast. I had a power bar."

I lifted an eyebrow. "A power bar?"

"Yeah, I was heading out the door."

"Do you want to get something to eat?" I asked. "Unless you have plans, that is."

He considered it, still moving the empty wine glass back and forth. His fingers were long and tapered. "Are you asking me out on a date?" His voice held a faint note of teasing.

No! said the Negative Nancy voice. I told it to hush. I was feeling a little lightheaded, probably because I hadn't eaten much lunch myself. "Do you want it to be a date?"

"I don't know," he said. "What if I said 'yes'?"

"Then I guess it would be a date."

"Well, okay then." He flashed me his trademark grin.

This is absurd, the Negative Nancy voice fumed. *You have no business getting involved with this man. Not just because he is in no place for any sort of long-term relationship, but because neither are you! You need to take care of yourself right now, not get involved with someone who is going to pull you in the wrong direction.*

The voice wasn't wrong. But in that moment, I didn't care. For one night, I wanted to go on a date and pretend I was normal. Pretend I wasn't in danger of becoming as crazy as my mother, and that I didn't have a terrible past I was hiding from anyone. That I could be happy, like everyone else.

Just one night. That was all I asked.

"Where do you want to go?" he asked. "Oh, actually, before you answer that, let me check my phone." He reached over and plucked up his phone from where it sat on the table.

"Check your phone?"

"Yeah. Since I have it off now, I turn it on periodically throughout the day to make sure I'm not missing any important messages." He fiddled with it for a moment, scrolling through the notifications. Then, his face froze. "The hospital called. I need to check this."

"Of course."

He dialed into the voicemail, and listening, the blood slowly drained from his face. "They're releasing her."

"What?"

"Yeah. Tomorrow. They want to make sure someone will stay with her." He dropped his phone back onto the glass coffee table. "They want me at the hospital tomorrow morning, so they can talk to me before releasing her." He looked shaken.

"But ... I thought she was still depressed," I said. "They wanted to watch her, to make sure she doesn't ... hurt anyone." I couldn't bear to add the other part of it—that she might try and do something to herself.

"That's what I thought," he said. "They told me that just a few days ago."

We looked at each other. There was a mixture of emotions on Cole's face: shock, concern, and exhaustion the most prevalent, but I saw another one starting to dawn, as well.

Hope.

"Do you think this means she's ready to talk?" I asked.

"I don't know," he said, but I could hear the excitement in his voice. "Maybe."

"Should we go visit her tonight?" Too late, I noticed I'd said, "we," and I wondered if I should correct it.

He mulled that over, not seeming to notice my mistake. "No. Tomorrow is soon enough. I think she would have reached out if she wanted to see me sooner. She has my number in her room, and I told her to call anytime." He tried to keep the hurt out of his voice, but it was there all the same. I had wondered why he wasn't at the hospital more, but maybe that was why. Along with stopping by every day, he had made a point of telling her how to get in touch with him if she was ready to talk, but she never did.

Of course, it wasn't a surprise she wanted to be left alone, and even if Cole knew that intellectually, especially being her twin, it probably still hurt.

He rubbed his face. "Man, I've got a lot to figure out before tomorrow. The first being, where should I take her?" He glanced up at me, giving me a sheepish look. "Would it be okay if we raincheck our date? Right now, my head is spinning around all the details involved with bringing her home."

My heart sank a little, even though I knew I was being ridiculous. "Of course," I said, forcing a note of cheeriness in my voice that I didn't feel. "I completely understand."

"Or ... what if we get some takeout? We could do pizza, or maybe Chinese?"

"We don't have to eat," I said. "Don't feel like you have to stay or anything."

"No, you're right. We both *do* need to eat. And I would love to talk through what to do. I don't want to take her to her condo ... talk about bad memories. And I'm sure it needs a good cleaning. My apartment is way too small; it's only a one bedroom. And I don't want to take her to my parents; they're in Redemption. Plus, my mom has enough to worry about." He frowned for a moment before catching my eye and giving me a crooked smile. "So, you pick. Pizza, Chinese, or something else?"

And here you are, getting involved AGAIN. This is why you shouldn't have even let him up here in the first place.

It's just one night, I argued back. *And I'm not helping him with his investigation. I'm helping him find a place to take his sister. Completely different.*

The Negative Nancy voice didn't buy it for a second. I wasn't completely sure I did, either.

But it *was* one night. And Cole was right. We both had to eat.

"I know a great Chinese place that delivers," I said, getting to my feet. One more night wouldn't hurt. Especially since he was already there. We would eat some dinner and brainstorm a plan for his sister. Period. "I'll grab the menu. More wine?"

He grinned. "You read my mind."

Chapter 17

I raised my hand, wanting to tug at my hat again but forcing myself to leave it alone. *It's fine,* I told myself. *I don't have to fiddle with it.*

I still wasn't sure how Cole had talked me into accompanying him to the hospital. I had been dead set against it, especially when he mentioned one of the reasons he wanted me with him was to help him navigate the media.

"Oh no," I had said, shaking my head vigorously. "No way. I want nothing to do with journalists.""

"But Tori, they're not going to have any interest in *you*," he said. "No one is even going to recognize you."

"You don't know that."

"Why would they care who you are?" he asked. "You're not family, or even a friend of Missy's. They aren't going to care."

"Until they dig up my past," I said. "They've been bugging my father. It's only a matter of time before they find me."

Baffled, he stared at me. "You changed your name," he said.

"You still found me."

"That's different."

"How?"

He breathed out hard through his nose. "Because I recognized you," he said. "I knew who you were. But no one else does. There's no reason to connect you to what happened in the past. And if you're that worried about it, wear a disguise."

The idea of a disguise was ridiculous, of course. It was far safer to not tempt fate and be nowhere near the hospital when Cole arrived to fetch his sister.

But Cole wouldn't let up. He needed backup, he said. Not just in case the media were there, which, it being Sunday, wasn't likely. Although he did grudgingly admit to me that a couple of reporters had been hanging around. "But more likely than not, they were chasing a few stories," he insisted. "I seriously doubt they would be staking out the hospital just because of Missy. Especially with what the M.E. just found."

That seemed like it ought to be true, but if it was, why were they still inundating his cell?

"Probably because I haven't given them an interview yet," he said.

All of his arguments made sense, but I still felt uneasy. Nonetheless, Cole kept insisting he needed help. Just because they were releasing Missy didn't mean she was cured. Who knew what kind of mood she would be in when he arrived? And once he got them settled in the hotel he found, someone would have to stay with her while the other went out for groceries and other errands. He wouldn't be comfortable leaving her alone until he had a sense of what shape she was in.

"I could meet you at the hotel," I said.

"That's too much like you're babysitting her," Cole said. "If you're coming with us from the hospital, then it's just natural for you to stay while I run some errands."

"I don't think I'm the right person," I said. "She was pretty upset with me the other day. Don't you remember?"

"She wasn't stable yet," he said quickly. "She'll be better now."

I wasn't convinced. Nothing about this sounded like a good idea. So far, I had been lucky. No one had connected me with little five-year-old Vicky. I shouldn't press my luck.

But Cole was right. He did need help. And I probably was the best person for the job. His parents weren't able, and Missy had argued with both of her friends, so even though I thought I might agitate her, her friends likely would, as well. Plus, if there were journalists lying in wait, her friends would be a target. More so than me.

In the end, despite it all—my better judgement, how sick the thought of being recognized made me, and Negative Nancy's shrieks—I agreed.

This is just like the last time, Negative Nancy warned.

It's nothing like the last time, I argued, and it wasn't. The circumstances were completely different. I was 15 then, and still going by the name "Vicky." It was easier for people to put two and two together. I was over a decade older now and calling myself "Tori." Plus, Cole was right—I was going to be there as Cole's friend who was helping his sister. No reason for anyone to dig into my background.

On top of that, it was the right thing for me to do. Face my fears and all that. Cole had been right, at least when it came to my father. Because I faced my fears and asked the hard questions, I now knew there was nothing sinister going on. This was probably the same thing.

But still, I felt uneasy.

I dressed carefully—plain white tee shirt and black leggings. No jewelry or anything that would bring attention to me. Oversized dark sunglasses. My hair piled up at the top of my head and covered with a black baseball cap with a smiling orange pig on it. It was from a promotion from a barbecue restaurant, and I rarely wore it, so I thought it a good choice for this venture.

I stared at myself at the mirror, wishing I had a wig. This would have to do.

Cole had done a double take when he saw me.

"I wasn't serious about the disguise," he said as I opened the passenger door.

"Just drive," I said grimly. My chest was tight, and I was having trouble forcing air into my lungs.

He shook his head slightly and started the car.

When we arrived at the hospital, I deliberately held back, trailing behind as Cole strode through the parking lot and lobby carrying a duffle bag in one hand. No one seemed to pay any attention to him. I started to breathe a little easier. Cole was right. The journalists weren't there, either because it was Sunday or because it seemed like an open-and-shut case. Crazy pregnant woman medicated herself with heroin and caused the baby to be stillborn. Tragic, but not criminal.

Cole held the elevator for me, although he didn't acknowledge me as I stepped in. I didn't think anything of it until the doors were closing and he had hit the button for Missy's floor. It was then that I noticed his lips pressed together in a thin, flat line. "Don't freak," he said under his breath. "But there was a reporter in the lobby."

My eyes widened as my throat tightened up. "Seriously?" I wondered if it was too late to dash down the stairs. I could call an Uber to take me back to my apartment and just forget this whole business.

He nodded. "But look. It's like I said. He's probably here for someone else. He didn't stop me or anything."

"Did he see you?"

He looked away. "I think so. But I can't be sure. I don't think it's a big deal, though. It's only him. I'm sure it's just a nothing-burger."

The elevator doors opened. I hesitated, wondering if I could just ride it right back down, but Cole gestured for me to walk ahead of him.

Get a hold of yourself, Tori, I told myself as I walked toward the psych ward, refusing to listen to Negative Nancy telling me what a fool I was being. The chances of anyone recognizing me were slim, and any journalist would be more interested in Missy and Cole.

All I had to do was keep my head down, and it would all be fine.

Cole signed us both in, giving the receptionist a friendly smile. Today was someone different—an older, gray-haired woman with thick, round glasses. It suddenly occurred to me that I had caught a huge break. If it had been the pink-haired woman, it was possible she would have recognized me, and maybe even wondered why I was taking such great pains to disguise myself.

This was such a bad idea. I wished for the umpteenth time that I had just waited in the car or insisted on meeting Cole at the hotel. But seeing as I was already in the hospital, I figured I might as well keep going. Besides, who else was going to recognize me from before? I had spent very little time when I first visited Missy.

Missy was sitting on a chair staring out the window. It wasn't much of a view, as it overlooked the parking lot, but that probably didn't matter, anyway. It was also covered with bars. She didn't turn as we entered the room.

"Missy. I'm so glad you're up," Cole said, his voice gentle. "I brought you some clothes to change into." He moved slowly toward her, almost like he was approaching a wild animal.

She didn't respond, just kept staring out the window. Her hair was oily and matted, and I wondered if anyone had even offered to wash it for her since she had been there.

He put the duffle bag on the chair next to her. "I brought a few outfits," he said. "I wasn't sure what you'd like. We can get you more clothes later … you just have to tell me what you want."

She still didn't move.

Cole glanced at me, his eyes helpless. My heart went out to him, and I suddenly wasn't as disgruntled about being there. Maybe it was less about Missy and more about supporting him.

He knelt by the chair, touching her hand. "You do know you're being discharged today, right? We're going to need to leave here soon, so you'll need to get changed."

There was a flicker, and Missy slowly turned her head toward him. "I don't want to go home," she said. Her voice was slow and hoarse, like she hadn't used it much.

"You're not going home," he agreed. "I'm taking you to a hotel."

"A hotel?" She looked puzzled. "Why would we go there?"

"We can talk about it in the car," he said. "Right now, you need to get ready. Can you handle dressing yourself, or do you need some help?"

She glanced at the duffle bag. "It doesn't matter. Nothing matters." She went back to gazing out the window.

"Missy, can you get dressed?" he asked tenderly.

For a moment, she didn't move, but then her head bobbed once, a tiny motion.

Cole stood up. "We'll wait for you outside."

Maybe it was the "we" that broke through whatever fog she was in, but her head suddenly swiveled toward me. For a moment, her face was blank, like she couldn't place me, but then recognition began to dawn, seeping over her face like water. "You," she said. "What are you doing here? And what's up with your hair? And that hat?"

"She's here to help," Cole said.

"She's wearing that silly hat because she wants to help? And what *is* that on it, anyway?"

"It's a pig," I answered. For the first time, I could hear the old Missy. And I could also remember why I didn't have much to do with her when we were kids. Even back then, she was brutally honest and in your face.

Missy shot me an "Oh really?" look. "And why are you still wearing your sunglasses? Are you trying to hide being on drugs, or something?"

"Can you get dressed first, and then we'll talk?" Cole interrupted.

Missy put a hand on the back of her chair and pulled herself to her feet. She was thin, way too thin. Her hospital gown hung awkwardly on her body, exposing the hollowness near her collarbone and under her cheeks and the waxiness of her skin. Dark circles stained her eyes like bruises. "We'll talk now. What is going on?"

Cole sighed and rubbed the back of his neck. "It was just ... easier. She didn't want to be recognized."

Missy jerked her chin toward Cole. "Recognized? Who is going to recognize her?"

"In case there were reporters ..."

"Reporters?" Missy's eyes grew very wide. "Why are there reporters?"

"Presumably to report on what happened to you," Cole said.

"But why? I'm not famous or anything. I'm just a nobody."

"Yes, but at least initially, it was, you know, a little sensational," he said. "But it's not a big deal. They'll eventually find something else to focus on ..."

"No reporters," she interrupted. A pale, white hand crept up to clutch at her neck.

"Yes, that's the idea. Now get dressed ..."

"No reporters," she interrupted a second time, her voice loud. Her face had gone white, although it was hard to discern as her skin had been pale before. Her eyes, though, had definitely shifted.

She was terrified.

I felt a surge of pity, and camaraderie, rise in me. I could relate to wanting nothing to do with reporters.

"No reporters," Cole said, picking up the duffle bag from where it sat on the chair. "Will you *please* get dressed now?"

She glared at Cole for a moment before finally nodding. He moved the bag to the bed and unzipped it. "We'll be right outside," he said, walking toward the door and gesturing for me to follow.

"Vicky can stay," Missy said.

We both gave her a startled look. "Wait. Me?" I asked.

"That's your name, right? Vicky?"

"Actually, I go by Tori now," I said.

She pressed her lips together and shook her head. "Of course you do."

"So, you want Tori to stay?" Cole asked.

"That's what I said. Is it so hard to believe?"

Cole glanced at me, raising an eyebrow in question. I gave him a quick nod. "Okay then," Cole said. "I'll go see about your discharge instructions."

"The doctor's an idiot," she said. "Find one of the nurses. They do a better job."

"I'll see what I can do," he said as he went out the door, closing it behind him.

Missy closed her eyes briefly after her brother left. She rubbed her face, then limped toward the bed. "Tell me the truth about these reporters," she said, rifling through the duffle bag.

"They're definitely interested in the story," I said.

She winced slightly as she pulled out a yellow tracksuit, grimacing as she looked at it. "Honestly, Cole," she muttered. "Could you have maybe found something less conspicuous?" She tossed it on the bed and continued to rummage. "Why are they so interested?"

"I'm not really sure," I said as Missy pulled out a grey pair of shorts and an oversized black tee shirt. "I haven't been following the news."

She eyed me. "Have they reached out to you?"

I shook my head.

She picked up a pair of panties and sat on the edge of the bed to put them on. "The name change probably helped," she mused.

"I changed my last name, as well," I said.

"Smart." She reached for the shorts. "So are there reporters here?"

"Cole said there was one in the lobby."

Her head whipped around to stare at me in horror. "Who?"

"I don't know. But Cole recognized him."

She muttered to herself and went back to dressing. I looked away as she removed her hospital gown and put on the black tee shirt. "I absolutely can't talk to the press," she said.

"I don't blame you."

"No." She was breathing heavily, her nostrils flaring slightly. "This is non- negotiable. I cannot talk to the press. I just can't."

"Okay," I said, feeling slightly alarmed. She was so intense, too intense, almost like she was still gripped in some sort of paranoid delusion. I hoped Cole would return soon.

She continued to stare at me, her eyes boring into mine. "Will you help me?"

"I'll do what I can."

She pressed her lips together and nodded. "It's just ... it's not about me," she said. "There are other people who could be hurt. It's better for everyone if this just stays quiet."

I wondered who she was talking about. If it was Cole or her parents, they were already hurt. I didn't think a newspaper article could change that. Was she talking about Sarah? Man, I hoped not, as I was pretty sure Sarah was at the bottom of what happened the night she gave birth, and the last thing any of us needed was for Missy to protect her.

Or maybe she meant the father of her child. She had been so quiet about who he was, even during the grip of her illness.

Why would the father need her protection?

"I get it," I said. "Truly, I do. But keep in mind that just because you're not interested in being interviewed doesn't mean they're not interested in writing the story."

"So, what does that mean? They'll make something up?"

I shrugged. "Possibly. But it's more likely they'll hound you for a while."

At that, she sat down heavily on the bed, almost like her knees collapsed. She looked toward the window. "What am I going to do?" she murmured.

She looked so lost and forlorn, her clothes draped loosely over her too-thin frame and her eyes full of despair. I reminded myself that she was still not completely well. Sure, she was stable enough to leave the hospital, but that didn't mean she was okay. She had just lost her child, the father wasn't in the picture, and the media were ready to burst through the door and hound her with questions, so they could splash her personal grief on the pages of their publications for money.

"Here," I said, taking off the baseball cap and handing it to her. She looked a little startled. "Do you want to pin your hair up, as well?"

"What are you doing?"

"Giving you my disguise," I said, removing my sunglasses. I pulled the pins out of my hair, refusing to think about the anxiety levels already shooting up inside me. Negative Nancy was about ready to have fit.

She didn't move. "You don't have to do that."

"It's fine," I said. Since she wasn't taking them, I moved closer to her and laid the items next to her on the bed, trying not to wrinkle my nose at the smell. She really needed to take a shower. I started fixing my hair into a simple ponytail.

"But … you don't want to be recognized, either."

"My name is different, so it's not like they're going to put two and two together immediately," I said, hoping it was true. "Cole knew me as a child. I doubt any of these journalists did." Another jolt of anxiety surged through me, and I pushed it down. Even if there did happen to be a journalist following the case who had seen me at five years old, would he really be able to recognize me as an adult?

She was shaking her head. "I wasn't trying to …"

"Take it," I said gently, interrupting her. "We know they want to speak to you. We don't know if they want to speak to me."

She gave me a hard look before reaching for the pins. "Thank you."

I nodded.

Behind us, the door opened. "Okay, I think we have everything," he said. "We'll have to pick up your prescription later, probably tomorrow morning, but I have samples to get us through until then … what's going on?"

"I'm borrowing Tori's baseball cap. What does it look like?" Missy asked as she finished pinning her hair.

"Yes, I see that. But why?"

"So that whoever is in the lobby doesn't recognize me," she said, pulling the cap on firmly and picking up the sunglasses.

He shot me a look. "I told you it wasn't a big deal," he said to me. "Tori shouldn't have said anything. There's no need to worry," he said to his sister, but she interrupted him.

"Don't blame Tori," she said. "I asked."

"I'm taking steps to protect you."

Missy's expression softened. "I know," she said quietly. "But she offered, and it makes me feel better."

They stared at each other for a moment, a wordless communication between twins, before Cole stepped forward to pack the yellow tracksuit back into the duffle bag. "You ready?"

"As much as I'll ever be."

I stepped back to allow Cole and Missy to go first, figuring I would lag behind. Maybe if I hung back far enough, no one would even realize we were together.

As soon as Missy stepped into the hallway, the red-headed nurse who had chased us out on our first visit appeared at her elbow. "All set to go home?" she asked.

Missy nodded. "Thanks for all your help. You were a Godsend."

"Just doing my job," she said, but her face flushed in pleasure.

"Thank you for taking such good care of her," Cole added.

The nurse nodded. "Good luck." She gave Missy one last smile before turning away.

Cole led us down the hall, him and Missy in front, me continuing to trail in the rear. "We'll go out the back way," Cole said loudly enough for me to hear.

"There's a back way?"

"Yeah. I asked the nurses. We can avoid the lobby altogether."

He reached the security door and started to wave through the glass, but then his body froze.

"What is it?" Missy hissed. "Is that him?"

Him? I took a few steps forward to peer through the window myself.

There was a man standing by the check-in desk. He wore a short-sleeve, red plaid shirt, torn jeans, and a red baseball cap. He lounged against the desk, his long limbs seeming to stretch everywhere as he talked to the older grey-haired woman manning the desk.

"Yeah," Cole said grimly.

Missy took a step backward. "We have to find another way out." Her voice was panicked.

"I'm not sure there is any other way out of this ward," Cole said nervously.

The man grinned at the older woman, clearly trying to charm her. He wasn't bad-looking, with his short brown hair and lazy smile, and was probably used to getting his way. But it didn't appear to be working on this woman.

"What's up?" It was the red-haired nurse again.

Cole gestured. "There's a journalist out there."

She swore under her breath. "Again?" She peered through the glass. "Margaret needs to call security." She picked up her hand as if to rap on the glass, but Cole stopped her. "Is there another way out?"

She gave him an uneasy look. "I shouldn't. He needs to be escorted out."

"He'll just wait in the parking lot," Cole said.

"Please," Missy begged.

She hesitated, turning her head toward Margaret and the man. Just then, some sort of movement must have caught his eye, because he snapped his head around. His eyes widened as he recognized Cole.

"Crap," Cole muttered.

He started gesturing wildly as he moved toward the door. Margaret threw her hands up in response and grabbed the phone.

"You gotta help us," Cole said.

The nurse pressed her lips together. "Okay. Follow me." She turned and headed back the way we came. Cole and Missy quickly followed.

I glanced over my shoulder as the man kept pointing to the glass and Margaret switched between yelling at him and talking on the phone. Then, the man looked up and directly into my eyes.

For a moment, I froze as we stared at each other. I was the first to break the gaze, turning swiftly and practically running down the hall after Cole, Missy, and the nurse.

It doesn't matter, I told myself. *It was a quick glance, nothing more. There's no way he recognized me. And besides, he's too young to have been working as a reporter when it all happened.*

Sure, keep telling yourself that, Negative Nancy said. *You didn't think you would be recognized at 15, either, did you?*

I refused to listen to her. What happened when I was 15 was completely different. There was no reason for that journalist to dig up my case.

Still, I couldn't push down the unsettled feeling.

Chapter 18

"I don't want to go to a hotel," Missy said.

We were in the car. I was driving, and Cole was sitting in the backseat with his sister.

The nurse had led us to a stairway with a locked door that required her key card. "You'll have to circle around once you get to the first floor," she said. "You may want to avoid the lobby …"

"Yeah, one of the other nurses told me about the side door," Cole said.

"Good. That's what I would do." She opened the door and gestured us inside.

After a couple of wrong turns, Cole finally got us outside and to the parking lot. There didn't appear to be any other media waiting for us. I wondered if the journalist trying to get inside had been detained by security. It felt like he could have caught us in the parking lot, if he had wanted to, but luckily, there was no sign of him.

"I know hotels aren't very homey, but we don't really have another choice," Cole said. "You know my apartment is too small."

"It's not just that," she said. "People are constantly coming and going at hotels. How can we possibly make sure the reporters won't find us?"

"They won't," he said. "I talked to the manager and booked it under a different name. It's going to be fine."

"You don't know that," she said. "What about the maid service? Are we just not going to get any? And what if I want to take a walk outside? I have to walk through a hotel lobby every time I want to leave? And food? We're going to cook every meal in a hotel?"

"You can stay with me." The words were out of my mouth before I could think through the ramifications. *What am I doing, inviting a woman suffering from bipolar disorder as well as grieving the death of her baby to* live *with me? Have I lost my mind?*

Silence from the backseat.

"I have a second bedroom," I continued, feeling more awkward and uncomfortable the more I spoke. Negative Nancy was uncharacteristically quiet, which made me wonder if she had fainted over the shock. "It was supposed to be my office. I knew I was going to be working out of the apartment when I got my job, so I thought a two-bedroom made sense. Except I never use it. I'm always sitting at the kitchen counter." I laughed self-consciously. "Anyway, there's a futon in there that pulls out to a bed and a mostly empty desk. I'll have to move some files out of the closet, and if you want a nightstand or something, we'll have to get one, but ..."

"Tori, you don't have to offer this," Cole broke in, his voice quiet.

I paused, suddenly realizing how much I was babbling. And why? Who was I trying to convince, myself or Missy? I glanced in the rear-view mirror and saw Missy staring at me, her eyes unreadable. Was it hope? Despair? A mixture of the two?

"I know," I said quietly.

He cleared his throat. "It's a ... a commitment ..."

"I know I need to take my meds," Missy broke in. "This isn't like before, Cole. I know what I need to do. I'll take my meds."

"But still," Cole started to say, but Missy put a hand on his arm.

"I don't need a babysitter," she said quietly. "I'll take my meds. Tori, I agree with my brother. You don't have to do this.

It's still a big imposition to have someone living with you, especially someone you barely know."

I met her eyes. "If you want to stay, I'm happy to have you. BUT there are a couple things we'd need to discuss."

I could see her tense. "Which are?"

"First, I do work from home. I'll be in the kitchen, but I need to be able to work. Sometimes I have to take calls and do meetings, so I can't be disturbed. Will that be a problem?"

She shook her head. "No."

"Two, you need to take a shower."

I saw a ghost of a smile touch her lips. "Deal."

***

It didn't take long to get Missy settled in. Cole had brought just one duffle bag, which along with shorts, a tee shirt, and the yellow tracksuit, also had a few changes of underwear and pajamas. He promised to make another run to her condo the next day and pack whatever she wanted—all she needed to do was give him a list.

While Missy was in the shower, Cole helped me move the files to a corner of my bedroom, which was already crowded, but after some rearranging of my shoe collection (which was painful), we got them to fit into one side of the closet.

"You didn't have to do this," he said again quietly, although it was doubtful that Missy could hear anything with the water running. "She would have been fine in a hotel."

"I know," I said. We were kneeling next to my closet, rearranging the boxes.

"So, if you don't mind my asking, why did you?"

Why did I, indeed? That was the question I kept asking myself, as well. It made no sense. The last thing I needed was a houseguest, especially one who was not well. This was supposed to be the week that I got myself back on track, not add to my stress load. And that wasn't even the worst of it. If a reporter caught wind that Missy was here, well, that would be the end of my being able to hide in the shadows. They would most certainly dig through my personal history and probably write it up for the world to see.

That thought made my anxiety skyrocket to the point of almost rescinding my offer and having Cole take Missy to a hotel the moment she finished her shower.

Almost.

"I'm not sure," I said quietly, not meeting Cole's searching gaze. "All I can think about is my mother ... the betrayal in her eyes as the cops led her away. I was too young to do anything then, but now ..." I shrugged.

He was silent for a moment. "What happened to your mother was horrible, and I have no doubt it was terribly traumatic for a five-year-old. And I know you know this, but Missy isn't your mother, and nothing you do here is going to change what happened."

"You're right, I do know that. I also know how strange this is. But I also feel like it's the right thing to do."

We both stood up then, and suddenly, I was acutely aware that we were alone in my bedroom. Sure, Missy was in the shower, but for all practical purposes, we were completely alone.

Cole seemed to become aware of it at the same time, as the tension between us suddenly electrified. We both stared at each other, and I saw him suck in his breath, almost like he was contemplating kissing me ...

I gave myself a quick shake and brushed my hands against my leggings. *That would be a massive mistake,* I told myself. I was already in way too deep with whatever this was. The last thing I needed was to get physically involved with Cole.

"I'll make a run to the supermarket, if you want to give me a list." I was surprised by how normal my voice sounded.

"Oh, you don't have to do that," he said. "Let me go to the store."

I shook my head and walked out of the bedroom and toward the kitchen. "Honestly, I need to go anyway. All I have is Pop-Tarts and frozen dinners. Actually, I think I might have eaten the last of my Pop-Tarts this morning."

"Yeah, but that's too much to ask," he said. "Seriously, let me go. I'm happy to buy whatever food you need, as well. It's the least I can do."

I strode into the kitchen to open the fridge and survey the contents. Yes, it was just as pathetic as I remembered. Condiments, a half-full container of cream, and some take-out boxes, including my salad from the day before. I had no idea what was even in the other boxes, or how long they had been in there. Surely, it was time to toss them. "I don't mind going," I said. "You and your sister should talk, anyway. Alone. I would just be in the way."

"Well, then, I'll be in charge of cooking," he said.

I was perusing the cabinets then, which were as bare as I remembered. A few cans of soup and a couple boxes of macaroni and cheese, but not a Pop-Tart to be found. I shut the cupboard and eyed Cole. "You can cook?"

"He's a great cook," Missy said. She had come out of the bathroom and was leaning against the door jamb, dressed in one of my robes and her hair wrapped up in a turban. "He's especially good at Italian, but he also makes some mean chicken enchiladas."

Cole's face was modest. "I'm okay."

I looked between them, feeling like I was missing something obvious, when my memory finally clicked in. "The cooking blog," I said, remembering our first conversation.

He nodded.

"Cole has always loved cooking, even when we were kids," Missy continued. "He used to bake bread when he was eight years old. Can you imagine? Mom hated it, because she always had to clean the kitchen."

"She ate the bread though," Cole said.

Missy rolled her eyes. "Well, of course she did. She needed the calories before tackling the cleanup."

It was both good and a little weird to listen to their banter. While it made me happy to see them reconnect, I also felt like an interloper—a trespasser in my own apartment. The sooner I headed off to the store, the better.

"If you say you're good at Italian, you better be able to back that up," I said, raising a hand. "Real Italian grandmother, here."

He raised an eyebrow. "Challenge accepted."

I opened up my junk drawer to find a notebook. "Okay, then. I'll buy the ingredients, and you cook them up. Wanna make a list?"

"Surprise me."

I looked at him in surprise. "Don't you have some favorite dish you want to make?"

He shrugged. "I'll manage."

Near the bathroom, Missy let out a rusty chuckle. I wondered how long it had been since she'd really laughed. It might have been months, even, back when she first conceived and went off her meds. "It's his shtick."

"'Shtick'?"

"What he does on his blog."

I looked between them. "I don't get it."

"You know how some people can walk into any kitchen and pull an amazing meal together with practically no ingredients?" Missy asked. "That's Cole."

"I wouldn't say that," he said. "But, yes, that's the essence of my cooking blog. How you can take whatever's in your kitchen, no matter how pathetic, and turn it into a meal. Good substitutions for things. Stuff like that."

"It's cooking lessons for people who can't cook," Missy said.

"Maybe I should start paying attention to it," I said. "The last time I tried to make an actual dinner, I almost burned the kitchen down."

"Well, if you want, I'll give you a private lesson," he said with a wink.

I looked away, feeling a little flustered. "Deal," I said. "I'll get the groceries. Missy, do you want anything?"

"Whatever," she said. "I'm not that picky. I haven't been all that hungry, either." From the corner of my eye, I saw Cole press his lips together tightly. Judging by how her clothes hung off her body, I wasn't surprised.

"Okay," I said brightly, picking up my purse. "I'll be back."

* * *

It was more difficult than I anticipated to shop for two people I didn't know very well. I had no idea what they liked or didn't like. I ended up buying as much variety as possible: all sorts of fresh fruit and vegetables along with pasta, tomato sauce, chicken, pork, and beef. I also got bread, deli meat, and cheese for sandwiches, and cereal and eggs for breakfast. At the last minute, I tossed in some bacon. Who doesn't love bacon?

Hopefully, something in the mix would tempt Missy's appetite. At the very least, the bacon should do it.

I paused by the Pop-Tart aisle and stopped myself from grabbing a box. I decided I would use this opportunity to improve my own eating habits, too.

When I returned to my apartment, Cole was in the middle of deep cleaning my kitchen. There was no sign of Missy.

"What, my kitchen doesn't meet your standards to cook in?" I asked, placing the first of several bags on the kitchen table.

Cole gave me a faint smile. "No, I just needed to do something. And I thought it might be a nice gesture, as I really do appreciate what you're doing for Missy."

"Where is she?"

He sighed. "In her room. We had ... well, not ..." he paused, pulling off the rubber gloves he'd found and rubbing his forehead. "Actually, that part doesn't matter. What does matter is she refuses to talk about anything to do with her pregnancy or that night."

I glanced over to the hallway, trying to see if Missy was listening, but it looked like the door was firmly shut. "She's been through a lot," I said cautiously. "We just got her out of the hospital. She probably just needs to rest and get a little food in her."

He snapped the gloves back on and went back to scrubbing the counters. "I know, but unfortunately, we don't have a lot of time. We already lost a week, and she still just refuses to talk. She won't even tell me Sarah's last name."

I watched him as he furiously scoured the stove. What I wanted to say was at this point, another day or two would hardly matter, but he didn't seem like he was in the mood. "I'll go get the rest of the groceries," I said instead.

His head snapped up at that. "Oh. I can help." He went to pull the gloves off again, but I put my hand out to stop him.

"I'm fine. You finish what you're doing, and yes, I appreciate help with any domestic chores." I threw him a quick smile before leaving the apartment.

It took three more trips before I'd emptied the car. By that time, Cole had finished scrubbing and had everything back in its place. As he examined my purchases, I put most of the food away, mostly so I would know where everything was.

He still seemed to be in a foul mood, muttering to himself, all hints of playfulness gone. I poured a glass of wine, fetched my computer, and disappeared into my own room, leaving him to work his magic. I figured it was a great time to go through my email and notifications, so I wouldn't start off Monday too far behind.

Oddly enough, I was unable to focus on work. Instead, I found myself listening to Cole in the kitchen and wishing I was in there with him, talking and laughing. Maybe Missy would join us, and the three of us could enjoy our time together, instead of me sitting alone in my room staring at my computer.

Yet this was the life I had created. Me, alone in my apartment, staring at a computer screen and trying to come up with new ways to sell beauty products, so other people could go out and have a life. In a few days, or maybe a week, whenever Missy and Cole decided it was okay for her to return to her condo, I would be alone again, still doing a job that meant nothing to me.

Where did I go so wrong in my life?

Did it really all stem from my childhood trauma? From losing Scott, my mother, AND my father? To having my father model workaholism as a method of dealing with emotional pain?

Maybe. Maybe that was where it started. But at some point, didn't I have to take responsibility for my choices rather than constantly blaming the past and what was done to me?

If I didn't like my life, wasn't it up to me to change it?

Cole called out that dinner was ready, interrupting my mulling, which was a relief. It wasn't like I could accomplish anything right then, anyway.

Cole had made pasta, something like spaghetti Bolognese, he said with a grin, since I didn't have all the ingredients for the traditional dish. There was also garlic toast topped with melted cheese and a salad. At first, Missy wasn't going to join us—she yelled from the bedroom that she wasn't hungry, but Cole, his expression flat, went in after her. I couldn't hear any actual words, only low voices, but whatever Cole said worked, because Missy emerged from the bedroom. She was wearing the yellow tracksuit, and her light-brown hair was bouncy with curls and waves framing her significantly cleaner face. But the spark I'd seen in her earlier was gone. Her shoulders were bowed, and her hazel eyes were dull and lifeless.

She joined us at the table, mostly picking at her food while Cole and I carried the conversation. Well, Cole, mostly. He told us stories about his former job and manager from hell. It was clear he was trying to make Missy laugh, and a few times, he got a wan smile out of her. But as soon as Cole and I finished, she disappeared back into her bedroom.

Cole sighed, staring at the food still left on her plate. "She needs to eat."

I stood up and started clearing the table. "Tomorrow is another day."

He rose to help, but I waved him away. "You did all the cooking. The least I can do is clean up."

"You're letting Missy stay here," he said. "The very least *I* can do is all the cooking and cleaning while she's here."

"It's fine," I said, bringing the plates into the kitchen. "I'm going to stick all of this in the dishwasher. You should go home. Get some rest."

"I was thinking I would sleep on the couch."

My back was turned, so he didn't see me falter and almost drop the plates. "That's really not necessary." The idea of him sleeping on the couch, a few feet away, was just … no. Way too much. I already had his sister to contend with in the next room. I didn't need to be worried about running into him in the middle of the night, too, if I had a night terror.

"I don't mind," he said. "In fact, I insist. Missy sometimes has trouble sleeping, and I should be the one to deal with her, not you. You need to get some sleep, too."

I put the plates into the sink with a clatter. "Honestly, I can handle it."

"I'm sure you can, but you shouldn't have to."

I took a deep breath and turned around. Cole was busy clearing the table. "It's really fine," I said. "I don't sleep much myself. If she wakes me, it's fine, but chances are, she won't."

Cole gave me a quizzical look. "What do you mean, you 'don't sleep much'?"

"Why does it matter?"

"I'm just curious."

"But why?"

He stopped clearing the table and stood there, studying me for a moment. "Because I really don't like the idea of leaving you alone with Missy and not being able to get a good night's sleep. I don't think that's fair to you. You're already doing so much for me, for her. So, I'm curious if you really don't sleep, or if this is something you're telling me just so I don't feel worse than I already do leaving you here."

Well, at least he was honest. I had to give him that. "I'm not exaggerating," I said. "I really don't sleep much. I'm lucky if I get four or five hours. That's why I don't want you on the couch, because if I want to go to the kitchen in the middle of the night for some tea or something, I don't want to worry about waking you."

He pondered my words for a moment. "That really sucks."

I huffed a laugh. "Tell me about it."

"Have you tried getting some help?"

I shrugged and turned back to the dishes. "When I was younger, I saw doctors, but nothing really helped."

"When you were younger? How long has this been going on?"

A figure in black, a too-white finger pressed to its lips. *Shhh.*

"Most of my life."

Cole brought the plates over to me. "That's awful. Is this somehow related to the night terrors you had as a child?"

I busied myself loading the dishwasher. I never liked talking about my sleep issues, because they invariably led to the night-terror discussion and, of course, Scott. "The doctors thought there was a connection," I said. "They all assumed I would outgrow it. When I didn't, well, there weren't a lot of options."

"What options did you try?"

"Things like going to bed at the same time every night, lavender, baths, avoiding caffeine later in the day. You know, all the same crap, as well as therapy."

I finished with the dishwasher just as Cole finished washing the counters and table. "Thanks," I said as he leaned past me to rinse off the sponge. I felt a sizzle of electricity between us and was suddenly conscious of the fact we were alone again.

I took a step back as he finished up. "We make a good team," he said with a grin.

"We do, but I think you did most of the work."

He laughed. "Isn't that how it's supposed to be?"

"Absolutely. I'm glad you've been well-trained."

I laughed with him, and as I did, I felt that same deep, dull ache inside that I'd had while going through my email earlier. This was what I missed. This camaraderie. I wanted it so badly, I could practically taste it.

But whatever was between Cole and me wasn't real. As soon as Missy was better, it all would dissolve, like cotton candy on the tongue—a brief, fleeting moment of sweetness before it all turned to crap.

"I guess I should get going," Cole said a little awkwardly, "just as long as you're sure you're okay ..."

"I'm sure," I said firmly.

"Okay. I laid out Missy's prescriptions and instructions on the counter over there." He nodded, and I saw the trial packages and a piece of paper. "I'll be back tomorrow with her refills and some more clothes for her. And I'll make dinner, too, so don't worry about that."

"Okay, sounds good."

"But if anything comes up before then, anything at all, feel free to call me. Anytime. I'm ten minutes away."

"I'm sure we'll be fine, but I promise I'll call if anything happens."

He hesitated, giving me one last searching look before striding toward the coffee table to collect his keys and phone. "I owe you, Tori," he said. "Big time."

"You better believe you do."

He let himself out, and I stood there for a moment in the living room, listening to his footsteps move away from me and down the hallway. The apartment was silent.

And I felt completely alone.

.

Chapter 19

It didn't take long to settle into a routine.

For the most part, I left Missy alone, and she generally stayed in her room. I kept an eye on her medications and would remind her to take them, which she dutifully did. I also reminded her to eat and take daily showers. I was a little less successful with both of those activities, but every day, I noticed improvement.

True to his word, Cole showed up daily. He ran errands, did laundry, vacuumed the floor, cleaned the bathroom and the kitchen, took Missy to her therapy appointments, and cooked.

He also asked Missy every day about Sarah and what happened during her pregnancy, and every day, he was rebuffed.

I could tell he was getting more and more frustrated, and nothing I said helped. It was clear that Missy was horribly depressed, but whether that was from her illness or because she was grieving, or both, I couldn't tell. Cole knew this, but still, I could see it was killing him to not be able to find Sarah.

But everything changed Wednesday night.

I awoke with a start, sweating and shaking, sure there was a shadowy figure in my room, clasping a bundle, one long, pale finger touching its lips.

Shhhhh.

I sat straight up in bed, straining my eyes in the darkness to see the figure disappear down the hallway, even as I chanted to myself, *It's just a dream, just a dream.* I rubbed my chest, trying to slow my breathing. *There's no one there*, I told myself. *I'm fine. I'm safe.*

But why could I still hear the "*shhhh*"?

I cocked my head, trying to hear over the pounding of my heart and the blood roaring in my ears.

Yes, there it was. That sound. Except it suddenly sounded more like a high-pitched wailing then shushing.

Missy!

I bolted out of bed and padded across the floor to the other bedroom. Her door was closed, but the noise was clearly coming from inside.

I paused on the other side of the door, uncertain what to do. Knock? Just open the door? I realized I had never asked what I should do in this situation.

But the keening was getting louder, and it sounded like Missy was in pain, so I took a chance and opened the door a crack.

"Missy?"

I peered inside and saw her thrashing around the bed, her breathing panicked while she shrieked. I ran to her, afraid she was going to hurt herself, and tried to grab her.

"Missy! Wake up. You're dreaming."

She fought me, nearly backhanding me with her flailing arms, but I was able to grab her and give her a good shake. "Missy!" I shouted. "Wake up."

"What?" she gasped as she continued to writhe. "Who are you? Where am I? What's going on?"

"It's me, Tori," I said. "You're in my apartment. You were having a nightmare, but you're safe."

She went limp, almost like the energy simply pooled out of her. "Safe?

"Yes."

She let out a harsh, bitter laugh. "That's a lie. I'll never be safe again."

What an odd comment. I wasn't sure how to respond, so instead, I focused on letting her go and making myself comfortable at the foot of the bed. "Want to talk about it?"

Missy didn't immediately answer. Instead, she slowly pulled herself up to a sitting position, bending her knees and wrapping her arms around her legs, so she was curled into a ball. "What happened?"

"I'm assuming you were having a nightmare," I said. "You were making a commotion, so I came to check on you."

She thought about what I'd said. The light from the moon shone through the window, revealing the sweat on her body. The back of her sleep shirt was plastered to her spine, and her hair was sticking to her face in clumps. "Sorry for waking you," she said.

"You didn't wake me. I was already awake."

"Couldn't sleep either?"

"I've never been a good sleeper. I'm lucky if I get four or five hours a night."

"Yeah, I don't sleep well, either," she said. "Haven't for years. I think it's my meds. Is it that you can't fall asleep or stay asleep?"

I smiled slightly. "A little of both. Depends on the night."

She blinked. "Well, that sucks."

"Yeah, it does." I paused, wondering if I should share more about my sleep habits—if doing so would get her to open up more. This was the longest conversation we'd had since the hospital. "I actually had a nightmare myself tonight."

She stilled, but I could still hear the faint sound of an indrawn breath. I could almost feel her gaze sharpen on me.

"Actually, it's closer to a night terror," I said. "I've had them for years."

"Years?"

"Yes. They started when I was child. I don't remember when exactly, but apparently, it was before Scott was born. That's why everyone thought I was in Scott's room that night."

"Now that you say that, I remember," she said. "They thought you were sleepwalking or something."

I nodded.

"There was even talk ..." she trailed off. "Never mind."

I could feel myself harden, my body tensing up. It was the same old, same old. It never changed, no matter how old I got. "What?" I asked, my voice sharper than I intended.

"Never mind," she said again. "I shouldn't have said anything."

"Say it," I demanded. I wasn't sure why I was torturing myself, but suddenly, I wanted to hear it ... wanted to hear again the words that had been on everyone's lips after my mother was taken away ... the words that caused my father to stop treating me like a daughter. "Say it. Please."

I could feel her eyes on me. "That you may have accidentally suffocated your brother while you were sleepwalking."

"You're being kind," I said, my voice full of contempt. "It was also said it wasn't an accident."

"I don't think anyone seriously thought that," she said. "You were five. There's no way it couldn't have been anything but an accident."

Did you kill your brother?

I looked away, realizing I was squeezing my fists together so tightly, I thought I might have drawn blood. I forced my fingers to relax.

"But you also must know that most people didn't believe you had anything to do with it," she said, her voice low.

"That didn't stop the whispering," I said. "That didn't stop my father from ignoring me or from eventually sending me away." It still hurt that he couldn't take care of me, his own daughter. I know Nanna would tell me it was his own pain that kept him from being the father he needed to be, but deep down, I was sure it was because he wasn't convinced that I had nothing to do with what happened to Scott.

She cocked her head. "I don't know why your father sent you away, but it wasn't you that people were whispering about."

Did you kill your brother?

"I know people thought my mother was self-medicating during her pregnancy ..."

"Yes, there was that. But a lot of people thought your mother's ... involvement was more than that."

"The authorities cleared her of everything, though."

Even in the dark, the look I knew she was giving me was clear. "You really think the rumor mill cares about that?"

"Wait, you're telling me that people really believed *my mother* suffocated Scott?"

"You honestly didn't know? Tori, look at the facts. Your mother was talking about faeries stealing her baby. She was so mentally unstable that to this day, over twenty years later, she's being cared for in a psychiatric home. How could people NOT think she had something to do with what happened to Scott? Especially when compared to a well-behaved five-year-old girl who had never shown any tendencies that would lead to her doing something so despicable to her baby brother."

I shifted uncomfortably on the bed. All those whispers and stares when I was a child ... I had assumed they had all thought I was the culprit.

But ... what if it was my mother?

Suddenly, it was as if I had been looking through a kaleidoscope—the whole time, I was seeing one picture, but now, it was as though someone had just violently shaken it, and everything was different. All the pieces of my childhood starting twisting and turning, and the picture was completely different.

Rather than judging me or even being afraid of me, what if all those people were feeling pity for me? Having a mother who could do something like that to one of her own children … keeping her locked up would be more about protecting others, especially me, than taking care of her.

Maybe there was a hint of worry, not about what I might do, but about what I might *become*. What if I inherited the same disease she had? It had always hung over me like a dark cloud— the fear that someday, I might wake up and be unable to trust my own thoughts. What if I was more like my mother after all? So far, I was fine, but what if that changed one day?

Now, though, with these revelations from Missy, I felt like a whole new world had opened up. Everything seemed different, and I wasn't sure if I trusted my old perceptions anymore.

"What do you think happened?" I asked.

She laughed, a short bark of laughter. "Why are you asking me? I wasn't there. You were."

"Yes, but I'm curious. What did you think happened that night?"

She was silent a long moment. "Growing up, I guess I thought it was your mother, too."

I felt a cold, icy shiver run through me. If she thought that, then Cole must have, as well.

"It's what my parents thought," she continued, her voice apologetic. "They were … well, after everything that happened, I see why they blamed your mother. But now …" her voice trailed off.

"What do you mean, you see why they blamed my mother?"

She sighed, a long, deep sigh. "Mental illness runs in our family. My aunt is bipolar, although she's medicated, so you wouldn't know it. But I also have a cousin who no one talks about. He refuses to take meds. Last I heard, he was on the streets. No one really knows where he is."

"Oh, Missy," I said.

She squeezed her arms tighter around her knees, like she was trying to self-soothe. "Growing up, we knew, of course. But we never really saw how, well, how awful it could be. Like we never saw my aunt at her worst. My mother, though, was another story. So, when I started to get sick … well, let's just say it brought up a lot of unresolved traumas, as they like to say in therapy. Cole, Beth, and my father were the ones who were there for me. My mother couldn't be. I don't blame her. I don't know the full story, but I do know how awful I was, so I can imagine. But that's why I think they blamed your mother, because they, of all people, knew how terrible and out of control it can make people."

I thought about that time. The strange things my mother said and did. How impossible it was to talk to her. But also, how after the birth of Scott, she rarely came out of the bedroom, even for something as basic as food.

"But something changed for you," I said. "What was it?"

She hugged herself even tighter, burying her face in her knees for a second. When she raised her head, I saw the tears glistening on her face. "I became a mother," she said, her voice so quiet, it was almost a sigh on the air.

You have to watch out for your little brother. Promise me. My mother, hunched over me, a worried frown between her eyes as she stared at me intently.

"I don't think my mother did it," I said, equally as quiet. "My mother rarely left her bedroom. And she was asleep when the cops came. I don't believe she had anything to do with it."

Her smile was twisted. "So, what do *you* think happened?"

I stared at the window, the moon shining on a patch on the carpet, making everything seem silvery and unreal. "I think he was taken," I said.

I peeked back at her, but she was frozen again, staring at me. "Tell me."

I took a deep breath. "I get that I was only five. I get that I had night terrors. But it felt so *real*. The figure in the room, the shushing. I think someone took Scott."

"But that would mean whoever it was also left a dead baby."

"I know. It's hard to get your mind around."

She paused. "I agree. That's difficult, but it's not the most difficult thing."

"What is?"

She uncurled herself, sitting cross-legged on the bed. "What was the official word on what happened to Scott?"

"That he died of crib death."

She nodded. "So, if you think Scott was taken and a dead baby put in his place, that means everyone who said Scott died of crib death was wrong."

"Exactly. Not that it's their fault. None of them saw Scott when he was alive, so how would they know if the dead baby was him or not? They just assumed it was Scott."

"But your father would have known the difference."

It was like a bomb went off, even though the apartment was totally silent. I slid off the bed, suddenly unable to sit, my mind seized up. "That's why I can't be right," I said hollowly as I moved toward the window. "I must be wrong."

Missy was silent. I stared out the window, studying the small square of grass that passed as a back "garden" for the apartment complex, complete with a bench and a couple of sad-looking trees. I thought of all the gardening I did growing up, both in Redemption and at Nanna's, and how much I loved it, and suddenly, I was disgusted with myself. Wasn't it just like me to move to an apartment building where the only bit of green was used by people walking dogs? Just one more brick in the wall of a life I hated.

But none of that was important right now. It was just a distraction from the real issue, the one deep inside me that no matter what I did—therapy, burying it, compromising with it, refusing to think about it—never went away.

Because no matter what I did, I couldn't reconcile the fact that the two absolute truths in my life couldn't both be true: That Scott was taken, and my father was telling the truth.

"My father loved Scott," I said, turning around to face Missy. "You weren't there during those first weeks. No one was. Except for me. He used to spend hours holding Scott, walking around with him if he was fussy. There's no way he would have done anything to hurt my brother. He was devastated after it happened."

Missy stared at me, her eyes glinting in the moonlight. "I'm not saying your father had anything to do with what happened to Scott," she said. "The whole thing is crazy. How would he even pull something like that off? But ..." she cocked her head, a movement so much like Cole's mannerisms, it took my breath away. "You know what you saw that night, as well."

"I don't know what I saw anymore." I turned back to the window, trailing a finger along the sill. "Over the years, I told myself over and over that I must have been dreaming or imagining things that night. For all the reasons you just said, it's an insane, crazy story. My father has assured me over and over that it was Scott in that crib. But no matter how much I've told myself none of it happened—that there was no figure in the room, and that Scott wasn't taken and another baby left in his place—a part of me simply refuses to believe it."

I turned back to Missy. "I remember how he looked. The sound of his voice. I even remember the smell ... damp and rotting ..."

Missy's eyes went wide. "You *smelled* something?"

"Yeah, it was really faint, just a whiff, but there all the same."

Missy untangled herself from the bed, straightening her spine. "Was it like something on the verge of decay, but not quite there yet?"

"Yeah, exactly like that."

Missy lowered her voice to just above a whisper. "Like the scent of death?"

It felt like the temperature of the room dropped. Cold, icy fingers trailed down my spine. "How did you know?" My voice was barely audible.

Missy wrapped her arms around herself, like she was feeling the cold, as well. "Because I smelled it, too," she said. "The night my baby was taken."

We stared at each other as the enormity of the revelation sank in.

Missy was the first to move, unwrapping her arms and sliding off the bed. "I think," she said as she stood up, "it's time for a cup of tea after all."

Chapter 20

"Her name is Sarah Ramsey," Missy said. We were sitting around the kitchen table, mugs of hot tea in front of us. She looked pale and haunted under the harsh lights of the kitchen, and her hands shook as she picked up her mug, cradling it for warmth. "She told me she was a certified nurse and midwife."

"Did she ever tell you where she worked?"

Missy worked her lip with her teeth. "The Riverview Women's Clinic. At least I think." She rubbed her forehead. "It's hard to sort out what was real and what was wasn't."

"It's okay," I said, reaching over to touch her hand. "There's no rush. Just do your best."

"We met at the coffee shop. I used to stop there after my therapy appointment. One day, I had some cramping—that happened sometimes—and Sarah was there. She introduced herself, and we started talking.

"We immediately clicked. You know how that happens sometimes? We liked the same things, had the same interests and sense of humor. It was awesome. Like finding an instant friend.

"So, of course, we started hanging out, and before too long, she was coming over to help keep an eye on things. And from there, since she is a midwife, it just seemed best for her to be the main person checking up on me."

"Were you paying her?"

Missy shook her head. "Sarah had a cousin who was bipolar. When she got pregnant, Sarah tried to help her, but she wouldn't listen. She ended up losing the baby. Sarah told me she was so haunted by what happened to her cousin that she still questioned whether there wasn't something more she could have done to help her. She told me helping me was a way for her to make up for that mistake."

I sipped my tea, careful to keep my expression blank, but Missy must have seen something on my face, because she gave me a look. "You think I'm an idiot, don't you? Or at the very least, too gullible?"

"It's a convenient story," I said. "Maybe a little too convenient. On the other hand, we have the benefit of hindsight right now. Plus, you were off your meds. I don't think this is your fault."

"Then whose is it?" she asked, and for the first time, I saw bitterness on her face. "I was the one who was pregnant. I was the one who let her into my home and life. If it's not my fault, then whose?"

"I think she took advantage of you," I said quietly.

Missy looked away. "Maybe. But what I lost that night ..." she shook her head, grabbing a paper napkin from the center of the table to dab her eyes.

I gave her a moment to compose herself. "When did you realize she wasn't what she seemed?"

She put her napkin down and gave me a crooked smile. "That's not as straightforward as you might think. I don't know what my thoughts are about Sarah. Maybe she was behind me losing little Jude. You and Cole certainly seem to think so. And maybe she is as bad as you both think. But maybe she's not. Maybe she was exactly who she said she was, and there is a good explanation for anything out of the ordinary."

"Maybe back up a bit," I said. "Why aren't you convinced of her guilt?"

She pressed her lips together again. "Probably because I'm not entirely sure what even happened," she said.

"So, let's talk it out. You said Sarah took over checking in on you. How were things going?"

Missy exhaled deeply and took a sip of tea. "Everything seemed fine, at least at first. She created a file for me, and every time she came, she'd give me a quick examination."

My eyebrows went up when she said that, but Missy didn't notice, her gaze remaining fixed on the cheap, white, ceramic salt-and-pepper shakers that sat in the middle of the table. "She would ask me a lot of questions. How was I feeling, how was my diet, was I taking my supplements, was I sleeping? That sort of thing."

More alarm bells were ringing in my bed. "What supplements were you taking?"

"Oh, the usual. Extra iron and a multi-vitamin. Dr. Greene had put me on them, but Sarah added some herbs to the mix. Plus, a special tea. Said it would help relax me and keep my emotions stable without hurting the baby."

"Did you ask Dr. Greene about them?"

She furrowed her brow. "Now that you ask, I don't think I did. It wasn't that I thought it was a big secret or anything, but I don't think he ever asked if I was taking anything else, and I didn't think about it." Her expression changed to a strange mixture of curiosity and fright. "You don't think there was anything in what I took that would hurt the baby, do you?"

"I don't know," I said. "But if I had to guess, I would say probably not. If Sarah was planning on stealing your baby, she would want to keep him healthy."

Missy's face instantly relaxed. "Oh, thank goodness. But ..." she paused, frowning at me. "Why did you look so concerned, if you don't think it affected the baby? What else would be the point, except ..." she sucked in her breath as she seemed to put the pieces together. "Me. You think she might have been trying to hurt me."

"It's possible," I said. "I don't know. But if that was her intention, she would have had to have been super careful to not hurt the baby in the process, and I don't know how likely that is. The other thing that could have happened is ... you delivered early, right? She might have slipped something in near the end to initiate labor."

Missy's eyes widened. "You think she really could have done that?"

I held my hands up. "I don't know. I'm just guessing. But if she wanted to get you in the habit of accepting supplements, tea, food, and who knows what else from her, it would make sense to start bringing you things early on."

Missy stared at me, a horrified look on her face. "How could I have been so stupid?" she whispered.

"What? No, you're not stupid. If this is true, you were taken advantage of, which doesn't mean you're stupid."

Missy didn't respond, instead pressing a shaking hand against her lips, as if to retrospectively stop herself from taking whatever Sarah had given her.

"It's okay," I said. "Whatever you did or didn't do, it's not your fault. You were in a very vulnerable position, and she took advantage of you."

"But that's the thing," Missy said. "I DID know, at least at the end, and I tried to stop it. But I let her override me." She shook her head, tears glistening on her lashes as she reached for a napkin again.

I paused, letting her get herself under control. She finished wiping her eyes and blew her nose, crumpling the napkin into her fist. "Did she give you something the day you went into labor?" I asked.

She nodded, confirming. "But you don't understand. It's more than that. It's just ... it's just so difficult trying to sort out what was real and what wasn't," she repeated.

Then, she sucked in her breath before saying, "I think I need to tell you everything."

"I'm listening."

"I think things started to go sideways two, three months ago. I'm a little hazy on time. I know it was after I told Renee she didn't need to come by so much because Sarah was taking care of things. She, Renee, was a little concerned, but told me if that was what I wanted, she would accept it, but she was only a phone call or text away if I needed anything. Beth was another story. She refused to stop coming. Said I needed someone who knew me more than five minutes checking in on me." Missy half-smiled at the memory. "She's always had my back. Always. I definitely owe her a huge apology."

"Beth understands," I said. "Try not to stress too much."

Her smile turned sad. "The story of my life. Relying on other people's capacity for understanding and compassion. Anyway, I remember when I told Sarah that Beth was still going to come over. She got this strange look on her face. It only lasted a second, and when I asked her about it, she brushed it off, but now … well, anyway."

"So, it was Sarah's idea? That you tell your friends to stop coming?" I asked.

Missy pulled another napkin out of the holder and started worrying one of the edges. "Yeah. Sarah thought it didn't make much sense for them to come over when she was the one with the medical training. She thought it made far more sense to rely on them once the baby was born, as I would likely need even more support then as I recovered. At the time, it seemed so reasonable. Even though deep down I knew I wasn't myself, I felt like I had things under control and, quite honestly, I didn't need anyone stopping by. But Sarah seemed so happy and eager to help, I couldn't say 'no' to her. She even used to thank me for allowing her to take care of me, so she could put her past mistakes to rest." Missy tore at the napkin more violently, little white pieces covering the table like confetti. "Just saying that out loud makes me cringe. You must think I'm such an idiot for still holding out hope she's innocent."

"Why would I think that?" I asked. "I think it's totally normal. No one wants to believe that someone they trusted would want to hurt them."

"Yeah, maybe," Missy muttered, continuing to pull apart the napkin, although less violently. "Anyway, Sarah was there late one night. She had made dinner and was cleaning up the kitchen as I rested on the couch. I tried to help, but she wasn't having any of it. This wasn't unusual. She made me dinner or brought me food to heat up later at least a couple of times a week.

"That night, I was half asleep when a loud crash jarred me awake. I stumbled into the kitchen as fast as I could. Sarah was standing by the sink, her face completely white. There was blood everywhere. I gasped and rushed forward, and it was then I saw the broken glass. She had been washing the dishes and dropped one. I had to carefully pick my way across the floor to get to her. The weird part was that Sarah wasn't responding to me at all. She just stood there, staring straight ahead. When I got closer to her, I realized she was whispering. So, I leaned closer to hear what she was saying."

Missy stopped talking and picked up her tea to take a sip. Her hand was trembling so much, the tea sloshed over the side. I knew it must have been cold by then, but I was too engrossed in her story to make more. She didn't speak again until she had replaced the cup on the table.

"She was saying, 'The faeries are watching.'"

I jerked back so suddenly, I knocked my own tea over. I leaped to my feet as the brown liquid sloshed over the side. "I … I'm … I'll get something to clean this up," I said as Missy pushed her own chair away from the table. "Do you want more tea?" I called out.

"Sure," she said. I turned on the stove to heat up the water as I grabbed a washcloth from the sink. Missy eyed me as I frantically scrubbed at the table. "Need help?"

The faeries. They're watching.

How could Sarah possibly know what my mother had said to me all those years ago? How could anyone? I racked my brain, trying to remember if I had ever told a reporter or a cop, but I couldn't pinpoint anything.

More importantly, why in the world would Sarah say it to Missy?

"I got it," I said to Missy as I finished my frenzied cleaning. I fetched more tea for both of us and sat down at the table. "Sorry for interrupting."

"It's okay," Missy said, a thoughtful expression on her face. She took a sip, her hand steadier. "Should I continue?"

"Please," I said. I was so grateful to her for not asking me what was going on. Clearly, she knew something she said had hit a sore spot, and she must have been curious … but she kept her questions to herself.

She put her mug back down. "The whole thing was really spooky. Sarah just kept repeating that statement, 'The faeries are watching,' over and over. I finally grabbed her shoulder and gave her a little shake while asking her if she was okay. Finally, she shuddered and started blinking, like she was coming out of a dream. She looked at me, and I could see her eyes were finally focusing. Whatever was going on with her passed.

"She asked me what I was doing in the kitchen, but when I told her, she didn't seem to believe me. The broken glass was all over the floor, and her hand was cut, but it was like she had no memory of what she'd been saying. I insisted on helping her clean up, despite her wanting me to go back to the living room. I didn't know what had happened to her, but I worried she might have had a ministroke or epileptic seizure or something. I wanted to call the doctor, but she wouldn't hear of it.

"After it was all cleaned up and we were sitting at the table, I asked her what happened, and she told me she thought she had seen someone lurking around outside. Well, of course, I immediately got up to check. The window above the sink looks out over the woods in the back, and I was trying to make out whether anyone was there. Sarah came over and pulled me away, saying she was sure it wasn't anything … probably just some kids messing around, or something, but that it had startled her, causing her to drop the plate she'd been washing. When I asked her why she was just standing there in some sort of trance afterward, she tried to laugh it off. Said she was afraid of blood, and sometimes, she gets so freaked out that she just freezes, like a deer in headlights. I said, 'But you're a nurse and a midwife—how can you be afraid of blood?' She explained that she wasn't afraid of other people's blood, just her own. I guess that's understandable."

"But, what about what she said? How did she explain that?"

Missy shrugged as she played with her mug, spinning it on the table. "That I didn't hear what I thought I had. Or misunderstood it. She insisted whatever I thought I heard was a mistake, but I knew better. I know what I heard. I didn't imagine it. But it didn't matter, as she constantly told me she had never said such a thing.

"And the night grew even weirder, because at first, she didn't want to leave. She was going to sleep on the couch. I, of course, wanted to know why. She had never stayed the night before. But she just kept saying it was super late, and she didn't want to go home to an empty apartment. I asked her several times if she was worried about whatever she saw outside, and she kept telling me she wasn't, but there was something off. I could tell she wasn't giving me the whole truth.

"I finally agreed, and she spent the night. Nothing else happened. The next morning, she made me breakfast and headed off to work, like nothing was wrong. But I of course couldn't stop thinking about it. What was outside? What had she seen? I spent the day pacing around, peering through all the windows, trying to see if there was anything out there.

"It was only later that I remembered what happened to you and your family." She shot me an apologetic look. "Once that thought entered my brain, I could think of nothing else. I got on the computer and started searching through all the old stories, sure if I could somehow track down where it all went south for you, I could prevent it from happening to me.

"Needless to say, it didn't take long for my paranoia to spin out of control, and I was sure the faeries were after my baby. Sarah ..." Missy paused to take another sip of tea and sighed. "You know, this is probably why I didn't want to talk about it. I thought it was because it didn't matter. Jude was gone, it was my fault, and I deserved everything coming to me. What did it matter if you found Sarah or not? It wouldn't bring Jude back. And maybe that was part of it, but now, hearing myself tell this story, I'm seeing all the little ways she manipulated me. She knew I suffered from paranoid delusions. What better way to feed into my insanity than by making a big deal out of whatever it was she saw that night? I was a fool for not seeing through it."

"You weren't a fool," I said. "You were vulnerable. And I think ... well, honestly, that she's evil."

"Maybe," Missy said after considering my words, her voice hopeless. "That doesn't change the fact that Jude is gone."

I reached over and put my hand over hers. Her skin was cold and clammy, almost like she herself wasn't human, but a faerie who had appeared to mock me all these years later. I kept my hand where it was, though, telling myself I was letting my imagination run away from me.

Still, I found myself wishing Cole was with us.

"Anyway," Missy resumed after clearing her throat. "I see now that Sarah continued to feed my paranoia. She would say things like, 'Oh Missy, you know there is no such things as faeries. Who has been putting those thoughts in your head? Is it

Beth? You know, now that you bring Beth up, there is something off about her. I didn't want to say anything sooner, because she is your friend and all, but are you sure she's ... well, forgive me for saying this, but do you think she's safe for the baby?'

"Or she would say, 'Missy, you know there's no such thing as faeries, and you shouldn't get so worried. It's not good for the baby. Isn't Dr. Greene helping you with your stress? Oh, he's not? Well, I didn't want to say anything sooner, because I know how much you like and trust him ... but are you sure he's the right obstetrician for you? Maybe a different doctor would be able to help you more with your stress.'"

"Wait a second. Are you saying it was Sarah's idea for you to stop going to Dr. Greene?"

She nodded.

"Was Sarah pushing you to choose another doctor?"

Missy frowned. "Not really. Now that you ask, that didn't really come up. Like I said, she was examining me every time she visited, and she kept telling me how healthy I was and how everything looked good. She said there was no rush to choose another doctor."

"What about the delivery? Did she talk about that?"

"Not in so many words. It was more like ... suggestions, I guess you would call them. Like she would tell me stories about her patients who had these beautiful home births, or she would talk about a new study that had just come out saying mothers who used a midwife were more satisfied with their birthing experience than those who went to a hospital. And if I said anything about having a hospital birth, like about packing a bag or who I should call to drive me, she would tell me not to worry about it ... that we had plenty of time before the big day arrived."

"So, she was actively trying to persuade you to have a home birth and for her to be your midwife."

Missy sighed and hung her head, as though ashamed. "Yes."

I sat back my chair. "Wow." I was strangely impressed by how coldly calculating Sarah was—how she had slowly and methodically not only broken down all of Missy's defenses, but also managed to manipulate her paranoia. But something was niggling at me too, and it took me a few moments to figure it out.

"Your therapist," I said. Missy raised her head to give me a questioning look. "How does she fit into all of this?"

"What do you mean?"

"Well, you told her about this, right? About Sarah and the faeries."

"Of course."

"So, what was her take?"

"Well, that there were no faeries trying to steal my baby," she said drily. "As for Sarah, she didn't say much, other than how lucky I was to have a friend who was also a midwife."

"So she knew?"

Missy looked confused. "Well, yeah."

I shook my head in disgust. "She told Cole she didn't know anything about Sarah being a midwife."

Missy's eyes narrowed suspiciously. "How do you know that? My therapist shouldn't be saying anything about me. That's all confidential."

"We weren't asking about anything confidential," I said quickly.

Missy's eyebrows shot up. "*We?*"

"Cole asked me to come with him, that's all."

"I can't believe this," Missy said, getting more and more agitated. She grabbed another napkin and started tearing that one into pieces, too. "Not only does he track down my therapist, but he brings a date?"

"It wasn't a date," I said. "We're friends."

Missy gave me a look.

"We are," I said.

"I've seen the way you two look at each other," she said. "But fine. He brought a *friend*. Still doesn't change anything."

"Look, the only thing we wanted from your therapist was Sarah's last name," I said. "Or, if that wasn't possible, where she worked. All we cared about was tracking Sarah down as quickly as possible. Each passing day made it more difficult to get to the bottom of what happened to you. And we didn't know who else to ask. Your friends and neighbors didn't know, and you weren't in any position to help. So, that only left your therapist."

Missy was still furiously demolishing the napkin, but her movements began to slow and then stop altogether. She seemed to deflate right in front of me, like a collapsed balloon. "You're right," she said quietly. "I can't fault you for wanting to find Sarah. I would have done the same thing if I had been in your shoes. Just because I didn't want to see the truth doesn't mean you shouldn't be searching for it."

"The important thing is, you're telling us now," I said. "And look, maybe Sarah didn't mean you or your baby any harm. It's possible there's another explanation, but we need to find Sarah to ask her."

"It would be good to hear Sarah's side of the story," Missy said. "Maybe I did misunderstand or make something up." Despite her words, she didn't look convinced.

"But back to your therapist," I said. "You're telling me she knew about everything and was fine with it?"

Missy shrugged. "Yeah, I think so. I don't remember every single thing we talked about or what she said, but nothing stands out."

"What about Dr. Greene?"

"What about him?"

"What did she say when you told him you were going to stop going to him?"

Missy frowned, her brow furrowing. "I don't really remember, to be honest."

"You don't remember? You talked about it, right?"

"Well, yeah. We must have. I guess ... I don't think it was a big deal. I think I told her Dr. Greene was making me feel stressed, and I didn't think that stress was good for the baby. I think she just ... agreed with me."

My eyes widened. "I can't believe it. How could she think it was a good idea for you not to have an OB/GYN?"

"Well, I did have Sarah," Missy said. "And Dr. Broomer knew Sarah was a midwife, so maybe she thought I was covered."

"Did she ask to talk to Sarah? Or ask you for her credentials or where she worked, so she could check up on her?"

Missy squished up her face as she thought. "I don't really remember, but she must have. I mean, she was my therapist. She had always helped me in the past. I can't believe she wouldn't have made sure I was being taken care of properly."

I didn't respond. Instead, I watched as Missy's expression crumbled into a strange mix of horror and confusion.

"You're not ... you're not really suggesting that Dr. Broomer was somehow ... involved?"

"I'm not saying anything," I said. "But there's something weird going on, don't you think? Does it seem normal to you that a therapist wouldn't be concerned that her bipolar patient fires her OB/GYN a few weeks before she's due to give birth? Because instead, she's trusting some woman she met just a few months ago?"

"But that doesn't make any sense," Missy said. "Why would Dr. Broomer do something like that to me? What would she have to gain?"

I thought back to the shiny new BMW in the parking lot, along with the designer handbag and suit. "Money?"

Missy looked confused. "But ... who would have paid her? And how would they even know she was my therapist?"

"Did you tell Sarah who your therapist was?"

Missy's mouth opened and closed, reminding me of a beached fish gasping for oxygen. "You honestly think my therapist had something to do with this?" she asked again in a strangled voice. "My *therapist*? Even if Dr. Broomer could be bought, who would do such a thing? And why?"

"I don't know for sure," I said. "I'm just guessing. But what I do know is that there's definitely a black market for infants."

Missy made a weird, choking noise. "Oh my God ... you think someone might have stolen my baby to *sell* him?"

"I know it's horrible to think about," I said, feeling terrible. "And I'm not trying to upset you ..."

She held a hand out. "I know you aren't. I'm just ... the idea I was somehow targeted for my baby ... that it was planned? I just ... I need a minute."

I was quiet as she pressed the wadded-up napkin to her face. I expected her to start to cry again, but she didn't. Her eyes were red-rimmed and shiny, almost like she had burned up all her tears.

When she spoke again, her voice sounded controlled, but underneath that, I could hear the frayed edges, where her rage was held barely in check.

"You probably need to hear the rest of it then," she said. "Even though it's going to sound completely and utterly insane."

Chapter 21

"I'm not sure this happened exactly as I remember it," Missy said, her face a mask of steely determination, as though it would require every ounce of control she had to make it through the story. "Even to me, it sounds completely unhinged. But ..." She gave her head a quick shake. "I have to tell someone. Even just to get it out of my system. I just need you to know I'm still not entirely sure it really happened."

"Understood," I said.

Missy paused to take one last sip of tea. She replaced the cup and straightened her shoulders. "I hadn't been feeling well the week before everything happened. Along with being really uncomfortable, I wasn't sleeping, because I was convinced the faeries were after my baby. I would be up all hours of the night, pacing the house. The only time I would rest was when Sarah was there. She would assure me no one was coming to take my baby, and that she would keep watch while I napped. As you can imagine, I was stressed beyond belief, but more than that, I was getting regular, blinding headaches and nausea.

"Sarah was basically doing everything by then. If she wasn't cooking a meal or brewing tea, she was leaving food for me to eat in the fridge, but I wouldn't eat much unless she was there coaxing me. I just wasn't feeling right.

"It was Saturday morning when things got, well, weird. It was early. It had been a bad night. Something was wrong, but I didn't know what. The one thing I was sure about was that the baby was in danger. I didn't know how or why I was so sure, but something was after my baby, and I had to be vigilant. I was even more agitated than normal Friday night, especially since I was convinced the faeries were most active when it was dark. So, when dawn finally came, I was more exhausted than normal. I must have sat down just for a moment on the couch to take a break and dozed off, only waking to the sound of a key unlocking the front door."

"Sarah had a key?" I asked.

Missy nodded. "She wasn't the only one. Maryanne and Beth both had one, as well. That way they could check on me if I didn't answer the door. However, the agreement was the same with all of them. They were to knock or ring the doorbell first. I was very clear; I wasn't an invalid. I knew I needed help, and I accepted that, but just because I gave them a key and told them they had my permission to use it if they thought I was in trouble didn't mean they could just come in and out of my home whenever they wanted.

"I was on my feet when Sarah opened the door, and I could tell by her expression she wasn't expecting to see me there. But she quickly covered it up. She insisted she had knocked, and I hadn't answered, so she was worried and let herself in.

"I knew she was lying. I would have heard her knock from the couch. But she told me I must have been sleeping.

"I remember getting upset. It was probably the closest we had ever gotten to a fight, at least up until that point. I was in the middle of telling her it was not okay for her to walk in without knocking when she froze, staring at the floor.

"'What's that?' she asked.

"'What's what?' I said, looking all around to see what she was looking at.

"'It looks like blood,' she said, and bent over as if to show me. She started rubbing a spot on the wooden floor. 'I think it is blood. Are you bleeding?'

"'No, no,' I said, clutching my stomach. All my fears and anxieties about the baby flooded over me at that point, and I could barely breathe. Was that what I had sensed? A problem with the baby? I wanted to see the blood, so I could get a sense of how bad it was, but when I asked, instead of showing me, she bundled me into the downstairs bathroom so she could examine me. I didn't protest, because I was desperate to know if there was something wrong.

"I was so scared about the baby, I forgot about everything else—her using the key instead of knocking, the expression on her face when I caught her, and also just how odd it was for her to be there that early. Sarah never came in the morning. Never. It was always afternoon, usually late afternoon, before she arrived."

Missy paused to sip her tea. She took a few deep breaths, as if gathering her thoughts before continuing.

"After the examination, Sarah told me the baby was fine and not in any immediate danger, but I needed to be very careful, because that could change. I wanted to go to the hospital, but Sarah said it wasn't necessary. I just needed to rest and not get so worked up. I tried to argue with her, but she just said all they were going to do was the same thing she just did—examine me, tell me I was fine, and send me home to rest. I was still upset, but then the baby started kicking, and that reassured me."

"The baby was *kicking* the day you gave birth?" I asked. "Had the baby been active before that?"

"Oh, all week," she said. "That was another reason why I couldn't rest properly. He was always moving around, kicking and punching me."

"Is that normal?"

She gave me a puzzled look. "What do you mean?"

I hesitated. I wasn't sure how to phrase my question without sounding terribly inconsiderate. "It's just … I'm just surprised that a stillborn baby would be so active right before birth."

Missy's face darkened. "That's what I tried to tell the cops. Over and over, I told them that couldn't be my baby. How could my baby have died so suddenly when he was always moving around? Nobody would give me an answer, though. They said once the coroner examined him, they would tell me more. It wasn't until later … well, I'm getting ahead of myself.

"Once I felt the baby move, I calmed down. Sarah then started asking me if I had eaten breakfast yet, which I hadn't, so she told me I should go lay down while she prepared something.

"I didn't want to. I tried to tell her I wasn't all that hungry, but she insisted. I wanted to keep watch for the faeries. I was sure they were getting closer … I could feel it, like an electric charge in the air. Something had shifted, and I didn't like it.

"But Sarah kept telling me everything was fine. She was there, and she would keep watch for me while I rested. I didn't want anything to happen to the baby, right? She helped me to the couch and went back to the kitchen.

"I don't remember exactly what I did on the couch, if I was staring out the window searching for faeries or if I dozed off again, but the next thing I remember is Sarah standing next to me holding a cup of tea. She seemed nervous. Her eyes kept darting around, and her hands were trembling. Some of the tea even sloshed over the side of the mug.

"I wasn't that interested in drinking it, especially since I was thinking she knew something about the faeries she wasn't telling me, but she insisted. Said it would relax me and would be good for the baby. I took a few sips, but it was bitter. I told her there was something wrong with it, that it didn't taste right, and she told me it was a different blend. She had added something to it because of my earlier scare. I asked what, and she rattled off the name of some herb … I can't remember what it was, now, but she said it was good for keeping the uterus 'strong and relaxed,' whatever that meant.

"I didn't want to drink it. In fact, every part of me was screaming that it wasn't right, but Sarah kept overriding me. She reminded me of the promise I'd made to her weeks before about trusting her judgement over my own. That my illness was playing tricks on me. That I needed to listen to her, for the baby.

"Finally, I pretended to drink a little more, and she went back to the kitchen to check on the food. I dumped the rest of the tea out in a plant.

"She made me an omelet with loads of onions, peppers, and cheese along with toast, and she hovered over me while I ate. Then, she insisted I go back to bed and rest. She promised me she would stay while I laid down. And I was so exhausted by that point, I let her talk me into it.

"I fell into a deep sleep. I'm not sure for how long, as I don't have a great sense of time. But I do know that when I woke up, Sarah was in my bedroom. She asked me how I was feeling. I was groggy and confused. She then asked if I was having any cramping. I told her no, and she said she was happy to hear that. But she didn't seem happy. She seemed a little upset. She had more of that bitter tea with her, except this time, she stayed and watched me drink it. I was so out of it, I did what she asked. She also gave me tomato soup with a grilled cheese sandwich. I ate about half before I fell back asleep. When I woke again, it was starting to get dark outside. It was the longest I had slept in weeks, months even, and I was still as groggy as I'd been earlier. But this time, the cramps had started."

Missy paused and rubbed the side of her nose. I wondered if she was thinking the same thing I was—that whatever Sarah had put in her tea, and maybe even her food, had not only caused her to go into labor, but to sleep so much beforehand. It was kind of brilliant, actually … giving her something to make her sleep, so she wouldn't be aware that she was in labor until it was too late. As long as mixing the sedative with whatever was inducing labor wasn't an issue, the plan was pretty impressive. It was also possible it was just a coincidence—that Missy's body finally collapsed from exhaustion.

"Anyway, I called for Sarah, who came running in. I told her maybe we needed to call a doctor, but she said, 'Let's just wait.' I wasn't full term, so I probably wasn't in real labor yet, and the cramping would pass. She brought me more soup and tea, which I didn't want. I told her it clearly wasn't working, considering the cramping. I just wanted water. She left and returned with water and her little black bag to examine me. She told me everything looked good, and all I needed was rest. I asked for my phone, but she told me I didn't need it—that the only thing I should focus on was rest. I wanted to get up and start my nightly patrol, but the cramps stopped me before I could get too far, so she told me to stay in my room … that it was too dangerous for me to try and walk down the stairs, as I could so easily fall if a cramp hit me at the wrong time. For a while, I was able to go from window to window on the upstairs floor, circling between the bathroom, my room, and the guest bedroom, as Sarah stayed with me, not letting me go anywhere near the stairs. Eventually, though, the cramping got so bad, I couldn't walk anymore, and she got me set up on my bed, where she had already created a 'nest' of old towels and sheets. She still refused to let me go to the hospital or call anyone, even though by then, we both knew I was in labor. At that point, she told me it was too late to go to the hospital. I wouldn't get there in time anyway, so I might as well stay and give birth at home."

Missy paused again, sweat beading over her upper lip and forehead. Her skin had turned a chalky white, and I was starting to worry that recounting the story was too much for her. I wondered if I should stop her and wait for Cole to arrive. I didn't want to set her back, as she was already so fragile. But after a moment, she seemed to dig deep inside herself, steeling herself to continue. She took a deep breath, squared her shoulders, and continued.

"Sarah had arranged me on the bed in such a way that I couldn't really see what was going on. I was propped up, with pillows behind me, and a towel was draped over my legs. Plus, she had piled more towels and sheets next to my legs, almost like a little wall. At the time, I didn't think much of it—after all, when you get examined by an OB/GYN, they always drape something over your legs. I was in full labor and in so much pain, I wasn't thinking straight, anyway.

"I remember the end ... Sarah telling me to push, the pain horribly intense. It felt like I had been torn in half. Broken. And then, it was over. I lay there panting and gasping, while Sarah was busy doing something.

"And then I heard a cry.

"Not a faint cry. A big, hearty, healthy cry. I was so happy to hear it! I'm sure I heard it. I'm sure it wasn't something else."

Missy stopped talking and took a big gulp of air. "I was so sure I heard a cry," she repeated. Her voice sounded hopeless, as if she were really trying to convince herself.

"Maybe you did," I said. "Which would mean your baby wasn't stillborn after all."

But she was already shaking her head. "I don't know. I just ... I don't know." She rubbed her forehead, as if trying to clear her brain so she could get a better look at the cloudy memory. She took another deep breath and resumed her story. "So, then I said to Sarah, 'Let me see him. Let me see my son.' But Sarah was already on her feet, the baby wrapped in a towel, so I couldn't see anything, just a bundle. She said I could see my baby in a minute. She wanted to clean him up and check him out first.

"She was backing out of the room as she was talking, moving quickly away from me. I could hear my baby crying, and I was crying, too. But maybe I didn't hear him cry after all. Maybe it was just my own sobs. I kept saying, 'No, let me see him first. I want to see him. He needs to be with me. I need to keep him safe.'

"But then, she was gone. She left the room with my baby and shut the door behind her, and all I could do was lay in the bed and sob. I could hear him crying through the door. I *know* I heard it then. I know it.

"I don't know how long she was gone. I tried to get up and go after her, but I was so weak and still in so much pain. I finally stopped moving and just lay there, trying to gather my strength.

"And that was when I heard it.

"The click of the front door closing.

"I immediately started panicking. Had Sarah left with my baby? This time, I didn't care. I hurled myself out of the bed and collapsed onto the floor, too weak to stand, as I called out for Sarah. I was crawling toward the door when she came back in. She was holding a wrapped bundle in her arms, and I remember the relief that flowed through me. Sarah hadn't left and taken my baby. She was still there. My baby was still there.

"But then I saw her face.

"She looked stricken. Just positively devastated. I knew the moment I saw her something was deeply wrong.

"'Why are you on the floor?' she asked me. 'You're going to make yourself bleed, if you're not careful. You need to stay in bed.'"

"'I want to see my baby,' I said. 'And who was at the door?'

"'No one was at the door,' she answered, but her face was squished up, and I knew she was lying.

"'Who was at the door?' I asked more loudly. 'And give me my baby. I want to see my baby.'

"She didn't move, just stood there frozen. It slowly started to sink in that the bundle Sarah was holding wasn't moving or making any noise. Why wasn't my baby crying or fussing?

"Then Sarah said, 'Missy, I'm so sorry.'

"I said, 'What are you sorry for? Let me see my baby.'

"And that was when I saw it. The blood smear on the side of the towel.

"I started to scream. That seemed to break Sarah's paralysis, and she rushed over, still holding the bundle. She was saying over and over, 'I'm so sorry, I'm just so, so sorry,' as she stooped down to place the bundle in my arms.

"I gazed into that little face, which was completely still. My brain couldn't even register what had happened. I touched his cheek, and it was cold. So very cold.

"I was a crying, sniveling mess by then, unable to process what was happening. I couldn't fathom that my baby was dead—that he'd died immediately after birth. How could it be? How could that happen? He was so healthy! He was moving and kicking in my womb just a few hours earlier.

"Then I remembered the click of the door closing. And I knew what happened.

"I stopped crying then. Everything seemed like it was moving in slow motion. I lifted my chin to look at Sarah, who was still standing there, stooped over me, her face filled with grief and something else ... something I couldn't identify.

"'Let me help you get back into bed,' she was saying. 'I need to examine you and make sure you're okay, and then I can get you started on your meds again.'

"'You did it,' I said.

"The blood drained from her already pale and exhausted face. 'You're confused,' she said. 'This has been a traumatic night. Let's get you back into bed ...'

"'You let the faeries take my baby,' I said.

"'There's no such thing as faeries,' Sarah replied, taking a hold of my arm, presumably to help me into bed. But I wrenched it away.

"'No,' I shouted. 'The faeries took my baby. And they left this ... this thing. This is not my baby.'

"'Missy, you need to calm down ...'

"'I won't calm down,' I yelled, my voice getting louder and louder. 'You let the faeries steal my baby! I heard him.'

"Sarah was shaking her head. 'Missy, that's not true. Your baby was in trouble the moment he was born. That's why I rushed out of here so fast. I was trying to save him, but he was too sick. No one could have saved him.'

"'I heard him cry!' I insisted. 'He was crying like a healthy baby.'

"'No, he wasn't. You were hearing things.'

"'I wasn't! I know what I heard. I heard my baby cry. I heard the front door close. This, this thing,' I held up the bundle in my arms, 'is not mine. It looks nothing like me. It looks nothing like its father. *It's not my baby.*'

"Sarah was still trying to calm me down, to get me into bed and to take my meds, but I wouldn't let her touch me. I just kept screaming how she'd let the faeries take my baby.

"Finally, she backed away. She put my meds on the table next to the bed with a glass of water and begged me to take them. She told me she would come back in a few hours to check on me. I told her to never come back, unless it was to bring my real baby back.

"She left then, and I went a little berserk. Screaming and howling and ranting. Somehow, I managed to drag myself and that infant out of the bedroom and down the stairs without killing myself. I made it into the kitchen, which was where the police and paramedics found me. I was covered with blood, and so was the baby, which is why they initially thought I had done something to it. But once they examined both of us, they realized it was all mine. I guess Sarah had been right about that part."

Missy paused, her head bowed. She looked like she had aged twenty years, telling me her story. Even her skin had turned grey and lifeless.

"Did you tell the cops the whole story?" I asked. "Because it really, really sounds like Sarah stole your baby."

Missy flashed me a faint, bitter smile, a ghostly echo of what I had seen so often on her brother's face. "Do you honestly think they would believe me? A bipolar woman off her meds who was ranting about faeries stealing her baby when they found her?"

"But you are lucid now," I said.

"Now I am, sure," she said. "But then, I was clearly in some sort of manic state. Maybe I was even hallucinating. Plus, I was in labor. How could anyone trust anything I thought I saw in that state?" Her voice shook. "I'm still not sure if I believe me. Maybe I was wrong about hearing the sound of the front door closing and him crying after I gave birth. Maybe I didn't feel him move near the end. Maybe everyone is right, and he did die. There were so many things I did wrong at the end. I wasn't eating enough, drinking enough. I didn't insist on going to the hospital, even though I knew there was a problem. Maybe it was something I did that killed him." Her sadness hung on her like a blanket, now.

Still, I had to ask.

"Did you do heroin while you were pregnant?"

Missy's jaw dropped open. "No! Of course not."

"Then you couldn't have killed him," I said reassuringly. Then, I gave her a sharp look. "You do know that's what the coroner found, right? That the baby died of a heroin overdose."

Missy had a pained expression on her face. "No, that can't be right. The coroner must have made a mistake."

"I don't think they make mistakes like that."

She pressed her fists against her temples. "It doesn't make sense. I wasn't on ANY drugs. The doctors and the cops asked me about that, too, but I wasn't self- medicating. This is proof it wasn't my baby! Because if it was, the coroner *would* be mistaken."

"What about what Sarah was giving you?"

Her face jerked up, her eyes wide with horror. "You can't think ... I thought you said Sarah wouldn't hurt the baby."

"I said if she was trying to steal the baby, she probably wouldn't do anything to hurt him. But that doesn't mean she didn't. It could have been accidental. The fact you were sleeping so much before you gave birth means it's possible that she was sedating you, and we don't know how that would affect the baby. That's the problem—we don't know WHAT she was doing."

Missy was shaking her head. "No, she couldn't have done that. I don't believe it." Her skin had turned grey.

I kept my voice gentle. "So, there are three options, as far as I can tell. One, the coroner made a mistake, but I think that's the most unlikely scenario. Two, you were taking heroin, either by accident or because Sarah was giving it to you or some other way." I didn't bring up the suspicious Dr. Broomer, because I didn't want to upset Missy more than she already was, but at that point, I wouldn't put it past the good doctor to have somehow slipped it to her. "Or, three, your baby was born perfectly healthy, and Sarah swapped it with a baby who died from heroin."

Missy stared at me. "You really think my baby is alive?" Her voice was tentative, like she was afraid if she said the words out loud, the possibility would cease to exist.

"Don't you?" My voice was perplexed. "You just told me a story that sure sounds like Sarah stole your perfectly healthy child. You said you weren't taking any drugs, yet they found drugs in the baby that was with you. Why don't you believe your baby is still alive?"

She didn't answer, instead turning her head to stare out the window. Night still pressed against the glass, but the edges were beginning to turn grey. Dawn would arrive before long.

She was silent for so long, I was sure she wasn't going to answer, but then she finally spoke, her voice low. "At first, I did. I was sure he was alive, and that he was stolen and replaced. Just like what happened to your family. But once the doctors got me back on my drugs, and the fog started to clear, two things started to happen. I became severely depressed, which isn't uncommon when someone like me is getting stabilized, and I started to doubt myself. I know how crazy that story sounds. But even more than that, all the physical evidence seems to point to none of it happening. The cops told me they couldn't find any evidence of *anyone* having been with me that night. Along with not being on my meds, I had lost a lot of blood after giving birth in a traumatic fashion. Had I hallucinated? It's possible ... the doctors didn't rule it out. I had certainly been acting like I was experiencing a psychotic episode.

"But even more than that, once I started to be able to think clearly and could look back at all the choices I had made while pregnant, it occurred to me that this was probably all my fault anyway, on some level. While I know I didn't willingly take heroin, or any drug or alcohol, I did invite Sarah in. I did let her manipulate me. So ..." She shrugged in a dejected way. "Since it was my fault anyway, what does it matter if the coroner made a mistake about how the baby died? It isn't going to change anything. My baby is still gone, whether he is the one who died that day or not. So, what difference does it make?

"The fact that I almost immediately went into a pretty severe depression didn't help, either. My baby was gone, along with all my hopes and dreams. So does Sarah, or the coroner's reports, or anything else matter? I know it's difficult to understand unless you've experienced it, but that's what happened."

"No, I do understand," I said, thinking about the major depressive episodes my mother had experienced. "My mother had similar swings."

She met my eyes, a knowing expression in hers. "Yeah, it sucks. It sucks no matter when it happens, but especially with a crazy story like mine. I'm not a hundred percent sure I even believe me. So how can I expect anyone else to?"

She had a point. Even if she couldn't, though, I could clearly hear the ring of truth in her voice.

Of course, I suspected no one would believe me, either, if I tried to go to the cops on her behalf. Especially if they knew my history. Nor would they believe Cole, as her brother.

No, there was only one person who could possibly get everyone, including Missy, to take Missy seriously.

Sarah.

"Maybe we need to reach out to Sarah and see what she has to say," I said. "Have you seen her or talked to her?"

Missy shook her head. "Not since that night. Although I haven't been on my phone much. Well, at all. It's possible she reached out. I can go get it."

"Doesn't matter," I said, thinking it would be a long shot if Sarah had reached out. "It's too early now to call or text her, anyway. Might as well wait for Cole to get here."

Missy nodded, her eyes starting to glaze over. Looking at her in the harsh overhead light that highlighted the dark, puffy circles under her eyes, the dullness of her hair, and the papery-thin texture of her skin, I was reminded that she wasn't well. She needed rest, food, and exercise. I couldn't do much about the last two, but I could try and help her with the first.

"Do you think you could rest now?" I asked.

Her gaze flickered up at me. I could see the wheels turning, as if she were trying to decide if talking about what happened had made things worse or better. "I could try," she said, her voice a little hoarse. The traces of fear and grief were still there, but there was something else, as well. Something I hadn't heard before.

Hope.

Chapter 22

"I can't believe you let her tell you that story without me being here," Cole grumbled as he furiously beat eggs in preparation for breakfast. It was late morning, and I had just finished filling him in on what had happened the night before.

Anxious to get his hands on her cell phone, Cole had peeked in on Missy and reported back that she was still sleeping. Really sleeping. Not the drugged, zoned-out sleep or the twitching, dozing, nap-like trance without drugs. It was probably the first real sleep she'd had in months. His concern for her health was stronger than his drive for her phone, and he gently closed the door before proceeding to make some sort of egg casserole that he could keep warm in the oven until she was ready. He had also whipped up a batch of blueberry bran muffins. "This is why I should be sleeping on the couch," he continued, taking out his frustrations on the hapless eggs. "All you would have needed to do was wake me, and I could have heard it all for myself."

I warmed my hands on my coffee. I was already on my second pot and was still exhausted. I was supposed to be in a meeting, but had called in sick. I knew I couldn't wait to tell Cole, and besides, there was no way I could focus on work after the night I'd had. Between what Missy had shared and my sleep-deprived brain, my mind was too unfocused to concentrate on work. Even though I had been more or less phoning it in for the past week and a half, I wasn't even sure I would be able to muster the energy to do even that.

No, it was better that Tess take over for a short time. It wouldn't be long before Missy would be gone, and my life would go back to normal. I could get myself caught up then.

Until that point, it was better to put my attention on helping Missy and Cole.

Besides, I deserved the break. I had spent years devoting my blood, sweat, and tears to the company I worked for. They could afford me a bit of a breather.

"Have you considered that maybe if you were here, she wouldn't have opened up?" My words were a little harsher and a less guarded than normal. Maybe it was because I was tired and a little uncomfortable about calling in sick when I wasn't, but I instantly felt ashamed.

"Sorry," I said, as Cole paused his literal egg beating. "I didn't mean it like that." I kept thinking about how it happened—how we had started in her bedroom, bonding over nightmares and shared experiences, and I truly didn't think if her brother had been there, she would have finally told her story.

He moved toward the chopping board to wreak havoc on a poor, unsuspecting onion. "But you might be right," he said, a hint of bitterness in his voice. "I have been asking her, begging her, all week to tell me what's going on, and in the middle of the night, while I'm not here, she finally opens up to you."

"We share a similar experience," I said. "I know you're her brother, and you love her to pieces, and she knows that, too. But that doesn't change the fact she's bipolar. She doesn't think 'normal' people are going to believe her side of the story."

"Why else would I ask about Sarah if I didn't believe her?" he fumed, grabbing a handful of mushrooms.

"It's not that simple," I said quietly. "You and I both know you think there's something fishy about that night, but Missy's having trouble trusting herself. She's grieving the loss of her baby and blaming herself for not being able to protect him. She's not even sure she completely trusts what she saw and heard that night. Why should you believe her, if she's having difficulties believing herself? But I'm different, because of my similar experience. I think she felt safe with me … that I wouldn't judge her, no matter how crazy her story sounded."

"But I …" Cole started to talk, then closed his mouth tightly. His dicing slowed down, became less violent. "You're right," he said with a huge sigh. "When she was first diagnosed, she was convinced that an alien species had invaded Earth and taken over certain humans, including the governor and the vice president. Like that old body-snatcher movie. She was convinced only she could tell who was human and who was 'infected.' She said she could hear the aliens inside the humans, making this hissing noise. Anyway, now that I think about it, it's sort of similar to this 'faeries snatched my baby' delusion, so it would make sense that she would be a little more … cautious, I guess, around those of us who lived through her first delusion."

"Wow." I was a little taken aback by how similar her old delusion was with the faeries snatching her baby. Maybe she had the right idea in finding a more receptive audience than either the police or her long-time friends and family.

"Anyway, based on what you're saying, it does sound like Sarah has some explaining to do," Cole said as he started sautéing the vegetables on the stove. "I just hope we can find her."

"I do, too," I said. "But at least now, we have a name and workplace."

"And hopefully, a phone number," he said, eyeing the hallway that led to the bedrooms as though hoping Missy would materialize. "But we can start with what we know. As soon as I get the casserole in the oven, we can begin digging."

He tried to inject an optimistic note into his voice, but we both knew it was going to be a long shot. Trying to find a Sarah Ramsey on social media was useless, as we had no idea what she looked like. Cole thought Missy might be able to help when she was awake.

Nothing promising resulted from our online searches, so we turned our attention to the Riverview Women's Clinic.

Cole clicked on the About page, and I started to skim it. I was amazed at how many specialties it offered. I didn't think Riverview would be a large enough city to have attracted such a big operation, but when I saw it was part of the Duckworth medical empire, it all made sense.

Cole slowed his scrolling down when he reached the pictures and bios of the staff. "Of course there's no Sarah here," he said glumly.

"You didn't think it would be that easy, did you?" I asked, trying to lighten the mood.

Cole gave me a slanted smile that didn't quite reach his eyes. I could see how discouraged he was, and how he was probably beating himself up for not being able to get this information out of Missy sooner.

"Let's call," I said impulsively. "It's possible she used to work there and doesn't anymore. Or maybe the website hasn't been updated in a while."

"Possible," Cole said doubtfully, but he dutifully fetched his phone and dialed the number, putting it on speaker so we could both hear. When the receptionist answered, he asked if there was a Sarah Ramsey who worked there.

"No, there's no Sarah Ramsey here," the overly bright voice answered.

My heart sank, even though I knew it was a long shot.

"Was there ever a Sarah Ramsey?" Cole asked.

"Not since I've been here, but I'm pretty new. Let me transfer you to someone who would know." There was a click, and music filled the line.

Cole rubbed his eyes. "This is a waste of time," he muttered.

"Probably," I said. "But what else are we going to do? At least until Missy gets up."

He sighed, but I could tell he knew I was right.

Another click. "How can I help you?"

"Hi, I'm trying to track down a midwife named Sarah Ramsey."

"Oh, she doesn't work here anymore."

My mouth dropped open. Cole was so surprised that he nearly knocked his phone on the floor. "Uh, ah, how long ago was it that she did?"

"Oh, it's been a while. At least a year."

A year? I could see the same questions I had mirrored on his face.

"Do you know why she left?"

"She retired."

Retired? I thought back to Beth's description of Sarah, which did not seem like someone near retirement age. I mouthed to Cole, *how old?*

"Oh wow," Cole said. "I didn't think she was old enough to retire yet."

The woman on the other end of the line laughed. "Oh, you're such a dear. She was nearly seventy, but that wouldn't have stopped her in itself. It was the arthritis in her hands. Poor thing. She loved being a midwife, and just hated having to retire."

Nearly seventy? Arthritis? My head was reeling with this new information.

Cole thanked the woman for her time and hung up. We both stared at each other.

"I can't believe it," Cole said finally. "There was an actual Sarah Ramsey who worked at the Riverview Women's Clinic."

"I know. Wild. Although she doesn't sound like Missy's Sarah Ramsey."

"No, she does not." Cole frowned. "Missy's Sarah must have known the original Sarah Ramsey. It can't be coincidence."

"Go back to the page with the staff members on it," I said. "Maybe one of them is Missy's Sarah, using a different name."

Cole clicked on the page and scrolled down through the list of bios and pictures. "I don't know. There's a few who look to be the right age. Missy will need to look at them."

"It's also possible she used to work there and doesn't anymore," I mused. "I'm not sure the best way to track that possibility down, though. I guess we need to start with Missy."

"Start with me for what?"

Missy was leaning against the wall in the hallway, still dressed in her sleep outfit. Her hair was a tangled mess and her eyes encrusted with sleep, and there were deep grooves on one side of her face, like she had been lying on something. Overall, though, she looked healthier than I'd seen her.

Cole immediately got up and went to the kitchen. "We found a Sarah Ramsey."

Missy's eyebrows raised. "You did?"

Cole opened the oven door, filling the apartment with the rich smell of the breakfast casserole. My stomach rumbled, and I realized I hadn't eaten anything since dinner the night before. "The key part of that statement is not 'Sarah Ramsey,' but the 'a,'" he said. "I suspect she's not your Sarah."

Missy inched closer to the kitchen, a hungry look on her face. I, too, found myself sidling toward the food. "What do you mean?" Missy asked.

Cole put the casserole on the counter and fetched a couple of plates and the bowl of bran muffins. "The Sarah Ramsey who used to work for Riverview Women's Clinic retired about a year ago."

Missy blinked in confusion. "Retired?"

"Apparently, she's nearing seventy." Cole started plating the food, one for each of us.

Missy's face went blank. "That can't be. There must be a mistake."

Cole put the plate down in front of her with a fork. "Coffee?"

"Please," she said, but her voice was distracted. I could see the worry starting to form behind her eyes, like early morning fog creeping over the streets. "I didn't get it wrong," she said. "I know what she told me. I even remember putting the info into my phone when she told me, so I would remember ..."

Cole reached over to cover her hand with his. "We believe you," he said, softly but firmly. "First of all, the odds of you plucking that name out of thin air and having it match up to a retired midwife who worked at the same place are slim to none. It's basically impossible."

"We think your Sarah worked at the clinic at some point and was using Sarah's identity to disguise her own," I piped in.

Missy looked at both of us, the lines around her forehead and eyes beginning to relax. "You believe me," she said, clearly relieved.

Cole and I glanced at each other. "Of course we believe you," Cole said. "Why would you think we wouldn't?"

Missy shook her head, her knotted hair bouncing around. "I don't know. I guess I feel like I've been trapped in this nightmare for so long, where no one believes me. I'm not even sure if I believe me. What I told you last night," here, Missy glanced at me, "was that really all true? Or did I imagine it? Even when I was telling you, there was a part of me that doubted ... that wondered if Sarah was right, and I was delusional. Especially when what I remember doesn't match up in the real world. I start to wonder if it's me. I just ... I don't always know if I can trust my mind."

I leaned toward Missy. "You're not alone anymore," I said. "We're going to help you figure out what happened to you and your baby."

She stared at me for a moment, the tears staring to pool behind her eyes. "Sorry," she said, fumbling for a napkin. "I'm just such a basket case."

"Don't worry about it," I said. She gave me a watery smile as she dabbed her eyes.

Cole caught my eye as well, and the expression I saw in his made my breath catch in my throat. I quickly looked away, not sure how to handle it with Missy sitting between us.

I suspect she sensed something, too, because I saw her take a quick peek at Cole before picking up her fork. "Smells delish," she said. "You've outdone yourself, Cole."

Cole cleared his throat. "Well, you need to eat," he said. "You're practically wasting away."

She nodded, forking up bites of the egg casserole. "I think I'm getting better now," she said. She turned to me and smiled, her eyes crinkling. "In fact, it shouldn't be long before I'm strong enough to go back to my own place. I'm sure you can't wait to have your apartment back."

My insides seemed to collapse inside me, like a deflated balloon. I forced a smile while playing with my food, no longer hungry. "No rush," I said. "I'd rather have you get completely better first."

"I second that," Cole said quickly. "If Tori's okay with you staying here, I'd rather not rush you home. It would be ideal if you could be here another week, if that works for you, Tori?"

A week. It would have to do, even though it felt like no time at all. I forced a smile. "Of course. However much time you need, take it," I said to Missy." That spare bedroom was just sitting there waiting for a purpose anyway."

Missy held up her hands. "Okay, okay. I'm just saying. I don't want to be a burden."

"You're not," I said. "Honestly." It was on the tip of my tongue to add that having her, well, *them* in my apartment was doing me just as much good as it was Missy, but I didn't want to sound as pathetic as I felt. I was 28 years old. I really ought to have more of a life, but the reality was that two people could basically move in for a couple of weeks without cramping my style at all.

"It's settled, then," Cole said briskly, picking up his fork. "Missy, once you finish eating, why don't you get your phone and let's try and call Sarah? I'm assuming you have her number."

Missy took on a thoughtful look. "Maybe I'd better get it now. It's probably dead. I haven't looked at it or charged it or anything in over a week."

"I'll get it," I volunteered as Missy started to get up. "You keep eating. Just tell me where it is." I needed a moment to collect myself and get my head on straight anyhow.

"Should be on the dresser," she said, and I headed to the bedroom.

I found her phone without much trouble. She was right; it was dead. I did a quick search of her room for a charger, but didn't find one, so I went to my room to grab one.

As I return to the kitchen, I could hear Cole and Missy talking in low voices. I couldn't make out any words until I heard Missy say, "Just drop it. I can't talk about it. Not right now."

They both stopped talking when they saw me. Cole straightened up and forced a smile while Missy stared at her plate. "Did you find the phone?"

"I did, and Missy was right—it's dead." I moved to an outlet to plug it in, wondering if I should ask what was going on. The reality, though, was that if they wanted me to know, they would tell me.

"It will probably take a while for it to reboot," I said, sitting back down in front of my breakfast. Missy nodded. She was moving food around her plate again, most likely having lost her appetite after whatever had just happened between her and Cole. For a moment, I wanted to throttle him. I knew he was anxious to get to the bottom of what happened, but this wasn't the time to be pushing Missy. She was still a long way from "fine," and to have her stop eating again felt like a setback.

No one spoke. Cole refilled coffee cups, and I forced myself to eat. If I was going to harp on Missy to eat better, I knew I'd better take my own medicine. Besides, Cole made this wonderful breakfast, and just because the silence hung around the table like a noxious cloud didn't mean I shouldn't enjoy my food.

The sound of the phone beeping out a string of notifications cracked through the silence like a sword. Missy leaned forward to look at the screen. "I guess it's been a while since I've checked it," she said as she scrolled.

"You said you hadn't looked at it since you went into the hospital," Cole said.

Missy's brow furrowed. "Yeah, it doesn't appear I was checking it much throughout the last couple of weeks of my pregnancy, either. I don't remember seeing a lot of these." She sighed.

"Did Sarah reach out after … that night?" I wasn't sure how to refer to the night Missy gave birth.

Missy shook her head as she studied the phone. "It doesn't look like it. I'll have to go back through."

"Do you want to try calling or texting her?" Cole asked.

Missy tapped on the screen and swiftly typed up a message. She hit send and did a double take. "That's odd," she said.

"What's odd?"

"I'm getting an error message. Says the phone number doesn't exist."

I could feel the energy shift. Cole straightened, making me think he felt it, too. "Try calling her," he said.

She tapped on the screen a couple more times and put the phone on speaker. Sure enough, the operator came on saying that the number was not in service or had been disconnected.

Missy sat back in her chair, a look of disbelief on her face. "It's all true," she said. "Sarah was lying to me from the beginning. She was manipulating me for my baby." She covered her face with her hands.

Both Cole and I leaned forward to touch her. "We don't know that," I said. Cole shot me a look. "Okay, so I know it looks bad, but there could be another explanation."

Cole raised an eyebrow. "Like what?"

I threw my hands up. "I don't know. Maybe she didn't pay her bill, and her phone got shut off. It's possible. She's not working at the clinic anymore. But I think we should do some more digging before we assume anything."

Missy pulled her hands away from her face, grabbing a napkin to dab at the wetness. "How should we start?" There was a shift in her voice … an edge of steel that hadn't been there before. It was almost like something had broken inside her, crushing the old Missy. What was rising in her place was a stronger, harder version.

Cole sensed it, too. "Well, we can start by looking at the Riverview Clinic website to see if you recognize anyone."

Missy nodded, sliding off the stool. We headed toward Cole's computer, where the website was still up. She took her time examining each face, but in the end, she shook her head. "No one I recognize."

Even though I'd expected that, my heart fell.

She glanced up at us. "Now what?"

"Now," I said. "I think we need to talk to Sarah Ramsey. The real one."

Chapter 23

Finding Sarah Ramsey was surprisingly difficult. She didn't have much of an online footprint. There was a Facebook profile that looked promising—both the profile picture and the banner displayed images of adorable babies. Plus, she had been tagged with newborn baby pictures as the midwife. But her account was private.

"Maybe one of us should friend her," Cole said, looking at me.

"Why would she accept my friend request?" I asked. "Besides, I barely use my Facebook account."

"Why don't you use Facebook?" Missy asked. "Do you not like it? Are you somewhere else?"

"I barely use any personal social media accounts," I said.

Missy's mouth dropped open. "*Any*?"

"I like my privacy," I said.

"I don't understand how you can survive without social media," Missy said.

"I've been informed by reliable sources that Gen Xers managed to somehow survive and make it to adulthood without social media," I said drily. "Besides, I'm on it enough for my job. I don't miss it."

"Well, I can't friend her, and Missy definitely can't," Cole said.

"Why can't you?" I asked.

He gave me an exasperated look. "Because of Missy."

"Why on Earth would she connect you with Missy?" I asked. "It's not like 'Cole Bennett' is a super-unique name."

"Plus, you have your cooking blog," Missy said. "It makes sense for you to be friending people on social media."

"What's the worst that's going to happen?" I asked. "She won't accept it. Big deal. It's not like we'd be any worse off than we are now."

Cole pressed his lips together like he wanted to argue, but then he thought better of it and instead sent the friend request.

"Even if she accepts," I said. "There's no guarantee she'll give you her number. You might have to find another way to contact her."

"Yeah, I was thinking that too," Cole said glumly.

"Why don't you reach out to the parents who have tagged her with newborn pictures?" Missy asked. "You can tell them that your girlfriend is expecting, and you are looking for a recommendation for a midwife."

"I suppose it's worth a shot," he said, turning the computer toward him to search out the profiles.

"Message them at the same time you friend them," I suggested. "Then the message is more likely to show up rather than get hidden."

He started typing. "Should I ask about Sarah by name?"

"Why not? They say in the post Sarah was their midwife, so might as well."

He focused on typing.

"It this doesn't work," I said to Missy, "I guess we can pay for the information from one of those sites for phone numbers. I doubt the Riverview Clinic will tell us."

Missy frowned, gnawing on her lip. "I suppose the police won't be much help, either."

"Probably not, but it's worth a shot," I said. "Maybe they could even track Sarah's old number."

"You know, I was going to prenatal yoga for a while," Missy said. "It's where I first heard of midwives and thought it might be good idea to find one. Of course, at the time, I didn't know one would find me, but that was another reason why I was so excited about Sarah. Anyway, back to prenatal yoga, I don't know if they'll talk to me, but maybe you could go and pretend to be pregnant ... see if anyone knows someone who has used Sarah in the past and could make an introduction or something."

The idea of pretending I was pregnant was making me uncomfortable for some reason, but before I could respond, Cole interrupted. "Okay, I reached out to four people," he said, leaning back and stretching. "If that doesn't work, I'll reach out to more. But I don't want to raise any flags ... I mean, some of them could be friends, and they could somehow end up comparing notes. It's possible Sarah responds before then."

"Well, it's a good first step while we try and figure out another way to find her," I said.

***

I was in the kitchen, pouring myself my first cup of coffee and trying to steel myself for the mess I would likely find when I logged into work, when Missy appeared, still looking puffy with sleep.

"You're up early," I said. "Want some coffee?"

She nodded, and I reached for a mug.

We had knocked off early the night before, our middle-of-the-night conversation finally catching up to us. I think Cole had wanted to stay later, but after about the third yawn from Missy, he decided to head off. There hadn't been any new developments—none of the people Cole reached out to had responded yet, and we hadn't landed on a decent plan B.

Even though we both turned in early, I had thought Missy would sleep in. I was sure her body needed it.

She shuffled over to the counter as I brought the two mugs over, but stopped when she saw my computer open. "Oh. I didn't think you'd be working this early," she said nervously.

"Well, I didn't do anything yesterday, so I wanted to get an early start on what I missed," I said.

"I won't bother you then," she said as she turned away, but not before I saw the disappointment on her face.

"It's fine," I said impulsively, even though my gut was telling me I ought to let her go. "It's still early, so it's not like I have to get on now. What did you need?"

She turned back. "Are you sure?" she asked. "You've already done so much. I don't want to be a bother."

"It's no problem," I said, patting the stool next to me. She hesitated for a moment, then sat down. "What's up?"

I thought maybe she had some new revelation she wanted to share … maybe something she dreamed about, but that wasn't the case at all.

"I was wondering," she said before pausing to bite her lip. "I was wondering about your mother."

For a moment, I could only stare at her. "My mother?"

"Yeah." She took a sip of coffee as if to steady herself. "How is she doing?"

"Okay, I guess. If you call being a permanent patient at Sunny Meadows 'okay.'"

Missy blanched. "So she never recovered from that night?"

I reached for my own coffee. "Unfortunately, no. For years, they messed around with her medications, trying to stabilize her. But nothing really took."

Missy's face softened. "Oh man. That's rough."

I couldn't bear to look at the mixture of pity and understanding in her eyes, so I instead fixed my stare on the plain black tea kettle sitting on the stove. It had been one of Nanna's. She had given it to me after she redid her kitchen and bought a brand-new, bright-yellow one to match her sunflower motif. It seemed to encapsulate my entire existence—living in an apartment surrounded by cheap furniture that didn't match, and in many cases, that I hadn't even picked out.

"So, I guess she never explained about the faeries then," Missy said, interrupting my train of thought.

"What do you mean?"

She pursed her lips. "I guess I'm wondering if she ever questioned whether there might be another explanation. That what she thought happened couldn't have actually happened ... that she was trapped in a delusion, or something."

I thought about those dutiful visits, when my mother was either drugged out and drooling or talking nonsense. "If she ever did, I wouldn't know," I said. "We never talked about it."

"Yeah, I guess that makes sense." She took another sip of her coffee and cocked her head at me. "Do you think it would be okay to visit her?"

I was so startled, I almost dropped my coffee. Instead, it sloshed over the side, soaking through my oversized tee shirt that ironically sported the letter I, a heart, and a mug of coffee.

"Oh! I'm so sorry," Missy said as I put my mug down and rushed to the sink to soak it with cold water. "I didn't mean to make you spill it."

"No big deal," I said. "A little coffee on my coffee shirt seems fitting."

She watched me dab at it for a moment. "Does your reaction mean that's a 'no'?"

I didn't answer for a moment, instead paying more attention to my shirt than I needed to. "I'm not sure," I said. "I mean, it's not against the rules, or anything. She can have visitors. I'm just wondering why you would want to."

"Fair question," she said, propping her elbows on the counter. "And to be honest, I don't have a great answer, other than

I feel like we're sort of, well ..." her face turned bright pink. "Soul sisters, I guess. That sounds so corny, especially saying it to her daughter."

"No, I get it," I said. In some respects, Missy and my mother were more alike than my mother and me. They shared something that no one else could—not even me, the five-year-old standing helplessly in her brother's room unable to prevent the tragedy that unfolded.

I finished mopping up my shirt and picked up the coffee pot to refill both of our cups. "Honestly, I don't know how helpful it will be," I said as I poured. "She's not exactly ... lucid. I don't think you'll be able to have much of a conversation."

"That's okay," Missy said quickly. "I mean, however it goes is fine. I just want to meet her."

I took the pot back to the warmer. "Okay, I can set it up," I said. "I'm probably due for a visit myself, anyway." I remembered what Nanna told me about my mother being in an excessively good mood lately. Maybe this wasn't such a bad idea after all. "When do you want to go?"

"Would later today be too soon?" she laughed, a little self-consciously. "I know you have to work, but maybe after? Or we could go tomorrow, since it's Saturday."

My first reaction was to say "no" to both options. It was too soon. Normally, I needed at least a week to prepare myself.

But when I saw the hopeful look in Missy's eyes, I knew I couldn't. For whatever reason, Missy had decided that seeing my mother might help her get better. And I wanted her to get better.

I couldn't imagine Missy's presence would make my mother worse. And if I had a chance to help Missy, especially since I had never been able to help my mother, why would I pass that up?

"Let me call," I said. "Maybe we can go this afternoon."

Her entire face brightened. "But don't you have to work?"

Yes. I absolutely did. No question about that. On the other hand, I had already called in sick the day before. Would one more day really make that much of a difference? Especially since it was Friday? I could start fresh on Monday, with all of this behind me. Maybe even more refreshed than I normally was, because I would have a four-day break versus trying to force myself to concentrate knowing a visit to my mother was looming.

I put a hand to my mouth and faked a cough. "Whatever bug I've come down with isn't going away. I'm sure I'll feel so much better after the weekend."

She smiled at me, and it nearly took my breath away. Not only because it was full of pure joy, but because of how much it reminded me of her brother.

* * *

I smiled at the attendant behind the desk as I picked up the gold pen to sign the book. She was tall and rawboned with bleached-blonde hair and a nose ring. I had seen her multiple times, but I still blanked on her name and had to search her dark-maroon uniform for the simple-yet-elegant gold-plated name tag. "How are you doing, Kim?"

"I'm doing fine, thank you for asking," she said. "And speaking of fine, boy has your mother has been in a fabulous mood lately."

"Really?" I glanced over at Missy, whose jaw was nearly hanging open as she looked around the lobby. It was true that Sunny Meadows resembled more of a high-end luxury hotel than a psychiatric ward: shiny hardwood floors, cream leather furniture, fresh pale-pink roses in gold vases that matched the pale-pink walls decorated with delicate watercolor paintings. Gold chandeliers lit the lobby with a warm glow as the staff moved soundlessly around. It even smelled lovely, like lavender and rose. I found myself wondering again how my father had been able to afford it for so many years. "Nanna told me she's been in a good mood."

Kim's eyes widened. "'A good mood'? She's been on cloud nine. I don't know what happened, but it's been wonderful to see."

I wondered what had shifted. Over the years, my mother certainly had her good days, but nothing this prolonged. Maybe the doctors finally got her medication right.

We found my mother outside, sitting in the sun in a gold-colored cushioned chair under the watchful eye of an attendant who stayed close, but not too close. Her eyes were closed, and in one hand, she held a crumpled piece of paper next to her heart. The air was filled with the scent of cut grass and flowers.

"Hi mom," I said, pulling up a second chair. "How are you?"

At the sound of my voice, my mother opened her eyes and slowly turned her head. "Vicky," she said with a smile. "How nice to see you."

I forced myself to smile back, trying to push down the automatic recoil I always felt when I looked at her. It was like looking in a mirror and seeing myself aged and sick. Her coal-black hair had highlights of silver in it, and her wide grey eyes were nearly lost in the puffiness of her face. She was pale and doughy, likely the result of years of prescription drugs combined with high-carb food and too little exercise.

If one day my brain decided to break in the same way, that could be me sitting there.

But she was still my mother, and I loved her. "It's great to see you," I said, taking her soft, plump hand still clutching the piece of paper. I often found my mother carrying around small pictures and trinkets when I visited, although a crumpled piece of a paper was a first. I wished I could get a look at what it was, but unfortunately, the way she was clinging to it made it impossible. "I brought a friend to see you."

My mother's eyes lit up. "You did? I love visitors. Who is it?"

It took me a moment to answer, because I wasn't expecting that response. My mother had never seemed overly interested in visitors before. Nor was she usually so lucid. No wonder why the staff were so excited about her recovery.

"Um, her name is Missy." I turned to gesture to Missy, who had been hanging back, likely gawking at the well-tended garden and lawn.

"Hi, Mrs. Hutchinson," she said, stepping forward. "It's so nice to meet you."

My mother's face seemed to freeze when she saw Missy. Her eyes widened, and her mouth dropped open. For a moment, I was worried she had just had a stroke and was about to call the attendant, but she reached out her other hand to Missy. "Oh my goodness, dear. It's so nice to see you again."

Again? Missy glanced at me in confusion as she took my mother's hand. "I'm so sorry, but I don't think we've met."

"Of course we have! I remember the day clearly." She sighed, a dreamy expression on her face. "I was so happy that day."

Missy looked even more perplexed, and I didn't know what to do. What was my mother talking about? Was she lost in another delusion? Or had she seen Missy on the news? Oh man, I hoped she wasn't going to bring up what happened to Missy. I couldn't imagine Missy wanted to relive that night again with my mother and the unnamed attendant listening in, even if she was pretending to be discreet about it.

"Mrs. Hutchinson, I'm sorry ..."

"Call me Cora," my mother said.

My mouth dropped open. *Cora?* What was going on? I had never seen my mother so friendly and chatty before.

"Uh, Cora," Missy said awkwardly. "We've, um, I really don't think we've ever met."

My mother's face was starting to look as confused as Missy's. "But I'm sure of it. I remember ..." She paused, her brow wrinkled as she tried to sort out the images in her head. "Aren't you here to talk about Scott?"

Oh no. It was exactly what I was afraid of. She had seen Missy on the news and was now going to ask her about her baby. I opened my mouth to try to salvage the impending wreckage, even though I wasn't entirely sure how or what I should say, when Missy interrupted me.

"Yes," she said, reaching to drag a chair closer to my mother without letting go of her hand. "Yes. I am here to talk about Scott."

My mom's eyes cleared. "I knew it," she said. Then, she leaned toward Missy, almost like they were conspiring together. "Did you see the faeries, too?" she asked in a loud whisper.

Missy nodded. "I did."

My mother nodded back, her eyes filling with tears. "They took Scott," she confided. "I know I blamed Vicky, but I shouldn't have. It wasn't her fault. She couldn't have stopped the faeries. No one could have." Her voice shook.

Automatically, I began forming my response in my mind, reassuring my mother that I didn't hold it against her. But Missy met my eyes and gave me a quick shake of her head. It was a small gesture, but I knew exactly what she meant.

For the second time in just a few minutes, I closed my mouth without speaking.

"It's not your fault, either," Missy said, also lowering her voice. "I couldn't stop them any more than you could."

My mother's face crumpled. "They're terrible, aren't they? I hate them."

Missy nodded solemnly. "I hate them, too." She lowered her voice even more, glancing at the attendant, who appeared to be paying more attention to her phone than to us. "They took my baby, too."

My mother's mouth fell open. "Oh no. Oh dear. It's so awful, so awful." She pressed a frail hand to her lips, shaking her head sadly.

"It *was* awful. I knew you'd understand," Missy said. "I can't stop thinking, why me? Was there something I did to get the faeries' attention?"

I'm not sure what I expected my mother's reaction to be, but it certainly wasn't what happened. Her face seemed to fold in on itself. She pulled back slightly, her eyes narrowing as she glanced furtively from left to right. "There was nothing you could do," she said. She sounded almost normal in that moment, like we weren't sitting in an expensive medical facility for the mentally ill, but there was also something ominous in her tone ... something that made the skin crawl at the back of my neck.

"What do you mean?" Missy asked, her face turning pale. She must have felt it, too. Even the birds and insects seemed to have gone silent, as if they too could sense the shift in energy.

My mother didn't respond. Her hands twitched, and she pulled them to her lap, where she began plucking at the yellow-and-white robe.

"It's my fault," she said, her voice low and broken.

Missy reached over and squeezed my knee, probably sensing how much I wanted to jump into the conversation. "What's your fault?" Missy asked, her voice gentle and soothing.

My mother's eyes traveled around the garden, and for a moment, I was five years old and searching our living room to see if I could see the faeries like she did. "I woke them up," she said.

"How did you wake them up?"

My mother dropped her gaze to her lap, her fingers still busily plucking. Her chin began to tremble. "I did a bad thing." Her voice was barely above a whisper.

I glanced at Missy and could see the same confusion in her eyes that I was sure was in mine. "What did you do?"

My mother shook her head violently. "I did a bad thing. It's all my fault. I shouldn't have done it."

I couldn't stand it. "Mom, what are you talking about? What could you possibly have done to cause all of this?"

At the sound of my voice, my mother's head jerked up. Her gaze softened as she looked at me. "Oh my dear Vicky," she rasped. "I'm so, so very sorry."

"Mom, I don't understand," I said. "What are you sorry about? What did you do?" I could feel my own agitation start to rise. What was she talking about? She couldn't have had anything to do with what happened to Scott. It didn't matter that other people seemed convinced otherwise. I knew for a fact she couldn't have. She was in her room, sound asleep when everything happened.

I was sure of it.

You have to watch out for your little brother. Promise me.

My mother kept shaking her head. "I did a bad thing. I'm so sorry. It's all my fault."

"Mom! What did you do?"

But she wouldn't answer. She just kept repeating over and over that she was sorry, and it was all her fault. Her voice was growing more and more frenzied the more she talked, and her fingers started to claw at the robe, like they wanted to tear it into little pieces.

"How are we doing, Cora?" The attendant swooped over. She was short and stout with blonde hair and dark roots.

"It's my fault," my mother said. "I'm so sorry."

"I know you're sorry," the attendant said smoothly, giving us the eye over my mother's head. "Let's get you inside, hmmm? Maybe we can get you some of that rice pudding you like." She put a hand gently on my mothers' frantic ones, slowing them down. At her touch, my mother seemed to calm. "That's probably enough excitement for one day," she said briskly. "Cora, would you like to say goodbye to your visitors before going inside?"

There wasn't much we could do. Clearly, we were being dismissed. We both said our goodbyes, and I leaned over and kissed her cheek like I normally did. She was still mumbling under her breath, but her words were less panicky, sounding more like a mantra that she was simply repeating over and over.

Missy and I didn't say anything until we were back in the parking lot, which somehow felt hotter than the garden. The asphalt seemed to shimmer under the bright sun, which was also reflecting harshly off the cars lined up neatly in the lot. I could feel the perspiration bead up on the back of my neck under my hair.

"Sorry," I said, although I wasn't sure why I was apologizing. I just felt like I needed to.

She apparently was on the same wavelength. "Why are you apologizing? You didn't do anything wrong."

I shrugged. "I know. But it feels like I could have done more."

"You did more than enough. Just bringing me here was enough." She gave me another sideways glance. "I take it you don't know what she was talking about either? About it being her fault?"

"Not a clue," I sighed. "I could ask my father and grandmother if they have any insight." Although even as I said it, I wasn't sure I would. What if I found out something about my mother I really didn't want to know?

Her eyes softened. "It's probably nothing," she said. "You know as well as I do that she's not in the best place to sort out what's real and what's imaginary."

"I know," I said as we reached the car. I started pawing through my purse for my keys. My hand knocked into my cell phone, lighting up the screen so I could see the notifications waiting for me. "But now that I know a lot of people in town

thought she had something to do with what happened to Scott
…"

"Doesn't mean she did," Missy interrupted. "Especially since we haven't a clue what she's talking about. Mothers blame themselves all the time for things they did and didn't do while they were pregnant. Not eating right, too little sleep, drinking a cup of coffee, having a glass of wine before they knew they were pregnant. It could be something as innocuous as that. Unless we know otherwise, it doesn't make sense to speculate."

"I suppose you're right," I said as I finally located my keys and unlocked the car. What Missy was saying made sense—it was far more likely that my mother was feeling guilty for some minor infraction.

Especially since I never saw her anywhere near Scott's room that night.

I just had to hang onto that, despite my gut telling me there was something more going on than my mother feeling bad about eating too many cookies.

"Let me check my phone before we get going," I said after getting settled in the driver's seat and digging it out of my purse. I saw some notifications. Maybe Cole was finally able to locate the original Sarah."

Cole had texted. Multiple times. I read them and then looked up at Missy, the surprise surely apparent on my face. "He not only located her … he made contact with her. And she's agreed to talk to us."

Chapter 24

"Do you have your phone?" I asked Missy while we were driving to Sarah's house.

She stared straight ahead. "No, I left it at home."

"Ah, well that explains why Cole couldn't get in touch with you."

Missy nodded but didn't say anything. I wondered at her lack of interest in her phone. It seemed peculiar to me, especially since she was so shocked over my non-existent social networking presence. While I get that she probably didn't want to be on social media at the moment, didn't she want to at least text her friends?

And what about the father of her child? Why hadn't she said a word about him?

I eyed her as I drove. She was sitting straight up, her back stiff, her face carefully blank. Actually, her entire body seemed stiff. Nothing like just a few minutes before, when she was relaxed and warm.

In fact, her demeanor had shifted right when I told her Cole texted about Sarah. Was it meeting Sarah? Or was it her brother?

The intense-but-quiet argument I'd heard earlier between them ... was that the cause?

"I'm surprised you didn't bring your phone," I said. "Aren't there people who would likely be reaching out to you?"

"Not really," she said.

The pain in her voice made me pause. Was it possible many of her friends turned against her? Believed the news reports?

Was it possible the father of her child did, too?

"I'm sorry," I said.

She shrugged. "It is what it is." She turned to stare out the window.

I chewed on my lip. Why wasn't she talking about the father of her child? At all? Not only that, but it appeared she hadn't even been trying to contact him. She didn't check her phone until that morning when we were trying to find Sarah.

What was going on? Had they broken up? Even if they had, one would think he would still be interested in what really happened to his child.

Unless, of course, he didn't know.

Or maybe he had been reaching out, but she had been ignoring him for some reason.

And if that was the case, why?

Missy had been so open about everything else ... why would she keep that a secret?

"Even the father of your child?" I asked. I knew it was a risk, but it was clear she was hiding something. I just wasn't sure what.

Her head snapped around. "Have you been talking to my brother?" Her voice was hard, angry.

I was taken aback. "No. Why would I be talking to him about the father of your child?"

"Because that's what he's been asking me."

"Cole and I have not talked about that," I said firmly. "I just think it's weird, that's all. The father is a pretty big part of the story, but you haven't brought him up at all."

"That's because it doesn't matter," she said. "He's not part of the story anymore." She went back to staring out the window.

Ah. So, maybe they had broken up, then. But still. Why was she so secretive?

"I'm sorry," I said for a second time. She just shrugged in response.

We didn't talk at all until I pulled up in front of the small, well-kept house on a dead-end street.

Cole was already there, sitting in his parked car waiting for us. As soon as we parked, he headed over to us. "Where were you?" he asked the moment I opened the driver's door. "Or did you just have your phone off?"

"Missy wanted to meet my mother," I said.

Cole's eyebrows went up. "In Sunny Meadows? How did that go?"

"Tell you later," I said. Missy had gotten out of the car and was standing facing the house, just staring at it.

Cole glanced over, saw his sister, and went over to her. "Are you okay?"

"I will be," she said. She took a deep breath and steeled herself. "Let's do this." Without looking at either of us, she marched up the driveway and onto the small porch decorated with pots of red geraniums and a friendly welcome mat, leaving the two of us lagging a few steps behind.

She rang the doorbell, not waiting for us to catch up, but we were all waiting together by the time the door opened. An older woman peered out at us from behind thick glasses. "Hello?"

Missy seemed to have lost her nerve at the sight of the woman. Maybe a part of her really thought it would be her Sarah opening the door versus the significantly older complete stranger.

Luckily, Cole was able to swoop in and save the situation.

"Are you Sarah Ramsey?" he asked.

She blinked owlishly at us. "Yes. Are you the young man who called me earlier?"

"I am."

"Come on in." She held open the door and shuffled back. She was tiny, but it was difficult to tell if it was because she was short or just stooped over. She wore black elastic pants with a loose blue tee shirt, and her hands were gnarled with oversized knuckles. Despite her obvious physical issues, though, her eyes behind the thick glasses were clear and sharp.

Cole stepped forward first, introducing us. Sarah smiled at each of us before leading us to the cheery red-and-white kitchen decorated with roosters. She waved to the round table near the sliding glass doors. "Have a seat. Would you like some lemonade? I just made it."

All of us said "yes," although lemonade was not something I was terribly fond of. It was clear Sarah was excited to have visitors, and as she was doing us a favor, it felt rude to refuse.

It took a few minutes for her to pour it into tall glasses covered with red and blue daisies and bring them all to the table. The kitchen smelled strongly of lemon and Lysol. As we waited, a fat ginger cat wandered into the kitchen, tail swishing.

"Thanks," Cole said taking a sip. I took one as well and tried not to make a face. It was overly sweet and tasted like it was made from concentrate. In fairness, looking at her hands, it seemed clear her lemon juicing days were likely far behind her.

"So, you're telling me there's a midwife out there pretending to be me?" she asked once she had settled into her chair. The cat leaped into her lap and made itself comfortable, and she began stroking its fur absentmindedly.

"Well, I don't know if she's pretending to be you per se, but she is calling herself 'Sarah Ramsey,'" Cole said. "So, we were wondering if you happen to know another Sarah Ramsey who is a midwife?"

Sarah let out a rusty chuckle. "Can't say I do. Where does this other Sarah work?"

"She said the Riverview Women's Clinic."

Sarah shook her head. "There's definitely not another Sarah Ramsey there. I would have known."

"We thought you might know her," Missy broke in. "Because I, we, think she may have been impersonating you."

Sarah studied Missy, those sharp eyes missing nothing. "Can you describe her?"

Missy hesitated. "She ... well, she isn't really memorable. Short brown hair, brown eyes, brown glasses. She wore a lot of brown and beige, as well. Almost like she wanted to be as inconspicuous as possible."

"Is she your age?"

"A little older. I think she said she was 32."

"And she is a midwife?"

"That's what she said."

Sarah grimaced as she reached for her lemonade. "It sounds like Marci, except Marci didn't wear brown clothes. She was always dressed in something bright and outlandish. It never suited her, if you ask me. But these youngsters never do, these days."

Missy sucked in her breath. Cole and I exchanged glances before he leaned forward. "Marci?"

The old lady nodded. "Marci McCabe. She was just as you described, minus the clothing, of course."

"Is she a midwife?"

"I assume so. Although she was fired from the clinic."

"Fired?" Missy stared at Sarah, her eyes round and shocked.

Sarah nodded, pursing her lips. "She was always troubled."

Missy's mouth was a thin, white line. "What did she do?"

Sarah shook her head. "Stole drugs."

"Drugs?"

"She was caught stealing the prescription samples. It was sad, really. The whole thing was. She wasn't a bad midwife. She had a nice manner with the patients, and as far as I could tell, she seemed to know what she was doing. I wasn't her mentor or anything like that, mind you, but from what I heard from the staff and patients, it seemed like she was giving them good advice. But …" she sighed. "She was definitely troubled."

"Was she taking the drugs or selling them?" Cole asked. "Do you know?"

Sarah glanced at him, her gaze a touch reproachful. "No, dear. I never asked. I didn't think it mattered."

"It probably doesn't," Cole said, looking a little chagrined.

Sarah went back to studying Missy. "So, what happened with Marci? Am I wrong about her midwife skills?"

"I … I don't know if I can really answer that," Missy said.

Sarah looked puzzled. "What do you mean? You were her patient, right?"

"I was," Missy said, staring into her lemonade. She seemed to be collapsing in on herself as the conversation shifted.

Sarah was still watching her, her expression pondering, when her eyes widened. "Oh, you poor dear," she said. "You're the one who lost her baby, aren't you?"

Missy kept her eyes glued to her lemonade, but she slowly nodded.

Sarah pressed her hand to her heart. "Oh, my poor dear," she said again. "That's just so awful. And Marci was your midwife?"

"It seems so," Missy said dully.

"Oh Marci, what did you get yourself into?" Sarah shook her head. "But you said she was pretending to be me? How did you even find her?"

"She found me," Missy said. "I was in a coffee shop and had some cramping. She saw me and helped me out."

Sarah's eyes narrowed, and you could almost see the midwife come to the surface. "When was this?"

"Last fall or so."

"I mean, where were you in your pregnancy when you met Marci?"

"Oh." Missy screwed up her face. "Either month three or four. No, it must have been near the end of month three, because I'm sure we talked about how I was still in my first trimester, although barely."

"And do you remember if that particular cramping you had the day you met Marci was easier or worse than other cramps?"

Now it was time for Missy's eyes to narrow. "What are you saying? Do you think there was a problem with the baby back then?" Her voice shook at the end, the note of fear clear.

Sarah shook her head. "Not at all, dear. Cramping is common throughout a pregnancy. It doesn't mean anything is wrong with the baby."

"Then I don't understand. What are you asking?"

Sarah paused to take a sip of her lemonade. "Even though cramping is common, I just find it … peculiar, I guess, that you got a cramp at the same time Marci just happened to be in the coffee shop. Especially since Marci decided to tell you she was a midwife, when she technically isn't anymore, as she lost her license when she was caught stealing drugs. Not to mention she lied about her name."

"You think she caused it?"

"Did you leave your coffee unattended? Perhaps to use the ladies' room?" She let out that rusty chuckle again.

"No. I had just gotten my coffee, and that's when the cramp hit." Missy frowned in thought. "I remember because it was so sudden and sharp, I put my coffee down on the counter. I nearly spilled it. Sarah, I mean Marci, noticed, and came over and helped me sit down. She explained cramps are fairly normal when you're pregnant, but if I wanted to go to the hospital, she would take me. She stayed with me, and we talked for a while. Eventually, I relaxed."

Sarah took another deliberate sip of her lemonade. "Well, cramping can be caused by all sorts of things. There are even herbs that can cause it. You can sometimes find them in herbal teas. Did you have any that day?"

"Maybe. It's hard to remember. I know I was drinking teas like chamomile, orange, lemon, raspberry ..."

"Raspberry or raspberry leaf?"

"I ..." she frowned. "No, I didn't start drinking raspberry leaf tea until later in my pregnancy. Sarah, I mean Marci, used to bring it to me. Why, is it bad?"

"Not necessarily. I recommend it as well, but usually later in a pregnancy, like what Marci told you. It can help tone the uterus and make for an easier delivery. But I would never give it to a woman in the first trimester, as it can cause a miscarriage."

Missy's face drained of color. "Do you think ..."

Sarah held out her hand. "I don't know. I'm just asking questions. And according to you, Marci wouldn't have had any time to give you that tea before you started cramping in the coffee shop. Correct?"

"Yes, and I'm sure I didn't have that kind before ..." Missy voice trailed off as her face turned an even chalkier color.

"Missy, are you okay?" Cole asked, alarmed.

Even Sarah looked concerned. "Oh dear, maybe I should make you a cup of tea."

"I'm fine," Missy said. "I don't need any tea, thank you." She didn't look fine—more like she was about to throw up. "You know, I think we might have overstayed our welcome. Thank you for all your help." She stood up, her legs shaking.

We all followed suit, including Sarah. "Why, of course, dear," Sarah said. "You probably need to lay down for a bit. This is all very shocking. Feel free to call me or come over anytime, if you have any more questions."

"Thank you," Missy managed as she headed toward the door. Cole and I followed her with Sarah bringing up the rear.

"Thank you again," Cole was saying as Missy flung open the front door and stepped outside, as if she were suffocating.

I followed her as Cole finished saying goodbye to Sarah. "Missy, are you okay?" I hissed.

Missy was doubled over, hands on her knees and breathing deeply. I put my hand on the small of her back, a little afraid she was about to be sick. She turned her head to eye me.

"Dr. Broomer," she said.

A cold breeze seemed to dart down my spine, making me shiver. "What about her?"

Missy gulped down a couple more breaths. "She used to give me tea during our sessions." She turned to look at me. "Herbal tea."

* * *

"Maybe we should go back to the police," I said. We were sitting around my kitchen table eating a casserole Cole had prepared and stuck in the freezer a few days earlier for just such an occasion.

"The police," Cole snorted. "They won't help."

"Why?" I asked. "We now have a link between Dr. Broomer and this Marci person, although I agree it's pretty tenuous, but still. It may be enough to make Dr. Broomer nervous enough to make a mistake."

"You heard Sarah," Cole said. "Cramps are common early in pregnancy. Missy doesn't even know for sure what she drank. How can we prove anything?"

I bit down on my lip, frustrated. Cole was right, but still. It was infuriating.

"I agree with Cole. The police can't help," Missy said. "But that doesn't mean we can't find out what Dr. Broomer has to say for herself."

Cole and I both started talking at once. "Oh no," I said as Cole proclaimed, "Absolutely not."

Missy gave us both a fierce look. "Why not?"

"Because it's not safe," I said.

Missy's expression was wild. "Safe? Safe?!" She was shaking so badly, I thought she might be having some sort of stroke. "Didn't you hear Sarah? She might have been poisoning me with something that could have made me miscarry! And why? So that there would be a plausible reason for me to meet a woman who would steal my baby! I trusted Dr. Broomer! I was paying her to be on my side!"

"Missy," Cole said, reaching out to touch her, but Missy snatched her hand away.

"Do you have any idea what this is like? What she did to me? I trusted her with my baby's life! I went off my medicine because I thought she would be my advocate … that she would make sure that me and my baby made it safely through the pregnancy. And what does she do? *She sells my baby to the highest bidder!*" Missy's voice ended on a scream.

Cole and I were both on our feet. "Missy, we don't know that," I was trying to say while Cole begged her to calm down.

"How can I be calm," she yelled at her brother, "after what I just learned?"

"Missy, we don't know," I said again, and this time, my voice seemed to cut through. She turned her head to stare at me, her eyes still crazed, but at least quieted.

"I know it looks bad," I said empathetically. "We need to check her out. But it could still be a coincidence. Just in case it's not, I don't think you should be by yourself when you see her."

She was still breathing hard. "I guess I can see that."

"AND," I continued, eying them both. "We should definitely tell the police. If this is true about Dr. Broomer, she shouldn't be seeing patients. While we don't have a lot of proof, we have some. We know Marci told Missy and her friends the wrong name. That's suspicious, if it is Marci, whether Dr. Broomer had anything to do with it or not."

"I had told her about Sarah," Missy said. "She didn't question me."

"Dr. Broomer could argue she didn't realize there was a problem, as there is a midwife named Sarah Ramsey in Riverview. Of course, the age doesn't match, but she could argue age never came up. It's plausible."

"You have a point," Cole said. "So, I think we need to do some searching for Marci. I'll start looking for her online, but if she took pains to dress differently around you, my guess is she's scrubbed her online presence, too. Still, you never know. I can come with you to your next appointment, and maybe on Monday, we'll find the detective and tell him what we've found out. Sound like a plan?"

Missy nodded. The color was returning to her face bit by bit, and her breathing was slowing down. The fact that Cole had outlined a plan with specific action steps seemed to steady her. Perhaps it was because she felt like someone was finally taking her seriously.

"We'll get through this," I said to her. "We'll figure it out."

She met my eyes and smiled at me. "Thank you," she said. "I don't know what I'd do without you."

I reached over and gave her hand a squeeze. "We're going to get to the bottom of this. I promise."

It wasn't until later that I realized sometimes getting to the truth isn't always what's best.

Chapter 25

That night, I slept better than I had in a long time. No night terrors or any dreams, as far as I could tell.

When I finally awoke, the sun was streaming through the window. The sky was dark blue without a cloud in sight. It looked like a beautiful day for a run, especially since it'd been a while since I had gone on one. Really, since Missy had arrived. Every day, it had felt like there was something else I should be doing in the morning.

There was a bluebird perched on my window ledge outside, also apparently enjoying the morning.

"A bluebird of happiness," I murmured. It felt like a good omen.

Maybe things are finally turning around, I thought as I pulled on my black running shorts and white top. Maybe I also had a new friend after all of this, and even when Missy moved out, I could still see her.

Maybe I could still see her brother, too.

My chest and neck felt warm just thinking about it, and I pushed the thought away. It was still a little too soon. We really needed to gather enough evidence to get the police interested again before I could even think about anything like that. Hopefully, we would be able to track down Marci soon, and that would get us moving in the right direction.

Missy was still asleep, so I quietly got the coffee started, put my running shoes on, and headed out the door.

I was right. It was a perfect day for a jog. And it felt so good to move my limbs and be outside, breathing the fresh cool air that held only a hint of humidity.

I did my usual five-mile circle, surprised by it being easier than I thought. As I rounded the corner that led to my apartment building, I noticed a couple of cars driving up and down the street rather slowly. Much slower than the speed limit.

Even though I was sweating, I felt a chill run through my body.

I swerved to the right, as if I were going into the apartment building next to mine, but instead, I ran across the back of the property and slipped into a side door of my apartment building. Through the glass window of the lobby, I watched one of the cars slowly cruise by again.

I didn't have a good feeling about it.

I took the stairs two at a time and ran down the hall to my apartment. Hopefully, it was nothing. Hopefully, this didn't mean the reporters had somehow managed to track down Missy and wanted to harass her. I had thought they had given up on the story. After all, the cops had, so really, what was there to talk about anymore?

I unlocked my apartment and grabbed my phone off the coffee table on the way to the kitchen for water and coffee. I powered it on, while sipping my coffee.

I had expected to see no notifications at all, other than maybe something from Cole.

That wasn't what I found.

I had dozens of texts from seemingly everyone.

The coffee turned into sludge in my mouth that I wasn't able to swallow.

I skimmed down the list.

Nanna: *Are you okay? Call me?*

Cole: *Call me!*

My boss: *Tori, we need to talk. ASAP. I don't care if it's the weekend. Let me know when you get this.*

As bad as that one was, it wasn't the worst.

Tess's definitely held that title.

Tori, are you really Vicky?

The sound of glass shattering made me jump. I looked around in confusion and saw my coffee mug in pieces on the floor and coffee everywhere, including on my new white running shoes.

"Tori?"

Missy was standing in the doorway, blinking sleepily at me, her hair the usual rat's nest she woke up with. "I thought I heard something break."

"I ... yeah, I dropped my coffee mug."

She blinked a few more times, glanced down at the mess and then back up to my face. Her brow furrowed. "Are you okay?" she asked. "You look like you've seen a ghost."

No, I think I saw a faery. I was suddenly overcome with the urge to giggle hysterically. *No, I haven't seen a ghost. There's no such thing as ghosts. But I have seen a faery!*

I was losing it.

"Tori?" Missy took a step closer to me. "What happened? What's going on?"

"Don't come any closer," I said. "There's broken glass everywhere. Here, let me clean it up." I bent down to try and pick up the pieces, but my fingers didn't seem to be working right. They were stiff and numb.

Missy disappeared for a moment. I heard her open and close a door, and she returned wearing flip flops and holding a broom and dustpan. She didn't say a word as she helped me clean up. Actually, she did most of the work, as I wasn't able to get my limbs to move properly.

When the glass was safely in the trash, she paused, tilting her head. "Wanna tell me what just happened?"

I busied myself getting two more mugs for coffee. "I'm actually not really sure," I said. "But what I think happened ..."

I was interrupted by the sound of the front door opening and slamming shut. Cole appeared in the kitchen, out of breath, his eyes huge. "Oh good. There you are, Tori. Did you see my texts? I have no idea how they found out."

They found out. I clutched the counter, afraid I might pass out. *See? I told you this would happen,* Negative Nancy spat at me. *You have no one to blame but yourself.*

I had no response. She was right.

Missy's gaze moved between me and Cole. "Who's 'they,' and what did 'they' find out?"

Cole glanced at me, but I couldn't speak. My tongue seemed to have stuck to the roof of my mouth.

Cole swallowed. "That Tori is Vicky."

Missy's eyes widened. "You mean ..."

"Yes. I don't know how, but they now know that Tori was the little girl whose mother had a very similar experience to what you just went through. Even worse, they also somehow figured out that Tori was visiting you in the hospital."

I closed my eyes. In my mind's eye, I again saw us standing at the nurse's station, my disguise on Missy, and the journalist staring at me.

"It was the day Missy was discharged," I said, my voice sounding dry and brittle. "That journalist you recognized? He saw me with you two."

"But just because he saw you with us doesn't mean he would know who you are," Cole said. "You're not online at all."

A cold numbness seemed to be slowly consuming my body, bit by bit. I felt like I was drowning in it. Idly, I wondered if I would simply cease to exist once it completely overtook me. I almost hoped I would. "If he found a picture of me as a child, he would see the resemblance. Then, it would just be a matter of tracking down my mother's maiden name and my name change, like you did. Who knows why he decided to look for me? Maybe he was doing research into your childhood history and stumbled upon my story. But the how doesn't really matter at this point."

"What do we do now?" Missy asked. She was wringing her hands together, and her face had turned pale.

Cole hesitated, but then addressed Missy. "You need to pack."

The cold numbness tightened around my chest, like icy bands. I was having trouble breathing. Missy looked confused. "Pack? What for?"

Cole shot me an apologetic look before moving to take his sister's arm. "It's not safe here for you anymore."

Missy's eyes went very wide. "Wait. You mean they know where I am?"

Again, Cole glanced at me, apologizing with his eyes. "I think so. There's some traffic congestion outside. I think it would be best if we left. The sooner, the better."

Missy didn't need to hear anything else. She swiftly turned on her heel and vanished down the hall.

Cole watched her go before coming closer to me. "I'm just so sorry," he said in a low voice. "I never meant for this to happen to you. Especially after all you've done for us."

It took me a minute to get my mouth to work properly. "It's okay," I said. "I knew the risk."

"I'm also sorry to leave you here like this," he said. "But I have to get Missy somewhere safe. You understand that, right?"

I forced my lips to curl up into some resemblance of a smile. "Of course I do. Missy has to be your first priority."

He turned his face away. "I wouldn't say that exactly, but if the media IS coming, I have to get her settled somewhere else.

But I'm not leaving you alone. I am going to try and help you out of this mess."

I had no idea what he, or anyone else, for that matter, could possibly do to help. My secret was out. There was nothing to be done.

But I also couldn't bring myself to say any of that. Cole's guilt was written all over his face. I couldn't bear to make him feel any worse than he already did.

"Don't worry about me," I said. "I'll be fine. Just take care of Missy. She needs you."

Cole started to say something, but then Missy was back, awkwardly carrying her unzipped duffle bag. She had dumped her belongings inside in such a rush, they were spilling out of the top. "I'm ready," she said. She still had on the shirt she'd slept in, but she had changed into a different pair of shorts. She also had my baseball cap shoved onto her head, and I didn't have the heart to tell her to take it off. "Cole, let's go."

"Missy, you can take a moment to zip your bag," Cole started to say, but Missy shook her head.

"No, you don't understand. The media can't find me." She quickly glanced at me. "I'm sorry, Tori, to run out on you like this …"

I waved my hand. "Go," I said. "We can talk later."

She bobbed her head once, a faint smile on her lips. "I knew you'd understand." She hurried to the door.

Cole trailed after her, a little more slowly. "I'll call you …"

"Go," I said again, waving my hand.

I stayed in the kitchen, listening to the apartment door open and close. I even heard the click of the deadbolt as Cole locked it for me.

As soon as they were gone, I collapsed, my legs no longer able to hold me up. The floor was still damp where Missy had helped me clean up the coffee, but I didn't care. I curled up in as tight a ball as I possibly could and bawled like a baby.

* * *

If I hadn't been numb with grief and shock, I would have been amazed at how quickly my life unraveled.

My boss fired me, although she was quick to say it wasn't because of what happened to me as a child or how being associated with me might affect the company's image and brand. The "official" reason was because the quality of my work had gone down the past couple of weeks. "Clearly, you're distracted by what happened," she said. "And maybe you just need some time off to figure things out. I get it; I really do. I'm truly sympathetic to what you must be going through. You've done a wonderful job for us in the past, so please don't think I'm not grateful. But this is business. We need someone in your position who is focused on growing our company, not on their personal lives, no matter how tragic. Especially now with the new line coming out. And I just don't think that's you … at least, not right at this moment."

She did offer me a decent severance package, which included a chunk of money for all my unused vacation days, so there was that, at least. Although I wondered if it would be enough to tide me over until another company would take a chance on me.

My so-called "friends" deserted me, although to be fair, I wasn't sure I even had any real friends. Tess was probably the closest, and while texting with her, it quickly became apparent that she was only interested in getting the lurid details around what had happened to me, probably so she could gossip about it with her actual friends. She was also cagey about work, sending only a terse "Sorry they let you go" message. It suddenly occurred to me that if I was gone, Tess would likely be first in line to get my job, at least temporarily, if not permanently.

Once I realized that, the entire sorry conversation made a lot more sense. I let her know I had to go and could talk later in the week. Her "Okay, great," said it all.

As for Cole and Missy, I received a brief text Saturday night that Missy was upset, and Cole didn't feel good about leaving her to come over. Plus, he thought it might make more sense to stay away from my apartment for the time being, as the media were still out there, and he didn't want them following him back to Missy. It felt like a punch to the gut, but I understood. I would stay away from me, too, if I were Cole or Missy. Clearly, I was tainted, and whoever was seen with me ran the risk of being tainted, as well. Guilt by association. It was one thing to be a five-year-old who may or may not have had something to do with her infant brother's death. That was a tragedy.

But an adult being involved with a woman who had nearly the same story?

Yeah, that sounded suspicious. Even to me, knowing I had nothing to do with it, it sounded suspicious.

I spent the day with the phone turned off, listening to the noises outside and trying not to think about the similarities to the last time my identity was discovered, thereby destroying my life. But, despite my best efforts, I found myself continually replaying the scenes over and over, like a streaming video stuck on repeat.

I was 15 years old and had gotten involved in one of those online cold-case clubs, where the members pour over old cases trying to solve them. Since what happened with Scott, I had been obsessed with true crime and cold cases. In fact, he had been my first "case"—as soon as I was old enough to be able to read the newspaper clippings, I started a case file, searching for evidence that he had been taken after all. Even though that project was destined to hit a dead end, it launched my love for investigating.

At the time, I was still Vicky Hutchinson. I had been living with Nanna in Riverview for roughly five years. No one had put two and two together to figure out that I was the Vicky Hutchinson who was the last to see her infant brother alive. Part of that might have been because I had told everyone I was from Milwaukee. No one questioned it.

Which is why I started letting my guard down more and more, and why I got a little too cute with my screen name for the online cold case club: victoryh. I also had used my real name to sign up for an account.

I should have been more prepared for when Scott's case would invariably be brought up. I don't think I was so naive to think it would never be mentioned, but by that time, it had been years since anyone had even talked about it, and I had let my guard down.

That was my first big mistake.

On the night in question, we were discussing the JonBenét Ramsey case—the six-year-old beauty queen found dead in her home in Boulder, Colorado. Actually, "arguing" was probably more accurate. Most of the people thought JonBenét's father had killed her, while the majority of the others felt it was the mother.

But there were a few who were convinced it was the nine-year-old brother.

Mistake number two? I should have realized it was inevitable someone would bring up Scott. And me.

His screen name (I assumed it was a "him") was "modern-sherlock." When someone else scoffed that it was highly unlikely that a nine-year-old would have been either physically or mentally capable of doing that to his sister, he replied, "What about Scott Hutchinson? His sister was only five when she suffocated him."

I never understood the saying "seeing red" until that moment. The rage descended on me so fast, I didn't have a chance. I was furiously typing a response before my brain could kick in with a warning.

I didn't remember what I actually wrote—only the black anger that was buzzing around me like a swarm of wasps. It wasn't until modernsherlock typed: "Wait? VictoryH? Is that short for Vicky Hutchinson? Are YOU Scott's sister?"

It was like a bright, white light had sliced through the fog of rage, and as fast as it had appeared, it disappeared, leaving me sick with horror.

What had I done?

I immediately logged out of the chat room, deleted my account, turned off my computer, and curled up in a ball on my bed.

I kept telling myself over and over it wasn't a big deal. It wasn't like anyone I knew in real life was in the online club. No one would possibly tie it to me.

My secret was safe.

As luck would have it, the older brother of a cheerleader in my school was friends with one of the club members. That person told the brother what happened that night, who mentioned something to his sister (the cheerleader), and well …

It was dreadful. It didn't take long for the entire school to know I was the Vicky Hutchinson who may have suffocated her brother when she was five. I was constantly harassed and bullied. My grades plummeted, and I stopped eating and sleeping. I spent all my time hiding in my room.

It all came to a head the day I took a handful of Nanna's sleeping pills.

That was last straw for Nanna. After a two-week stay in the hospital, where I could be fully evaluated to determine whether I was going down the same path as my mother, Nanna decided she was transferring me to a different school.

I could still remember the day she told me. I was lying on my bed, staring listlessly at the ceiling.

"You're done at South Riverview," she said. "Next week, you're starting at Sherwood."

I tilted my head to look at her. She was standing in the doorway, arms crossed. I remember thinking she seemed angry, but I think she was more scared than anything.

"No," I said.

Her jaw dropped. "No? You want to go back to South Riverview?"

"No."

"Then I don't understand. You don't want to go to Sherwood?"

"I'm not going anywhere as Vicky Hutchinson," I said.

She paused for a moment, cocking her head as she studied me. "Who do you want to go as?"

"Tori." The name fell out of my mouth, even though I hadn't given a thought as to who I wanted to be until Nanna asked. All I knew was Vicky Hutchinson was dead.

Her lips twitched up in a half-smile. "Tori who?"

I met her eyes. "Tori Agnello."

She stared at me for a moment, her eyes softening. "Tori Agnello is a lovely name."

My name wasn't the only thing I changed. I also went to a hair stylist and had them chop off my long, thick, black hair and give me a pixie cut. I bought a pair of glasses with plain glass frames to wear. I wore those glasses until I got my job working at home. By then, I thought enough time had passed that I was safe.

Safe. The word tasted bitter on my tongue. Again, I had thought the worst was behind me. Again, I had let my guard down.

And again, I had lost everything.

How could I have been so stupid?

Just like I had all those years ago, I spent most of the afternoon curled up in a ball, beating myself up. Occasionally, a journalist would interrupt me, pounding on my door, calling out to me, but one of my neighbors would eventually call the cops and have them escorted out.

One of those times, the cops returned and asked if they could have a few words. I let them in, mostly because I couldn't think of a reason not to. The interview was short. Basically, they asked me about my relationship with Missy and if I had any idea where Jack Spade, the "journalist" who broke the story, came up with his wild accusations. I told them I didn't have a clue, as I had never even met the guy. They nodded, took a few notes, and left.

And if all that wasn't enough, what happened on Sunday was the cherry on top. My landlord left me a voicemail, threatening to evict me. "I'm getting complaints from the other residents," he barked into the phone. "We can't have the media blocking access, taking parking spaces, and making a nuisance of themselves here. You have to get this under control."

His idea of getting things "under control"? Me moving out, "either temporarily or permanently. I don't care which, but you have to do something."

While I was pretty sure he couldn't evict me because the media had chosen to camp outside the apartment building, by that time, I was too exhausted to argue. I texted him "Fine," and turned my phone back off.

Maybe he was doing me a favor. With no job, the fewer expenses, the better. But still, it left me feeling hollow inside.

The one bright spot was Nanna. She of course told me I could stay with her as long as I wanted. I packed a bag and waited until it was dark to slip out of the building. I left my car in the lot and cut across to the next street, where Nanna was waiting to pick me up.

"I can't believe those vultures," she spat after I slid into the passenger side door. "Bunch of bottom feeders. They should all be ashamed of themselves."

I closed my eyes and leaned my head back against the head-rest. "It's all about the clicks, Nanna. The more sensational, the better."

"When I was a child, we called it 'yellow journalism,'" she said. "No self- respecting reporter would ever do anything so lewd or indecent."

"Things change," I said.

The article, when I finally brought myself to read it, was most definitely a lewd and indecent piece of work. Not only did Jack Spade dredge up the whole Scott story, but he also tracked down the fact that Missy and I had been in the same class, along with the fact we were "seen together recently." From there, he had made the astonishing leap that we were either somehow "in it together," in terms of Missy's loss, and had planned for it to happen for whatever unfathomable reason, or that I had been the mastermind behind the "stunt" and Missy the inno-cent victim. If it were the latter, he proposed that, again, for reasons unknown, I had tricked her into thinking that faeries were going to steal her baby.

The fact that neither Missy nor I had actually benefited from the tragedy didn't seem to factor into the article. Jack did toss out a few theories—we wanted attention and publicity, or may-be because the baby had died, whatever we were planning had just gone horribly wrong. But to me, they seemed pretty lame.

Lame or not, the article had still managed to destroy my life.

I was now jobless, friendless, and homeless. I had no con-nections or opportunities. I was back in the same house and the same room I had grown up in.

I had been so close to changing my life for the better—to growing up, maybe getting a real social life and real hobbies, and maybe even going out on a real date. To finally *living*.

Instead, I had somehow regressed back to being a child … one who had lost nearly everything and would have to start over. Again.

I felt like a complete and utter loser.

Chapter 25

Nanna poked her head into my bedroom. "Knock, knock."

I sat up, pulling my earbuds out of my ears. I had spent the day staring out my bedroom window and listening to songs from old bands such as Pink Floyd, Simon and Garfunkel, and Metallica.

Nanna forced a smile. "Dinner is ready."

"Thanks," I said. I could still hear the tinny sounds of *Dark Side of the Moon* floating from my earbuds.

"I made homemade deep-dish pizza ... your favorite."

"Thanks," I said again.

"I opened a bottle of a nice red, as well. A pinot noir. Your other favorite."

"The perfect wine for pizza."

There must have been something in my voice she didn't like, maybe a dullness or lack of interest, because she put a hand on her hip and narrowed her eyes at me. "You need to eat. I know you didn't eat much breakfast or lunch."

I sighed. "I know. I'll be right there."

Nanna nodded and walked away, leaving the door open.

I sighed again, turning off my old iPod and putting in on the nightstand next to my powered-off phone. I hadn't touched it all day. What was the point? Nobody wanted to get in touch with me except for journalists, anyway, who I definitely wanted nothing to do with.

Slowly, I swung my legs out of bed and headed toward to the kitchen. Nanna was right. I did need to eat, even if I wasn't that interested in food. I had barely eaten anything for three days, since Saturday morning when my life came crashing down around me. It was hard to believe it had only been that long. It felt like much longer.

Nanna's smile was more natural when she saw me taking my seat at the kitchen table. "Help yourself," she said, placing the salad next to the stuffed pizza and cheesy garlic bread. "There's plenty."

"I see that," I said, putting a little bit of everything on my plate. I eyed the wine, which was the most appetizing thing on the table, but I refused to let myself have any until I got some food in my stomach.

Nanna's eyes had a little gleam to them, and I realized she had done it on purpose—poured a glass for me as a way of encouraging me to eat. She knew I wouldn't want to get sick in front of her.

I took a bite of pizza. My stomach rumbled, and I was suddenly conscious of how empty it was. "It's good," I said.

Nanna gave me a slight nod. Her glasses had fallen down her nose, giving her a slightly owlish expression. "Want to talk about it?"

I took another bite of pizza as I reached for my wine. "What's the point?"

"Well, it might help you process what happened, so you can move forward quicker," she said.

I made a face. "What, you're going to be my therapist now?"

She gave a slight laugh. "Hardly. But I do think it would be good for you to talk about it."

I sipped my wine. "Well, the exact thing I have always been afraid of happening again happened again. Even after I had structured my life so it wouldn't. So, yeah, it's a struggle."

She studied me for a moment, looking like she was about to say something, then pressed her lips together and shook her head.

"What?" I asked.

"Nothing," she said, reaching for the salad.

"It's something," I said. "What is it?"

She hesitated. "It's just … I think it's a little too soon."

"A little too soon?"

She waved the salad fork. "It's only been a few days. I know you're still processing everything."

I rolled my eyes. "When has that ever stopped you? What is it? I know you want to tell me."

Her lips curled into a small smile. "Fine. Don't say I didn't warn you."

I rolled my eyes again.

"Have you considered whether a part of you maybe wanted this to happen?"

My mouth dropped open. "What?"

"I don't mean you losing your job and moving back here," she said quickly. "Or …" she paused, cocking her head. "Maybe I do."

"What are you talking about?" I asked. "My life is a mess right now. Why would I want that to happen?"

Her expression softened. "Because, my love, you were stuck in a life that didn't suit you. Now, you're out."

I opened my mouth and closed it. I had no idea how to answer her.

Because she wasn't entirely wrong.

"My worst nightmare has come true," I said. "I was so careful, changing my name, keeping as low a profile as possible, especially online. How could you possibly say I wanted this?"

She reached over to take my hand. "Sweetie, think about it. You've built your life around a lie. Around pretending your past never existed. Of course you're unhappy. How could you not be? And how can you possibly build a new life if the truth isn't out there? So, while what happened is pretty drastic, I think a part of you wanted it to, so you could finally stop hiding in the shadows and create a more fulfilling life."

I moved my hand away. "I don't buy it."

"Then why were you hanging out with that girl ... what's her name? Missy, right?"

I blinked in surprise. In my mind's eye, I saw myself in the hospital that first day, standing in the waiting room until Cole got a look at me. Over and over again, I saw myself investigating with Cole, accompanying him in public. People knew Missy was his sister. If they had decided to dig around, they of course would find me, which Jack the reporter proved.

Had I really wanted this after all?

"But ... I was just trying to help her. I know what it's like. She needed someone in her corner."

"I'm sure she did, but she has a family, right? A brother, for sure. She didn't necessarily need you. Were you even friends before this happened? Even when you were kids?"

"I ... ah ..."

Nanna patted my hand. "It's okay. I know this has all been a huge shock. You're stronger than you think. You'll be okay."

"I wouldn't be all that sure," I muttered darkly into my pizza.

Nanna studied me, her expression considering. "I know that right now, it feels awful and unfair. And it *is* awful and unfair. But sometimes, the reason bad things happen is so we can heal from our past and move on. Maybe that's the opportunity here."

I stared at her. "How is any of this going to help me heal? It feels like all it's doing is re-traumatizing me."

Nanna's expression was full of love and compassion. "Oh, honey. That's certainly one perspective. But you can also choose to let this be a fresh start … one where you're done hiding and running from your past."

I wanted to argue with her. What she was saying was ridiculous. Of course I needed to hide from my past. Look what happened when everyone found out the truth. I lost my job, my apartment, my friends. Everything.

But some part of me, deep inside, recognized the truth in what she was saying. What if I just decided I didn't care who knew or didn't know about my past? What would that look like? Was it even possible?

Just contemplating a life where I wasn't spending all my time and energy hiding felt so … freeing. Like a huge boulder had rolled off my shoulders. I wondered if the hiding was protecting me like I'd always thought … or if it was actually draining me.

Have you lost your mind? Negative Nancy piped up. *Do you want to live the rest of your life as an outcast? Hiding in Nanna's house with no job or friends?*

But what if that wasn't what happened? I answered. *Other people have terrible pasts and are still able to live their lives and have relationships and jobs and be a part of a community. Why is it different for me?*

It just is, Negative Nancy snapped. *This never would have happened if you had just listened to me and not gone to the hospital. Everything was fine before then. You had a good job, a nice apartment, everything you could ever want. But instead, you throw it all away. And for what? For a guy who dumped you the moment it became inconvenient.*

That's not true, I argued, but there was a sinking pit in my stomach even as I answered.

Of course it is, Negative Nancy said smugly. *If it isn't, then where is he?*

I was still trying to figure out a response when the doorbell rang.

I froze. The media. They must have finally found me.

A tiny crease appeared between Nanna's eyes. "Are you expecting anyone?"

I shook my head slightly.

She picked up her napkin, pressed it to her lips, and got up. "I guess we better see who it is."

"Don't," I said. "It's better to ignore them."

"We'll see about that," she said, and marched out of the kitchen.

I squeezed my eyes shut, wondering if I should get my phone to call the cops. They could escort them away, right? Tell them to leave us alone?

I heard voices, but I couldn't hear specific words until I heard Nanna say, "Come in."

What? I jumped to my feet, ready to run out of the kitchen. Why would she invite reporters inside? Didn't she know I had no intention of talking to them?

I was edging away from the table when Nanna appeared, her face wreathed with smiles. "Tori, look who came to see you."

I was getting ready to tell her I didn't want to see anyone when I realized the two people following her were Cole and Missy.

Relief coursed through me (along with a little *Ha!* sent to Negative Nancy, who wisely didn't respond), and I pressed my hand against my chest. "I thought you were inviting a reporter in."

"Nonsense," Nanna said cheerily. "Pull up a chair," she said to Cole and Missy. "There's plenty."

I moved back to my seat as Cole and Missy sat down. Nanna disappeared into the kitchen for more plates and silverware. "How did you know I was here?" I asked.

"We didn't," Missy said as Nanna placed a plate in front of her.

"You didn't?"

"Your phone is off," Cole broke in. "Which I don't blame you for, of course. We didn't want to go to your apartment for obvious reasons, but I thought maybe Nanna would have a way to get a message to you."

"How did you find Nanna?"

Cole gave me a look.

I held out my hands. "Okay, stupid question. Why were you looking for me?"

"Because we have news," Missy said. Her cheeks were flushed, and her eyes sparkled with excitement. She bounced a little on her chair. "We found Marci."

"Really? That's wonderful! What did she say?"

"We haven't talked to her yet," Missy said, eying her brother. "Cole wanted to wait for you."

"It only made sense," he said, paying careful attention to putting a piece of pizza on his plate. "You were a part of all the other interviews. It didn't feel right not having you there."

Missy hid a smile.

A little ball of heat bubbled up in my stomach. I busied myself topping off my wine and filling Cole's glass.

"How did you find her?"

"Well, it was much easier knowing her name," Cole said. "We found her Facebook and Instagram accounts."

"Which were private, of course," Missy chimed in.

"But we were able to go through her friends' list on Facebook, and believe it or not, Missy has two shared friends with her."

"Really? Wow. That worked out."

"They aren't good friends," Missy said. "I met one of them at a party a couple of years ago, and she tagged me in a couple of pictures. I can't remember where the other one came from, but I think she might have been a friend of Renee's."

"So, did you private message them, or ..."

Missy shook her head. "We were going to, if we couldn't find another way, but I couldn't figure out a way to word it. 'Hey, do you know how to get in touch with Marci? I think she was my midwife when I gave birth and might have done something to my baby' didn't seem like the best way to open a conversation."

My lips curled in a smile. "Probably not."

"So, instead, we went through their newsfeeds." Missy rolled her eyes. "It took a while, believe me. I was looking for a picture or something with Marci tagged or mentioned."

"One of them had a few pictures of Marci, usually at a bar," Cole said. "Which still wasn't that helpful, but eventually, we found a picture of when Marci graduated from midwife school."

"That's a relief. At least she went to school," I said.

"Right," Missy agreed. "And in the post, it mentioned how Marci didn't have to work as a bartender anymore."

"It was a long shot," Cole said. "But we decided to call all the bars. I mean, if she wasn't working as a midwife anymore, it made sense she would go back to her old career."

I stared at both of them. "Wait. Are you serious? She's working as a bartender?"

"I know, right? Not only that, but she's working tonight. Her shift starts in an hour." Missy scooped up a mouthful of pizza. "This is wonderful, Mrs. Agnello," she said to Nanna.

Nanna beamed. "You can call me 'Bea,'" she said.

Chapter 27

"You sure you're up to this?" Cole asked his sister for probably the tenth time.

"I'm fine," Missy said through gritted teeth. While I could appreciate her frustration with her brother, I was on Cole's side with this one—Missy did not look well. The closer we had gotten to the bar, the paler she had become, and now that we were standing in front of it, she was nearly as white as a ghost.

I could see the worry in Cole's eyes, but he kept his mouth shut. He probably knew as well as I did that she needed to be a part of this for her own mental health.

Even if, in that moment, it looked like she was about to experience a massive setback.

Marci worked at what appeared to be a dive bar called Brews 'N Cues. Despite the fact it was in the middle of the week, there seemed to be a fairly decent-sized crowd.

"Should we go in?" I asked.

Missy nervously shoved her hair behind her ears. She was dressed in skinny jeans and an off-white peasant top and had even put on makeup. She looked good, the best I'd seen her yet, but it still couldn't mask her anxiety. "Let's do it," she said with a smile, but it appeared forced and uncertain.

I gave her a quick smile back, and with a slight nod at Cole, we headed for the front door.

The sound of pool balls knocking into one another greeted us when we stepped inside. Nearly half of the bar was all pool tables, and all of them were in use. There were also several dartboards and a foosball table, but those were less popular. High, round tables and stools were scattered about, and a good number of people occupied them, drinking mugs of beers.

Next to me, Missy's entire body went stiff. Both Cole and I paused, as well.

"See her?" I asked quietly.

Missy's lips were pressed together in a thin line. She gave a quick, sharp nod.

"Behind the bar?" Cole asked.

Another nod. I glanced toward it.

There were two women working. Both had short hair—one was white-blonde with pink tips and the other was nut-brown. They both wore tight black tee shirts, making it obvious that Pink Hair was definitely more endowed than Brown Hair, who was fairly flat-chested. Neither wore glasses.

"The one on the right?" Cole asked.

Another quick, sharp nod. That would be Brown Hair.

While I wasn't surprised that of the two, Brown Hair fit Beth's description more than Pink Hair, she didn't look nearly as mousy as Beth described. She was actually quite attractive, with an elegant, heart-shaped face with high cheekbones and huge brown eyes. Looking at her, I wondered if the reason she had worn such huge glasses was to cover up her face as much as possible.

Missy swayed slightly, and Cole reached out to steady her, his face alarmed. "Missy, you don't have to ..."

"I do," Missy interrupted. "Cole, I have to." She turned to look at her brother, but not before I saw the pain flash in her eyes. "I'll be fine." Her voice was gentler, then, but I could hear the steel behind it.

Cole met her eyes and nodded. "Then what are we waiting for?"

Missy straightened, squared her shoulders, and marched toward the bar. Even though Cole and I hadn't planned it, we both hung back a little, letting Missy go first.

She strode through the bar, winding her way around the people and tables. Pink Hair noticed her first and started to shift, as if to move to where she thought Missy was heading, so she could take her order. Missy ignored her, all her focus on Marci.

Marci was busy talking to a customer and pouring a beer and didn't notice Missy until she was practically at the bar. Her eyes widened, and for a second, she froze. Something flitted across her face, but it was so fast, I couldn't tell what it was. Instead, Marci plastered a professional smile on her face. "I'll be with you in a minute."

"Fine. I'll wait. *Sarah.*" Missy exaggerated the name as she leaned against the bar.

Marci's face didn't change, but I thought I saw something flicker in her eyes. "I'm sorry, are you talking to me?"

"Of course I'm talking to you, Sarah. Or would you rather I call you 'Marci'?"

Marci's expression was puzzled. "Do I know you?"

Missy's hands balled into fists. Her entire body seemed to be vibrating. "You helped deliver my baby, so yes, I would say you do know me."

Marci's eyes widened. "What? I don't know what you're talking about. You must have me confused with someone else."

"Everything alright, Marci?" Pink Hair asked, moving closer.

"I don't have you confused with anyone," Missy said, her voice getting louder and more agitated. "You pretended to be my midwife for months!"

"Midwife?" Pink Hair asked before glancing at Marci. "Is this one of your former clients?"

For the first time, Marci looked rattled. "Gigi, you know I haven't worked as a midwife in over a year now."

"You were working as one a month ago," Missy said.

Marci looked closely at her. "Wait a minute. I DO know you. You're the girl who thought the faeries stole her baby."

"That wasn't my fault," Missy said. "You tricked me."

The other patrons were starting to turn to watch the exchange. Gigi's expression had turned to a mixture of pity and wariness. "Honey, I'm so sorry for your loss, and I can totally understand why you want a drink right now, but maybe it would be better if you found a different bar."

"I don't want a drink," Missy said, getting more and more agitated. "I want my baby back."

This was definitely not going well. Gigi's expression turned flat, and she started to gesture at someone behind us, most likely a bouncer.

Cole took a quick step forward, placing a hand on Missy's arm. "Marci, would you be willing to answer a few questions for us? It won't take long. And then we'll go. Quietly."

Marci's face was cool. "I don't know what answers I could possibly have for you. I've never met this woman in my life."

"Liar!" Missy hissed.

"That's enough. I'm going to have to ask you to leave now," Gigi said.

"I'm not leaving until I get some answers," Missy said.

I stepped forward. "You should probably know our next stop is the cops. And they do have fingerprints they'll likely want to compare." Inwardly, I crossed my fingers, hoping it was true. And that she wouldn't call my bluff. I wasn't sure if the cops would take Missy seriously enough to question Marci.

Gigi didn't look impressed. "So what if the cops have fingerprints? If Marci wasn't there, then Marci wasn't there." Marci had quickly ducked her head and was focusing on the beer she was still pouring, so I couldn't see her expression.

"Yes, but do you really want all the aggravation of dealing with the cops in the first place?" I asked.

Gigi put her hands on her hips. "Are you threatening us?"

I held my hands up. "No, not at all. It's an honest question."

"Marci has nothing to hide. Right, Marci?" Gigi glanced at Marci, whose head was still down.

"I'm just saying Missy has a couple of her friends and neighbors who say they've seen her midwife, so I'm sure they could identify her," I said. "Between that and the fingerprints, there might be a certain amount of ... shall we say, 'red tape' that Marci is going to have to sort through. But if you'd rather deal with the police than us, then hey, that's fine. We can do it that way."

"Will you leave quietly if I talk to you?" Marci asked.

Gigi's mouth dropped open as she spun around to face her. "Marci, you don't have to give this ... this person any of your time. Let them call the police."

Marci held a hand up. "It's fine, Gigi. I'll give you five minutes, and no more, and then you'll go."

"Fine," I said quickly, before Gigi could talk her out of it.

"You've got this?" Marci asked Gigi.

"You don't have to do this," Gigi said again.

"It's five minutes," Marci said. "It's not a big deal. And it's better than having the cops poke around."

Gigi opened her mouth and then shut it again, pressing her lips together. "Five minutes," she said, mostly to me. "Any longer, and I'll be the one calling the cops."

"Deal," I said.

Marci took her apron off and fumbled around for her bag before leaving the bar. She indicated we should follow her by tilting her head.

She strode through the bar, moving swiftly and paying no attention to whether we were keeping up with her or not. She led us to a back hallway, which was where the bathrooms were, and through the back storage area, which was filled with boxes of booze and smelled of sour beer. Finally, we filed out a door that led to an alleyway.

By the time we made it outside, she was standing a few feet away in front of a garbage bin, facing the door, arms crossed. "What do you want?" she snapped. The only light was above the back door, and she was far enough away that most of her face was in shadow. The alley smelled of urine, rotten food, and puke.

"I want to know why you stole my baby," Missy said.

"I didn't steal anything," Marci said. "Your baby is dead."

Missy blanched, and her whole body shuddered. Cole put a hand on her arm. "So, you admit it. You ARE 'Sarah.'"

Marci didn't say anything for a moment. "It wasn't supposed to be like this," she said, her voice heavy. "No one was supposed to get hurt."

"What are you talking about?" Missy asked. "What about my baby?"

"I tried to help you," Marci said. "I tried to save you and your baby. Don't you understand?"

"But you lied to me," Missy said. "Why would you do that?"

"Because that was part of the deal," Marci said.

"Deal? What deal?" Missy asked.

"To keep you and your baby safe," Marci said.

"What?" Missy asked, completely perplexed.

"I think you need to start from the beginning," Cole said. "Starting with why you told Missy your name was 'Sarah.'"

Marci paused again. "You don't understand," she said, her voice low. "I made a mistake. I lost my medical license. It was stupid. But ... well, I was an addict. I loved being a midwife ... but I lost everything. So, this just seemed like such a perfect opportunity. I could be a midwife again, and help someone who really needed my help. I really admired you, you know. Going off your meds so you could have a healthy baby."

"Just stop," Missy said. "You used my disease against me. I still can't sort out the truth of what really happened."

Marci bit her lip. "I didn't want to do that."

"Wait, hold on," Cole said. "You did it on purpose?"

"I didn't want to," Marci said. "I didn't want to do any of that. But it was part of the deal ..."

"You need to start from the beginning," I repeated. "What deal are you talking about? Who approached you, and why?"

Marci sighed heavily. "He called himself 'Pan.'"

"'Pan'?" Cole asked. "Like a cookie pan?"

"Or Peter Pan," I said.

Marci nodded. "Yes, like that."

"Was that a first name or a last name?" Cole asked.

"I don't know."

"What about where he worked?" Cole continued.

"I don't know. All I know is he offered me a lot of money if I would become your midwife."

"How much?" Missy asked.

Marci looked away again.

"How much?" Missy asked again, taking a step closer.

"A hundred thousand dollars," Marci said.

"A *hundred thousand* dollars?" Cole asked, his voice disbelieving. "And you didn't question it?"

"Well, of course I did. I was told that your baby was very special and needed extra care. Money was not an issue. But it was important that Missy not know about the arrangement."

"Why?" Cole asked.

Marci shrugged. "I don't know. Something about the father. It was supposed to be anonymous. The father's identity needed to be kept a secret, or something. He made it seem like he was a celebrity." Marci gave her a hard look. "Was he a celebrity? Or a politician?"

Missy had gone very still. "None of your business," she said, her voice cold.

Marci let out a bark of laugher. "I probably deserve that. Anyway, if the father is rich and famous, it makes sense he wouldn't want the tabloids to know that he had gotten a bipolar woman pregnant, especially since you were going to be off your meds, and it all could get very messy. So, I agreed."

"The coffee shop?" Missy asked, her voice strangled. "You planned that?"

"No, someone else did," Marci said. "I was supposed to show up there at a certain time and look for you. I was told there would be an opening for me to introduce myself and get you to trust me. I was ..." she swallowed hard. "I was given information about you, so I would know the things to say to make it easier for you to trust me. I'm ... I'm sorry about that."

"So, it was all a lie," Missy said. "From the very beginning."

"I'm sorry," Marci said again. "I know you won't believe me, nor should you, but despite the fact I was briefed about you, I did come to genuinely like and care about you."

"Then why did you lie to me?" Missy threw her hands up. "All the things you said to me. The faeries taking my baby. Why would you tell me that?"

"I didn't want to," Marci said. "It was part of the job. Pan told me to do it."

"But why would he do that?" Cole asked. "If your job was truly to just to keep Missy and the baby healthy, why would you say such a thing to her?"

"Because Pan wanted Missy to have a home birth," she said. "They didn't want the attention a hospital birth would attract."

"But why?" Cole asked. "No one knows who the father is. Why would giving birth in a hospital change that?"

"I don't know," Marci said. "Although my impression was that Pan wanted to isolate Missy as much as possible, because they were afraid she might let something slip about the father or the father's identity. That's why they didn't want friends or neighbors looking in on her. Just me. Once she gave birth, I was supposed to get Missy back on her meds as quickly as possible, and once she was stabilized, then it would be safe for her to be around people again."

"I wasn't going to tell anyone," Missy said quietly.

"Well, I guess they couldn't take that chance," Marci said. "Truly, I'm sorry. I hated doing it. But Pan insisted."

"What happened the night I gave birth?" Missy asked, ignoring her apology. "I heard Jude cry. I know I did. What did you do to him?"

Marci was shaking her head. "I don't know what you heard, but your baby was dead. I'm just so sorry Missy."

"No! I don't believe it," Missy cried out. Tears were streaming down her face. "You took my baby."

"I didn't," Marci said. "You must believe me."

"No, no, no," Missy said, her legs giving out as she collapsed onto the broken asphalt.

"How could you leave her alone?" Cole asked. "You just left. Why didn't you stay with her, or get her to the hospital?"

Marci was staring at her. "I … I had to leave. Don't you see? I had … failed."

"My baby died, and you were worried about failing?" Missy asked.

"I'm just so sorry. I have to go," Marci said, turning to walk down the alley toward the front of the bar.

"No!" Missy howled. "I don't believe you. What happened to my baby?"

Marci's footsteps seemed to shudder for a moment, but she kept going, without turning around or saying another word.

Missy remained in a heap on the ground, like a broken doll, sobbing. Cole was kneeling next to her, holding her in his arms.

I had a feeling this was the first time she had really cried over the loss of her baby, which made what I had to do feel even worse.

I knelt down next to them. "Missy, you have to get up," I said quietly, my voice urgent. "We need to get out of here."

"Why?" Cole asked, as Missy continued to bawl.

"Because Marci isn't going back into the bar," I said. "She had her purse with her. She's probably getting ready to reach out to Pan right now to tell him that we're on to them, and she had to spin a story to send us on a wild goose chase."

Cole's eyes widened as the implications sunk in. "Missy, we gotta go. Now. We're in danger."

"I don't care," Missy said between sobs.

"Missy," I said, my voice urgent. "I know Marci was lying to us. About a lot of things. I suspect she may have been lying about your baby, and if I'm right, we need to get out of here. Now."

Missy let out a strangled sob. "You really think so?" she hiccupped.

I nodded. "I really do. But we have to go. Now."

Chapter 27

"You really think she was calling Pan?" Missy asked. We were back at Nanna's house, settled in the living room with new glasses of wine and freshly baked peanut butter cookies, although we were all too full from the huge dinner to touch them.

Missy had disappeared into the bathroom as soon as we arrived at the house. I had thought she just needed a place to continue her crying, as she had spent most of the drive to Nanna's sniffling in the backseat. But instead, she had cleaned herself up. Her eyes were still bloodshot, and her cheeks were flushed, but otherwise, she looked almost like herself.

"She went down the alley rather than through the back door," I said.

"We were in front of that door though," Missy said. "Maybe she thought it would be easier to go around to the front."

"Or maybe she was leaving and didn't want to answer any questions from Gigi," I said.

"She couldn't have left," Missy said.

"Why not?"

"Well ..." Missy waved one hand. "She told Gigi she'd be back."

I raised an eyebrow. "You think that would stop her?"

"And she would need to get her stuff," Missy added.

"She left her apron and grabbed her purse before she took us out to the alley," I said.

"That's right," Cole mused.

"But that still doesn't mean she was calling anyone," Missy insisted.

"Why are you defending her so much, when you know she lied to you?" Cole asked. "Everything she did was a lie. Why would you put calling Pan past her?"

Missy paused, twirling the straw in her club soda. "She could have killed me," she said, her voice low as she stared into her drink. "I was weak and completely at her mercy. But instead, she tried to help me. She tried to get me back on my meds. I just don't believe she would do anything to hurt me."

I took a sip of wine, pondering my next words. "You're more of a threat now," I said at last. "You're stable and on your meds, and you have two other people with you. You're not a half-out-of-her-mind woman who has just given birth, and you're starting to put it all together. Before, it would have likely caused more headaches to have killed you. But now? Knowing the truth? They may feel like they don't have much choice anymore."

Missy continued staring into her drink. "Maybe it's illogical, but I don't think she's a killer."

"She might not be, but that doesn't mean she isn't working for one," Cole said.

Missy gave Cole a sharp look. "You really think Pan is a killer?"

"He arrived at your home with a dead infant," I said. "Although it's true he might not have been responsible for the infant's death, I certainly wouldn't want to meet him in a dark alley."

Suddenly, in my mind's eye, I could see the dark, shadowy image from my nightmares, the white finger pressed against the bloodless lips. *Shhhh.*

Could that have been Pan?

My stomach churned, and I put my wine glass down, trying to keep myself from throwing up. I had been alone in a room with someone who was likely a killer. How much danger had I been in? Was I only still alive because I was so young when it happened?

Missy was staring at me as I struggled to keep myself from being sick. "Are you okay? You look like you've seen a ghost."

I pressed my fingertips against my mouth, feeling both hot and cold. "I'll be okay." I didn't feel like it was the right time to share my suspicions. I had to focus on keeping Missy safe and finding her baby.

Missy didn't look convinced, but she didn't push it. "You really think my baby is still alive?"

I nodded. This felt like much safer ground. "I do. I also think Marci knows more than she told us. It's possible she's in this deeper than she made herself out to be, as well. But it seemed clear she was lying about something, and I think one of those lies is that your baby died."

"If that's true, no wonder she didn't go back into the bar," Cole said. "She would have wanted to get as far away as possible, and quickly."

I nodded. "Which is why you need to tell the cops as soon as possible. So maybe they can track Marci down before she disappears again." While Missy was in the bathroom, I had convinced Cole to call the detective and tell him everything that happened and try to persuade him to bring Marci in for additional questioning as soon as possible. Cole reported back that the detective had promised to look into it, but it wasn't clear when that would happen.

"Maybe we need to track her down ourselves," Missy said, reaching over to place her drink on the coffee table. "If she knows where my baby is ..."

"I doubt she knows," I said. "That part, she probably wasn't lying about. Pan is probably the only one who knows that."

"But you just said you think she knows more than she told us," Missy said.

"Yes, but that's probably not it. Her job was to deliver a baby to Pan. She did that. There's no need for her to know the details after that."

"Besides, we have no idea where she lives," Cole said.

Missy slumped over. "This is impossible. The cops are never going to believe us."

"I wouldn't be so sure," I said. "If Marci doesn't return to work after tonight, that's going to look awfully suspicious."

"And that might trigger a deeper investigation," Cole said. He leaned over to lift up her chin. "We're not going to rest until we find your baby. I promise you."

"I second that," I said.

Missy looked between us, blinking her eyes rapidly as if to hold back tears. "You guys are the best," she said.

* * *

Shhhh …

I bolted straight up in bed, sure there was a dark, shadowy figure in the doorway, white finger pressed against his lips.

But of course, my bedroom was empty.

I collapsed backwards, rubbing my chest and trying to slow my breathing. I probably should have taken a Valium before going to sleep, as it should have been obvious that I was destined to have a nightmare after the evening I'd had. It wasn't like I had to get up and go to work in the morning, so I considered taking one right then. Based on the silvery-grey moonlight that lit my room, it was clear it was too early for me to be up. I needed to get back to sleep.

But I knew that would be impossible. At least until I calmed myself down. Or took a Valium.

I sighed as I stared at the ceiling. Normally, I would quietly make my way to the kitchen for a cup of tea, but as I knew both Cole and Missy were staying the night, I felt strangely reluctant.

The detective had called Cole back about an hour after we'd contacted him to let us know that Marci had not returned to work nor her apartment. They were still searching for her, but the fact she couldn't be found had raised his interest level. He also wanted to warn us to be careful.

Once Missy heard that, it was clear she didn't want to leave. Even though she and Cole were staying at a hotel, and Cole hadn't been using either of their real names, she didn't want to risk going there. Plus, neither of them wanted to leave Nanna and me alone, in case Pan was also tracking me.

"It just makes more sense if we stick together," Missy said.

Nanna had a spare bedroom with a double bed along with an air mattress, so Missy slept in the bed and Cole on the floor.

I knew the chances of running into Cole were minimal, and even if I did, what did it matter? But still. Just the thought of it made me uncomfortable.

C'mon Tori, get a grip. It's not like anything is going on between you.

Nor did it look like anything was going to start, what with all that was happening with Missy and our search for the truth.

After tossing and turning, I finally gave up and decided to get that cup of tea after all. Hopefully, I wouldn't disturb anyone.

I eased my way out of my room and padded down the hallway to the kitchen. I had just put the water on the stove to boil when a voice from behind me said, "I guess you really do have chronic insomnia."

Startled, I jumped back, just missing the kettle before whirling around. Missy was standing in the doorway. She gave me a sheepish smile. "Sorry. Didn't mean to scare you."

"That's okay. Do you want a cup, as well?"

"That would be great."

We were both silent as I made the tea and brought it to the table. Missy immediately cupped her hands around the mug, reminding me of the first night we sat at my kitchen table, when she told me the harrowing story of her pregnancy.

"So, what's keeping you up?" I asked.

"Can't turn my mind off," she said.

"Oh. Too many thoughts whirling around, huh?"

She nodded. "I can't stop thinking about Sarah. I mean Marci. I've been going through all my memories over and over, analyzing them, trying to figure out how I could possibly have been so stupid."

"You weren't stupid," I said. "You were manipulated by some horrible people."

Missy's smile was twisted as she sipped her tea. "It wasn't just her, though. That's the problem. How did this Pan person know I would have cramping at the coffee shop? Had he bribed one of the employees to put something in my coffee without my knowledge? Had someone snuck into my kitchen and put something in my food?"

I shivered. "That's a creepy thought."

"It is." She put her cup down. "Although not as creepy as thinking it was Dr. Broomer, after all."

My eyes widened. "That's right ... you mentioned that Dr. Broomer gave you something to drink."

Missy nodded. "Herbal tea. So, yeah. Cole was probably right." She was silent, staring at the wall. "I don't know what to do or who I can trust. I can't even trust myself. I'm still not clear how reliable my memories are." She slumped, her sorrow visible. "Maybe I didn't hear my baby cry after all."

"Well, I for one believe you," I said.

She eyed me. "Why?"

"Because Marci winced when you said it."

Missy looked surprised. She clearly hadn't expected that answer. She took a sip of tea, mulling it.

I watched her, wondering if now was the time to bring up the one thing that Missy had never addressed during this whole sordid mess.

The father.

Was he actually some sort of celebrity or famous person after all? Was he the one behind hiring Pan and Marci, as Marci said? Or was that another of Marci's lies?

It felt like the big missing piece. But Missy continued to avoid talking about it.

Why?

"Let's just say my baby was born alive. That would mean Marci did steal him," Missy said slowly. "And she was paid by someone to do so. But why? Why did they want *my* baby?"

"Well, there is a lot of money to be made on the black market for a healthy baby," I said, keeping my voice intentionally soft. "It's possible you were picked because you seemed like an easy target."

Missy blanched, wrapping her arms around her middle. "Because of my illness." Her voice was full of self-loathing.

"That and because the father wasn't in the picture."

My hope was that Missy would take my gentle hint and finally tell me about him. "You think my baby was *sold*?" she replied.

Inwardly, I sighed. "Probably to a rich couple who desperately wanted a child," I said.

"He should be with me," she choked out, her voice fierce.

"And we'll keep looking," I reassured her.

"But why me?" she asked. "If I'm right, not only was Marci in on it, but so was Dr. Broomer. That seems like a lot of money and effort to go after me. Wouldn't it be easier to snatch a baby out of a stroller?"

I spun my teacup around the table. "It might not have been you."

Missy looked confused. "What do you mean?"

"Well, it's possible it was because of the father," I said, eyeing her. "Marci seemed to think the father was a celebrity or something."

Missy's face shut down. "It's not the father."

"How do you know?"

"Because I know. He ..." She shook her head. "No one knows who he is. So, it's impossible."

"Why is it such a secret?"

"Because it is." For the first time, Missy looked angry. "The father would never be behind something like this."

I wasn't sure if I should press or not—on one hand, I was a little afraid she might leave in a huff and maybe never talk to me again, but on the other, if we wanted to find her baby, she had to stop keeping secrets. "If he had nothing to do with it, why won't you tell us his identity?" I asked. "What does it matter now?"

Her hands clenched into fists. "Because ... because ..." her jaw worked for a moment, and her face seemed to collapse. "You're making a bigger deal than it is. He knew his family wouldn't approve of me, so we kept our relationship a secret. It wasn't supposed to be a big thing. Just us having a bit of fun. But then ... well, we got more and more serious. And then I got pregnant. So, we decided we needed to continue to keep it a secret until the baby was born. Then, his family would have to accept me. We'd get married, and we could be a family. But ..." she stared into her tea. "It doesn't matter now. I lost Jude, one way or another, so it's over."

Her chest heaved a couple of times, but she didn't cry. Maybe she had wept all of her tears for her baby. "Have you talked to him?"

She shook her head violently. "I can't bear to face him. Regardless of which way it happened, I was responsible for taking care of our baby. That was my one job. He had been quietly supporting me, so I didn't have to worry about money or a job. All I had to do was take care of myself and our baby. And I couldn't do that. I failed him and our baby."

My heart broke seeing the pain and misery on her face. No wonder she didn't want to talk about him. "You said you were in love. Maybe you should reach out to him. He's probably suffering, too."

"Maybe," she said, her tone flat. "But before I do, I need more answers. I need to be able to look him in the eye and tell him what happened to his son." She looked away again, and it was clear from her body language that she was done talking about the father.

I wished there was something more I could say to her … something to comfort her, but at that point, the only way I could do that was by helping her find answers.

Maybe that would be enough.

"There's something else I wanted to ask you, if that's okay," she said after a long pause.

I looked at her in surprise. "Of course. Why wouldn't it be okay?"

She shifted in her chair, her expression uncomfortable. "It's just … well … one of the things that I keep going over and over in my head is why Sar .. Marci brought up the faeries?"

I stilled, my limbs suddenly unable to move, instantly very much afraid as to where this was going.

"I know it wasn't me who came up with the faery idea," Missy mused. "I know she was the one who said it first. I suppose it's possible she said something else, and I misunderstood, but she kept bringing it up. So why did she do that? And if you believe what she said tonight, Pan was the one who told her to do that. Why would he want me to think faeries were going to kidnap my baby?"

I squeezed my teacup between my hands, trying to soak the warmth into my chilled body. "Probably to discredit you. Everyone would think you were crazy, just like my mother was crazy. No one would take you seriously."

"Possibly," she said, lifting her cup to take a sip and eying me over the rim. "But it's also possible that maybe I wasn't the first to ever hear that particular suggestion."

You have to watch out for your little brother. Promise me.

I was squeezing the cup so hard, I was surprised it didn't shatter in my hands. My voice seemed to come from far away. "You think someone, like this Pan person, also suggested to my mother that the faeries were going to steal her baby?"

She cocked her head. "You don't think it's possible?"

"I … I don't know what to think."

She smiled a little. "You and me both." She put her cup down. "It would be interesting to know where your mother got the idea of the faeries. Do you think it would be worth it to ask her?"

"You want to see my mother again?" There was a frantic edge to my voice. I had just seen her. I couldn't go through that again.

Missy's face softened. "I know it's tough. But it might be helpful. Maybe you can even ask her about Pan … see if that name rings a bell."

So many thoughts were racing through my head. Was it possible my mother had been targeted because of her illness? And by the same person or organization that targeted Missy? Were they trying to steal babies from mentally ill women who wouldn't be able to defend themselves or their children?

With Missy, it made some sense. She was all alone. She would have been an easy target.

But my mother wasn't alone. She had a family. She had my father. She had me, although I wasn't much older than a baby myself at the time.

She shouldn't have shown up on any baby kidnapper's radar.

And yet …

The shadowy figure in Scott's room. My mother's insistence that Scott was in danger from faeries.

It had to be a coincidence. Or, maybe what happened to my family had inspired Pan to see if he could repeat history.

It couldn't be connected. If it was …

No. I wouldn't go there. The two events couldn't have anything to do with each other.

Because if they did, the unthinkable would have to be true.

My father was involved.

Chapter 29

"Tori, how lovely to see you again," Kim greeted me as I signed my name in the book. "Your mother is going to be thrilled to see you."

I gave her a quick, forced smile. "Still happy?"

"As a clam," Kim said, giving me a big smile. "I wish all our residents were as happy as she is."

I had told Missy I would consider asking my mother about the faeries, even though I had no actual intention of doing so. I made some noise about not wanting to upset her, and that I should maybe talk to her doctors first to see what they said. Missy agreed it was a long shot, and that upsetting my mother wasn't ideal. From there, the conversation was dropped.

But I couldn't let it go. I couldn't stop thinking about what happened to our family over twenty years ago, and what had just happened to Missy.

After Missy and Cole had left to go back to the hotel and check in with the detective, I found myself asking Nanna if I could borrow her car for a bit. I had the lie ready on my lips, but it turned out I didn't need it. All she asked was if I wouldn't mind stopping at the store for a few items.

Before I could think through the possibilities, I found myself parking Nanna's car in the spacious Sunny Meadows parking lot.

I found my mother in the large recreational room, sitting near the window. It was a comfy room with lots of couches and chairs, a fireplace on one side, a large screen TV on the other, and plenty of tables and chairs in between. A variety of games and puzzles were spread invitingly out, although only one person, an extremely thin younger woman who seemed to have lost big chunks of her hair, was interacting with the activities. She was slowly doing a jigsaw. Two other men were sitting in front of the television, their faces slack and drugged-looking, their eyes nearly catatonic.

My mother was looking out the window and humming to herself. The moment she saw me, her face lit up in a smile. "Vicky! You came back!"

"Hi Mom," I said, leaning over to kiss her cheek. Her hair was freshly shampooed, and I could detect a hint of floral lotion. Maybe this wasn't such a bad idea after all. Maybe I would finally get some answers, and maybe, just maybe, I would finally be able to put what happened to us all those years ago behind me once and for all ...

She squeezed my hand, and then craned her neck around. "Where's your sister?"

I stared at her blankly, my stomach slowly slithering to my feet. So much for her having a good day. "Mom, it's just me. I don't have a sister."

She squeezed my hand again. "Of course you do, dear. Maybe it's not official yet, but it will be soon." She laughed, a little tinkling laugh.

Official? What was she talking about? Did she think she could adopt another child? Was that why she had been so happy these past few weeks, because in her muddled mind, she was going to have another daughter? "What do you mean by 'official'?"

"Oh, well, you know." She seemed so giddy, so unlike the mother I normally visited. "I'm probably jumping the gun a little, but a mother always knows when her children are getting serious about someone."

Children? "Mom, it's me," I said, feeling hopeless and wondering if I should even try and correct her. "I'm ..." my voice caught in my throat. "I'm your only child."

My mother sighed. "Oh, Vicky. I know you've had your issues with your brother in the past, but that's no reason to pretend he's not your brother."

I squeezed my eyes shut. Why did I even bother to come? I should have known better. No wonder my mother had been in such a great mood—her current delusion was that she still had two children, not one.

Except … that wasn't actually true. Her current delusion was apparently that she had THREE children, not one.

My mind flipped back over the conversation we'd just had … "not official yet" … "a mother knows when her children are getting serious about someone."

I thought about how she had immediately warmed up to Missy, acting like they already knew each other.

It's probably nothing, I told myself. *My mother just inserted Missy into her current delusion. That's all.*

Nothing else made any sense.

Slowly, my knees buckled, and I sat down on the couch beside her. "Mom," I said, trying to keep my voice casual. "When you asked about my sister …"

My mother's eyes lit up. "Yes, how is she?"

"Missy is doing great," I said, seeing if the name triggered anything. My mother continued smiling, so I kept going. "She was so happy to meet you last time."

"Oh!" My mother clasped her hands together. "Tell her I was thrilled to meet her, too. I was so excited when I realized Scott was getting serious about someone, especially someone as lovely as her. It's going to be so exciting to plan a wedding." She tittered gleefully.

"Yes, it will," I said. "And how is Scott doing? I haven't seen him in a while."

"Oh, he's doing great. Did I tell you he came by to see me?"

My mouth was dry. I told myself I shouldn't be doing this … I shouldn't be feeding into her delusion, but I also found I couldn't stop. "No, you didn't."

"Oh!" My mother's eyes fluttered. "He was so handsome in his suit. He's doing so well, too. I'm so proud of him."

"That's wonderful," I said, forcing the words out through numb lips. "Was Missy with him?"

"Well, of course! Otherwise, I wouldn't have seen her." My mother's face seemed to shift, her brow puckering in confusion. "I think. But it doesn't matter. What matters is they'll be getting married soon, and it will all be wonderful."

"I'm sure. Um, do you happen to remember when you saw them?"

My mother frowned in concentration. "It was yesterday, right? Or maybe it was last week? No, it was longer than that. Heavens, it's so difficult to keep track of time in this place. One day blurs into another. I'm sure Dr. Janson would remember. Or Nurse Chelsea."

Yes, it might be a great time to have a chat with one of the staff members. "Good idea," I said, and I took a deep breath. I wasn't sure if I should ask my next question or not, but at that point, I felt like I had no choice. "Also, I was wondering, did you ever have a chance to ask Scott about the faeries?"

My mother's face clouded over, and she shook her head violently. "Don't say anything to Scott about that. He doesn't remember anything about the faeries."

"He doesn't?"

She continued to shake her head. "No." She leaned closer, whispering to me. "They wipe your memory, you know. So you don't remember."

I kept my voice low, as well. "Did they do that to you?"

"They did, but it didn't work." She tapped her forehead with her index finger. "They think they got me. They think I don't remember. But I do. I remember it all. I know what they did to me. They set me up. They took away my son, and they locked me in here. They thought they could erase my memories, but I showed them. I'm stronger than they think."

I was suddenly overcome with a deep sadness. "You are, Mom. You're definitely stronger than they think."

Her gaze shifted, and suddenly, she was seeing me. Really seeing me, in a way I didn't think she had since before she was pregnant with Scott. "Oh, my dear Vicky." Her voice broke, and I saw the shine of tears in her eyes. "What I did to you ... it's unforgivable. I'm so very sorry."

My own throat was tight. "It's okay, Mom. You weren't yourself."

"No, it's not alright. I should have known better. I shouldn't have listened to them. I was so, so wrong."

I swallowed, trying to keep myself together even though I really wanted to burst into tears and throw myself into her arms, like I did when I was child. But I couldn't do that, if I wanted the truth. And this was the moment. "Who's 'them'?"

My mother pressed her lips together in a thin straight line. "The faeries."

The moment had passed. My heart sank. "The faeries?"

My mother's face seemed to crumble, like she was going to cry. "I'm so sorry, Vicky. They told me they were going to take Scott, and I should have listened. I thought I could protect him, but I couldn't. I messed everything up. It's all my fault."

"No, it's not your fault," I said, alarmed. My mother seemed to collapse in on herself, tears running down her face. She started rocking and muttering to herself.

"Everything alright, Cora?" One of the nurses had materialized next to us. "Oh dear. It might be time for a little break, don't you think?" She put her hands on Cora's shoulders and gave me a compassionate smile. "She's been in such a good mood. We probably just need to let her rest a little, and she'll be right as rain."

"Of course," I said as my mind continued to replay the words my mother had just said.

They told me they were going to take Scott, and I should have listened.

"They." Who was "they"?

I met the nurse's eyes and smiled my most professional smile. "Would it be possible to speak to Dr. Janson?"

* * *

"It's so nice to meet you," Nurse Chelsea said with a big smile as she ushered me into a small, well-lit, private waiting area. Dr. Janson wasn't available, but Nurse Chelsea was, and said she would be delighted to speak to me.

My head was buzzing with all the thoughts, and it took all my energy to focus on taking deep, steady breaths. If I didn't, I felt like I was going to shatter into a million little pieces, and I had to keep it together.

Nurse Chelsea was younger than I pictured her, which was my age or maybe a few years older. Her long blonde hair was in a top knot, and her eyes were a startling shade of blue. The room she had led me to was decorated in soft peach and cream, elegant and tasteful, like everything else at Sunny Meadows. The smell was even understated—a faint whiff of roses and lemon. Nurse Chelsea shut the door behind me as I perched uncomfortably on the edge of the sofa.

"Your mother is a joy," she said as she sat on the matching chair. A glass coffee table with a basket of peach plastic flowers was between us. "We love having her with us."

"I'm glad to hear that," I said.

Nurse Chelsea smoothed down her white pants and laid a file folder on her lap. "So, you have some questions for me?"

"I do. Everyone has been telling me what a good mood my mother has been in for the past few weeks or so."

Nurse Chelsea smiled broadly. "Yes. It's been wonderful to see."

"I agree. So, I was wondering if there was something that occurred to make her so happy."

Her smiled dimmed slightly. "What do you mean?"

"Well, was there a medication change or something like that?"

"Oh, yes. Of course." She opened the file and started flipping through the pages. Her nails were polished and looked freshly manicured, even though they were cut very short. "I don't think there were any changes to her medication, but I'll double check. Sometimes, things just finally start to click. We don't always understand why."

She seemed a little nervous, although maybe I was reading more into the situation. It was all I could do to not leap across that glass coffee table and snatch the file from her lap. My entire life, I had been waiting for answers, and now, when I was right at the edge of finally getting some, it felt like pulling teeth.

"Of course," I murmured. "But maybe it was something else. Like maybe something happened?"

Her fingers trembled for a moment, and she closed the file. "Look, I know what happened was unacceptable, but we've taken steps to rectify it, so it will never happen again."

Alarm bells started going off in my head, so loud I could barely hear the sound of the blood roaring in my ears. "Maybe you better start from the beginning," I said. My voice sounded hollow, like it was coming from far away.

Nurse Chelsea just sat there for a moment, her hands clasped, her head bowed. After a moment, she seemed to steel herself, and she lifted her chin to meet my gaze. "No one could have known she would have reacted the way she did. We can't be blamed, when she's never done anything like that before."

I pressed my hands against my thighs, like I was physically keeping myself on the couch and away from throttling her until she told me every last word she was hiding from me. "Please start from the beginning."

"It should have been like every other time Mr. Duckworth came to visit," she fretted.

I blinked at her, trying to figure out if I heard her right over all the noise in my head. "Mr. Duckworth?"

"Yes." She gave me a sharp look. "You do know the Duckworths own Sunny Meadows, right?"

Did I know that? I couldn't recall, but it seemed to me there was a faint connection in the corners of my memory. It certainly fit what the Duckworths generally invested in. "So, Mr. Duckworth visits?"

"Yes. He visits all his properties a few times a year. He looks around, talks to the staff, the residents … you know, that sort of thing."

There was something about the Duckworths I thought I should be remembering. This wasn't the first time that family had come up in the past couple of weeks. But my mind was too overwhelmed in that moment to place it. "Go on."

"So, it should have been like every other visit. But it wasn't. Cora, well, she got really excited. She wanted to touch Mr. Duckworth and talk to him. Of course, we got her under control."

"Was Mr. Duckworth upset about this?"

Nurse Chelsea's eyes widened. "Oh no. He was very gracious. He understood these things sometimes happen. And we thought it was fine, but then …" she bit her lip, her eyes glancing everywhere around the waiting room. "We're still not sure how it happened, but she somehow got ahold of Mr. Duckworth's phone."

This was so not what I thought she was going to confess. I could only sit there, dumbfounded. "My mother ... stole Mr. Duckworth's phone?"

Nurse Chelsea nodded unhappily. "Yes. Worse, she managed to unlock it, although we think Mr. Duckworth had put it down on a table after he had gotten a text and she ...well, took it."

I was flabbergasted. "Weren't you watching her? How did that happen?"

"I can assure you we keep a very close eye on our residents at all times, but ..." she shook her head. "We had a situation with another resident, who we've been having some challenges getting stabilized on her meds, and that caused another resident to act out, and it was ... well, it was a perfect storm. Somewhere in the middle of all that chaos, Cora slipped away with his phone."

I was still trying to get my head around all of what she was saying. "So ... did she do anything to it? Like break it, or anything?"

"Oh no. Nothing like that. I'm not really sure what she was doing, but Mr. Duckworth said it didn't look like she had hurt anything."

"Was he ... upset?" I was starting to wonder if my mother was in some sort of legal trouble.

She bit her lip again. Her pale-pink lipstick was starting to smear. "He understood. He knows when you're running a home like this one, sometimes unexpected things can happen."

She didn't really answer the question. "Is my mother in trouble?"

"Oh, no! Not at all. I didn't mean to imply that. No, she isn't. He was ... well, he was upset. You understand he has private, confidential information on his phone, and one of our residents going through it is not ideal. But it didn't seem like she had done much other than scroll through his photos."

Scrolled through his photos? Could there have been something in his photos that reminded her of Scott?

Or … Missy?

But Nurse Chelsea had said that my mother had been excited when she first saw Mr. Duckworth, wanting to touch him and talk to him. Was it possible he reminded her of Scott?

"How old is Mr. Duckworth?"

She looked a little surprised at the question. "Oh, he's close to sixty, I would imagine."

I felt deflated. There was no way a sixty-year-old would remind my mother of Scott. "And you said Mr. Duckworth had been here before?"

"Yes, he's here a few times a year."

None of this was making sense, and suddenly, I was exhausted. The entire afternoon was a wild goose chase. My mother finding Mr. Duckworth so interesting out of the blue made no sense. "And my mother has never shown any interest in him before?"

"Well, she hadn't seen him before."

I looked at her in confusion. "I thought you said Mr. Duckworth is here a few times a year. How could my mother not have seen him before now?"

Nurse Chelsea's eyes widened. "Oh! I thought you knew. Mr. Duckworth had sent his son this time. Will."

"Will?" I vaguely remembered that Mr. Duckworth had a son. He was a couple years younger than me, if I recalled.

"Yeah, since he's going to take over the business, Mr. Duckworth sent him."

The roaring was back in my head. "So this was the first time my mother had seen Will."

"Yes." Nurse Chelsea shook her head. "And she was so excited. I don't know what got into her that day, or why she would take his phone the way she did, but something sure got into her."

***

The sun was just beginning to set, casting long shadows across my father's house.

The house from my childhood. The house from my nightmares.

I was parked across the street. I had no concept of how long I had been sitting there. I couldn't even remember driving to Redemption. Actually, I couldn't remember anything since I'd left Sunny Meadows.

The roaring was back in my brain. I couldn't think over the noise.

Why had my father never moved? It was a large house—four bedrooms, three bathrooms, a family room, and a living room. It was much too big for a single man, but even if it wasn't, why would he choose to stay in a house that contained such terrible memories? The death of his son, the madness of his wife, the breakup of his family?

It made no sense.

Unless ... he was forcing himself to relive those failures and sufferings over and over.

Punishing himself, because he wasn't able to save his family.

Or ... maybe it was some other, darker reason.

My parents had bought the house when my mother was pregnant with me. Clearly, they had high hopes of growing their family, despite my mother's mental issues, although according to all accounts, her symptoms were much milder when she'd had me.

Something changed. I wondered what.

Did it have anything to do with Scott?

The buzzing was growing louder in my head. I couldn't stand it anymore. I opened the door, climbed out of the car, and began the long trek up to the front door.

I knew my father was home. I had seen the lights on in the house and him moving across the living room window. He was working at home more often now, out of an office he'd set up in one of the bedrooms.

I reached the front porch and slowly climbed the steps. Three more steps, and I was in front of the door.

I rang the bell.

I listened to the footfalls, imagining my father walking through the hallway, down the stairs, and past the kitchen. There was a pause as he reached the door, no doubt looking through the peephole, before flinging it open.

"Tori," he said. He wore navy sweatpants and a light-blue tee shirt. His hair was sticking up on one end, as if he had been running his hands through it. He was smiling when he opened the door, but as soon as he got a closer look at my face, it dried up. "Oh no. What's going on? Did something happen to Nanna?"

"Nanna is fine," I said. "Can I come in?"

"Of course, yes, of course," he said, moving back to allow me to step inside. "Was there another story about you in the paper? Those jackals. I'm so sorry you've had to deal with that."

"Let's sit down," I said, walking toward the kitchen without waiting for him. I went to the table—the same one I had seen him sitting at all those years ago, surrounded by bills and booze. I pulled out a chair and sat down. Confused, he joined me, sitting across from me.

"Tori, what's going on?"

"I saw mom today," I said.

His eyes widened. "Oh no. Did something happen to your mom? Sunny Meadows should have called me."

"Mom is fine," I said. "She's happier than she's been in years."

"Oh." My father sat back in his chair, looking even more perplexed. "Well ... that's good news, right?"

"It could be. Except she apparently thinks Will Duckworth is her son. Why would she think that?"

He blinked, and something flickered across his face, so fast I couldn't tell what it was. "Because she's not well. You know this."

I slammed my hand onto the kitchen table, so hard I made the white ceramic salt-and-pepper shakers tip over. "Don't lie to me," I hissed.

His expression shifted to anger. "Now, you listen to me, young lady. You don't get to come into my house and accuse me of lying to you. And why on Earth would you believe your mother, knowing her background, over me?"

"Because both my mother and Missy had the same story fed to them while they were pregnant. That the faeries were going to take their babies."

"Missy? You mean the bipolar woman who was off her meds when she gave birth? Tori, I'm not trying to be cruel, but neither of these women were in their right minds at that time. Their word is hardly credible."

"Yet they both had stories fed to them from other people about faeries taking their babies," I said. "You don't think that's strange?"

"How do you even know that? Because that bipolar woman is telling you?" His tone was scornful.

"Because we found the woman who was feeding her the lies, and *she* told us," I said.

My father's face shifted slightly. "Oh. Well, that's unfortunate. I'm sorry your friend had to go through that. It still doesn't have anything to do with your mother."

"Except that Will is also the father of Missy's son," I said. "The same man who my mother happens to think is *her* son. Quite a coincidence, wouldn't you say?"

He stared at me, his mouth slightly open, like he wanted to say something, but nothing came out.

I leaned across the table. "I want the truth. No more lies. I'm sick of them. What really happened to Scott?"

He didn't answer. I could see his Adam's apple bob when he swallowed. He seemed to have aged in that moment, appearing twenty years older than when I had first walked in. Again, I saw him as he was all those years ago, propping me up on the couch so I could feed Scott with a bottle, playing with both of us on the floor, me giggling as he tickled me.

He was my rock back then. Even at that age, I knew I couldn't completely trust my mother, as I was never sure about her mood swings.

But my father? Him, I knew I could trust.

Until now.

My father took a deep, shuddering breath.

"The year before Scott was born was a terrible year," my father began. "Your mother and I were having problems, and we agreed to a trial separation."

I blinked. "I don't remember that."

"You were pretty young," he said. "And we tried really hard to keep it from you. You and your mother continued living here, but I got another place. I would still stop by several times a week to see you. Your mother," he swallowed again. "Well, she was with someone during that time. I don't know who. But eventually, she broke it off with him and told me she wanted to try again, so we did. I hadn't wanted the separation anyway, so I was happy to come home.

"It wasn't until later that I learned she was pregnant. And that the baby wasn't mine."

I sucked in my breath. "Wait. Scott was my half-brother?"

He nodded unhappily. "Your mother swore she didn't know when she came back to me. She told me as far as she was concerned, he was mine, no matter what. But she also said she would understand if I didn't want any part of it. I was pretty upset at first, but after a few days, I calmed down and decided I was okay with it after all. We had both wanted a large family with lots of kids ... that's why we bought a big house to begin with. And we had always talked about adoption being an option for us if Cora couldn't handle the pregnancies. So, for me at least, it wouldn't be any different from adoption.

"For the first few months, everything was fine, but then, everything went downhill at once. I lost a couple of big clients, but even worse, none of my proposals were being accepted. Suddenly, all my jobs just ... dried up. I couldn't pay my bills, the bank was threatening to call in my loan, and your mother was getting more and more mentally unstable. I had no idea what to do.

"So ... I did something I never thought I would."

"You *sold* Scott?" My voice was high-pitched and brittle, as though each word shattered in the air as it left my mouth. "Is that how you got the money? Because you sold your 'son'?"

My father winced. "It wasn't like that," he said. "That thought never crossed my mind."

"Then what did you do?"

My father seemed to shrink into his seat. "I called George."

"George who?"

"George Duckworth."

Again, the Duckworths. "George Duckworth? The head of the richest family in Riverview? Why on Earth would you call him? How do you even know him?"

"He's my half-brother."

My jaw dropped. "Half-brother? I thought you were an only child."

"My mother was George Senior's secretary. They had an affair, and she got pregnant."

"Seriously? You're telling me I'm related to the Duckworths?"

"Yes. He's your grandfather." My father sighed again. "Of course, it was all hush hush. No one was ever to know. My mother got some money to help raise me, and I got some money once I turned 21, with the stipulation that what I received would be it—there'd be no more. I used that money to start my company and put the down payment on this house.

"But then, I was in danger of losing it all. The house and the business. I had to do something, and the only thing I could think of was to see if George would help. I thought he could maybe lend me some money, or speak to the bank about my loans, or maybe even help me land a few projects. Anything, really. I was desperate.

"Well, as it turned out, he did happen to want something."

My mouth was so dry, my tongue was stuck to the roof of my mouth. "He wanted Scott."

My father dipped his head. "Yes. He wanted Scott."

Even though his voice was quiet, his words slammed into me, like bullets into my gut.

My entire life was a lie.

And I felt like a fool.

"All these years, you let me think I was crazy," I said. I wanted to scream the words, to howl in frustration, but instead, they came out broken and jagged.

"And I'll never forgive myself for that," he said. "But it was better you didn't know. Don't you see that?"

"No, I don't. Everyone thought I was crazy. *I* thought I was crazy. And some people even thought I killed Scott! And what about mom? Look what it did to her!"

"I know, I know. I just … I was so desperate. I was losing everything. And your mother was in no position to help. Not only that, but she was in no position to move. If we lost the house, and I had to take her somewhere else, in her condition … I couldn't chance it."

I pressed my fingers against my temples. "I can't believe I'm hearing this. So, you just said 'yes'?"

"Not right away," my father said heavily. "It took a few weeks of things continuing to spiral out of control and get even worse. But yes, eventually, I agreed. I figured your mother was so sick, she wouldn't bond with the baby much anyway, and you were so young, you probably wouldn't remember much. So it would just be me who would remember. I also figured we could have another child. As soon as your mom was better, we could try again, or maybe look into adopting."

"I just … I don't understand any of this. Why would George Duckworth even want Scott anyway?"

"I guess it was a stipulation in his father's will. If he didn't have a child, he wouldn't inherit the fortune. It would end up going to charity. Viola couldn't have children, and they didn't want to adopt the normal way, because he was supposed to have his *own* child, not an adopted one. So, that's why he wanted Scott. He figured since I was his half-brother, it would be close enough."

"He didn't know Scott wasn't yours?"

My father shook his head, his expression defeated. "I didn't tell him."

My head was pounding. I dug my fingers into my temples. "I don't understand. How was this supposed to work? Wouldn't anyone be suspicious when Viola suddenly had a baby despite not being pregnant?"

"Remember, the Duckworths were in Riverview, and I was in Redemption. Once we made the arrangements, Viola went to Europe, where she stayed for several years with Scott. She had some family living there, and George was visiting. They told everyone they wanted their son to have the opportunity to be immersed in other cultures and languages while he was still young. I think he was four or five when they brought him back."

I couldn't believe what I was hearing. I felt like my entire life was crashing down around me, shattering into millions of pieces. How would I ever be able to put it back together again? "Who else knows?" I asked, my voice cracking, as if it were as fractured as my life.

"No one."

"What about Nanna? Did she know?"

"No! No one else knew."

"So, you mean to tell me you've kept it a complete secret all these years?"

"What choice did I have?" he asked, his voice bitter. "You have no idea. George is ... well, let's just say he's not at all like his public persona. He can be ruthless. If anyone had found out the truth, he would have ruined me. Ruined our entire family."

"And you let someone like that raise your son? My brother?"

"I didn't want to! I didn't have a choice. Besides, I'm sure he was good to Scott. He was raising Scott as his son. That's completely different from a competitor or even a half-brother he viewed as competition."

I pressed my fingers against my temples again. The roaring in my head was so loud, I thought I might go mad. I couldn't think or focus. "You lied to me," I said. "My entire life has been built on a lie."

"Tori, that's not true," he said, his voice desperate. "You must see how it was better you didn't know. It's better that no one knew. And it's not like I sold Scott on the black market or anything like that. He was raised by one of Riverview's wealthiest, most powerful families. He had the life most people only dream about." He reached for me, but I jerked away so quickly, I nearly fell backwards.

"Tori! Be careful ..."

"Don't touch me," I hissed, untangling myself from my chair and backing toward the front door.

My father stood up as well. "Tori, wait. Don't go like this. Let's talk about it ..."

"Oh, *now* you want to talk?" I interrupted, my voice on the edge of hysteria. "All those times I asked you for the truth ... I *begged* you for the truth, and you refused! You've lost the right to ask me for anything anymore."

"Tori ..."

I held my hand up. "Stop. Just stop. I have to go."

"Tori, please." My father's voice was broken. He stood in the hallway, head hanging, the picture of defeat. "You shouldn't drive in this condition. Stay. Let's talk about it."

Another time, another place, I would have gone to him and given him a hug. My heart would have swelled, finally feeling the love from him I had desperately longed for all my life.

But not after what I'd just learned. And maybe not ever again.

"I never want to speak to you again," I snapped before stalking out the door.

Chapter 30

Cole's eyes widened when he saw me. "Tori, what happened?"

"I need to speak to Missy." My voice was eerily calm, betraying the storm that continued to rage in my head.

I have no idea how I got back to Riverview, or how long I drove aimlessly around. I couldn't remember any part of the drive. A part of me supposed I should be grateful I hadn't gotten into a wreck.

Eventually, the chaos in my head cleared up enough for me to realize I needed to talk to Missy.

Immediately.

I texted Cole to find out where they were, telling him I had urgent news. I wasn't sure what I would have done if he hadn't texted me back right away, but he did, including the name of the hotel and the address. Springhill Suites.

"Of course," he said, stepping back to allow me to enter.

Missy was sitting on the couch, dressed in her sleep outfit. Was it that late? I had no sense of time anymore. She looked shocked as well when she saw me. "Tori, what happened? Is everything okay?"

I ignored her question. "It's Will, isn't it?"

She went pale. "I … What?"

"Who's Will?" Cole asked.

"Will Duckworth," I said.

Cole stared at me. "Will Duckworth? What does he have to do with anything?"

Missy swallowed hard. "I don't know what you're talking about."

I took two steps toward her. "Don't lie to me," I hissed. "I've had it up to here with lies."

Missy's eyes were huge in her face. "You don't understand. I can't ..."

"You can," I snapped. "And you will. I want the truth."

"Wait," Cole said. "Are you saying *Will Duckworth* is the father?"

Missy's eyes never left mine. "How did you find out?"

"*What?*" Cole yelped. "It's true? You were dating Will Duckworth, and you never told me?"

I closed my eyes. All the strength seemed to drain out of my legs, and I simply collapsed on the floor. I hadn't realized until that moment how much I didn't want any of it to be true. Even after my father had told me everything, a part of me still hoped there was another explanation—that my father hadn't done what he said ... that he was somehow trying to protect me by making the whole thing up. But now, hearing Missy corroborate my suspicions sucked that final, tiny sliver of hope right out of me.

How was I possibly going to pick up the pieces after this?

"You don't understand," Missy was saying to Cole. "I couldn't tell you. I couldn't tell anyone."

"I'm not just anyone," Cole said. "I'm your brother. Your twin. You should have told me you were dating the son of the most of powerful family in Riverview."

Missy was shaking her head. "I just ... I can't think. Cole, can we talk about this later? Tori, I need to know. How did you find out? What does this have to do with Jude?"

My mouth was so dry. I licked my lips. "Will is my brother."

Silence. They both stared at me, their expression blank and uncomprehending.

Cole was the first to speak. "I ...I thought you were an only child now." His voice was cautious, as if he was approaching a cornered wild animal, and he wasn't sure how it would react.

I let out a laugh that sounded more like a yelp. "You know I'm not an only child. This whole nightmare started because of my brother."

He was watching me carefully. "But your brother isn't ... here."

"You're right." I looked at Missy. "That's why you need to call Will. Get him over here. Now."

Missy had the same careful expression on her face. "You're not possibly suggesting that Will is ..."

"Scott? Yes, that's precisely what I'm suggesting. Actually, I'm not suggesting it at all. I'm telling you. That's why you have to call him."

Cole and Missy's eyes flickered toward each other. "Tori, you must see how impossible this is ..." Cole began.

"How old is Will?" I interrupted, turning back to Missy.

"I don't see how ..."

"How old is he?"

She glanced at Cole. "He's twenty-three."

"Which makes me five years older than him."

"That doesn't prove anything," Cole said gently. "There are lots of twenty-three-year-olds."

"Okay," I said, feeling the energy drain out of me. "It doesn't even matter. You need to call Will and get him here, because he's the only one who's going to be able to find Jude."

Missy paled. "Will had nothing to do with this. He would never hurt his son."

"I didn't say he had anything to do with it," I said. "In fact, I'm fairly certain that he didn't. But that doesn't mean he's not the only one who can fix it."

Missy chewed on her lip and shot Cole a helpless gaze. Cole breathed out loudly from his nose. "I'm still having trouble processing how Will Duckworth is suddenly involved," he grumbled. "But regardless, maybe if you told us why you think Will is your brother, Missy would have an easier time convincing him to come here."

Suddenly, I was exhausted. I wanted nothing more than to curl up in bed and go to sleep. I felt like I could sleep for hours, maybe days. Maybe I would never wake up.

"I'm sure it would be easier for you," I said. "But I'm only telling the story once. So, when Will gets here, I'll tell it to all of you. In the meantime, the longer you wait, the longer Jude is away from you, and who knows where they'll end up taking him."

That was enough for Missy. She jumped off the couch to find her cell phone, going into her bedroom and shutting the door.

* * *

I don't know what Missy said to get Will to come to the hotel room in the middle of the night. She was gone for a while, and while I could hear her voice on the other side of the door, it was too low to make out the words.

Cole paced around the room muttering to himself, mostly about Will and his sister, as far as I could tell.

I stayed where I was, splayed out in the middle of the floor on the thin and worn carpet that smelled faintly of cigarettes. I wasn't sure I could move even if I wanted to … my limbs felt like they belonged to a different person.

Eventually, Missy emerged from the bedroom, announcing Will would arrive in twenty minutes. Cole paused his pacing to stare at his sister.

"How did this even happen?" he asked.

"We'll talk about it later," Missy said.

"But I don't get it," he said. "How did you even meet Will Duckworth?"

"Cole, not now," Missy said. "Why don't you get us all something to drink?"

We ended up sitting in silence, drinking wine out of plastic glasses as we waited.

When the knock at the door finally came, we all jumped, although Missy was the one who almost spilled her wine, as she hadn't drunk much of it.

"I'll get it," she said, getting up from the couch and striding past her brother. Cole followed her. I stayed where I was, my back to the door. My entire body had tensed up, and my stomach was in giant knots. This was such a stupid idea. Why would I have demanded Missy bring Will to us? He wasn't going to believe me. Who would believe such a ridiculous story? This was crazy.

Worse, what would he do with the information? Would he tell his father and get my father in trouble?

I was still so angry at my father, I (almost) didn't care. He should pay the consequences for what he did. In fact, I reminded myself, he was the last person I should be worrying about.

I wasn't sure if I completely believed that, but my head was spinning around so furiously, I couldn't think straight at all. The doubts rushed in.

Maybe I should leave, before I did something I would come to regret. Maybe I really do need to sleep on it and see how I feet in the morning, when I might at least be able to order my thoughts in a cohesive manner.

Although it wasn't just about me. Missy was a part of this, too. Not to mention an innocent baby. I couldn't walk away, especially if I had the missing piece that could bring Jude back to Missy right in front of me. I had to at least try.

No matter the cost.

"Tori," Missy said, circling around so she could stand in front of me. "This is Will."

The man standing next to her was quite good-looking, with dark hair and grey eyes like mine. Actually, they had more blue mixed in them than mine, and his face was broader than mine, but there were elements of it—like his straight nose and the curve of his chin—that were like looking in the mirror.

"What's this all about?" Will asked. He was trying to look at all of us at once. "Why are you all staring at me like that?"

"Cole, do you see it?" Missy asked in a low voice.

"See what?" Will asked.

"I'm ... I'm not sure," Cole said. "Yes, I see what you're talking about, but is it just because Tori suggested it?"

"What?" Will asked.

Missy was shaking her head. "No. It's there. Besides, it's easy to test."

"Test what?" Will demanded, his frustration rising. "Missy, what is going on?"

Missy blinked, and finally seemed to see him. Her expression softened, looked a little sad. "Why don't we sit down?" she suggested quietly. "Tori has some things to tell you."

"I don't want to sit down," Will said. "I want to know what's going on, and I want to know now. What do I need to know about our son?"

"Please trust me. You're going to want to sit down for this," Missy said. She sat on the couch and patted the seat next to her. "Just sit. Cole can bring you a drink."

"I don't want a drink," Will said, but he did sit next to her. His expression was disgruntled. He also had a wrinkle between his eye that matched mine, when I was disgruntled.

"Well?" he demanded, meeting my eyes. "What is it? And why do you keep staring at me?"

I couldn't seem to bring myself to stop staring at him. This was Scott. My brother. The one who I was supposed to have protected all those years ago. I knew it. I could feel it deep in my bones.

It was really him.

No wonder my mother had been so happy. She had seen it, too.

I took a deep breath. "There's no easy way to say this, and I'm fairly certain you aren't going to believe me ... but I'm your sister."

Chapter 31

Will stared at me. "Is this some sort of joke?" He squinted around the room. "This *is* a joke, right? Am I on camera? Dean is behind this, isn't he? I knew it. Still trying to get back at me for the April Fool's Day joke. Very funny, Dean," he shouted, as if to a hidden audience.

I shook my head. "No joke. I'm really your sister."

"What, are you looking for money?"

"I don't want money."

'Then what? Are you trying to blackmail me?"

"No. I just want the truth."

"The truth." He snorted. "You come to me with some ridiculous story, and you try to twist it into 'the truth'?"

"I thought you might want the truth, as well."

He shook his head and leaned forward to look directly into my eyes again. "You know you're not going to get anything, money or anything else, without some sort of proof, like a DNA test."

"Again, I don't want anything from you. But I'll take a DNA test," I said quietly.

His nostrils flared. He was starting to get agitated. "Why are you telling me this? If you're insinuating that my father had an affair with your mother, you're going to have to take it up with him. I don't have anything to do with it."

"It's more complicated than that," I said. "We actually have the same mother."

His expression went blank before completely shutting down. "That's enough," he said, starting to get up. "What you're suggesting is impossible. Missy, what is going on? Why would you bring me here to listen to such nonsense?"

"I think you should hear her out," Missy said quietly. "Just give her a few minutes to explain."

He flung his hands up. "I don't have to give her a few minutes to explain. I already know this is absurd. My mother didn't have any other children. She only had me."

"Actually, she didn't have you, either," I said. "She can't have children."

He whirled toward me, his eyes narrowing. "She *did* have a child. She had me. What do you know about it, anyway?"

"She had you in Europe, right?" I asked. "You were a year or so before you came home?"

"I was two and, yes. So what? Lots of people give birth in other countries. That doesn't prove anything."

"Did you know your father has a half-brother?"

That stopped him. He paused, studying me suspiciously. "What does that have to do with anything?"

"Your father's half-brother is named Simon, right?" I asked.

Missy gasped, her hands flying up to her face. I didn't realize she knew my father's name, but she must have, given her reaction. Will noticed it, too, turning to her, the furrow between his eyes growing deeper. "I still don't understand. What is this about my mother not giving birth to me?"

"My father is your half-uncle," I said carefully.

There was a long silence. Will slowly sunk back down on the couch. "I don't … I'm still not understanding."

"Want that drink now?" Cole asked.

"Please," Will said faintly.

I waited for Cole to bring him a glass of wine before I began the whole story. He didn't stop me or interrupt me, just listened as he drank his wine, his face growing blanker and more shut down with every word I uttered. In contrast, Missy and Cole's expressions grew more horrified and shocked, as they both struggled to process what I was saying.

When I finished, there was complete silence. None of them even looked at me. Instead, they all stared at the floor or around the room. I looked into my wine glass, which was now empty. Cole hadn't offered to refill it, and I was too exhausted to get it myself. I was actually so tired, I wasn't sure if I would ever move from that spot again.

Will was the first to speak. "You're expecting me to believe I am your brother, who was stolen out of my crib and replaced with a dead baby." His tone was flat.

"Yes."

He cocked his head as he studied me. "Do you have any proof?"

"No."

He didn't move, just continued staring at me. "No one is going to believe you, you know. Not my father or anyone else."

"Do you believe me?"

He didn't answer. "My father will destroy you, you know."

"I told you I'll take a DNA test."

He let out a laugh that was devoid of any humor. "You honestly think that will save you? In fact, it would be better for you if the results proved you were lying."

I continued to look directly into his eyes. "As I said before, I'm not looking for money. I just want the truth. I'm tired of living under lies. I thought you might be, as well."

He didn't answer, just continued to stare at me.

Missy cleared her throat. "What about Jude?" she asked. "How does he fit into all of this?"

I nodded toward Will. "That's up to Will."

"What does *that* mean?" Will snarled. "I didn't have anything to do with what happened to Jude."

"I didn't say you did," I said. "I bet your father did, though. I suspect he orchestrated Jude's kidnapping, just like he orchestrated yours. Which means he also knows where Jude is."

Missy's head snapped toward Will, her expression so filled with hope, it was almost painful. "Will? We could get Jude back!"

Will didn't meet her gaze. "Missy, you heard her story. What she's suggesting is absurd."

"But it's not. I ..."

"No!" His voice was final. "You should be ashamed of yourself," he said to me. "Giving false hope to a grieving mother."

I didn't waver. "It's not false hope, though. It's the most likely scenario."

"No, it's not. The most likely scenario is Jude died during childbirth. Not this nonsense."

"If it's such nonsense, why don't you dig around? See what you find out? Or, better yet, set up that DNA test for me. If it's not a match, I'll do whatever you want. Apologize publicly, privately, disappear forever. But, if I'm right, and it is a match ..." my voice trailed off.

Will abruptly stood. "I wouldn't waste my time," he snapped. "If I were you—any of you," he said, including Cole and Missy, "I would forget I heard any of this. For your own sake." He strode toward the door.

Missy scrambled to her feet, her expression horrified. "Will, no! Don't you see? We have to try! For Jude's sake! We have to find him."

"Missy," Cole said, but there wasn't any strength behind it. Missy ignored him as she ran after Will, pleading and begging with him.

Cole shifted his head to meet my eyes. His expression was haggard, like he had aged ten years in a matter of hours. "What a mess." His voice was empty. "I don't even ... I don't even know what to say."

I was so tired, my entire body hurt. "I know the feeling."

His eyes flickered toward his sister. "I have to go to her, but ... what about you? How are you handling all of this?"

"I'll survive." I had to. What other choice did I have?

Again, his eyes, full of concern, went to his sister. "I don't know if this was the right choice. Telling us, I mean. The Duckworths are a powerful enemy."

"The truth needs to come out," I said, automatically. Even if he didn't know that now, he would someday. He would know this was the only choice available to me.

"Despite the cost?"

"You assume the cost of hiding the truth and living a lie is less than revealing it," I said. Behind us, I heard the door of the hotel room slam and Missy's desperate, heartbreaking sobs. "I can assure you, it's not."

"I hope, for your sake, you're right," Cole said quietly.

Chapter 32

I watched the sleek black Mercedes pull smoothly into the empty parking lot and park next to the one lone tree that created a small pool of shade.

It had been three days since that terrible night, when I finally revealed the painful truth. I hadn't spoken to anyone else since, including Nanna. As soon as I was able to gather myself enough to get to my feet, I had left without a word, leaving Cole holding a hopelessly weeping Missy on the floor.

Neither looked up as I left, numb and broken. I stepped around them and quietly shut the door behind me.

I went back to Nanna's, who thankfully was asleep, and immediately showered. I turned it as hot as I could stand it and scrubbed every inch of me. I felt filthy and disgusting, like I would never be clean again.

I didn't leave the shower until the water ran cold. Then, I headed straight to bed, where I fell into a deep, dreamless sleep for over twelve hours.

I couldn't even remember the last time I had slept like that without the help of drugs. In a way, it felt like the end of my night terrors.

I was sure it was Pan who had taken Scott, well, Will, all those years ago, and now that I had a name for that shadowy, dark figure, he no longer had any power over me.

Nanna knew something had changed, but after I made it clear I wasn't ready to talk about it, she stopped asking. I knew I would have to say something to her eventually, but between what my father had said about George and Will's parting threat,

I kept my mouth shut. I needed more information before I did anything, especially since I was not willing to put Nanna's life in danger in any way.

Neither Cole nor Missy reached out to me, which didn't surprise me, although it did leave me with a hollow sadness. If the pain of dealing with my father's terrible choices hadn't been so all-consuming, I suspected I'd feel a lot worse. But for the time being, I needed all my energy just to process my past.

My father did reach out twice, which I ignored. I was definitely not ready to talk to him.

That morning, though, I received a text from an unknown number asking to meet me. I had a pretty good idea as to who it was.

I invited him to Nanna's house. She was gone all afternoon for her bridge club, but he wasn't ready for that. So instead, we decided to meet at a small, neighborhood park about a half-mile from Nanna's, so I could easily walk to it. Eventually, I was going to have to do something about my car, which was still sitting in my apartment's parking lot, not to mention my things and the apartment itself, but that could wait for another day.

I headed over to the car as the driver stepped out.

"I didn't think I'd hear from you," I said to Will.

He leaned against the car door and looked at me. His face was pale, and there were dark, bruised circles under his eyes, like he hadn't slept. When I asked him how he had gotten my cell number, he told me Missy had given it to him.

"I didn't think you'd hear from me, either," he replied.

As I came closer, I heard the soft sounds of an infant cooing from the backseat. I stared at him. "Is that who I think it is?"

"Meet Jude," he said, waving his arm with a flourish. I moved closer to the window, peering inside. There, tucked safely in a car seat, was Jude, wearing a bright-yellow onesie with a duck on it. He was gnawing on small stuffed penguin sporting a bright-red stocking hat and a red-and-white-striped scarf.

I looked at Will. "Does Missy know?"

He shook his head. "I wanted to see you first, before I deliver him to her."

I looked back at Jude. He was watching me with his blue, unfocused eyes, his fist clutching the penguin.

"Who convinced you I was telling the truth?"

"No one," he said, shoving his hands into the pockets of his jeans. "Or, I guess I did. There was always something … off, growing up, although I know a lot of kids don't feel like they fit into their family. But something shifted inside me when I heard your story, and I just … well, it suddenly made my childhood make a lot more sense."

"I'm sorry," I said.

He gave me a small smile before turning away, shuffling his feet and staring at the ground for a moment before meeting my gaze. "We can never talk about this again," he said.

I nodded.

He gave me another hard look before turning away to look across the empty park. A small breeze stirred his dark hair against his head. "My father is … ruthless. Although you probably already figured that out, after what he did to your father."

"I blame my father," I said. "Yours wanted a baby for money. Mine was willing to sell his."

He turned back to me. The sun had gone behind a cloud, darkening the day and turning his blueish-grey eyes closer to my color. "What mine did was worse. Trust me."

"I don't understand."

He looked away again. "Mind you, I don't have a lot of proof. But I know my grandfather had a clause in his will that kept my father from his inheritance if he didn't have a child. The part that isn't true is that my father's inheritance would go to charity, if he didn't."

"Where would it go?"

"To your father."

My mouth dropped open. "What? I thought my father wasn't getting anything."

"He's not. Since my father 'had' a child."

A freezing numbness started creeping down my neck and into my chest, making my blood feel like it was turning to ice.

"That's not all," he said. "Do you know when my grandfather added that clause?"

I shook my head. I didn't think I would be able to open my mouth.

"Four-and-a-half years before I was born."

My knees buckled, and I staggered, reaching an arm out to brace myself against the car. "But that's ..." I whispered.

"Yes," he said, nodding. "After you were born."

I had so many questions, they couldn't possibly fit into my mouth, but I didn't think I could spit any of them out right then, anyhow.

"My grandfather was always big on family," Will continued. "Family was the most important thing to him. My father? Not so much. I'm not sure he even wanted children. Which is probably why he didn't realize my mother couldn't conceive until years after their marriage." His mouth turned up into a small, twisted smile. "I don't know that for a fact, but it's true there were always a certain amount of ... questions, surrounding my birth. It also seems like my mother's inability to get pregnant wasn't clear until after my grandfather discovered this way of forcing my father into having children."

When I learned the truth from my father, I believed there was nothing else that could shock me. But now, knowing that my family had been torn apart because of a power play? I thought I might be sick.

"There's more," Will said, his voice quiet. "Although I have absolutely no proof of any of it."

I eyed him, wondering how it could get any worse.

"After my grandfather changed his will, there were whispers that my father was going to leave my mother, because she couldn't give him child. My father denied that, and my mother denied she was barren. But the whispers were there. They grew louder when my father was supposedly having an affair, about a year before I was born."

I gave him a confused look. "An affair? But I don't ..." I stopped talking, the pieces starting to click together.

"My father denied the affair, of course. And there's no proof, but he clearly set out to financially ruin your father. He was on the board of the bank your father had his business loan with. And while I don't know who your father's canceled contracts were with, it's safe to say if my father wanted to ruin a construction business in this town, he could."

I continued to prop myself up against Will's car. "Are you saying what I think you're saying?"

He looked into my eyes. "My grandfather was a terrible father. He was a great grandfather, but as a father, he sucked. He was strict and I think abusive, and my father hated him. And it seems some of that hatred spilled onto your father."

"But why? What did my father have to do with any of that?"

"Because your father wasn't raised by my grandfather. My dad was so jealous of your father for that. Never mind that your father grew up relatively poor compared to mine. He saw your father still benefiting financially from his family without having to put up with any of the crap. Never mind that the amount was miniscule compared to my family's wealth—the small monthly sum your father's mother got to raise him and the money he received when he was 21. The fact your father was getting any money at all from the Duckworths without having to put up with everything else gnawed at him.

"My guess is that the final straw was when my grandfather threatened to cut my father out of the will if he didn't have a child and give it all to his hated half- brother. He came up with a plan that would not only ensure he got his rightful inheritance, but also allow him to take revenge on my father."

"He had an affair with my mother, made her crazy, and nearly drove my father into bankruptcy … all so he could steal you? And all because he had a lousy childhood?" I asked, finishing the story for myself.

Will lifted his hands up helplessly. "There's no proof of any of that, of course."

"Of course," I murmured. I wanted to scream and howl … to tear my hair out in sheer frustration. My entire family had been destroyed for something we had absolutely nothing to do with. The unfairness burned inside me like an inferno, threatening to destroy me right along with it.

But I kept it all inside. There was no point. One look at Will's face, and I could see the same inferno of pain burning inside him. What good would it be to take it out on him?

Instead, I turned back to Jude, still chewing on the penguin. "What about him?" my voice was hoarse with unshed tears. "Why did your father do that to Missy?"

There was a long pause. "My father didn't approve of Missy," he said. "I'm not entirely sure how he found out we were dating, but he did. I guess it shouldn't be a surprise. He kept tabs on everyone else, so of course he would keep them on me." Will's voice was bitter.

"I assured him it wasn't serious, even though it was. I already knew she was the one, but there was something … unhinged about my father when he brought her up. At the time, I thought it was because he considered Missy beneath me. He had made it clear he was expecting me to marry well. Ideally, into a much wealthier and more powerful family than ours. We're a big fish in the small pond of Riverview, but even the entire state of Wisconsin is still too small for him. He had also made it clear he wanted me to go into politics one day. I think that was his real dream for me. I would marry a woman with a well-connected family and make my national run for political office. Never mind I wasn't interested in politics. That was beside the point.

"But now, after learning the true story of my birth and who my mother is, I think the reason Missy frightened my father so much was because of her mental illness. Any children we had would be tainted—not just by her genetics, but mine, too ... my mother. *Our* mother. And I think that's the deeper reason he was so dead set against me being involved with Missy.

"Unfortunately for him, I never had any intention of letting Missy go. I kept our relationship quiet, biding my time to figure out the best way for him to accept her. But before I could figure it out, she got pregnant. At first, I thought maybe the baby was the answer. Once he was born, my father would have to accept Missy and his grandchild. I knew my mother would be beside herself. She couldn't wait to be a grandmother. I figured that would help my father warm up to the idea.

"But I thought it best to keep the pregnancy a secret. So, I pretended to break up with Missy, thinking my father would stop watching her. I told my father Missy was moving, which she did—to that condo that I bought in secret, under a different name. I thought I had it all planned out. I was so, so wrong." His voice was filled with self-loathing and disgust.

"You shouldn't beat yourself up," I said. "There's no way you could have known the real reason, which is why he went to such lengths to keep you two apart."

He shook his head. "It doesn't matter. I know my father. I should have known he wouldn't be fooled by some financial maneuvering and my not seeing her anymore." He glanced toward the backseat of the car. "I'll never forgive myself for what I allowed to be done to my son. And to Missy."

"But you fixed it now," I said. "How did you find Jude? And how did you get your father to agree to return him?"

"It's complicated," he said. "And it doesn't really matter now. The good news is, he was being well taken care of. Even my father couldn't hurt his own flesh and blood. He was in a suburb of Milwaukee with a paid nanny, thank goodness. If he had been adopted out, that would have raised all sorts of legal issues, but this will make it fairly straightforward."

"Make what straightforward?"

"The official story." He looked intently into my eyes. "Jude was kidnapped by a black-market infant ring. My father was tipped off that this might have occurred, so he hired a PI at his own expense, who recovered the baby. In terms of the kidnappers, my family will be working with law enforcement to see about bringing them to justice."

I gave Will a skeptical look. "You really think that's going to fly?"

He shrugged. "That's my father's issue, really, but yes, I do. He has enough people on his payroll and who owe him a favor that I'm sure it won't be a problem. Remember, we're talking about a man who was able to procure two dead infants from the hospital morgue and pay a coroner to not look at either of them too deeply. He'll get it to work."

In my mind's eye, I saw the dark, shadowy figure, and smelled the scent of death. I shivered. "That must have been why he smelled the way I remember. He probably came straight from the morgue."

"Probably," Will said. "While I'm sure they were watching the hospital closely for male stillborn babies, so they could time the death as close as they could to Jude's birth, there would still be a delay. Why do you think Marci induced Missy? Most likely because 'Pan' had an appropriate baby, and they couldn't wait long to do the swap." His eyes narrowed. "Probably induced your ... *our* mother, as well."

That stopped me. I rifled through my memories, trying to remember the day Scott, well, Will, had been born, but it was a blank. "That's a horrible thought."

He nodded slightly.

"I suppose you know who 'Pan' is, then?"

He grimaced. "Unfortunately, although I wish I didn't. He's my father's go-to guy for all his dirty work." He tilted his head and narrowed his eyes. "Just like most of this conversation, it would be better if you simply forgot him."

I looked away, feeling the anger start to bubble under the surface. "Just like that, then? My family is ripped apart, but I'm not supposed to say anything or do anything about it?"

He took a step toward me. "Trust me on this. You don't want to mess with my father. It's better this way."

I lifted my chin. "Better for who?"

"Everyone."

I turned away, shaking my head. "He shouldn't be allowed to get away with it. It's not fair."

Will stepped closer to me, so close I caught a whiff of his scent. And just like that, I was transposed to a child, holding him as I fed him his bottle. Even though it was mixed with his aftershave and his shampoo instead of baby powder, the essence was still him.

Still my brother.

I fought the urge to wrap my arms around him right then and there.

"Look," he said quietly. "I know it doesn't seem like it, but we won. We got Jude back. Eventually, Missy and I will be together, as my father will want Jude to be a part of the family. We need to take the win. At least for now. Especially since we're not in any position to get back at him yet. But one day, we will."

I stared at him, the set of his jaw, the grim look in his eyes, and I felt a shiver. In that moment, I wouldn't want to be Will's enemy. But then I thought again about everything George had done, and the same surge of anger shot through me. I looked again at Jude and his penguin, reminding myself that something good had come out of this mess.

"Don't get me wrong—I'm thrilled you got him back. But when I think about what happed to me ... to us ... it doesn't feel like a win."

"Maybe not in this moment," he said. "But it's the best we can do. And, besides, we at least both know the truth. Does it matter if anyone else knows it?"

"Easy for you to say," I said. "Your life wasn't ruined because of a lie. Your father deserves to be held accountable for what he did."

"It sucks what happened to you," he said, his expression softening. "And I agree with you, and wish there was another way. But there's not. We'd be no match for him. So, at least for now, you're going to have to figure out a way forward through the lies."

I could feel the frustration and rage bubbling up inside me, and I squeezed my hands together into fists. Still, I knew he was right. Someone as powerful as George Duckworth? I was in no position to challenge him. I would be better off focusing on how I could put my life back together in such a manner that I wouldn't have to worry about it blowing up if another journalist starting sniffing around.

"If it makes you feel any better," he continued. "It's not always going to be this way. He WILL pay, someday. Just not now."

I glanced at him. The cold, hard look was back in his eyes. "You sound confident."

He smiled. "You forget. I'm my father's son. And I'm an excellent student."

There was an edge to the smile, and it made the skin on the back of my neck crawl. Again, I found myself being glad he was on my side.

He gave himself a quick shake and took a step back. "I should go. I shouldn't keep Missy waiting any longer."

"Good idea," I said as I backed away from the car. "She needs to see him."

He moved to the driver's side door and paused with his hand on the handle. "You know you're welcome to see him, as well. Any time." He smiled again, but this time, it was more relaxed … more like an actual smile than a veiled threat. "After all, you're family."

Family.

The word felt warm and bubbly inside me, chasing away all the negative emotions, the numbness, the grief, the fear, the anger, that had seemed to dominate my entire existence lately.

I had a family now, in addition to Nanna.

I smiled back at Will, a true smile. My brother.

Chapter 33

As much as I had my doubts that the "Jude was kidnapped by a black-market infant ring, but we got him back" public cover story would actually work, I should have known better.

Money and power talks, after all.

Plus, I had no doubt Missy was so overjoyed to have her son back, she would agree to parroting just about any story.

Will was true to his word, and started reaching out to me more. His time was too tight to hang out a lot in person, but we texted and called each other fairly often.

Missy also made it clear I was welcome any time to visit her and the baby, my nephew, which was still a little hard to get my head around, but so far, I was staying away. The media was still way too interested in the case, interviewing Missy multiple times for different stories and features, and the last thing I wanted was for them to resume their interest in me.

I knew Cole had moved in with her. Until Will felt more able to openly date Missy, Cole wasn't leaving her side. Which I understood, of course. But that also meant Cole had a media target on his back, along with not having any time to pursue a new relationship.

I was disappointed, but not as much as I might have been. Truth be told, I needed space and time, as well, to figure out who I was without the lie, because I had no idea.

I didn't even know if I would like her very much.

But even if I didn't, I knew there was no going back to the old Victoria.

The new Tori was definitely here to stay.

The biggest sticking point was my father. He continued to call, and I continued to ignore him. I was nowhere near ready to even have a conversation with him.

I wasn't sure if I ever would be.

I finally told Nanna the truth, after she questioned why I kept ignoring him. I hadn't wanted to, as I was a little worried about what George Duckworth might do if he found out, but I also thought she deserved to know.

She didn't say much after I told her. Or for days after. Instead, she seemed to age before my eyes, getting older and grayer far too quickly.

It scared me to see, but I kept reminding myself I had a brother now, even if no one else could know. At least for now.

I wasn't alone in the world.

"He's still your father," Nanna said one day after I had sent my father's call to voicemail again.

I glanced up, surprised she was taking his side. "He's no father," I said. "He sold his child."

She pressed her lips together, so tight they turned white. "You do understand he did it for you," she said, her voice quiet.

My mouth dropped open. I hadn't thought of it like that.

"I'm not saying he didn't make a terrible, terrible mistake," she continued. "But you also don't realize the pressure he was under. He was losing everything, including his wife. Yes, he sold one of his children. But he did it to save you."

And with that, she turned and walked into the kitchen.

I swallowed hard and picked up my cell phone. I stared at my father's name in the call list and put the phone back down.

Not today. I wasn't ready.

But maybe someday, I would be.

Author's Note

Hi there!

I hope you enjoyed *The Taking* as much as I enjoyed writing it. If you did, I would really appreciate it if you'd leave me a review and rating.

The Taking is one of the books in *The Riverview Mysteries* series, which is currently a series of standalone psychological suspense mysteries. However, that will change as I have more Tori and Cole books planned (the next installment will be released sometime in 2023).

In the meantime, I'd like to invite you to continue your exploration of Riverview, along with its sister city, Redemption, Wisconsin, which is about forty-five minutes away (and has a much darker past).

If you decide to stay in Riverview, you can check out the other two standalone books, *The Stolen Twin* and *Mirror Image*.

If you want to take your chances in Redemption and are interested in another standalone, you may like *The Third Nanny*. Or if you want to see where it all starts, you can dive into *It Began With a Lie*, which is the first book in the *Secrets of Redemption* series. In fact, if you turn the page, you'll get a sneak peek of *It Began With a Lie*.

You can also grab a free standalone psychological thriller short novella called *Today I'll See Her,* on my website at MPWNovels.com. I've got lots of other fun things there to check out as well, including more on all my books, short stories, giveaways and more.

For now, turn the page for a sneak peek at *It Began With a Lie*.

It Began With a Lie - Chapter 1

"You're right. It's perfect for us. I'm so glad we're here," I said, lying through my carefully pasted-on smile.

I tried to make my voice bright and cheery, but it sounded brittle and forced, even to me. I sucked in my breath and widened my smile, though my teeth were so clenched, my jaw hurt.

Stefan smiled back—actually, his mouth smiled but his dark-brown eyes, framed with those long, thick lashes any woman would envy, looked flat ... distracted. He hugged me with one arm. "I told you everything would be okay," he whispered into my hair. His scent was even more musky than usual, probably from two straight days of driving and lack of shower.

I hugged him back, reminding myself to relax. *Yes, everything is going to be okay. Remember, this move represents a fresh start for us—time for us to reconnect and get our marriage back on track. It's not going to happen overnight.*

His iPhone buzzed. He didn't look at me as he dropped his arm and pulled it out of his pocket, his attention already elsewhere. "Sorry babe, gotta take this." He turned his back to me as he answered the call, walking away quickly. His dark hair, streaked with silver that added a quiet, distinguished air to his All-American good looks was longer than normal, curling around his collar. He definitely needed a haircut, but of course, we couldn't afford his normal stylist, and not just anyone was qualified to touch his hair.

I wrapped my arms around myself, goosebumps forming on my skin as a sudden breeze, especially cool for mid-May, brushed past me—the cold all the more shocking in the absence of Stefan's warm body.

He has to work, I reminded myself. *Remember why we're here.*

I remembered, all right. How could I forget?

I rubbed my hands up and down my arms as I took a deep breath, and finally focused on the house.

It was just as I remembered from my childhood—white with black shutters, outlined by bushy green shrubs, framed by tall, gently-swaying pine trees and the red porch with the swinging chair. It sat all by its lonesome in the middle of a never-developed cul-de-sac, the only "neighbors" being an overgrown forest on one side, and a marshy field on the other.

Okay, maybe it wasn't *exactly* the way I remembered it. The bushes actually looked pretty straggly. The lawn was overgrown, full of dandelions going to seed, and the porch could definitely use a new paint job.

I sighed. If the outside looked like this, what on earth waited for me on the inside?

Inside.

I swallowed back the bile that rose in the back of my throat. It slid to my stomach, turning into a cold, slimy lump.

The house of my childhood.

The house of my nightmares.

Oh God, I so didn't want to be here.

Stefan was still on the phone, facing away from me. I stared longingly at his back. *Turn around*, I silently begged. *Turn around and smile at me. A real smile. Like how you used to before we were married. Tell me it's going to be okay. You don't have to leave tonight like you thought. You realize how cruel it would be to leave me alone in this house the first night we're here, and you don't want to do that to me. Please, tell me. Or, better yet, tell me we're packing up and going back to New York. Say this was all a mistake; the firm is doing fine. Or, if you can't say that, say we'll figure it out. We'll make it work. We don't need to live here after all. Please, Stefan. Please don't leave me alone here.*

He half-turned, caught my eye, and made a gesture that indicated he was going to be awhile.

And I should start unpacking.

I closed my eyes. Depression settled around me like an old, familiar shawl. I could feel the beginning of a headache stab my temples.

Great. Just what I needed to complete this nightmare—a monster headache.

I turned to the car and saw Chrissy still in the backseat— headset on, bobbing to music only she could hear. Her long, dark hair—so dark it often looked black—spread out like a shiny cloak, the ends on one side dyed an electric blue.

Oh, yeah. That's right. I wouldn't be alone in the house after all.

Chrissy closed her eyes and turned her head away from me.

It just kept getting better and better.

I knocked on the window. She ignored me. I knocked again. She continued to ignore me.

For a moment, I imagined yanking the door open, snatching the headset off and telling her to—no, *insisting* that—she get her butt out of the car and help me unpack. I pictured her dark brown eyes, so much like Stefan's, widening, her pink lip-glossed mouth forming a perfect O, so shocked that she doesn't talk back, but instead meekly does what she's told.

More pain stabbed my temples. I closed my eyes and kept knocking on the window.

It's not her fault, I told myself for maybe the 200th time. *How would you act if you were sixteen years old and your mother abandoned you, dumped you at your father's, so she'd be free to travel across Europe with her boy toy?*

I squelched the little voice that reminded me I wasn't a whole heck of a lot older than said boy toy, and started pounding on the window. Stefan kept telling me she was warming up to me—I personally hadn't seen much evidence of that.

Chrissy finally turned her head and looked at me. "What?" she mouthed, disgust radiating off her, her eyes narrowing like an angry cat.

I motioned to the trunk. "I need your help."

Her lip curled as her head fell back on to the seat. She closed her eyes.

I had just been dismissed.

Great. Just great.

I looked around for Stefan—if he were standing with me, she would be out of the car and helping—a fake, sweet smile on her face, but he had moved to the corner of the street, still on the phone. I popped the trunk and headed over to him. Maybe I could finally get him to see reason—that it really was a dreadful idea to leave the two of us alone in Redemption, Wisconsin, while he commuted back and forth to New York to rescue his failing law firm. "See," I could say, "She doesn't listen to me. She doesn't respect me. She needs her father. I need you, too. She's going to run wild with you gone and I won't be able to deal with her."

Stefan hung up as I approached. "The movers should be here soon. You probably should start unpacking." Although his tone was mild, I could still hear the underlying faint chords of reproach—what's going on with you? Why haven't you started yet? Do I need to do everything around here?

"Yes, I was going to," I said, hating my defensive tone, but unable to stop it. "But there's a problem I think you need to deal with."

His eyes narrowed—clearly, he was losing his patience with me. "What?"

I opened my mouth to tell him about Chrissy, just as her voice floated toward us, "Can I get some help over here?"

I slowly turned around, gritting my teeth, trying not to show it. Chrissy stood by the trunk, arms loaded with boxes, an expectant look on her face. The pain darting through my head intensified.

"Rebecca, are you coming?" Stefan asked as he headed over to his charming daughter, waiting for him with a smug expression on her face, like a cat who ate the canary. I took a deep breath and trudged over, the sick knot in the pit of my stomach growing and tightening.

What on earth was I going to do with her while Stefan was gone?

Chrissy threw me a triumphant smile as she followed her father to the house. I resisted the urge to stick my tongue out at her, as I heaved a couple of boxes out of the trunk.

Really, all the crap with Chrissy was the least of my worries. It was more of a distraction, than anything.

The real problem was the house.

The house.

Oh God.

I turned to stare at it. It didn't look menacing or evil. It looked like a normal, everyday house.

Well, a normal, everyday house with peeling paint, a broken gutter and a few missing roof shingles.

Great. That probably meant we needed a new roof. New roofs were expensive. People who had to rescue failing law firms tended to not have money for things like new roofs. Even new roofs for houses that were going to be fixed up and eventually sold, ideally for a big, fat profit.

Would there be *any* good news today?

Again, I realized I was distracting myself. New roofs and paint jobs—those were trivial.

The real problem was *inside* the house.

Where all my nightmares took place.

Where my breakdown happened.

Where I almost died.

I swallowed hard. The sun went behind a cloud and, all of a sudden, the house was plunged into darkness. It loomed in front me, huge and monstrous, the windows dark, bottomless eyes staring at me ... the door a mouth with sharp teeth ...

"Rebecca! Are you coming?"

Stefan broke the spell. I blinked my eyes and tried to get myself together.

I was being silly. It was just a house, not a monster. How could a house even BE a monster? Only people could be monsters, which would mean my aunt, who had owned the house, was the monster.

And my aunt was dead now. Ding, dong, the witch is dead. Or, in this case, the monster.

Which meant there was nothing to fear in the house anymore. Which was exactly what Stefan kept telling me back in New York, over and over.

"Don't you think it's time you put all this childhood nonsense behind you?" he asked. "Look, I get it. Your aunt must have done something so dreadful that you've blocked it out, but she's dead. She can't hurt you anymore. And it couldn't have worked out any more perfectly for us—we have both a place to live rent-free right now, while I get things turned around. And, once we sell it, we can use the money to move back here and get a fresh start."

He was right, of course. But, still, I couldn't drop it.

"Why did she even will the house to me in the first place?" I persisted. "Why didn't she will it to CB? He was there a lot more than I was."

Stefan shrugged. "Maybe it was her way of apologizing to you all these years later. She was trying to make it up to you. Or maybe she changed—people said she was sick at the end. But, why does it matter why she willed it to you? The point is she did, and we really need it. Not to mention this could be a great way for you to finally get over whatever happened to you years ago."

Maybe. Back in New York, it had seemed so reasonable. So logical. Maybe the move wouldn't be a problem after all.

But, standing in the front yard with my arms filled with boxes, every cell in my body screamed that it was a really awful idea.

"Hey," Stefan whispered in my ear, his five o'clock shadow scratching my cheek. I jumped, so transfixed by the house that I hadn't even realized he had returned to me. "Look, I'm sorry. I should have known this would be rough for you. Come on, I'll walk in with you."

He rubbed my arm and smiled at me—a real smile. I could feel my insides start to thaw as all those old, exciting, passionate feelings reminiscent of when we first started dating swarmed over me. I remembered how he would shower me with red roses and whisk me off to romantic dinners that led to steaming, hot sex. He made me feel like a princess in a fairy tale. I still couldn't fathom how he ended up with me.

I met his eyes, and for the first time in what seemed like a long time, I felt the beginnings of a real smile on my lips. *See, he does care, even if he doesn't always show it. This is why the move was the perfect thing for our marriage; all we needed was to get away from the stress of New York, so we could rekindle things.* I nodded and started walking with him toward the house. Over her shoulder, Chrissy shot me a dirty look.

The closer we got to the house, the more I focused on my breathing. *It's going to be okay, I repeated to myself. It's just a house. A house can't hurt anyone. It's all going to be okay.*

An owl hooted, and I jumped. Why was an owl hooting in the daytime? Didn't that mean someone was going to die? Isn't that what the old stories and folklore taught? My entire body stiffened—all I wanted to do was run the other way. Stefan hugged me closer, gently massaging my arm, and urged me forward.

"It's going to be okay," he murmured into my hair. I closed my eyes for a moment, willing myself to believe it.

We stepped onto the porch, Chrissy impatiently waiting for Stefan to unlock the door. He put the boxes on the ground to fumble for his keys as I tried hard not to hyperventilate.

It's just a house. A house can't hurt anyone.

After an eternity that simultaneously wasn't nearly long enough, he located the keys and wrenched the door open, swearing under his breath.

His words barely registered. I found myself compelled forward, drawn in like those pathetic moths to the killing flame.

I could almost hear my aunt excitedly calling, "Becca? Is that you? Wait until you see this," as I stepped across the threshold into the house.

It was exactly like I remembered.

Well, maybe not exactly—it was filthy and dusty, full of cobwebs and brittle, dead bugs lying upside down on the floor with their legs sticking up. But I remembered it all—from the overstuffed floral sofa where I spent hours reading, to the end table covered with knick-knacks and frilly doilies, to the paintings lining the walls. I found myself wanting to hurry into the kitchen, where surely Aunt Charlie would have a cup of tea waiting for me. It didn't feel scary at all. It felt warm and comforting.

Like coming home.

How could this be?

Stefan was still muttering under his breath. "I can't believe all this crap. We're going to have put our stuff in storage for months while we go through it all. Christ, like we need another bill to worry about." He sighed, pulled his cell phone out, and started punching numbers.

"Dad, what do you mean our stuff is going into storage?" Chrissy said, clearly alarmed.

Stefan waved his arms. "Honey, look around you. Where are we going to put it? We have to put our things into storage until we get all this out of here."

"But Dad," Chrissy protested. I stopped listening. I walked slowly around, watching my aunt dashing down the stairs, her smock stained, arms filled with herbs and flowers, some even sticking out of her frizzy brown hair, muttering about the latest concoction she was crafting for one of the neighbors whose back was acting up again ...

"Earth to Rebecca. Rebecca. Are you okay?" I suddenly realized Stefan was talking to me, and I pulled myself out of my memories.

"Sorry, it just ..." my voice trailed off.

He came closer. "Are you okay? Are you remembering?"

There she was again, the ghost of Aunt Charlie, explaining yet again to the odd, overly-made-up, hair-over-teased, forty-something woman from the next town that no, she didn't do love potions. It was dangerous magic to mess around with either love or money, but if she wanted help with her thyroid that was clearly not working the way it should be, that was definitely in my aunt's wheelhouse.

I shook my head. "No, not really. It's just ... weird."

I wanted him to dig deeper, ask me questions, invite me to talk about the memories flooding through me. I wanted him to look at me while I spoke, *really* look at me, the way he did before we were married.

Where had it all gone wrong? And how could he leave me alone in a lonely, isolated and desolate house a thousand miles away from New York? Sure, Chrissy would be there, but the jury was still out as to whether she made it better or worse.

The memories pushed up against me, smothering me. I *needed* to talk about them, before they completely overwhelmed and suffocated me. And he knew it—he knew how much I needed to talk things through to keep the anxiety and panic at bay. He wouldn't let me down, not now, when I really needed him.

Would he?

It Began With a Lie - Chapter 2

The empty coffee pot mocked me.

It sat on the table, all smug and shiny, its cord wrapped tightly around it.

I had been so excited after unearthing it that morning—yes! Coffee! God knew I needed it.

The night before had been horrible, starting with the fights. I ended up in the living room, where I spent the night on the couch, a cold washcloth draped over my face in a feeble attempt to relieve the mother of all headaches.

Several times, I'd have just dozed off when the sound of Chrissy's footsteps would jerk me awake, as she paced up and down the upstairs hallway. I couldn't fathom what was keeping her up, so finally, after the fourth or fifth time of being woken up, I went upstairs to check on her. She must have heard me on the stairs, because all I saw was of the trail of her white nightgown as she disappeared into her room. I stood there for a moment, wondering if I should go talk to her, but the stabbing pain in my head drove me back downstairs to the safety of the couch and washcloth. I just couldn't face another argument then, in the middle of the night.

She must have decided to stay in her room after that, because I finally drifted off, only waking when the sun shone through the dirty living room window, illuminating all the dust motes floating in the air.

Coffee was exactly what I needed. Except … I had no beans to put in the coffeemaker. Not that it mattered, I realized after digging through the third box in frustration. I didn't have any cream or sugar either.

Well, at least my headache was gone, although what was left was a weird, hollow, slightly-drugged feeling. Still, I'd take that over the headache any day.

I sighed and rubbed my face. The whole move wasn't starting off very well. In fact, everything seemed to be going from bad to worse, including the fight with Stefan.

"Do you really need to leave?" I asked him again as I followed him to the door. He had just said goodbye to Chrissy, who had immediately disappeared upstairs, leaving us alone. I could see the taxi he had called sitting in the driveway and my heart sank. A part of me had hoped to talk him out of going, but with the taxi already there the possibility seemed even more remote.

He sighed. I could tell he was losing patience. "We've been through this. You know I have to."

"But you just got here! Surely you can take a few days—a week maybe—off to help us unpack and get settled."

He picked up his briefcase. "You know I can't. Not now."

"But when? You promised you would set it up so that you could work from here most of the time. Why can't you start that now?" I could tell his patience was just about gone, but I couldn't stop myself.

He opened the door. A fresh, cool breeze rushed in, a sharp contrast to the musty, stale house. "And I will. But it's too soon. There are still a few things I need to get cleaned up before I can do that. You know that. We talked about this."

He stepped outside and went to kiss me, but I turned my face away. "Are you going to see *her*?"

That stopped him. I could see his eyes narrow and his mouth tighten. I hadn't meant to say it; it just slipped out.

He paused and took a breath. "I know this whole situation has been tough on you, so I'm going to forget you said that. I'll call you."

Except he didn't. Not a single peep in the more than twelve hours since he had walked out the door. And every time I thought of it, I felt sick with shame.

I didn't *really* think he was cheating on me. I mean, there was something about Sabrina and her brittle, cool, blonde, perfect elegance that I didn't trust, but that wasn't on Stefan. I had no reason not to trust him. Just because my first husband cheated on me didn't mean Stefan would. And just because Sabrina looked at Stefan like he was a steak dinner, and she was starving, didn't mean it was reciprocated.

Worse, I knew I was making a bigger mess out of it every time I brought it up. The more I accused him, the more likely he would finally say, "Screw it, if I'm constantly accused of being a cheater, I might as well at least get something out of it." Even knowing all of that, I somehow couldn't stop myself.

Deep down, I knew I was driving him away. And I hated that part of myself. But still nothing changed.

To make matters worse, it didn't take long after Stefan left before things blew up with Chrissy. I asked her to help me start organizing the kitchen, and she responded with an outburst about how much she hated the move. She hated me, too—her life was ruined, and it was all my fault. She stormed off, slammed the door to her room, and that's how I ended up on the couch, my head pounding, wishing I was just about anywhere else.

Standing in the kitchen with the weak sunlight peeking through the dirty windows, the empty coffee maker taunting me, I gave in to my feelings of overwhelm. How on earth was I ever going to get the house organized? And the yard? And my aunt's massive garden? All the while researching what it would take to sell the house for top dollar, and dealing with Chrissy? My heart sank at that thought, although I wasn't completely sure which thought triggered it. Maybe it was all of them.

And if that wasn't difficult enough, I also had to deal with being in my aunt's home. Her presence *was everywhere*. I felt like an intruder. How could I do all of this, feeling her around me? How could I be in her home, when she wasn't? It wasn't my house. It was Aunt Charlie's. And I wasn't even sure I WANT-ED it to feel like my home.

Because if it did, then I would probably remember everything.

Including what happened that night.

The night I almost died.

God, I felt sick.

I needed coffee. And food.

Maybe I should take Chrissy out for breakfast as a peace offering. We could get out of the house, which would be good for me at least, and then go grocery shopping before coming home to tackle the cleaning and organizing.

I wanted to start in the kitchen. It was Aunt Charlie's favorite room in the house, and I knew it would have broken her heart to see how neglected and dingy it had become. When my aunt was alive, it was the center of the home—a light, cheery place with a bright-red tea kettle constantly simmering away on low heat on the stove. Oh, how Aunt Charlie loved her tea—that's why the kettle always had hot water in it—she'd say you just never knew when a cup would be needed. She was a strong believer that tea cured just about everything, just so long as you had the right blend. And, surprise, surprise, you could pretty much always find the right blend outside in her massive garden, which I had no doubt was completely overgrown now. I didn't have the heart to go look.

I could almost see her, standing in that very kitchen, preparing me a cup. "Headache again, Becca?" she would murmur as she measured and poured and steeped. The warm fragrance would fill the homey kitchen as she pushed the hot cup in front of me, the taste strong, flavorful, and sweet, with just a hint of bitterness. And, lo and behold, not too long after drinking it, I would find my headache draining away.

I wondered if I would still find her tea blends in the kitchen. Maybe I could find that headache tea. And maybe, if I was even luckier, I would find a blend that would cure everything that ailed me that morning.

With some surprise, I realized just how much love encompassed that memory. Nothing scary. Nothing that could possibly foretell the horror of what happened that dreadful night.

Could my aunt actually be the monster?

My mother certainly thought so. She forbade any contact, any mentioning of my aunt even, refusing to allow her to see me once I woke up in intensive care following the stomach pump. She refused her again when I was transferred to a psych unit, after becoming hysterical when I was asked what had happened that night.

My mother blamed my aunt.

And, I, in my weakened, anxious, panicked state, was relieved to follow her lead. Actually, I was more than relieved; I was happy, too.

But sitting in that kitchen right then, I felt only love and comfort, and I began to question my choices.

My mother had been completely against us moving back here, even temporarily. At the time, listening to her arguments, I had chalked it up to her being overly protective. Now, I wondered. Was that it? Or was something deeper going on?

Chrissy chose that moment to stroll into the kitchen, her hair sticking up on one side. She was wearing her blue and red plaid sleep shorts and red tee shirt—the blue plaid almost an exact match to the blue highlight in her hair. Staring at her, something stirred deep inside me—a distinct feeling of wrongness ... of something being off—but when I reached for it, I came up empty.

She leaned against the counter and started checking her iPhone. "How sweet, you're being domestic."

I shook my head—that off feeling still nagged at me, but I just couldn't place it. I really needed coffee. Coffee would make everything better.

She tapped at her iPhone, not looking up. "Anything to eat in this God-awful place?"

I sighed. Maybe I should be looking for a tea that would cure Chrissy.

It Began With a Lie - Chapter 3

Chrissy wrinkled her nose. "What a dump."

She said it under her breath, so neither the bustling waitresses nor the other customers could hear. But I could. I gave her a sharp look, which she ignored.

We were in what *I* thought was a cute little diner called Aunt May's. It felt friendly and familiar and had a respectable number of customers in it for a Monday morning. In fact, on the drive over, I had been amazed at how bright and cheery the town was—it was almost like I had expected to see dark, grimy, stains tainting the buildings, the streets, even the deep green grass. Instead, the sun shone down on clean, well-kept houses and cute stores complete with maintained lawns and pots of colorful flowers.

Chrissy clearly wasn't impressed by any of it.

She poked at her menu. "Do you think anything here is gluten-free?"

I sighed, flipping over my coffee cup. "You'll have to ask."

Chrissy made a face and stared darkly out the window.

Despite the inauspicious start, she seemed to be in a better mood. Well, maybe "better" wasn't quite the right word—"subdued" was probably more accurate. It was almost like our fight had drained vital energy from her, leaving a shell of her former self.

The waitress appeared, coffee pot in hand. "Are you two visiting for the summer?" she asked as she filled my cup. I shot her a grateful look. She looked familiar with her dark, straight hair cut in a chin-length bob and Asian features. Japanese maybe. But I couldn't really place her. Maybe I had run into her years ago, while visiting my aunt.

"No, we just moved here," I said, pulling my coffee toward me, doctoring it with cream and sugar.

The waitress raised her eyebrow at me. "Really? Where?"

"Charlie, I mean Charlotte Kingsley's house."

The waitress set the coffee pot down. "Becca? Is that you?"

Something inside me seemed to twist in on itself, hearing that name out loud. *I'm not Becca*, I wanted to say. *Becca's gone. It's Rebecca now.*

At the same time, I found my brain frantically searching for a wisp of something, anything, to give me a hint as to who this waitress was. "Uh ..."

"It's Mia—Mia Moto. We used to hang out, remember?"

I blinked at her and suddenly, it was like the dam opened— memories crashed down into me. I sucked in my breath, feeling physically jolted by the impact. "Mia! Oh my God, I hardly recognized you!"

She laughed in delight and held out her arms. Somehow, I found myself on my feet, swept up in a giant bear hug—impressive, considering how tiny she was. She smelled spicy, like cinnamon and coffee.

"It's so great to see you," Mia said, when we finally separated. "I mean, after that night, we were all so worried, but the hospital wouldn't let any of us visit you."

"Yeah, well, my mom ..." I fumbled around, not really sure what to say. The truth was, I hadn't wanted to see them. I had become hysterical again, when one of the nurses said I had visitors. And, until that very moment, I had never even considered how it must have looked from their point of view. They were my friends; they cared about me, and I had almost died. Of course they would want to see me. I felt sick with shame.

"I can't believe it's you," I said, changing the subject. "Who else is still here? Is ..."

"Daphne's still here," Mia interjected. "In fact, she's still living in the same house, right by you. She moved in after her mom got sick to help her out. I know she'd love to see you."

"And I'd love to see her too," I said, jolted again by how much I really did miss hanging out with Mia and Daphne.

"And Daniel is still here, too." Mia continued. "He's engaged now."

A rush of conflicting feelings started swirling through me at the sound of his name, anger being the most prevalent. "I'm married," I said shortly, smiling at the last second to soften my tone.

Daniel. God, I had totally forgotten him, too. For good reason, considering he had not only stood me up, all those years ago, but he also had then ignored me completely .... like I didn't even exist. Talk about painful. Snapping back to reality, I turned my attention back to Mia. "In fact, this is my stepdaughter, Chrissy."

Mia turned her 40-thousand-watt, infectious smile on Chrissy. "Great to meet you, Chrissy. Make sure you ask your stepmom where all the hot places are to hang out." Chrissy's lips twitched upward in a semblance of a smile, and her "nicetomeetyoutoo" almost sounded friendly.

I elbowed Mia. "I don't know if that's such a good idea."

Someone near the kitchen yelled Mia's name, but she waved him off. "We definitely need to catch up."

"Yes," I agreed, sliding back into my seat. "I'm really surprised you're here. I thought you would be long gone—California, right? Stanford? Law school?" I had vague memories of Mia going on and on about being the next Erin Brockovich. She had nearly memorized that movie, she had seen it so often.

Mia's smile slipped. "Well, yeah. It's complicated. After that night … you … Jessica …" her voice trailed off and she pulled out her order pad. "I better get your order."

Jessica.

It felt like all the air had been sucked out of the room. I could hear Chrissy asking about gluten-free options, and not getting the answer she wanted, but it seemed like the conversation was taking place outside of the bubble I was trapped in, as I could barely hear anything but a warbling echo.

Jessica. How could I have forgotten about Jessica?

Mia, Daphne, Jessica, and me. We were the four amigos that summer. The four Musketeers. Hanging out at the beach, the mall, at my aunt's house (because she was by far the coolest of all the adults we had to choose from).

Until that night, when Jessica disappeared … and I ended up in the hospital, broken, mentally and physically.

I rubbed my eyes, the faint wisp of a headache brushing my temples like a soft kiss. I realized that while my memories from that summer were finally returning, that night was still a total blank. Actually, the entire day was a black hole. I didn't even remember taking the first drink, one of many that would put me in the hospital, having to get my stomach pumped, followed by a complete and utter nervous breakdown.

"Becca?" Mia asked, pen poised on her pad. "You okay?"

I reached for my coffee cup, glad to see my hands weren't shaking, and tried on a smile that felt way too small. "Yeah, I'm fine. Just still recovering from moving."

Mia didn't look like she completely believed me, but I could tell she needed to get back to work. I ordered the American breakfast—eggs, bacon, fried potatoes with onions and pep-pers, and rye toast—even though I was no longer hungry. I knew I had to eat. I had barely eaten anything the day before, and if I didn't start eating, I would probably trigger another headache.

I figured chances were decent I'd get one anyway, but at least eating something would give me a fighting chance.

Along with the lack of gluten-free options, Chrissy also voiced her displeasure around the coffee choices, wanting a mocha, or latte, or something, made with some other type of milk than, well, milk from a cow, so she ended up with a Coke. I restrained myself from pointing out that soda was probably a lot less healthy choice than something with gluten or dairy in it. Ah, kids.

She blew the paper off the straw and plopped the straw in her soda, then pulled out her iPhone. "Who's Daniel?"

I didn't look at her as I added a little more sugar to my cup, and carefully stirred. "Just a guy I knew from back when I would visit during the summer."

"Hmmm," Chrissy said, lifting her head from her iPhone to narrow her eyes at me. "Sounded like more than that."

"Well, it wasn't," I snapped. Chrissy looked up at me in surprise, one eyebrow raised. I took a deep breath and reminded myself that I was the grown-up.

"Sorry, I didn't sleep well last night. All your pacing kept me awake." *Oh, great, Rebecca. Fabulous apology right there. Maybe I just should have just cut to the chase and said "Sorry, not sorry."* I tried smiling to soften my words and turn it into a joke.

But, Chrissy was frowning at me. "Pacing? What are you talking about? I slept like the dead."

I stared at her, that sense of "wrongness" I felt in the kitchen that morning rushing through me again. "But, I mean, I saw you …" my voice trailed off as images flashed through my mind.

The white nightgown disappearing into Chrissy's room.

Chrissy standing in the kitchen wearing her red and blue sleep outfit.

I rubbed my temples, the coffee turning into a sick, greasy lump in my stomach. Oh God, I hoped I wasn't going to throw up.

Chrissy was looking at me with something that resembled concern. Or maybe it was alarm. After all, I was the only adult she knew within 1,000 miles. "Are you okay, Rebecca?"

I reached for my water glass. "Yeah, I'm fine. It's an old house. Old houses make all sorts of noises. I'm sure that's what kept me awake."

Chrissy didn't look terribly convinced, but she went back to her iPhone. She was probably texting her friends about how I was losing it. Or worse … texting her father.

I drank some water to try and settle my stomach. I was being ridiculous. Old houses make all sorts of creaks and groans and can sound exactly like footsteps, which is what kept waking me up last night. And as for what I saw … well, clearly, I hadn't seen anything. Just a trick of the light, or the moon, or something. And with the pounding of my head, I really wasn't paying that close attention.

I just needed to get some food in my stomach. And hopefully, some decent sleep that night. Then I could forget about all the house nonsense. Stefan and I could laugh about it … assuming he finally got around to calling me back, that is.

Okay, I so didn't want to go down *that* road. Instead, I sat back in my seat, sipped my coffee, and watched Mia top off the cup of a cute guy who looked like a contractor, laughing at something he said. I still had trouble believing Mia was waiting tables at the diner. Of all of us, she was bound and determined to get out and never come back. I remembered how driven, how passionate she had been about all the injustices in the world, and how determined she had been to right them. She was going to be a lawyer and fight for everyone who couldn't help themselves. What had happened?

A couple of older, neatly-dressed women sitting at a table next to us were staring at me. They wore nearly identical pantsuits, except one was baby blue and the other canary yellow. Their half-eaten food sat in front of them. Taken aback at the open aggression in their eyes, I looked back at them, wondering if I should know them.

Were their stares really directed at me? Did I do something in my youth my traitorous memory had yet to reveal? Maybe they were actually looking at someone sitting behind me. I turned around to look, but no one was there. When I swiveled back, their identical gaze looked even more antagonistic.

I dropped my eyes, only half-seeing the paper placemat covered with local advertising, feeling a growing sense of unease in my belly. They didn't look familiar at all. Who were they? And why me?

"Why did the waitress call you Becca?" Chrissy asked, startling me. For once, I was glad she was there to distract me, even though part of me instantly wanted to scream at her to stop calling me that.

"It was my nickname," I said, willing those older women to get up and leave. Out of the corner of my eye, I saw them lean toward each other, whispering, hostile eyes still watching me. I adjusted my head until I couldn't see them anymore.

Chrissy went back to her iPhone "It's cute. Better than Rebecca."

I ignored the twist of pain inside me and put my hand on my heart. "Wait. Did I just hear an almost compliment there?"

Chrissy rolled her eyes. "I'm just saying. I think I'll call you Becca."

"Don't," I said, before I could stop myself.

Chrissy looked surprised. And, if I didn't know her any better, a little hurt. "What, only people you *like* can call you Becca?"

Cripes. I could have smacked myself. Why on earth wasn't there a manual out there on how to be a stepmom to a daughter who is only fifteen years younger than you?

"That's not it," I said, stalling for time as I tried to put the feelings that had swamped over me into words. "It just ... it just triggers bad memories. That's all." I cringed—I sounded so lame, even to myself.

Chrissy gave me a withering look as she furiously pounded on her iPhone. I opened my mouth to say something—I had no idea what ... something to bridge the gap that yawned between us—but Mia's voice interrupted me. "Daniel! Look who's here! It's Becca!"

I closed my mouth and turned to look. A police officer was standing at the counter watching Mia fill up a to-go container with coffee. Could that be Daniel? I searched the room, but only saw only a handful of people finishing up their breakfast. It had to be him.

I looked back at the cop. Broad shoulders and dark blonde hair—Daniel. Mia glanced at me and winked. I made a face back at her.

He turned. He was older of course, but yes, it was most definitely Daniel. He wouldn't be considered traditionally handsome—not like Stefan with his almost pretty-boy looks. Daniel's face was too rugged, with sharp cheekbones and a crooked nose. But his lips were still full and soft, and his eyes were still the same dark blue. I found myself suddenly conscious of my appearance. I hadn't taken a shower in two days, and I was wearing an old, faded New York Giants tee shirt. I had scraped my unruly mass of reddish, blondish, brownish hair back into a messy ponytail in preparation for a full day of cleaning and organizing. But I quickly reminded myself that I was being silly. I was a married woman, sitting with my stepdaughter, and he was engaged.

Besides, he had made it more than clear years ago he wasn't the slightest bit interested in me.

"Becca," he said coming over, his face friendly, but not exactly smiling. "Welcome back to Redemption." It didn't sound much like a welcome.

"Thanks," I said, mostly because I couldn't think of anything better to say. Instinctively, I reached up to smooth out my hair, since as usual, a few curly tendrils had escaped and hung in my face. "Not much has changed."

He studied me, making me really wish I had taken an extra five minutes to jump in the shower and dig out a clean shirt. "Oh, plenty has changed."

"Like you being a cop?"

He shrugged slightly. "Pays the bills."

I half-smiled. "There's lots of ways to pay the bills. If I remember right, you always seemed more interested in breaking the law than upholding it."

"Like I said, things change." He lifted his to-go coffee cup and took a swallow, his dark-blue eyes never leaving mine. "I take it you're still painting then."

I dropped my gaze to his chest, feeling a dull ache overwhelm me—the same pain I felt when I heard the name Becca. "As you said, things change."

"Ah." I waited for him to ask more questions, but instead, he changed the subject. "So, how long are you staying?"

I shrugged. "Not sure. We've actually moved here."

His eyebrows raised slightly. "To Charlie's house? You aren't selling it?"

"Well, yes. Eventually. That's the plan. But, at least for the foreseeable future, we'll be living in it." I sounded like an idiot. With some effort, I forced myself to stop talking. Why on earth did I share so much detail? How was this any of his business?

He looked like he was going to say something more but was interrupted by a loud snort. The two pant-suited women both scraped their chairs back as they stood up, glaring disgustedly at all of us before heading to the cash register.

"What's with them?" Chrissy asked. I had forgotten she was there.

I shrugged, before remembering my manners and introducing Chrissy to Daniel. I made a point of gesturing with my left hand to flash my wedding ring.

His head tipped in a slight nod before looking back at me. "Will you be around later today? I'd like to stop by and talk to you."

There was something in his expression that made me uneasy, but I purposefully kept my voice light. "What on earth for? I haven't even unpacked yet. Am I already in trouble?"

The ends of his lips turned up in a slight smile, but no hint of warmth touched the intense look in his eyes. "Should you be in trouble?"

I let out a loud, exaggerated sigh. "Why do cops always answer a question with a question?"

"Occupational hazard. I'll see you later." He dipped his chin in a slight nod before walking away. I noticed he didn't give me the slightest hint as to what he wanted to talk to me about. That sense of unease started to grow into a sense of foreboding.

"Well, for an old friend, he wasn't very friendly," Chrissy said.

I sipped my coffee. "That's for sure."

She smirked. "He was pretty cute, though. For an old guy, I mean."

Man, she did have a knack for making me feel ancient. But, unfortunately, even that didn't distract my mind from scrambling around like a rat in a cage, worrying about what he wanted to talk to me about.

Acknowledgements

It's a team effort to birth a book, and I'd like to take a moment to thank everyone who helped, especially my wonderful editor, Megan Yakovich, who is always so patient with me, Rea Carr for her expert proofing support, and my husband Paul, for his love and support during this sometimes-painful birthing process.

Any mistakes are mine and mine alone.

About Michele

When Michele was 3 years old, she taught herself to read because she wanted to write stories so badly.

As you can imagine, writing has been a driving passion throughout her life.

* She's an award-winning, bestselling fiction author, writing a range of mystery novels, from psychological suspense to cozies.

* She's a bestselling nonfiction author, creating the popular "Love-Based Business" series of books.

* She's also a professional copywriter, blogger and journalist.

She holds a double major in English and Communications from the University of Wisconsin-Madison. Currently she lives in the mountains of Prescott, Arizona with her husband Paul and southern squirrel hunter Cassie.

Made in the USA
Middletown, DE
03 February 2023

23882870R00223